NIGHTHAWKING

RUSS THOMAS

**SIMON &
SCHUSTER**

London · New York · Sydney · Toronto · New Delhi

First published in Great Britain by Simon & Schuster UK Ltd, 2021

This paperback edition published 2021

1 3 5 7 9 10 8 6 4 2

Simon & Schuster UK Ltd
1st Floor
222 Gray's Inn Road
London WC1X 8HB

Simon & Schuster Australia, Sydney
Simon & Schuster India, New Delhi

www.simonandschuster.co.uk
www.simonandschuster.com.au
www.simonandschuster.co.in

A CIP catalogue record for this book
is available from the British Library

Paperback ISBN: 978-1-4711-8143-6
eBook ISBN: 978-1-4711-8142-9
Audio ISBN: 978-1-3985-0031-0

Typeset in Bembo by M Rules
Printed and bound by CPI Group (UK) Ltd, Croydon, CR0 4YY

MIX
Paper from
responsible sources
FSC® C020471

raise for
RUSS THOMAS

'Comparable with the best of Michael Connelly's Bosch
books and James Lee Burke's Robicheaux novels, and –
naturally – Ian Rankin; but there's an elegiac quality here
that reminds me of Kate Atkinson's Jackson Brodie titles
and the Dublin Murder Squad novels by Tana French'
AJ FINN

'I loved it! *Nighthawking* turns Sheffield into a dark and terrifying
underworld, and the plot is wonderfully fresh and original'
KATE RHODES

'Superb. Every part of *Nighthawking* is so well woven
together ... the end dragged me around and spat
me out a broken man. Highly recommended'
JAMES DELARGY

'I loved it'
LEE CHILD

'Clever and compulsive'
LOUISE CANDLISH

'Devoured in three days. A cracking read with a terrific new
detective lead'
SARAH HILARY

'A great read. Totally absorbed me'
CASS GREEN

'Intelligent, pacey and compelling, it's everything you
could want from a crime novel'
SARAH WARD

Russ Thomas was born in Essex, raised in Berkshire and now lives in Sheffield. After a few 'proper' jobs (among them: pot-washer, opticians' receptionist, supermarket warehouse operative, call-centre telephonist and storage salesman), he discovered the joys of bookselling, where he could talk to people about books all day. His debut novel, *Firewatching*, was selected as a Waterstones Thriller of the Month. *Nighthawking* is his second novel.

Also by Russ Thomas

Firewatching

For the People of Sheffield,
who welcome strangers with great generosity

NIGHTHAWKING

breaking
ground

the first nighthawker

<u>Record of Finds</u>

Date: Mon 6th Nov
Time: 04:45 (approx.)
Location: Botanical Gardens, Sheffield
Finds: shilling coin (indecipherable year), ring-pull (circa 1980s), arm

He climbs the wall slowly, the equipment strapped to his back working with gravity to pull him down to the pavement below. When he reaches the top, he pauses for a moment, sweat on his brow mingling with rainwater before trickling down his neck. A car swings around the corner, its headlights threatening to pick him out. He flicks left leg after right, launches himself into a freefall, and drops like a stone into the silent garden below.

He crouches in the flower bed and waits for his heartbeat to slow. There are no cameras here. No lights other than from

3

the street beyond the wall, and the odd yellow square of a window in the row of terraced houses beyond the treeline. Sheffield is far from being 'The City That Never Sleeps', but it is still a city. He consoles himself with the thought that if he gets caught, the penalties won't be all that harsh. Not from the police anyway.

He moves through the dark of the Botanical Gardens, staying clear of the more open spaces, hugging the walls and darting from tree to tree. The rain begins to ease, which is a bonus. As long as the clouds don't dissipate; the last thing he needs is an almost full moon to pick him out. There's still a faint whiff of smoke in the air from the bonfire parties and firework displays that took place earlier in the evening, in spite of the weather.

When he reaches the smaller, walled rose garden he hesitates, his eyes flicking towards the houses now clearly visible beyond the park boundary. This area is more overlooked than the rest of the Gardens but it's where he needs to be. He has a job to do. He reaches up and takes hold of the strap cutting across his shoulder. The metal detector is light enough but it's still a relief to lift it from his back. He slips on the headphones and hears the sharp whine of the machine as he switches it on. Time to go to work.

The detector arcs across the ground in long sweeps, its black plastic coil turning over fallen leaves and parting the stems of plants. The wind whips at his jacket and makes him shiver as it cools the sweat on his back. He listens carefully to the background hum of the detector's negative response, his eyes focused on the digital control box. The glow from the display is small but it could be seen. It wouldn't be the first time he's been caught, thrown off some irate farmer's property or given a telling-off by a poorly paid security guard. Some people threaten to call the police or let the dogs loose, and once, an old man came out of his house and fired a shotgun over his head. But these are the hazards of the trade. He's a *Nighthawker*, after all. A trespasser. A thief. He chuckles to himself.

He works for more than an hour, quartering the area, stopping to dig occasionally at the wet earth when he gets a reading, uncovering small items that for the most part will turn out to be worthless and shoving them into his backpack to examine later.

The clock ticks on. Four o'clock. Four-thirty. It won't be long before lights begin to flick on in bedroom windows and early-morning workers glance out to check the weather for the day ahead. He digs carefully, trying not to leave too much evidence in case he has to come back. Again. For this isn't the first time he's been here and each time he worries about the traces he leaves behind. Footprints in the flowerbeds, broken branches, flattened stems.

The wind is bitingly cold now the rain has stopped and he starts to lose the feeling in his nose and toes. His back is aching. He checks his watch again. Almost five. Perhaps one last sweep towards the wall and then call it a night. It's disappointing, but it's better than being caught.

He's halfway to the wall when the detector screeches and

he stumbles to a halt, desperate not to lose the reading. He backtracks, checks the display for confirmation — '32'. A mid tone. Too high for aluminium or iron, too low for silver. The sweet spot for gold. But also the sweet spot for bottle caps, ring-pulls, other low-conducting metals. He sweeps the ground a couple more times, triangulating the exact location, then he puts down the detector and begins to dig.

The soft wet earth of the flower bed parts easily and he's down inches in mere seconds; the soil here is freshly dug. And then he hits something. Is this it? He changes the angle and digs down again, finds the same stiff resistance. It's something, but is it what he's looking for? He can't tell anything with the trowel and despite the light pollution from the city, he still can't see much. He uses his hands now, his fingers sinking into the mud and feeling their way along and around the squishy protuberances. There are several of them. Thin tree roots, perhaps? Gnarled and sticky with some kind of sap. He grabs hold and pulls.

The hand emerges from the mud with the quiet pop of something snapping.

He lets go and falls backwards, stifling a small cry, his own hands sinking into the muddy earth behind him, grateful to be washed clean of the contamination of rotting human flesh. He pants into the darkness, feeling the adrenaline flooding his weary limbs. He glances left, and right, suddenly sure there must be someone else here, someone watching him in the night.

He looks back at the hand lying flat on the ground before

him, an arm bone trailing back to the hole he pulled it from. The whole thing is little more than a skeleton but there are remnants of tatty skin still visible that hang loosely around the bones like a torn glove. Around the middle finger of the hand is a thin gold ring. That must be what the detector registered. It looks as though the body it belongs to has begun to crawl its way from slumber. Because there *is* a body, there has to be. There was that slight resistance as he pulled. That small sound, more of a vibration really, that travelled along the bones and up through his arm. He shivers.

The smell hits him now. A curiously sweet scent mixed with the fetid earthiness of the soil. Rotting meat. The bile rises in his throat even as he realises he can't allow himself to be sick. He can't leave behind any DNA. Assuming he hasn't already.

He needs to go, but he still hasn't got what he came for and now there's zero chance he can come back. A light flicks on in the nearest house beyond the wall. He can make out the garden in its entirety now, the bushes, the wall, the entranceway he slipped through a couple of hours ago. He can hear traffic beginning to build outside. Passing cars, every few seconds or so, making it so much harder to escape undetected. He hesitates, making new plans, discarding them, trying to work out how this development changes things. But then another light comes on somewhere. And another.

With a small cry of frustration, the nighthawker grabs the metal detector and runs.

one

The man with the scar on his cheek looks down at the cold steel of the railway tracks and the morning sun glints back up at him. He wonders what it would be like to meet your end in this place. The wind picks up for a moment and he pulls his thick coat around him against the chill. The sharp breeze cuts into the scar on his cheek and makes it ache.

A dozen or so separate railway lines branch here, in a complex spider's web of iron that stretches out to meet the platforms at Sheffield station. Another man, in a bright orange safety vest with reflective flashings, stands a few paces ahead, holding a black and white communications paddle. He's there for protection, in case there's a mix-up and a train gets shunted through on the wrong line. A radio crackles on his belt.

There's not a great deal to see, of course. The body found here thirteen years ago is long gone, the parents of the teen-age boy have put him to rest, and the blood and any other evidence has been washed away by countless rainstorms. And yet, the man tries to imagine what it was like.

It had been late evening, snowing heavily, and East Midlands Trains were already running a reduced service. There were no witnesses passing on the final trains in from Manchester or Nottingham. The original investigation posited a rival gang, some turf beef that ended in a knife to the guts. Tragic and unnecessary but sadly not unusual. The death of young boys is an embarrassing stain on the reputation of this city, which once had a different reason for the fame of its knives. His parents and friends said he wasn't in a gang but then they always say that, don't they?

The boy's corpse had been found the next morning, half-buried in a snowdrift and an unnaturally deep shade of blue, the body so unrecognisable the driver who reported it assumed it was an animal hit by a passing train. The woman sent out to check had needed weeks of counselling.

After a few months the investigation stalled. The case was filed away with all the other unsolved cases. Which is what has brought the man with the scar here.

'Finished?' The railway worker has returned from the tracks ahead. 'Only, the eight-fifteen to Plymouth'll be through soon and if they have to divert it'll throw a right spanner in the works.'

They begin the short walk back to the platform.

'Can't imagine what you thought you'd find after all these years. Reckon this was a bit of a waste of your time.' The railway worker clearly considers it a waste of his.

But the man with the scar *has* found something. A building that overlooks the crime scene. He knows no one in those offices was interviewed in the original investigation. Maybe someone in the building was working late that night. Maybe they saw something they didn't fully understand at the time. Maybe they'll remember it, thirteen years later. Maybe.

He thanks the railway worker and takes his leave of the station, following the curve of the Cutting Edge sculpture in Sheaf Square as it glistens in the morning sunlight. He walks up the hill past the university buildings and crosses Arundel Gate, cutting through the Millennium Galleries and the Winter Garden and onto Surrey Street.

Outside the coffee shop, a barista stares in disgust at a young homeless guy tucked up close to the wall against the chill. The man with the scar drops a couple of quid into the lad's polystyrene cup.

'You shouldn't encourage them,' the barista scolds, and disappears back inside.

At the counter, the man orders his drink while the barista pointedly continues his conversation with a colleague, extolling the merits of his one-man war on destitution.

'I've a good mind to call the police,' the barista says and holds a Sharpie poised against a cup. 'What name is it?' he asks distractedly.

'Tyler,' says the man with the scar. '*Detective Sergeant* Adam Tyler.'

The barista manages a sick smile and hurries away to steam some milk.

Dave Carver arrives at the Botanical Gardens early that morning, just as he always does. His official shift starts at ten but he likes to get here earlier. Sometimes he's even here before the council workers who open the gates, and he has to wait patiently until they arrive.

He likes to grab a takeaway coffee – black, filter – from one of the High Street chains that have sprung up like mushrooms along Ecclesall Road. He remembers a time when there were far fewer coffee shops in Sheffield, when people made do with what they had at home. Now, you can't move for cardboard cups and the smell of roasted coffee beans. He's filled with disdain for these capitalist multinationals, enslaving the downtrodden poor of South America so some middle-class student can part with £3.50 of Daddy's money for a syrupy concoction that costs the purveyor no more than eight pence a cup. It's obscene and he despises himself each time he goes into one of these places. But he goes anyway, every week. Because she loved them so much.

Once through the entrance to the Gardens he wanders up the steep path that leads to the greenhouse with the signing-in book. Then he tracks right, never left – he stays clear of that side of the Gardens if he can – and turns right again into the small walled area they call the Marnock Garden.

He finds it peaceful here, a small enclave within the busy, breath-taking city, like the eye at the centre of a storm. Here he will sit, until the start of his shift, on a wooden bench with a small brass plaque. Sometimes he gets so lost in memory he ends up late for work. So often in fact that he has a reputation for tardiness and poor timekeeping among the other volunteers. It has become a running joke. Speedy Dave. So early, he makes himself late.

This morning is different though. As he enters the garden he glances once at the giant stainless-steel ant sculpture made from scrap metal and idly wonders, as he often does, if any of the parts were made with steel he had a hand in tempering. But then, as his eyes swing back round to the rose garden along the left-hand side he sees something that causes him to stop short.

At first – and later he'll laugh at the absurdity of this notion – he sees it as a living organism. Some new plant he hasn't seen before, pushing its way out between the succulents. Five stubby branches and a long, thick trunk. And then, of course, he realises what it really is. A human arm. Five fingers loosely clenched, as though it has begun crawling its way towards the path.

The blood drains from Dave's face and his knees lock. He stands perfectly still, staring at the hand. It seems to beckon him in some way, even as it crawls its way ever closer. *Come over here. Join me.* Then, behind him, a woman screams, and as though the noise has given them permission, his legs give way beneath him and Dave falls to his knees on the gravel path.

Detective Constable Mina Rabbani braces the desk with the back of her neck and head, and lifts, shoving a folded-up copy of yesterday's Sheffield *Star* as far under the front left leg as she can manage before the weight becomes too much for her and she has to let go. She hears the monitor above her rock back and forth and then settle, and breathes a sigh of relief.

That would really go down well with IT, if she managed to smash her PC so early into her new role.

PC. Personal computer. Or Police Constable. Except it's DC now. *Detective* Constable. She wonders whether she'll ever get used to that. She knew there was nothing particularly glamorous about the role but she'd hoped she might get to see a bit more action than fixing a wobbly desk. Still, it means something. She finds herself smiling. It means a lot.

She straightens up and glances around the room. Still no sign of Tyler. Well, there was no reason to suppose today would be any different to yesterday but it's becoming more and more difficult to cover for him. If Jordan finds out she's going to lose the 'Detective' bit before she's even got used to it.

She decides to keep her head down in the hope no one will notice her. Or the fact that Tyler's missing. She goes back to the case she's been reviewing but within a few minutes her mind is wandering again. For some reason she finds herself wondering if her brother, Ghulam – he's a doctor, you know! – ever has to stop his desk wobbling with yesterday's newspaper. She leans forward and puts her head in her hands, digging the heels of her palms into her eye sockets. It isn't that she's ungrateful. Really, it's not. She's got a lot to be thankful to Tyler for, not least for saving her life. It's just that none of this is what she expected. None of this is what she wanted!

She knows police work isn't like it is on the TV or at

the movies. Cases like the one she was involved in last year don't just crop up every day, she gets that. She's grateful for it, really. Otherwise her mother wouldn't even let her out of the house. *Ay, Mina! Jaan, why can't you get a* different *job?* She knows the job involves a lot of paperwork and maybe it isn't as hands-on as it is for the Murder Room team. It isn't as though Doggett had wanted her anywhere near his squad after what happened anyway, but that was fine. She was happy to give up her original dream for a chance to work with Tyler. It's still CID and, to be fair, she would have taken anything as long as she got that word 'Detective' in front of her name. It isn't even that she doesn't believe Tyler when he tells her how important it is to review cases. It's there in the name, after all. Cold Case *Review* Unit. She gets that. She's done every crappy job Tyler's asked of her, and more. It's beyond boring, but has she complained? No. Not even once.

But it would all just be a lot more bearable if he was there leading by example. Instead of doing whatever the hell it is he does all day.

There's a loud cheer and Mina swivels in her chair in time to see Guy Daley walk into the office. It has been a year since she last saw him, being hurried into the back of an ambulance. The room erupts into a chorus of 'For He's a Jolly Good Fellow' but, for all that she's happy Daley hasn't suffered any long-lasting effects from his knock on the head, she can't bring herself to join in with it. She turns back to her screen and begins reading the notes again.

Half an hour later she gives up and makes her way to the watercooler with an empty plastic bottle. You're not supposed to refill bottles. There's a printed sign, laminated and stuck to the wall with Blu Tack that says, 'In the interests of hygiene, please do *NOT* refill water bottles. Use the paper cups provided!!!!!' Despite the underlining, bold, and excessive use of exclamation marks, no one ever uses the paper cups provided.

Her bottle is half full when Daley appears alongside her. He smiles at her without speaking and it's even worse than the encounters she used to have with the man.

'Welcome back, Guy. How are you doing?'

'Cheers, Mina. Yeah, I'm good, mate.'

Mina? Mate? Perhaps the knock on his head dislodged something. She immediately feels the shame of that thought. He was badly hurt last year and from what she's heard, it's been a long recovery. He might be an ignorant bastard but he didn't deserve that. Still, *mate?* Maybe it's the fact she's a detective now. She hasn't considered that before. Is she now 'one of the lads'?

As though he's read her thoughts he says, 'Congratulations, by the way.'

'Right. Yeah, thanks.'

'Look, I . . .' He trails off and they stand in silence as her water bottle fills slowly to the brim.

She lets go of the dispensing button and turns to face him. She wants to head straight back to her desk, but it's obvious he hasn't finished yet.

'Thing is, Mina,' he says, and steadfastly fails to reveal the thing. 'I just wanted to say . . . look, thanks. You know.'

She's so shocked to hear the words coming from him it takes her a few seconds to work out what he's talking about. But then it comes to her. He must have found out from someone that she was the one who sat with his split scalp cradled in her hands as he bled all over her best jeans. With one hand she'd pressed a t-shirt as hard as she dared against his head to staunch the blood loss, while with the other she called for help, chasing up the ambulance, the fire brigade, and every police officer South Yorkshire had to spare.

'No problem,' she says. She can't really think of anything else to say.

'No, really, Mina. I mean it.' And she thinks that maybe he does. 'You . . . you proper saved my life. I owe you one.'

Bloody hell, that knock must have been harder than the doctors thought! He's probably still concussed.

'It's good to have you back, Guy.' The words stick in her throat but she manages to get them out, and a half-smile to go with them.

'So . . . you've joined CCRU, then?' He says it the same way everyone does, 'sea-crew', as though she's a deckhand on a trawler. She's never sure if the nickname's meant to be disparaging or not.

Oh, God! He's trying to make small talk. She preferred it when he was being a dick. She knew how to deal with that.

'It seemed like a good fit,' she tells him. And it had done, at the time. She glances back at the screen and the case notes waiting for her. 'You didn't happen to see DS Tyler on your way in, did you?'

Daley can't help the involuntary scowl that crosses his face and it's so familiar to her, Mina almost smiles.

'No,' he says, and then, like the shark that he is, he smells blood in the water. 'Why? What's he up to?'

'He went down to look at some evidence, I think.' The lie comes easily to her after months of practice. 'Just a case we've been looking at. Listen, I'd better get back to it.'

'Oh, right, yeah, course.' But he makes no effort to let her go. 'Listen, I was wondering ... some of the lads said they want to take me out for a few drinks after work tonight and I thought—'

But whatever he's thinking is cut off as someone shouts, 'Oi-oi, saveloy! *Daley Thompson's* back!' and three of Daley's colleagues begin slapping him on the back and shaking his hand and Mina uses the distraction to slip back to her desk.

She sits down and takes a long, hard swig from her water bottle, trying not to think about whatever it was Daley had been about to suggest. She's just grateful she didn't have to say no to whatever it was.

Breakfast with Paul does not go according to plan. It was supposed to be a chance for them to reconnect but, as is so often the way when they meet up, Tyler finds his attention wandering. Paul slaps butter and jam onto a croissant – the man shovels food into his mouth faster than anyone Tyler's ever encountered, and burns it off just as quickly – and talks about a factory that went up in flames last night, out towards Doncaster. It's been a busy weekend for the fire service, with Bonfire Night falling on a Sunday and Paul's voice is weary and strangely soporific. Tyler listens to his words without really registering them and then, too slowly, realises the conversation has stopped. He looks up from the table to find Paul watching him.

'Look,' Paul says, 'I know you've got a lot on your plate at the moment ...' He holds up a hand as Tyler begins to apologise all over again. 'Just, let me get this out. It's fine, I understand there's stuff going on and I'm not going to ask, you've made it clear you don't want to talk about it. But I'm beginning to get the impression it's not just that.' He absently wipes the crumbs from his grey t-shirt. 'I'm beginning to think it might just be me.'

Tyler senses this is the pivotal moment. If he says the wrong thing – or is it the right thing? – the relationship's over. He doesn't think he wants it to be, but neither can he offer Paul exactly what he wants. Not right now, anyway. Maybe never. He's conscious he hasn't said anything at all yet and Paul's face is beginning to harden.

'I want to tell you about it,' Tyler says, and realises as he says it that he actually does. It will be good to get Paul's input, to apply that cool, considered, analytical mind of his to the problem that has been dogging Tyler for so many months. He even finds himself with the urge to talk about Jude, and he hasn't mentioned that to anyone yet. But, as always, he finds himself asking the same question – *is it fair to involve him in all this?* He needs more time to think. 'Not here,' he says, checking his watch. 'Dinner, tonight? My place?'

Paul hesitates, perhaps considering if Tyler's worth another chance. There have been so many already. Finally, he agrees. But when they leave the coffee shop there are no hugs, no kisses. Tyler can feel them both teetering on the edge of something, he just isn't sure which way they will fall.

When he gets to the office, the first person he sees is Guy Daley back from his convalescence. He'd forgotten the man was due back today. They manage exactly two words between them.

'Tyler.'

'Daley.'

And that appears to be that. Still, at least it was civil. Sort of.

Rabbani's at her desk. She greets him with a somewhat less civil, 'Where the fuck have *you* been?'

'Morning, Mina. How are you?'

Rather than answering she gives him a look, raising those shaped eyebrows of hers into an arch.

Tyler suppresses a smile. Since gaining the Detective moniker, she's grown into herself. DC Rabbani is a far greater force to be reckoned with than PC Rabbani ever was, and that's saying something.

'Now look,' she says, forgetting her irritation with him, or parking it at least. 'I think I found something.'

He grabs an empty swivel chair and Rabbani calls up the relevant files and outlines the cases to him, the connection she thinks she's made. He listens and allows that there could be something in it. But it's thin. Still, he's not going to dismiss her theory out of hand.

'Okay,' he says. 'Good.' Her back stiffens, perhaps it's the unexpected praise. 'Carry on, then.'

'What?'

'It's your case, look into it. You know what to do.'

'I just thought . . . I mean, don't you want to . . . ?'

'Come on, Mina. You're a detective now, you don't need hand-holding. Just keep me up to date on progress.'

It's better if they work separate cases for now. For one thing it will increase their chances of getting a result and, for another, he has the feeling that the more he distances himself from Rabbani, the better it will be for her professionally. He tries not to think of the real reason he's keeping her at arm's length. The reason he's been keeping everyone at arm's length, including Paul. *There are things we need to talk about . . .*

'Look,' he goes on. 'You're a capable police constable, better than that, you're *good*. We're a team, sure, but there's no need for us to both work the same case until we need to. Dig a bit deeper and if you need my help, you know where I am.'

Her mouth opens but then she closes it again without speaking.

'Right, I'll leave you to it then.'

'But . . . ?' Rabbani turns on her chair. 'Where are you going *now*?'

'There's something *I* need to look into, and then I have a lunch appointment. You can call me if you need me.'

She looks as though she wants to argue further, but in the end she lets it go and turns back to her screen.

Tyler pulls out his mobile and holds the number 2 until the speed dial clicks in. There's no answer at the other end, just a curt demand that he leave a message. 'I need to see you,' he says. 'Tonight. Usual time, usual place.' When he hangs up he sees Rabbani watching him. 'Dentist,' he tells her, not caring that even Guy Daley would be able to see through that one. Rabbani certainly can.

Mina watches Tyler disappear back through the door he came through less than twenty minutes ago. She can't decide how she feels about that. On the one hand, she's beyond stoked he seems to be trusting her with more responsibility, and that talk he gave her about how good she is and how they're a team and all that was … well, uncharacteristically nice of him. But on the other hand, it was exactly that – out of character. *What the hell's going on with him?*

Maybe it's love. People sometimes act funny when they're at the start of a new relationship, don't they? *Ay, Mina, when are you going to get a husband?* That's what she's heard anyway. And the phone call would back up that theory. The usual time. The usual place. It certainly sounded like a romantic meeting. But from what she's pieced together about his relationship with Paul, she didn't think things had been going all that well. The thought of Tyler in love seems even more ridiculous than the thought of her agreeing to one of her mum's attempts at matchmaking. So he genuinely has confidence in her? No, she can't believe that. He's up to something, she's sure of it. And whatever it is, he's trying to keep *her* out of it, which probably means it's something dodgy and he's trying to protect her.

She buries her head in her hands for the third time that morning. Maybe she should have joined the dog-handlers after all.

Across the room a telephone rings, and then another, and a third, and within a few minutes the room is buzzing in that way that always speaks of something big. It's juicy by the sounds of it. She could just go and insert herself into a conversation. No, she has her own case to see through.

After a few minutes Guy Daley's voice cuts across the noise in the room and puts her out of her misery. 'All right, that's enough! Quiet! Carla, I need you to set things up at this end; Dev, Cat, Mina, you're with me.'

It takes her a moment to realise he means her. 'What?' By that time, he's joined her at her desk.

'Grab your jacket, it's cold out there.'

'I can't! I'm busy. And anyway, I report to DS Tyler now.' Even as she says it, she knows it sounds petty and ridiculous. She doesn't even know what the case is yet. It could well be something more important than a case that's been lying dormant for eight years that Tyler doesn't think is important enough to bother with.

'Come on, Mina. You know we're short-handed and your

case isn't going anywhere, is it? It's waited all this time, it can wait a few more days.'

It pisses her off to hear him speak the thoughts in her head again. *What is he, a mind-reader now?* She wants to argue with him and remind him that what she does is just as important but she can't quite find the words.

'Look,' he goes on. 'You don't really want to be digging around in dusty old case files for the rest of your career, do you? Do yourself a favour. If this goes well I'll talk to Doggett. You're a good . . . cop.' She can't be sure, but she'd put money on the fact he'd been about to say 'WPC' before he stopped himself.

She glances back at her monitor. It would be good to get back out on a case. Something recent. Something with real evidence to follow up. Of course, Daley could just order her. But he hasn't. He's being annoyingly nice. Is that what she's waiting for? An order? So that later she can tell Tyler it was all Daley's fault. Or is it just that she feels more confident when someone's telling her what to do?

'Mina. It's my first day back. Do me a favour, eh?'

'Fine,' she says, grabbing her jacket.

Daley beams at her like a child who's just got the extra sweets he asked for.

The arm's just lying there, looking like it belongs in one of those zombie B-movies Ghulam was always so obsessed with when they were teenagers. As though it's just crawled its way out of a grave.

Mina shivers in the wind and pulls her jacket tight. She can't smell the body from this distance; she's not sure how much it would smell anyway, given the desiccation of the flesh on the skeleton. It's in an advanced state of decay and would appear to have been buried for a while. But there's a fecund earthiness to the air that's unusually turning her stomach. This isn't her first body, and she finds the buried ones are usually a bit easier to deal with than the fresh ones, the scenes where life has so recently been snuffed out that the arterial blood is still dripping down the walls. But there's something about this one that's bothering her.

She wonders if it's the location. The Botanical Gardens has always been one of her favourite places in the city. She used to come here when she was studying for her police entrance exam and sit on the grass with all the students reading and drinking and snogging, imagining a life she never had a chance to experience. Not that she isn't happy about where she's ended up. And if she had gone to uni, like Ghulam, she doubts she would have got on all that well. She just isn't academically minded in the same way he is. She can accept that, even if their mother can't. But she'd enjoyed that summer, lying in the sun, half-experiencing a life she would never have, while simultaneously planning for the one ahead of her.

Of course, the Gardens feel different at this time of year. The evergreens are still beautiful but the deciduous trees so recently turned to flame are already sporting bare branches. And this part especially, this walled inner garden full of sparse flower beds, feels bleak and dead, even at the tail-end of autumn. The only real sign of life is the sound of children screaming and shouting in the schoolyard on the other side of the red-brick garden wall.

The arm is obscene. It looks almost as though it has been planted there, quite literally. Maybe it has. Maybe it's just an arm. There doesn't have to be a whole body underneath, does there? She can't decide if that would be better or worse though. If it *is* just an arm then maybe the person it belongs to is still alive out there somewhere, although that seems a bit unlikely. But if it *is* just an arm, it's going to make their job so much harder.

The man standing next to her is shaking. He's wearing the grubby overalls that mark him as one of the volunteers who help tend the garden. He can't seem to take his eyes off the thing, but that's hardly surprising. The crime scene manager, Jill Harris, hadn't wanted to let him back into the scene but Mina convinced her. She wants to see how he reacts when he retells his story and, since he's already been in here, as long as they stick to the Common Approach Path, the damage is minimised. Jill had reluctantly agreed.

'Can you tell me how you found it, please, Mr Carver?'

He doesn't answer straight away.

'Mr Carver?'

'Wha . . . ? Oh, sorry, love. It's just . . . the shock.'

'I understand. I'm sorry I have to ask you this now but it's important we go over it all while it's fresh.' She baulks at her choice of words. The only thing fresh around here is the wind. Unless it changes direction.

His eyes stay fixed on the wasted limb. 'I did tell the other policewoman.'

'If you could just go over it with me, please, Mr Carver.'

He still fails to meet her eye. 'I'm not sure how much I can tell you. I came in at the usual time, about eight-thirty, I suppose. I do the early shift so Alice can see to her husband before she leaves the house and—'

Mina cuts him off. 'Just what happened today, if you don't mind?'

'Oh, sure, sorry. Well, like I said, it were around eight-thirty. I came into the Marnock Garden and there it was.'

'Do you always come here first? At the start of your shift?'

Carver meets her eyes for the first time. 'I like it here. It's always . . . peaceful.'

'But the Gardens open at eight, is that right? Could someone have been here before you?'

'I can't say for sure, but most people that early are just passing through. The volunteers don't start 'til ten and we're mostly working on the Mediterranean Garden at the moment, which is further over that way so . . . no, I doubt anyone came into this area before me. I mean, they couldn't have, could they? Or they'd have found . . .' He trails off and gestures at the arm.

'So you saw the arm straight away?'

'As soon as I came through the wall.'

This is what Mina had wanted to follow up. *ABC. Assume nothing. Believe nobody. Check everything.* She glances back at the entranceway into this smaller garden. 'I don't mean to contradict you, Mr Carver, but I can't see the entrance very well from here. That tree blocks the view.'

Carver glances across to the entrance. 'I don't . . . I don't know then. I suppose I must have walked in a ways, an' then seen her.'

'Her?'

'What?'

'What makes you say, "her"? We don't know who the arm belongs to yet?'

'I just . . . it looks like a woman, doesn't it? Small?'

'Go on. So you walked into the garden a bit?'

Carver huffs and splutters. 'Look, I don't know. Why are you asking me all this?'

'It's just routine, sir. It's important we know where you've trodden.'

Carver thinks for a moment and studies the grass. 'I walked in along the path there, I think. I sometimes sit on the bench over there for a spell, just to gather my thoughts, but I didn't get that far. I must have glanced across and that's when I saw her . . . it.'

Mina makes a note to tell Jill about the increased area of potential contamination. 'And did you know what it was, or did you have to move closer to see?'

'I might be getting on a bit to you, love, but I'm not *that* far gone.'

Mina smiles to herself. David Carver can't be much over fifty. If that. 'What did you do then?'

'I don't know. I just … froze, I suppose. And the next thing I knew, Lynda were screaming.' He points to the orange-haired woman Daley is talking to over by the entrance. She has her hands thrust into her fleece jacket and is talking animatedly at Daley as though she's never going to stop. It's funny, Mina thinks, how some witnesses love to talk while others clam up.

'I think she'd seen me come this way,' Carver goes on. 'And she followed me to say good morning. Poor lass, she shouldn't have had to see that.'

From what Mina can see, Lynda's dealing with the trauma far better than Carver is.

'All right, Mr Carver.'

'Look, it's just Dave, all right?'

'Okay, Dave. We've got your contact details. Maybe you should get yourself home, eh? You've had a nasty shock.'

'Yeah. I'm all right, love. You don't have to treat me like an invalid.' But he glances again at the severed arm and swallows.

Mina steers him back along the path so that he doesn't tread anywhere he hasn't already.

'What will happen to her now then? Or him, or whatever.'

'Well, we don't know for sure there's a whole body there yet, it might just be the arm.' She sees Caver wince at her feeble attempt to reassure him. 'But if there is, there'll be an autopsy and then we'll make sure it … *she* gets a decent burial.'

Carver nods. 'That's good, then, isn't it? That's something.'

Mina and Daley watch as Lynda and Dave negotiate their way under the police tape and up the hill towards the main office by the park entrance.

'Anything?' Daley asks.

'Not really. Sounds like he didn't disturb the body at least. You?'

'A recipe for rhubarb and ginger crumble among other exciting tips, but nothing relevant. Oh, here he is!' This last statement is made as Dr Elliot strides his way forcefully down the path towards them.

'Good morning, detectives! Nice day for it!' The skinny Geordie ducks under the tape in a well-practised manoeuvre. 'In here, is it?'

Daley starts to follow but Mina grabs hold of his arm. He stops and looks at her. She points to the crowd beginning to gather just the other side of the taped area. 'Do you not think we should close the *whole* Gardens?'

Daley frowns at the masses. 'That's Jill's call.'

'But you could suggest it.'

'Uniform'll keep them out of this bit.'

'Yes, but we don't know how big the crime scene is yet, do we?' Always assume the worst. *Think meningitis; hope for a cold.* She'd read that somewhere.

'Ah, come on, Mina. That hand's been there ages. Any forensics will have been long lost.'

She suppresses the urge to sigh. 'But someone dug it up, didn't they? More recently than ages ago. Someone who might have left trace evidence.'

Daley thinks about this. 'I suppose. Fair enough. You go deal with Elliot and I'll have a word with Jill. Should be easy enough to close the whole place, they close it every night anyway.'

'Be nice,' Mina tells him. 'Try not to make it sound like you're telling her how to do her job.'

Daley walks away shaking his head, the irony of her last statement lost on him. She heads back down the path and into the walled garden.

Elliot's bent over, staring at the skeletal arm as though it's the most fascinating thing he's ever seen.

He glances back at her. 'Detective ...'

'Rabbani,' she reminds him, even though they've met countless times before. 'Mina.'

He nods without any visible attempt to commit her name to memory. 'Well, I'd say it's gonna take us the best part of the day to get her out of there.'

'Her?'

Elliot tilts his head. 'Looks like a woman's hand to me. Could be a child, of course, but children don't usually wear gold rings.'

Mina hadn't thought of that. She hopes it isn't a child. 'And the rest of her's definitely under there?'

'Well, I can't tell you if any bits are missing but there's more than a forearm, that's for sure. Look, you can see the elbow joint under these leaves. Looks like something pulled the radius and the ulna away from the humerus.' He clicks his tongue to make a popping sound. 'It wouldn't have taken much force. You can also see where the ground has sunk as the body decayed. Classic sign, that. Saw hundreds like that in Kosovo. A bit less obvious with all these bushes and plants on top mind. Mmm . . .'

'What?'

Elliot breaks from his reverie. 'Oh, nothing, I'm just surprised they've survived, that's all. Plant life tends to die off when the body purges its liquefied organs. Doesn't usually grow back until skeletonisation and, judging by the hand here, that process is only just beginning. See?' He points to the bony digits. 'Her nails have fallen out but there's still a fair bit of skin holding things together.'

'So can we tell how long she's been there?'

Elliot sighs dramatically. 'There's no set time frame for when skeletonisation occurs but I'd say we're looking at months rather than years.'

'Who dug her up? Could it have been an animal?'

Elliot raises an eyebrow at her. 'Well, I'm not a bloody psychic but . . .' He leans forward, turning his head from side to side, examining the earth around the disturbed hole. 'Looks like it's been dug with something sharp. Spade or a trowel, I'd say.' He turns back to examine the arm again. 'We'll take her out slowly, try and preserve as much of the matter around her as we can. We'll need the soil to help determine how long she's been there.'

She watches him crouching and staring at the arm as though it's an art exhibit.

Daley crosses from the entranceway and joins them. 'How old?' he asks.

Elliot barks out a laugh. 'Bloody hell, Detective, I'm not a magician either! I've no idea how old she is.'

Daley's face flushes. 'I meant, how long has she been there?'

Elliot shakes his head and laughs. 'You're all the same, you lot, aren't you? No bloody patience.'

Thankfully, Daley decides not to respond to that.

Elliot turns and looks at them both. 'Who's leading on this then?'

'I am,' Daley tells him. 'For now, anyway. Probably DCI Jordan though, DI Doggett's got his hands full with the Talbot case.'

'Aye, nasty business, that.' Elliot flicks his eyes from one of them to the other. 'All right, fine. All these bushes will have to come out. If we manage to get her out before dark we'll do the autopsy in the morning. I've got a new forensic archae-ologist just started so I might well get her to handle things.

'For now, we'd best get a tent up in case it rains. Or in case things take longer than we think. Plus it'll stop those little shits from seeing what we're up to.' He points to the wall at the back of the garden where the heads of three boys disappear from view in a flurry of giggles.

'Oh, great,' says Daley.

'I'll go round and have a word with the school,' Mina tells him, and heads back down the path.

Daley hurries after her. 'Fucking parasite,' he mutters.

She frowns at him.

'Elliot. I swear to God he gets off on this stuff. And all that business about a forensic archaeologist. What he means is he's got a golf game planned for tomorrow and he doesn't want to cancel.'

Mina ignores him.

'So, er . . . do you think there's anything else we should be doing?'

She stumbles to a halt, hardly able to believe what she's just heard. He's asking for her advice?

As though he realises he's gone too far, Daley backtracks. 'It's good for your development, a case like this. What would *you* do?'

So he hasn't brought her along just because he feels he owes her, or worse, fancies her. He's brought her along as a crutch. How does she manage to get herself into these situations? She now has one superior who does nothing but distance himself from her, and another who needs his hand holding and his nose wiping. Mina takes a deep breath and, as she begins to tell Guy Daley how to do his job, she tries to concentrate on the fact that one day she'll be the one sitting in Jordan's office. When that day comes, she tells herself, these bastards will do exactly what she tells them, and not the other way around.

Tyler's halfway through a plate of breadsticks by the time Diane Jordan arrives. He sees her coming along the street since, despite the cool weather, the maître d' has chosen to seat them outside. There are huge orange heat lamps positioned over every table, an extravagant waste of resources.

'Sorry, I'm late,' she says, kissing him absently on a cheek and dropping a leather handbag that's seen better days onto one chair as she sinks into another. She goes straight for a menu. 'I'm starved.' He offers her the breadsticks and she snatches one without looking and crams it into her mouth along with a couple of strands of grey hair that have come loose from their bun. She notices without really noticing and curls a finger round the strands to hook them back out again even as she chews and swallows.

He tries to remember the last time he saw her out of uniform. A long time ago. Probably not since the Cartwright case. They've not exactly been on the best of terms since then and have seen each other so rarely out of the office that their relationship has become little more than that between any detective chief inspector and her sergeant. He regrets that but wonders if it isn't for the best right now. He wishes he could change what happened, some of the decisions he made, but he can't. The only thing he can do is try to prevent it happening again. Try not to compromise his friendship with this woman who has been his protector and confidante any further than he has done so already. It's one of the reasons he hesitated when she suggested this get-together in the first place. One of them.

The waiter arrives and they order drinks, Tyler a black

coffee, Jordan a large glass of sauvignon blanc. 'You don't mind, do you? I thought I'd take advantage of the rare day off.'

It worries him to see her drinking at this time of day. There was something in the way she ordered it, emphasis on the word *large*, that makes him wonder how badly she needs this. Their relationship has passed the point at which he can intervene though, if it ever really reached that point in the first place.

She notices him studying her and smiles. 'Stop worrying, Adam. I'm fine.' Then she adds, 'Really.'

'I know we haven't spoken much recently,' he begins. He's been rehearsing this for a while now but it doesn't make it any easier. 'I just wanted to say—'

But she cuts him off with a raised hand. 'Please don't start apologising again. I think we've done all that to death. It's over. You had your reasons for not coming to me, I understand them, even if I don't agree with them. It's over, Adam. Really. You have to let it go. I have.'

It's more than he deserves but then, she's always given him more than he deserves. 'I thought maybe you were avoiding me,' he says.

'I was giving you space. I learned a long time ago that to do anything else was counterproductive.'

There's a pause in the conversation while the waiter returns with their drinks and takes their order. As Jordan selects items from the menu, Tyler notices the homeless guy across the street. It's the same lad that was outside the coffee shop this morning, he's sure of it. The guy appears to be watching them. Entirely unashamed, he makes no effort to look away when Tyler catches his eye.

When the waiter takes his leave Jordan smiles and says, 'I'm glad you decided to come back.'

Tyler smiles as well, the scar tugging at the corner of his mouth as it always does. 'Thank you for taking me back. I'm sure Superintendent Stevens had to be persuaded.'

She laughs. 'You can leave the Eel to me,' she says. It's an unusual breach of etiquette from her, using Slippery Stevens' nickname rather than his title. He wonders if it's just because they're not at work or whether it's some deliberate attempt to broker peace between them, a bonhomie designed to remind him she's still on his side. Regardless, there's a slight tightening around her eyes that tells him he got it right. His reinstatement after the Cartwright business has cost her. What has she given up for him this time? Another chance at promotion?

Jordan takes a long swig of her wine and puts down the glass. It's already half empty. 'I've been meaning to ask you, what changed your mind?'

'About coming back?'

Take a few weeks, then come find me, Doggett had said over the sound of the drumming rain. *There are things we need to talk about.*

'A friend convinced me.' He doesn't like lying to her, and maybe, in one sense, he's not. Jim Doggett isn't a friend exactly but, in a wider sense of ... someone who consistently annoys you but who you can't quite manage to hate?

Is there a word for that? Perhaps what he's told her is not so far from the truth then. Even so. He *is* keeping things from her. Again. This is how it starts.

He takes a mouthful of coffee, enough of a pause so it's not too obvious he's changing the subject. The homeless guy's still watching them. But then Tyler decides he's being paranoid. Maybe he's just watching the restaurant. There's something Dickensian about the scene that makes Tyler think of Tiny Tim in *A Christmas Carol*.

As though it has just crossed his mind and hasn't been nagging away at him for days now he says to Jordan, 'I thought I saw Jude the other day.'

'Jude?'

It's a small thing. A pause before she says his name, a *lack* of reaction more than a reaction in itself. But it's there.

'It *was* him, wasn't it?' he asks her. 'He's back.' He doesn't say it aloud but in his head he adds, *and you knew about it*.

To give Jordan her due she makes no effort to prevaricate now he's guessed the truth. 'He's been back a few months or so, just after Easter. I'm sorry, Adam, I should have told you.'

'Why didn't you?'

'He asked me not to until he was ready.'

'And you agreed to that?'

Jordan takes another mouthful of wine. This time she doesn't put the glass down. 'I understand you're upset about this but I'll explain it as best I can. He came to me when he first got back to the city, I assumed at the time because he didn't have an address for you and because I was still at the same place. He told me he wanted to see you but not until he was back on his feet.'

'He came to you for money.'

She doesn't deny it but she won't confirm it either. She's stubborn about private stuff like that. He's also fairly certain that, however much money was involved, Jude won't have paid her back yet.

'I tried to convince him to contact you but he said he wanted to get a job first, and an apartment. You're his baby brother, Adam, he didn't want to disappoint you.'

Too late for that. 'When was the last time you spoke to him?'

The glass is almost empty and she's looking round for the waiter, to order another. 'That *was* the last time.'

'But you've not mentioned it, in all the months since?'

The waiter returns with their meals, more quickly than Tyler appreciates; he hopes that doesn't indicate the use of a microwave.

Jordan orders another glass of wine. As the waiter leaves, she goes on, 'At first, I was just trying to respect his wishes, and besides, I wasn't sure you were in the best frame of mind to hear about it.' She doesn't mention the fact they've barely spoken in a year but the words hang there nevertheless. 'In the end, and since I didn't hear any more of him, I assumed he'd moved on. I figured the matter was best left. Raising your hopes for them to be dashed again seemed unnecessarily cruel.'

They finish the rest of the meal in silence.

It's while Jordan is winding the last of her linguine onto a fork that Tyler sees the homeless guy make his move. He's very good, passing in close proximity to the tables but without alarming the occupants. But then, it's easy not being seen when you're someone no one wants to see. The two women seated a few tables behind Jordan are so deep in conversation they don't register the man's approach. He reaches out with the expertise of a silent waiter removing an empty glass, lifts the mobile phone from their table and moves on.

Tyler excuses himself to Jordan and follows but the man has a good head start and is hurrying away. Instead of following him back to the street, Tyler turns into the restaurant, flashing his warrant card at the waitress hovering by the door. He asks her if there's a back exit to the building and she points to an emergency sign at the end of the corridor. He hurries past assorted diners and staff, and pushes the metal bar on the rear door without worrying if it will set off a fire alarm; presumably the waitress would have warned him if it did. The exit brings him out into a service yard and then to another set of fire doors that open near the front of the Winter Garden.

The homeless guy's a few metres ahead of him, not hurrying in the slightest now, confident that if anyone had seen him he would have heard about it by now. Tyler closes the gap, takes hold of the man's arm and spins him round.

'Hey! Watch it, mate!'

He's just a young lad, can't be far past his eighteenth birthday, and for some reason Tyler thinks of the pictures he's been studying of the bruised blue boy on the railway. He has stretchers in his ears and a piercing in his nose that looks as though it might be infected. He also has a small cut on his left cheek and the beginnings of a black eye. His clothes are dirty, but not filthy, and he has a brightness to his eyes that tells Tyler he's not on anything. It doesn't surprise him, he doubts the lad would have been able to pull off the snatch-and-grab quite so easily if he was high.

Tyler shows the guy his warrant card. 'Where's the phone?'

The lad looks away and says nothing but Tyler simply holds on to his arm and squeezes. Not enough to hurt, but enough to make a point.

'Dude! All right!' He reaches into a pocket and pulls out the mobile.

Tyler takes the phone from him and lets go of the guy's arm. He expects the lad to bolt and has no intention of chasing after him if he does, but he just stands there, staring.

'Well?' the lad says, after a moment. 'Aren't you gonna arrest me, then?'

'Should I?'

A shrug. 'Prob'ly.'

'Are you gonna do this again?'

'Not when you're around.'

Tyler resists the urge to smile. Not Tiny Tim, at all. The Artful Dodger. 'What's your name?'

'Ca ... Callum.' There's a resignation to his expression that tells Tyler he's accidentally forgotten to lie.

'Callum what?'

'Smith.' He's a lot surer of himself this time. 'Callum Smith.'

This time Tyler does smile and again he feels the scar on his face turn it into a sneer. 'All right, Callum *Smith*. Thank you for returning this lady's lost property. I'll make sure it gets back to her. You got a bed for the night?'

Callum narrows his eyes. 'I'm not sharing yours, if that's your game,' he states flatly.

Tyler ignores him. 'I can make some calls, get you into a hostel.'

'I got a place.'

Tyler pulls out his wallet and extracts a ten-pound note and a business card. 'Here.'

He tries to snatch it but Tyler holds on for a moment. 'For food,' he says. '*Just* food.' He knows throwing money at the problem isn't the answer but he's damned sure locking the lad up isn't either.

Tyler lets go of the note. It disappears into an inside pocket with one hand while Callum examines the card with the other.

'I need to get back to my friend. Look after yourself, Callum. If you need help with anything, call me.' Maybe this one won't end up dead by the side of the tracks. He turns to walk away and then spins back again. 'Oh, and if I see you do anything like that again, I'll come down on you like a ton of bricks, understood?'

Callum sneers at him. 'All right, DS *Tyler*. Fair play.'

When he gets back to the restaurant Tyler uses the front entrance. As he passes the table with the two women he reaches down and pretends to pick up the mobile. 'Is this yours?'

The woman looks at him quizzically. 'Oh ... yes! I can't imagine ...'

'You should probably keep it tucked away somewhere,' he tells her. 'There are a fair few thieves operating in this area.'

'What was all that about?' Jordan asks as he sits back down.

'Nothing.'

She lets it go. He notices her glass has somehow refilled itself.

'Look. About Jude,' she says.

'Never mind.'

'He'll be in touch when he's ready. I'm sure of it. If he's still around after all this time then maybe we've both misjudged him. Maybe he's just waiting for the right time to reconnect.'

'Maybe. He didn't tell you anything about where he was living then?'

'Just give him time, Adam. You two have a lot of history to deal with. He knows that. He'll do the right thing in the end.'

But Tyler's far from sure of that.

'So what are you working on at the moment?' she asks.

He outlines the case of the boy on the railway tracks without going into too much detail in case they can be overheard.

She nods along, sadly. 'I remember. Anything in it?'

'Maybe. Maybe not.' He pauses before adding, 'Doubtful.'

'Look, I don't want to put any more pressure on you, Adam, but you could do with a win here.'

Stevens again, no doubt. Sure enough, Jordan begins talking about resources and financial cuts, and for a moment Tyler can hear the Eel's voice speaking through her. He wonders again just what she had to do to keep his head from the chopping block after the Cartwright case last year. And he realises something else. She's scared for him. The worry's present in the creases around her eyes, and in the way she moves her finger through the condensation on her glass.

'Anyway,' she says, abruptly changing tack, 'enough about work. How's that handsome fireman of yours? Things getting serious yet?'

Yet another subject he's not that comfortable with but he allows her to move on. He's got the message. CCRU needs a result. And soon. Or at the very least he'll lose Rabbani, and if the super has his way, Tyler will probably lose his job as well. For some reason, it's the former of these thoughts that bothers him the most. He wouldn't have expected that.

It's the sheer size of the Gardens that's giving them the biggest headache. There's just no way to say how far the crime scene extends. Jill had agreed it was a good call to close the gates but, assuming someone broke in last night to dig up the corpse – deliberately or otherwise – there's no way of knowing which parts of the Gardens they passed through. She simply doesn't have enough crime scene examiners to search the entire space.

It had been Mina's suggestion that she and Daley might help. Jill had agreed, reluctantly, when Mina pointed out there was a pressing time factor. The rain threatening overhead might well wash away significant evidence.

She and Daley keep to the paths as much as possible, watching carefully where they tread and scanning the lawns and flowerbeds around them in the hope of spotting something that's obviously out of place. Jill has them under strict instructions that if they find anything, they're to report it to her immediately.

Mina feels her stomach gurgle. They'd manage to commandeer a small office in the gatehouse to use as a makeshift incident room but they hadn't had time to arrange any lunch. She's had nothing all morning but one cup of weak tea served in a chipped mug.

'What the fuck's this?' Daley's voice echoes back to her from down the path. She hurries to catch up to him. He's found the old Victorian Bear Pit and is circling around inside it, craning his neck to peer up at the thick stone walls.

Mina stops at the arched entrance. 'Have you never been here before?'

'What is it?' Daley asks, his voice full of the wonder of a small boy.

'It's the Bear Pit. See, there's a bear.' She points at the steel statue of the brown bear, rearing up on its hind legs before them.

'Sick!' Daley's still staring up at the railings high above them. 'Did they used to fight them here, or summat?'

'I think they just kept them for show.' Mina kicks at the bark chippings that cover the floor of the pit. It's a big circular area, several metres across, with two smaller caves built into the walls of the pit where presumably the bears were able to take shelter from the elements. As Victorian zoos go, she imagines, it was probably fairly comfortable, but she can't help wondering what happened to the poor creatures who were kept here. She's always found the place a bit . . . macabre. She shivers.

'Mina!'

They both look up to find her old colleague from Uniform, Danny, looking down on them from above. She'd forgotten how deep the pit is. The walls tower above them, maybe fifteen or twenty feet.

'How'dya get down there?'

She tells him to stay where he is. 'I'll come to you.' The pit's built into the side of a small hill, with a path leading up either side of the thick stone walls to a viewing area above. It's muddy from last night's rain, and she wonders whether they should be preserving footprints, but it isn't as though this area is anywhere near their crime scene. Still, she does her best to avoid disturbing anything.

'Elliot's looking for you,' Danny announces as she joins him at the railings circling the top of the pit.

'Me?'

'Either of you, I think.'

Mina glances down at the ground far below them but the brown bear's standing all alone. Daley's wandered off again.

'He said it's urgent.'

'Fine.' She follows Danny back down the other side of the

hill and onto one of the wide gravel boulevards that dissect the Gardens.

'Did you hear about Nadine and that flasher bloke?' Danny asks with a wide grin. She lets him tell his story, and then another about Dawson getting covered in horse shit out at some farm somewhere. As he rambles on at her, though, she finds her interest waning sharply. In the end she cuts him off in mid-sentence and sends him to go check on the perimeter, to make sure no one from the media has found a way past the closed gates. He looks a bit stunned, as though she's slapped him or something, but agrees readily enough and takes off with a cheery, 'See you later, Mina.'

She feels bad then, but it's not as though Danny ever minded being told what to do. Even when she'd been his equal back in Uniform. *You're still his equal,* she reminds herself. Technically. She might be a detective now but there's no difference in their rank. *Technically.*

In the Marnock Garden, an enormous tent has been set up across the grave site and, as Mina feels the first drops of the threatened drizzle, she thanks Elliot for his expertise. There are a dozen SOCOs here, clad in the same white suits that Jill had forced her and Daley into an hour ago, cataloguing rubbish, broken plant stems, casts of prints and tool marks. No telling at this point which part of it's essential evidence and which is not. Mina treads carefully along the delineated path with her covered shoes until she reaches the part of the tent Elliot's working in.

'Ah,' he says, looking up. He has that look in his eye

that says he's done something very clever. Or is about to. 'I thought it would be the other one.'

'DS Daley's tied up.' Before Elliot can ask where he is, she adds, 'What have you found?'

'We've identified the grave cut so she was definitely buried here deliberately, in case there was any doubt. Oh, and it *is* a woman. Modern clothing, and from the rate of decomposition she hasn't been here much longer than a few months, I'd say. We've taken up all the plants and we'll check the soil and the surrounding detritus as well, which should give us a better idea of the postmortem interval.'

He has something he wants to tell her but he's dragging it out. She listens patiently while he witters on about soil acidity and stratigraphy, whatever the hell that is. She doesn't ask any questions even though she can see he's dying for her to.

'Yes, well, anyway,' he says after he realises she isn't going to bite. 'As I said before, we have a new lass at Watery Street, fancies herself something of a forensic archaeologist or some such. I might get her input on this.'

Mina realises something. He's showing off. She's seen this before, a million times. She wonders if he finds this 'new lass' a bit threatening.

'Okay. Great,' she says, attempting to force his hand. 'If that's everything then I'll head back and wait for you to finish up—'

'Hang on, love. I didn't call you down here because I was bored and like the sound of my own voice.'

'I did wonder,' she says, smiling to take the sting out of the words.

After a swift flick of his head, Elliot turns back to the corpse. 'Take a look at this,' he says, and with a sadistic flourish, he flicks off the plastic cover draped over the corpse.

Mina gasps out loud and takes a physical step backwards. Even as she does so, she notes the look of triumph on Elliot's face. *Damn him!* And damn her for giving him the satisfaction. She feels the cold tea sloshing around in her stomach and suppresses the urge to gag. She won't give him the satisfaction of being sick.

She forces herself to look again at the skull. Sunk into each of the sockets where the eyes should be, there is a small golden coin. On each of the coins, a tiny head is visible.

'They're Roman,' says Elliot, delighted.

Mina closes her own eyes, positive that the image of a dead woman staring back at her with golden eyes will stay with her forever.

Tyler sits in the Red Deer and sips at his pint, staring into the flames in the fireplace. His thoughts take him back to another time, another place; the still-tender skin on his shoulder crackles and itches with memory.

'Penny for 'em,' says a voice over his shoulder.

Jim Doggett stands over him, holding two pints of ale.

'Not worth it.' Tyler drains the last of the pint in his hand and takes one of the glasses from Doggett. He feels something brush against his leg and looks down to see Doggett's Yorkshire terrier sniff urgently at the table leg before chasing its tail for a couple of revolutions and then settling on his foot.

Doggett sits down as well and takes a long glug from his own glass.

Tyler says, 'Thank you for meeting me,' and Doggett shrugs. It makes Tyler smile. The DI's always shrugging. Or tapping, or clicking his fingers. He has zero ability to sit still any longer than a couple of seconds. He wonders, not for the first time, if this is some kind of medical or genetic condition. It certainly isn't nerves. DI Jim Doggett is the least nervous person Tyler's ever met.

'Sounded urgent,' Doggett asks without asking.

Tyler ignores him. 'How's the case?'

'Christ! You don't want to know.' He takes another long swig of beer and smacks his lips. 'I'm not the god-fearing sort, but what he did to that boy . . . It's enough to make you believe in the Devil.'

Five-year-old Jason Talbot had been missing almost six months by the time they'd found his frozen, mutilated corpse on a building site in the Don Valley. There wasn't an officer on the force who hadn't spent time looking for that little boy, and there wasn't an officer who didn't want his killer caught. That had been six weeks ago but the press interest hadn't faded and neither had Doggett's determination. Tyler can see it in his eyes.

'Still think it's the father?' Tyler asks him.

'It's always the father,' says Doggett. 'Except when it's the boyfriend or the husband. I heard you got a murder case of your own to look into.'

Tyler's surprised. He's only just told Jordan what he's working on and he doubts she would have mentioned it. 'There's not much to it, to be honest.'

'She didn't dig her own way out from under the roses.'

'What? Who?'

'You haven't heard?'

'I haven't been into the station this afternoon.'

The DI tuts. 'I can guess where you *have* been.'

Doggett fills him in on the top story of the day, the finding of a body buried in the Botanical Gardens. The Roman coins left on her eyes. Tyler listens and wonders how they've reached this place. If someone had told him a year ago he'd be sitting here swapping war stories with this belligerent little Yorkshireman and his scruffy dog, he wouldn't have believed them. When they first met, it had taken all of his restraint not to clock the man.

Doggett finishes his story. 'Anyway, I heard your young protégée was there this afternoon, figured you were involved.'

'Rabbani? No, I've not had anything to do with it.'

Doggett shrugs again, takes another mouthful of ale. 'So what did you want to talk about?'

'I think you know.'

Doggett drums his fingers on the table top. 'I thought we agreed to leave all that for now.'

'Did you think I would?'

'No,' says Doggett. 'I guess I didn't. But I've got to tell you, lad, I don't see where we go from here.'

'You were the one who started this. You can't tell someone you think his father was murdered and then just say you've changed your mind.'

They'd met in the same pub, a few weeks after Doggett had said those words that still kept Tyler awake at night. *There are things we need to talk about.* They sat in the opposite corner to this one, Tyler full of questions and Doggett nursing a cold, sniffing and twitching, and telling Tyler what he later realised he'd known all along, that he didn't think his father, Richard, had committed suicide.

'I knew your father well,' Doggett said, stopping to blow his nose on an oversized hankie. 'We came up together and we'd worked with each other closely for years. He used to tell me things. Things he maybe didn't tell anyone else. I mean, he was close to Diane too, of course, but it's different with a woman, isn't it?'

Tyler wasn't sure he agreed with that sentiment but let him go on.

Doggett sniffed again. 'That was how I knew things weren't right, those last few weeks, because he stopped talking to me.'

'They said he was depressed.'

Doggett shook his head, violently. 'It wasn't just that. I tried to talk to him the week before he ... before he died.

I knew he was working on something, but he wouldn't tell me what it was exactly.'

'But he told you something?'

Doggett looked up, his red nose glistening in the crackling light from the fire. 'He called it a conspiracy.'

'What? On the force?'

Doggett shook his head but turned it into a shrug halfway through. 'I dunno. That was all he said. He was distracted, scared even. I'd never seen your dad scared. Ever. But he wouldn't say any more, tried to backtrack on that even. The more I pushed him, the more he backed down, wouldn't give me any more details. He said there was one more piece to the puzzle he needed to figure out and then he'd play his hand. Less than a week later, he was dead.'

For Tyler it was like a sudden light coming on in a dark room. He'd known. He'd always known. Without really knowing. Nothing about his father's death ever added up. He was sixteen at the time and after messing about in town with a friend after school, he'd come home to find his father's body swinging from the banister in the hallway. His memory of the weeks after that is vague. It had sent him into a downward spiral of alcohol and drugs, and nights spent in dodgy clubs. He had his godmother, Diane Jordan, to thank for rescuing him from it.

He realised at that moment, sitting in the pub listening to Doggett's story, that he'd dealt with all the unanswered questions by blaming his father, choosing to accept the story he was told. He'd had to. But deep down he'd never believed it.

'Why didn't you say anything?' Tyler asked.

Doggett sniffed and fidgeted and shook his head. 'I tried, son. I promise you, I tried. I kept telling people and I kept getting shut down. In the end they made me take leave, told me I needed to get my head together if I wanted to come back. I still tried. I broke in and searched your house once. I did my best to talk to Diane but she was a mess, barely holding it together herself, and trying to cope with you at the same time. I sometimes think if she hadn't had you to look after she wouldn't have made it through herself. I didn't want to add anything to her troubles. So I kept quiet. I had no idea who was involved, or even what it was they were involved in. I even tried talking to you once, but Diane put the kibosh on that one. She was just looking out for you. And then not long after that I was transferred away. I played my part. I pretended to let it go.'

'But you didn't.'

Doggett sneezed and swore and blew his nose again. 'I've been quietly digging away over the years but I haven't found very much. I'd put it all to the back of my mind, to be honest, something that kept me awake some nights, but not as often as it used to. And then you were transferred back to Sheffield last year ...'

'And you asked for me on your team.'

'You're my last hope, son. You need to think. You've got to rack your brain and think back. Try to remember everything he did and said to you in those last few weeks.' Doggett paused for a moment, his eyes red raw as though he'd been crying. 'But before you do that, there's something I need to show you.'

Doggett took him home that night, to show Tyler his work. The dining room table was covered in box files, folders and reports. Most of it was copies of police files. Illegal copies. The last cases Richard Tyler worked on. A record of his movements from that time, as far as Doggett had managed to piece them together. Phone calls, CCTV footage, car number plate recognition traces. Doggett had kept it all for years. It was obsessive. Tyler dived in there and then.

They worked on it for months, with Doggett gently – and sometimes not so gently – prodding Tyler for what he remembered. They went over everything he had so far which, considering the amount of paperwork involved, equated to very little.

There was a receipt for paracetamol that Richard had supposedly bought on the day of his death. It had been found, somewhat conveniently, left in plain sight on the kitchen table. Suspicious, but hardly a smoking gun. If Richard *had* committed suicide then by definition he wasn't in his right mind. Maybe he just forgot he had a cupboard full of paracetamol in the bathroom cabinet already.

They had a list of the cases Richard was looking into before he died, thanks to some diligent detective work on Doggett's part, and a favour from a now retired colleague who helped him compile the list of files Richard had accessed. They had gone over and over those cases again and again and neither of them could see any connection, other than the fact they were all unsolved. What *hadn't* been found anywhere in the house, or on Richard's desk at work, were any of the investigative notes he had told Doggett he'd been compiling. Again suspicious, but only Doggett had heard anything about this so-called 'conspiracy' and, again, if Richard was out of his mind then how much did his word count for anything? Maybe the whole thing was in his head?

Then there was the fact Richard had told the cleaner not to come to the house the day he'd died but hadn't thought to warn his son not to come home. This was the most inconceivable part for Doggett. Again, the argument had been made that people who committed suicide were not in their right mind, but if Richard's death was to be taken on face value he put forethought and planning into it. If that were the case, he would never have put his son through that. 'He loved you,' Doggett said that first night back at his place, the warm centrally heated air in his house blocking his nose and further distorting his words. 'He loved both his boys but you were the one he talked about most, especially after his bust-up with your brother. At full stretch, if I accept he was depressed and at a very low ebb, I might – *might* – just accept he could take his own life. But no one will ever convince me that if he did, he would have allowed you to find his body. He would have engineered a way to get me there instead.'

But at the end of the day that was all they had. Tyler could see why no one would take Doggett seriously.

In the weeks and months that followed, Doggett's obsession became his own. Gradually, the box files were transferred to Tyler's spare room. He'd bought a fold-up trestle table from a DIY store that was really designed for pasting wallpaper but now functioned as a foldaway desk. The foldaway bit was important, as he wanted to keep what he was doing from Paul, as far as possible. Despite his efforts, there were times the room looked like the incident room back at the office, with pictures stuck to the wall and pieces of string drawing connections between them, even if they were only connections he was making in his own, desperate head. Paul began asking questions and Tyler avoided answering them. Soon, Paul stopped coming round quite so often, and the trestle table and the wall of imagined connections took up permanent residence.

And for all the months of late nights and early mornings, Tyler hadn't been able to add anything to Doggett's original case. Try as he might, his memories of that time were sketchy at best. He was sixteen. Not in the least bit interested in anything his father did. If anyone had told him that one day he would follow in his father's footsteps and become a police officer, he would have laughed in their face. But maybe it had been inevitable. If, somewhere deep down, he had always known what Doggett was now telling him for sure, then what other choice did he have? Since the day he'd joined the force, he'd only ever really had one case to solve. He just hadn't known he was working on it.

*

Tyler stares at Doggett across the pub table. He looks sheep-ish; the dog whimpers in sympathy.

'Look,' says Doggett, 'we've been over this a dozen times. I only told you as much as I did because I thought you might remember something.' He studies Tyler's face for a moment. 'Have you remembered something?'

'No,' Tyler has to admit. 'But there's a chance someone else might know something.' He pauses for a moment. 'My brother's back in town.'

Doggett's brow wrinkles as he takes another sip of beer. 'He wasn't around when your father . . . when he died.' Even now, neither of them are comfortable calling it murder. Any more than they are calling it suicide.

'But he was here in the lead-up to it. He's older than me. It's possible Richard told him something about what he was working on, something Jude never connected with his death. Something . . .' He knows he's clutching at straws, but straws are all he has left after a year of investigation.

The dog whines, sits up and wags its tail, thumping Tyler against the leg and bringing him out of his reverie.

Doggett's eyeing him closely. 'Look, I know what I told you but maybe we just have to accept I got it wrong.'

'You don't mean that.'

'Even if I'm right, maybe we have to accept there's nothing we can do about it.'

'You don't mean that either.'

Doggett sags back against the wall and scratches his stub-ble. 'I'll get us another pint.'

'It's my round.' Tyler heads to the bar.

When he gets back Doggett's fidgeting in his seat, stroking the dog behind the ears and bouncing his leg up and down under the table. He downs half a pint and says, 'I know you're not just going to walk away from this but you need to be careful. You're risking your career.'

Tyler knows he's right. Doggett's obsession has become Tyler's and his work is suffering for it. Jordan's warning about getting a result is still ringing in his ears.

'Rabbani's too, for that matter,' Doggett goes on. 'There's been a lot of talk about "reallocation of resources" lately.'

'Yeah, I heard.'

Doggett taps the frayed beermat on the table, sending up a fine spray of spilled ale. 'If the worst happens, I'll do my best to fold you both into my team but . . .'

'You already have a DS.'

'Yeah, and he's bloody liability enough on his own without adding you into the mix.'

Tyler smiles.

Doggett checks his watch and then stretches his arms over his head. 'Right, I'd best be off. I've got a booty-call planned and I'm running late.'

'I think a bit of sick just came up. Who's the lucky lady then?'

'Just this lass I've been seeing.'

'Going well, is it?'

Doggett wobbles his head from side to side in a 'so-so' manner. 'She's a bit of a pain in the arse, to be honest. Insists on trying to improve me by taking me to galleries and the like.'

'She's got her work cut out then.'

Doggett smiles. 'Fucks like a rabbit though.'

'Spoken like a true Renaissance man.'

'Ah, the voice of a man who's not getting any. What happened to the fireman then?'

'Shit!' He's supposed to be cooking dinner. 'I've gotta go.'

Doggett chuckles as Tyler downs his pint.

As he races back to his apartment Tyler reflects on their conversation. He knows Doggett's right. The people around him – Rabbani, Diane, Paul, even Doggett himself – deserve more from him than this. But how's he supposed to just forget it all? How is he supposed to forget the possibility that someone killed his father?

Dave can't sleep. He lies awake in the darkness and listens to the sounds coming through the wall. Thump, thump, thump; a persistent squeaking; and those high-pitched squeals, like the daybreak cry of some exotic jungle creature.

He thinks she's Greek-Cypriot, although he isn't entirely sure. Almost everyone in the building is a student, and the vast majority are from overseas. She continues to cry out, loud, high-pitched squeals of pleasure that should be exciting him but instead turn his bowels to jelly. He wants to hammer on the wall and tell them to 'Shut the fuck up!' But he can't bring himself to do that just in case he meets her in the corridor one day.

There comes a last volley of loud, carnal utterances from both her and her partner and they are finished. Dave sighs, much as they must be doing next door, though for somewhat different reasons, then he gives up on sleep altogether and decides to get up.

The clock on his bedside table says 3.32am in enormous red figures designed for tired, ageing eyes. It's one of the few things he kept of his mother's belongings when she died. Then he remembers it's actually 2.32am, since the clocks went back last week and he's lost the instruction manual and has no idea how to press the right combination of buttons to correct the hour. Despite his lack of sleep, he finds himself disappointed it isn't closer to morning.

He gets up slowly, levering his heavy legs over the side of the bed and pushing himself up from the lumpy mattress. He walks to the toilet and relieves himself. The walls are thin in this old Victorian building and he would normally sit down on the throne, aghast at the thought his closest neighbour might hear the splashing of his urine. But this morning he stands and pisses freely. Let them listen to his own pleasure. His only pleasure these days.

In the living room he fills the kettle and prepares a cup of tea. He won't sleep any more tonight, so to hell with the caffeine. He picks up the photo frame on the windowsill and strokes her face with a soil-crusted finger. He smiles, closes his eyes and presses the frame against his chest so she's close to his heart. He opens his eyes and looks out the window at the quiet garden. It's a good view, even in the pale orange glow of the street lighting.

His flat might be cold and damp, and the neighbours might fuck too loudly, but at least he has this. He considers taking his mug out onto the patio at the back of the house but decides against it. If one of the neighbours sees him they'll consider him even stranger than they no doubt already do.

Dave drains the last of his tea, puts the photo frame back on the windowsill and gets dressed. Then he slips into his donkey jacket and heads downstairs to the front door. The night's crisp and there's a cool breeze; the long winter is just around the corner and is making its presence felt. He pulls his ancient bike out from the lean-to at the side of the house, straps on his equipment, and leads it down the path to the front gate. He's out on the road and freewheeling down the hill before he realises where he's headed.

He can't shake that image of her arm out of his head and he knows he won't be able to sleep again tonight until he knows she's all right. Stupid, really. It isn't as though the police are going to let him in, assuming they're still there, and anyway they've probably already carted her off to some cold slab in the morgue.

He pulls up by the turnstile but everything's locked up for the night. He supposes he could break in if he wanted to. He knows a half-dozen ways to get into the Gardens other than through the main gate, but his reason for coming begins to seem less urgent now he's here. Whoever dug up her corpse didn't find what they were looking for. His hand idly strokes the metal detector attached to his bike. It's too risky to go back in now.

Nighthawking

How awful her hand looked. He can't bear to think of her that way, all cold and dead and wasting in her grave beneath the rose bushes. He'd always pictured her whole, whenever he thought about her. All peaceful and sleeping. The way she'd looked when he buried her.

two

the second nighthawker

<u>Record of Finds</u>

Date: Sun 9th Apr
Time: 22:15
Location: Sheffield Botanical Gardens
Finds: N/A

Dave slips off his backpack and holds it awkwardly against his chest as he squeezes through the turnstile. He doesn't have his detector with him this evening, which he's grateful for as he presses his skinny waist up against the cold metal of the bars. He takes a deep breath, pulls the turnstile tight against his body until he hears the click, and then pushes back the other way. The metal bars slip away from him and Dave unfolds himself into the Gardens. It's a trick she taught him a few months ago and he supposes he should have told someone about it straight away. He's glad he didn't now.

The thought that he's on his way to meet her sends a shiver

of excitement down his spine. Once again, he considers his motivations in this matter. But it's not a sexual thing, no matter how others might see his friendship with her. She's half his age for one thing, and he's never really been into younger women, quite the opposite in fact. Lizzie was six years younger and look how that turned out. It's undeniable she's beautiful though. Stunningly so. In that exotic way foreign women have about them. But it isn't that. He's attracted to her, obviously, but it isn't that kind of attraction. He doesn't really understand it himself, which is perhaps why he's analysing it so much. He wants to feel that his motivations are . . . pure.

She understands, though, which is the main thing. She doesn't flirt with him the way he's seen her do with other men. It's something far more indefinable than sexual attraction. An unspoken bond. And despite the clandestine circumstances they find themselves in tonight, he feels the same lightness of heart he always has when he's on his way to meet her.

He crosses the Gardens on light feet, the dark around him somehow demanding he make no excessive noise, even though there's unlikely to be anyone else here at this time. The coins in the rucksack clink and clatter against each other but the sound doesn't carry very far.

That was the second most incredible piece of luck to befall him in the past year — the first was meeting her — but then, after the past few years, wasn't he due a bit of luck? He hadn't set out to do anything illegal. It was just a bit of fun at first. He hasn't slept properly for years, not since the hospital. All those half-hearted attempts to grab a couple of hours in a cramped chair next to her bed. And afterwards, when she was gone, he couldn't shake the feeling there was something treasonous about sleep. He would always associate sleep with guilt and it would never come easily to him again. So that's why he'd started metal-detecting, going out at nights on digs to keep his mind off things. Shortly after that he'd joined the detectorists group and he'd realised he wasn't the only one. The *Nighthawkers*, they called themselves, partly a joke, partly a secret 'club within a club'. And though it was technically a bit shady to go digging up private land without permission, as long as you declared what you found, where was the harm? And truth be told, it wasn't as though they ever found anything of value anyway.

Then Nick had got that tip. A mate of his who worked in the planning department at the council who let slip that building work was about to start on a new school development. The site chosen was an area that was likely to have been part of the old Sheffield Castle, razed to the ground at the end of the Civil War and famously the home of Mary Queen of Scots for fourteen years of her exile. An archaeological dig had been taking place there but was about to conclude. The conversation had started as a remonstration on how sad it all was. Who knew what fascinating historical artefacts were waiting to be found, buried just beneath the topsoil? The university had been digging there for weeks and had found walls that were part of a settlement dating back to at least the Norman invasion, possibly even earlier. It was criminal that it was all about to be concreted over.

Dave can't remember whose idea it was, exactly, but of the four of them only Deepak put up any resistance, and it was a weak one at that. The university moved out, the builders were yet to move in. Where was the harm in having a quick look, in between? They had a period of just three days before the trenches that the university had dug were due to be filled. They all agreed to leave Colin out of it, since he was such a stickler for the rules, and Mike had insisted they not tell Ronnie given, in his words, 'she's not exactly great at keeping her mouth shut'. And anyway, the four of them had got used to going out together by that point. It seemed right that it should be just them.

The thing is, they didn't really discuss what they'd do if they found anything. None of them really thought they would. And then, on the second night, after they'd been searching for hours and Nick had already started to grumble about calling it a night, Dave's detector screeched like some tortured animal and they all came running. It had taken a fair bit of digging, but without the university's earlier intervention it would have taken a fair deal more. Of course, without the university dig, the detector would not have registered anything buried that deeply.

It was a leather sack of some sort as far as they could tell but they barely had time to examine it before it disintegrated in their hands and spilled its clinking golden contents across the ground.

They laughed, all of them. And Dave heard himself

declaring, 'Roman! They're Roman!!' over and over again while the others laughed and patted him on the back.

But as excited as they were, they had no idea what they'd found. Not until a few days later, after they'd done some research. Thirteen golden aurei, still almost as fresh as the day they were minted, each bearing the head of the Roman usurper-emperor Allectus. Just one of these coins had sold recently for half a million and that one hadn't been in anywhere near as good condition as these. Even accounting for a reduction in value — their find would significantly increase the supply of these coins given that, so far, only twenty-four had been found worldwide — they were looking at hundreds of thousands of pounds, maybe more! Even split four ways — Dave had made that offer immediately — this was so much more than any of them could have hoped for.

They knew the rules, of course: any more than two gold coins is officially classed as treasure. And given the condition of the coins, the very clear outline of the Emperor's head visible on each, this would be classed as an enormously significant find. Nick said he'd read somewhere that there had been very few Roman finds in Sheffield, but it was thought that a minor Roman road once ran through the land now covered by the city, connecting the Roman forts at Templeborough and Brough-on-Noe. So not only were the coins intrinsically worth money but this was a significant archaeological find as well. Perhaps enough to delay the building of the school and get the site opened up again. They *had* to report it, obviously. No question. They would still get half of the haul's worth.

But over the next couple of days this urgency towards honesty faded. Mike pointed out the fact they didn't have permission to be digging on the site in the first place. It was possible the haul would be confiscated and they wouldn't see a penny. More days passed and still they did nothing. Work began on the new school. In the meantime, they split the coins between them for safety — three each, with Dave taking the extra one since he'd been the one to actually find them. There was only minor wrangling over who should hold the coins in the best condition. And slowly, over the following weeks, a plan began to form. A plan that had led Dave here, tonight. With all thirteen coins in his backpack.

He sees her then, darting between the trees at the back of the Mediterranean Garden. He calls out her name but then alters it in mid-sentence to a whisper. They still have to be wary in case someone else is around. He follows her through the trees, wondering why she's headed this way when they were supposed to be meeting at the Bear Pit. But when he emerges onto the path there's no sign of her.

Odd. Maybe it's just his mind playing tricks on him. It wouldn't be the first time. The episodes come less frequently now but they still hit him on occasion. Moments when he feels outside himself, looking in. As though the world around him is a film he's watching or . . . no, more like a videogame. Something he can interact with but isn't a part of. After she'd nagged the information out of him, Lizzie had diagnosed them as panic attacks and badgered him to go to the doctor. But doctors were always finding things wrong with you if you let them. They both knew that better than anyone. And it wasn't as though the episodes didn't pass.

No, perhaps he hadn't seen anything at all, his mind just conjuring an image in expectation of their meeting. He retraces his steps and doubles back towards the Bear Pit as arranged.

When he gets there, his first thought is that she's sleeping, curled up on the blanket of bark chippings that carpet the ground. She works all those long hours in the lab. What right did he have to force her into this illegal enterprise, causing her to go gallivanting about in the middle of the night? He walks towards her, still unable to say her name out loud. But she isn't asleep.

'No!' Dave drops to his knees.

There's blood everywhere. Her eyes are wide open but he can already see she's gone. 'Nonononono . . .'

She's folded up like a broken doll, her left leg pinned under her body in a manner that's so far from natural it's hard to believe he could have ever taken it for sleep. He glances up to the top of the pit. She must have fallen, he realises. There's a gaping wound on her head and a long smear of red blood dripping down the statue of the bear. She's fallen from above and been so very unlucky. Had she landed clear of the statue she might well have survived, suffering not much more than a broken bone or two.

He crouches down beside her and takes her head in his arms, cradling it in his lap. He sits there and the mist descends on his mind, just as it did for the first time in the hospital six years ago. Pulling him into that other world. The safe place, where he can act without consequence. Tears streak down his face in much the same way her life's blood drips from the pelt of the brown bear towering over them.

Mina's first into the conference suite next morning. They call it that, but in reality it's just a corner of the Murder Room that has been partitioned with MDF walls to create a room within a room. It has a door, and a long window with Venetian blinds that can be closed for privacy, but none of this is of particular use since the ceiling tiles aren't sound-proofed. Confidential conversations held in anything louder than a whisper can easily be overheard by anyone taking up a position two paces to the left of the watercooler. There *is* a coffee machine, though, so the room's popular for meetings.

Jordan has called the meeting for nine but it's gone ten past by the time she finally arrives with a folder of paperwork under one arm and Guy Daley in tow. Mina's already fetched them a drink each from the machine: Earl Grey for Jordan, a milky latte for Daley. There's a black coffee waiting for Tyler too, but no sign of him yet.

Jordan sits at the head of the table and takes a sip from her cup without a word of acknowledgement or thanks. Mina waits until Daley pulls out a chair before choosing a place on the opposite side of the table, furthest from the door.

'Right, we'd better get started,' Jordan says, opening the file. 'Any sign of DS Tyler?'

Mina has a number of responses rehearsed to answer this

predictable question but now it comes to it, she can't think of any of them. She opens her mouth to say something – anything – but is saved by Jordan raising a hand.

'All right, Mina, don't bother. If I hear you cover for him one more time I might have to start shouting and I really don't have the energy this morning. Let's just get started and—'

The door opens and Tyler walks into the room. Jordan shoots him a withering look but he makes no attempt to apologise or explain, simply picks up his coffee and skirts around the table to Mina's side. Despite the irritation she feels at having been put on the spot yet again, Mina can't help but feel a small jolt of satisfaction that he's chosen to join her rather than Daley.

'Guy,' says Jordan, 'can you bring us up to speed, please?'

Daley looks up as though puzzled to have been asked to contribute. 'Er ... Sure. Yeah. We have an unidentified body found in the Botanical Gardens. Elliot's confirmed it's a woman but we don't have much more than that.'

'When's the postmortem?'

'Er ...'

'Scheduled for ten this morning, ma'am,' Mina interrupts. 'By the time they got her out yesterday it was too late to start.'

Jordan checks her watch. 'I'm not going to be able to make that. Guy, I'll have to leave that to you.'

'Huh? Oh, right, yeah sure.'

'What else?'

Daley appears to have nothing, so Mina takes over. 'As far as the SOCOs can tell, it looks as though the arm was dug up. The area has markings consistent with the use of a trowel so it seems likely it wasn't an animal. There are no paw prints either. There are footprints, though. Size-nine trainer. The lab are processing now to see if we can get a make.'

'So someone dug her up? Or part of her, at least. Any idea why?'

Mina glances at Daley, who lifts his shoulders as if to say, *It's your funeral.*

'I think,' she says carefully, 'someone was looking for something else but maybe found her by mistake.'

'What makes you say that?'

Mina outlines her theory. 'The woman who's head of the volunteers who work at the Gardens says people are always digging up plants and stealing them. They have quite a few rare specimens and people take them for their own gardens.'

Jordan takes another sip of tea. 'It never ceases to amaze me; the lack of civic-mindedness of some people.'

'She reckons they're usually pretty brazen about it though. There's so many volunteers and members of the public coming and going, you can pretty much help yourself.'

'Like shoplifting,' Jordan says. 'It's the fear of being caught that stops people, not the lack of opportunity.'

'Or maybe it's the fact most people are pretty civic-minded?' Tyler suggests, cradling his coffee.

Jordan stares at him. 'How glass half-full of you.' She turns back to Mina. 'Go on.'

'The point is, they don't normally break in at night. They get a few students climbing over the walls for . . . er . . .'

'Assignations?' Jordan supplies.

'Er, yes, ma'am, but they don't normally dig stuff up.' Mina realises she's only pouring water on her own theory. 'Anyway, there doesn't seem to be any other reason someone would break in there.'

'Are the plants in that area particularly valuable?'

'No, ma'am.'

'Okay,' Jordan says thoughtfully. 'Then if it wasn't an accident, we're left with the possibility they knew exactly what they were looking for.'

'The killer coming back for something?' Mina asks.

Daley jumps in, perhaps aware he should contribute. 'We interviewed the people at the Gardens. They're mostly volunteers but there's a core group of council workers who open and close it, and make the real decisions. The head woman's given us the use of an office there to finish the interviews. She reckons that area of the Gardens is tended pretty regularly, you know, weeded and all that, but it had a big overhaul just a few months back. Around Easter, she reckons, but she's looking into the dates for me.'

'So she hasn't been there any longer than that?'

'No,' Daley says. 'The woman said there's no way the body could have been there before then or they would have found it when they re-landscaped.'

'It fits with Elliot's rough time of death as well,' Mina adds.

Jordan nods, thoughtfully. 'And then there's the coins,' she says.

Mina turns to Tyler to fill him in. 'When they finished extracting the corpse they found she'd been buried with two old coins placed over her eyelids.'

'And by old, she means ancient,' Daley chips in. 'Roman, Elliot reckoned.'

'Yes,' Tyler says. 'I heard.'

'You've got some catching up to do,' Jordan tells him. There's a look that passes between them and then Tyler nods, shortly.

'Okay,' Jordan goes on after a moment's pause. 'I'm not going to lie to you, we have precious little resource for this. Jim's going to be tied up on the Talbot case for the foreseeable so I've asked DS Tyler to join you both since he's not working on anything essential or time-sensitive at the minute.'

Daley opens his mouth to argue: 'Ma'am—'

But before he can go on, Jordan cuts him off, 'I don't want to hear it, Guy. You need to find a way to work together, both of you. Understood?'

Daley backs down but it's Tyler who Jordan's looking at. He looks as though he isn't bothered either way. He *is* bothered, though, Mina knows him well enough to know that. This obviously isn't the first he's hearing about it. She wonders when Jordan read him the riot act.

Apparently satisfied there'll be no more argument, Jordan moves on. 'I'll remain Senior Investigating Officer on this but to be honest, the three of you are pretty much all we've got.'

Mina wonders whether she's the only one who feels that's a bit less than complimentary.

'What about Dev? And Cat maybe?' Daley asks, betraying his order of preference.

'I appreciate why you took them yesterday, Guy, but Jim needs them back. I can let you have a couple of Uniforms when you need them but *only* if absolutely necessary. Superintendent Stevens is not going to authorise any over-time on this. The only reason the case is getting the attention it is, is because of the unusual location of the discovery. The media are already all over it. I had to give them something last night and now they're predictably baying at my heels.'

'That could work in our favour,' Daley says. 'The more attention from the press, the more likely Stevens is to put his hand in his pocket.'

Jordan raises the eyebrow again. Mina makes a mental note to practise that.

'Leave the media to me, DS Daley, is that understood?'

'Yeah, all right, I'm not gonna talk to anyone.'

'Your focus needs to be on ID-ing the victim. That's the best chance we have of scaling up the investigation.' And with that, Jordan gets up, gathers her papers and steps out of the room.

There's silence for a moment and then both Tyler and Daley speak at once.

Daley says, 'Mina, I need you to—' and at the same time Tyler begins, 'Take a look through the—' They both stop and stare at each other.

Mina throws down the pen in her hand and stands up. 'Oh my God, will you two stop snarling at each other for five minutes! I'm not going to be the one caught in the middle. You don't like each other, I get it. But you've got to work together so . . . just get over yourselves, will you?'

'Couldn't've said it better myself, Mina,' Jordan shouts from the other side of the wall.

She hadn't realised her voice had carried that far but she's not going to apologise. Instead she crosses her arms. 'Right,' she tells them. 'I'll tell you what I'm going to do. I'm going to go through the database and start looking for a missing girl. What you two do is up to you. Obviously.' It isn't the best finish but she's conscious she's probably pushed things about as far as she can. Tyler has a slight curl to his lip that might be a smile or might just be that scar on his face.

Daley is full-on snarling. 'Fine,' he says. 'Let me know what you find.' And with that he leaves the room.

Mina's about to head out herself when Tyler touches her arm. 'Careful, Mina,' he says. 'You can't trust Daley.'

He seems genuinely concerned for her but she resists the urge to point out that she's not sure she can really trust either of them.

'What are you going to do?' she asks as they follow Daley back into the Murder Room.

'There's something I need to check out.'

'I don't suppose it has anything to do with *this* case, does it?'

He stops for a moment and uses Jordan's eyebrow trick. She's really going to have to practise that one.

'Don't push your luck,' he tells her, and with that he's gone too.

Tyler pulls up opposite a dilapidated house on Shoreham Street, in the shade of the Bramall Lane football ground, and kills the engine. He sits for a minute with his hands on the wheel and leans back against the headrest. He'd avoided the talk with Paul last night by taking things straight to the bedroom, and then he'd left early this morning before Paul was awake. He figured if he put some time in at the station it might make up for his absence yesterday. But Jordan had been waiting for him and ushered him into her office.

It started as a rehash of their talk in the restaurant, Jordan telling him how CCRU needed a result, and quick. He tried to get her interested in the boy on the railway again but she didn't want to hear it. He realised afterwards she must have already made the decision to co-opt both him and Rabbani into this 'Girl in the Gardens' case, as everyone was already calling it, but by the time she'd made that clear, he was annoyed she'd let him waste his time wittering on for so long before telling him. It led to an argument neither of them had needed and he was already regretting it. But what was he supposed to do? If he just accepted this without a fight, he was in danger of allowing them to side-line CCRU and everything he'd put into it in the past couple of years. *How much have you actually put in, this last year?* He'd asked her for just one more day, to tidy up his thoughts and notes on the case he was working on before moving across. If he let her – or Stevens, more to the point – believe he could be co-opted at a moment's notice, it would set a dangerous precedent for the future. She'd paused for a long while before shaking her head. 'Half a day,' she'd told him, and he knew that she wouldn't have granted it to anyone else. He was exploiting their relationship again, but right now he was too furious with her to care.

In the meeting, he'd done his best to hide his irritation but he knew he hadn't done very well. He'd tried to focus, but his thoughts kept flitting away to other places. It was as he was sitting there, while Rabbani outlined the case, that the real reason he was pissed off with Jordan hit him. It had nothing to do with work at all.

How could she not tell him that Jude was back?

It was that epiphany that had led Tyler here. It's been years since he last came here. He wasn't sure he'd be able to remember the right house, but now he sees the faded purple of the window frames and realises it hasn't changed a bit. All those years and not so much as a lick of paint. He dreads to think what the inside must look like. It was hardly a palace back then. Now it must be close to derelict. He looks up at the bedroom window, steamed up and dripping with condensation. There's someone living here at least.

It's the longest of long shots but he doesn't have much to go on. He knows Jude's back in Sheffield. He knows he's short of money. Even without Jordan's input he could have guessed that much. Jude was always short of money. Where would he stay? If not with Jordan, or himself, where would he turn? This is the only place he can think of.

It had been years ago when Jude first brought him to this place. Their mother had already gone by that point, and Richard was tied up with work. Jude had been left to babysit his brother. Not that Tyler had ever needed babysitting; sometimes he wondered if his father insisted on these arrangements so Tyler could look after his older brother rather than the other way around.

Jude was always the one who was far more likely to get them in trouble. He hated babysitting, and wouldn't let a little thing like Tyler's well-being get in the way of having a good time. So, often, Tyler got dragged along on whatever mildly dodgy endeavour Jude was embarked upon.

Tyler never really blamed Jude. Whatever trouble they inevitably found, he'd learned a lot about life thanks to his older brother's wild behaviour. And they were both sensible enough to get out before anything too serious happened, usually. Playing on the railway lines, smoking in abandoned buildings, it was fairly ordinary kid-stuff for the most part. Until Elly.

Jude met her at some party or other. He told Tyler at the time she was 'a student or something'; he remembers thinking even then that the 'or something' didn't bode very well. Jude and Elly started hanging out more; Jude and Tyler less so. But he doesn't remember being upset about this particularly, understanding instinctively that his brother was growing up and had certain interests that a younger brother did nothing but hamper. But occasionally Jude would let Tyler tag along. Most notably the day they came to this place. To Elly's house.

At first, Tyler thought Elly was just one of several roommates who shared the place, but he found out later she was the owner of the property and everyone else rented from her. She was older than Jude by quite a bit, maybe ten or fifteen years. Jude would have been eighteen at that point, Elly in her late twenties or early thirties; it was hard to tell because sometimes she seemed very young and other times as old as some of Tyler's teachers at school. He was never clear exactly what she did for work but he supposes now it must have been something flexible because a great deal of her time seemed to be spent in this house, drinking, getting high, fucking guys. And Jude started to spend a lot of time here too.

Tyler only came once and sat on a mildew-coated beanbag and watched his brother stick a needle in his arm. He waited until they were out of it and then he picked up his school bag and walked the five miles home alone. He never went back. Jude did. Tyler never told his father what Jude was up to. He wonders now if he should have. Would it have changed anything between them? Or just made things worse?

Tyler's brought back to the present by the front door opening. An old woman steps out and pulls the door closed behind her. She totters slowly up the path and then he realises it isn't an old woman at all. It's Elly. He's so shocked that for a moment he doesn't move. But then he realises this is exactly why he's here and jumps out of the car and darts across the road.

'Elly!' He reaches out to touch her arm but at the last moment stops himself. He has an instinct she won't be predisposed to help him, and invading her personal space is unlikely to help his case.

She slows and looks up. She's still recognisable as the woman he remembers, but only just. If she was in her early thirties back then, she should be mid-forties max by now, but she looks far older. The skin on her face is creased and dried out, and she's painfully thin. She looks him up and down as though trying to work out how she should know him. There's no hint of recognition in her eye but he supposes that's hardly surprising.

'What do you want?' she asks, without giving anything away.

'My name's Tyler, Adam Tyler. I'm Jude's brother.' He leaves it at that.

'Right,' she says noncommittally. 'Well, I haven't seen him for years.'

She's lying. For a hardened drug addict she's not very good at it.

'I didn't ask,' he says. 'But thanks anyway. So, how are you?' He's about to say she's looking well but decides it's a statement so far from the truth neither one of them would be able to take him seriously.

'What do you want?' she asks again.

'I just saw you as I was passing, thought I'd say hello.'

'Yeah, well, you've said it.'

'Okay, then. I guess I'll see you around.' He lets her turn away and then he does take hold of her arm. She turns again, pulling away from him and raising her own arm as though he's going to hit her.

'I'm sorry.' He raises his palms to show her he means no harm. 'I just wanted to give you this.' He reaches into his inside jacket pocket and pulls out a business card. She takes it and reads it slowly, her lips moving as she sounds out the words. Her eyes widen when she realises he's police. This is what he was hoping for, that Jude hadn't told her what his little brother does for a living. That she might decide to give him up rather than risk any trouble. 'If you should see Jude, maybe you could pass that on, tell him I was asking after him. I'd be grateful. It would save me having to come back here again.' He lets the threat settle.

Her hands shake as she holds the card. She grunts something that he hopes is agreement and shuffles off up the road. He watches her, now and again turning back to check if he's still there. If she *is* in touch with him, Jude will get the message. He supposes it's the best he can hope for.

As he turns away he glances once more at the dilapidated house and sees a movement at the front window. The filthy net curtains, falling back into place? Perhaps. Or maybe he imagined it. He considers knocking on the door but it's not as though he can force Jude to talk to him even if he's there. Instead he writes a short message on the back of another business card and posts it through the letter box. Then he heads back to his car, wondering if his brother's watching him from a window.

'There's some American woman on the phone asking for DS Daley.'

Mina looks up from her screen and squints at Carla, her eyes adjusting to the new focus. 'O-kay?'

'I don't know where he is.' Carla looks stricken, as though answering the phone has been too much for her. Clearly, taking a message is.

'Put her through.' Mina rubs her eyes. The phone on her desk trills and she picks up the receiver. 'Detective Constable Mina Rabbani.'

There's the expected pause while the caller realises she's through to yet another person who's not the person she wanted to speak to. 'I'm looking for Detective Sergeant Daley,' she says, in a voice rich with a southern US accent.

'Yes, I'm sorry, he isn't available at the moment. Is there something I can help you with?'

The woman at the other end of the phone tuts quietly. 'What about DS . . .' she pauses again as though checking her paperwork. 'DS Tyler?'

'I'm sorry, he's not available either.'

There's a palpable silence and what might be a blast of irritated breath.

Mina says, 'Can I ask who this is?'

The woman apologises. 'I'm Dr Ridgeway. DCI Jordan left a message to say DS Daley would be attending the autopsy.

I guess I'm a little shocked he's not here. I was told the case was urgent. Do you know if he's on his way here, now?'

Crap. Now she's got *two* superior officers who've disappeared. Is anyone doing anything except her? Not that what she's doing is achieving a great deal. She glances at the surprisingly long list of candidates from the Missing Persons' database, open on her screen. She needs more information if she's ever going to narrow down the search. Information that she'd been banking on getting from the autopsy.

Ridgeway goes on, 'I can't wait much longer. We already gotta backlog here and if I have to delay 'til tomorrow there's—'

'I can be there in ... twenty minutes?' Rabbani says, checking her watch.

There's another short pause, presumably while Ridgeway factors this further delay into her plans. 'Fine. DC Rabbani, was it? I'll leave word at the desk to expect you.' She hangs up without another word.

Tyler's on his way back to the station when a voice addresses him from the pavement.

'You stalkin' me or summat?'

The young snatch-and-grab lad from yesterday is sitting cross-legged on the pavement outside the Co-op. 'Callum Smith.'

The lad grins. 'Yeah.' He looks down at his feet. 'But it's Morgan, actually. Callum Morgan?'

He looks better than he did at the restaurant, the cut on

his cheek has closed, and the black eye hasn't developed any further. He's wearing the same grubby jacket but still seems clear-eyed and alert. Again, Tyler's struck by the Dickensian quality of the lad. There's something likeable about Callum Morgan. A lovable rogue. If he manages to stay out of trouble, gets back on his feet, he might end up doing quite well.

'How's it going then?' Tyler points to his own eye. 'No more trouble?'

Callum glances up and down the street as though mentioning it might bring the trouble back down on him. 'Ah, it was just a disagreement. No biggie.'

Tyler checks his watch. He really should get back to the office before Jordan notices he's missing. His half day's grace is rapidly evaporating and even the lightest digging on her part would expose the fact he wasn't doing anything remotely related to CCRU. No doubt he'd already earned himself a ticking-off from Rabbani. That was something to look forward to.

'Have you eaten anything today?'

Callum shrugs a mighty indifference.

Tyler glances across at the front entrance to the office. He might as well give Rabbani something to really shout about.

Mina's shown into a small, featureless room. There are half a dozen chairs or so, lined up in front of a glass window that fills the entire wall. The window looks down onto the autopsy room below. The room is bright and stark, with two metallic tables taking pride of place in the centre. There are two trolleys as well, one laden with assorted instruments of torture as far as Mina can tell, and another bearing the withered corpse recovered from the crime scene.

She's never had a weak stomach but looking down at that wasted, ragged corpse, she's glad for the glass wall that separates her from the smells that no doubt fill the room.

Dr Ridgeway's a tall woman but other than that, Mina can't tell much as she's wrapped from head to toe in scrubs – a mask and visor covering her face, her hands encased in gloves. She's holding a large saw and her front is spattered with a dark substance Mina can only think of as *gore*. Ridgeway looks up and raises the saw in casual greeting. Her voice comes into the viewing room via a speaker mounted high on the wall behind Mina. It's a bit eerie, especially since she can't see the woman's lips moving.

'DC Rabbani. I'm glad you could make it.' She's obviously still pissed off at having had her time wasted. It won't have helped that Mina's optimistic twenty minutes had turned into something closer to an hour by the time she'd fought her way through the traffic on the ring-road.

Mina smiles down at her. 'I'm sorry,' she says. 'I appreciate you taking the time to—'

Ridgeway's shaking her head. Again the woman's tinny voice echoes from behind. 'You gotta press the intercom button before you speak.'

Mina looks down and feels her cheeks heat. She presses the button and apologises all over again.

'You're here now,' says Ridgeway. 'Let's do this, huh? As

you can see, I've already gotten started. I'll catch you up at the end.'

Ridgeway talks as she works, describing the remains for the benefit of the recording. A lot of the technical stuff Mina doesn't understand but she decides to wait to ask questions rather than risk raising the wrath of the good doctor any further. Instead, she forces herself to watch as Ridgeway digs and cuts her way through bone, removing unidentifiable masses, weighing and measuring. Another doctor enters the room and goes about some unknowable but related business. The two of them work in tandem, passing instruments and samples back and forth in a complicated dance, with little need for communication. It reminds Mina of the way the dentist and nurse work together when she gets her teeth checked. She hopes she won't think of that the next time she's there.

Eventually the business is concluded and Ridgeway indicates Mina should leave, back through the door she came in by. She heads out as directed and a woman she hasn't seen before escorts her into a conference room with a long table and asks her if she'll wait. Ten minutes later, Dr Ridgeway steps into the room.

Mina notes she was right about Ridgeway being tall. She's blonde, her hair tied back in a functional ponytail. She's changed out of the scrubs and is wearing a bright-red skinny-fit cardigan and tight blue jeans. She's younger than Mina expected, perhaps just early thirties. And she's very pretty. Mina knows girls like this: confident, classically beautiful.

She'd bet any money the woman was a cheerleader at school. Ridgeway's the sort of woman who life falls to on a plate. She doubts she's ever had to fight for anything.

Mina prepares herself for another spiky encounter but in fact, the woman smiles warmly at her.

'Detective Rabbani, I'm Emma Ridgeway.' She steps across and holds out her hand.

Mina takes it and decides that a bit more buttering up won't harm anyone. 'Thank you for your time, Dr Ridgeway. I really appreciate how busy you must be.'

Ridgeway waves the comment away as though her time's endless and waiting on AWOL detective sergeants is all in a day's work. 'Don't worry about it. And it's Emma.' She's still smiling, a line of bright white teeth showing her perfect American dental care.

'Mina.'

'Mina. Please, take a seat.'

Emma sits to Mina's left and presses a remote that activates a screen on the wall at the end of the table. Immediately, pictures of the skeletal corpse appear, its decayed frame held together with soil-encrusted clothing.

Mina swallows.

'Your victim's a young woman, East Asian descent, early twenties at most. She was in good health, no signs of any long-term malnutrition or serious disease of any kind.'

'Can you tell how she died?'

'Not conclusively. She has a broken clavicle and left tibia, two cracked ribs, and a fractured skull. She also has a number of hairline fractures in other places and I would say all of this is consistent with a fall from a significant height. All of these injuries were pre-mortem but no one of them would have been fatal necessarily. The head wound might have made her groggy or incapacitated but it wasn't enough to kill her. She was, however, stabbed in the stomach with what looks like a serrated blade, maybe five or six inches long. Most of the flesh in this area has decomposed so I'm going by damage to the skeleton mostly. She certainly would have bled out if the wound wasn't treated and there's no obvious sign of her receiving treatment of any kind.' She stops and smiles apologetically. 'I appreciate that's not very conclusive.'

'Can you tell how long she's been in the ground?'

'Given the insect activity and the fact the ground in the Gardens is moist and fertile, it wouldn't take more than a few months for the body to reach this level of decomposition.'

'Six months?' That would fit with the information they had about the re-landscaping of the garden.

'Not much more than that, certainly. There are some more tests I can do that might help narrow it down, but they're gonna cost. I'll need a signature from you to authorise them.'

Mina takes her eyes off the screen. 'I . . . I'm not really sure if I'm authorised to . . . I'll speak to the SIO.'

For a moment the annoyance Emma displayed earlier returns to cloud her face, but when she speaks her voice remains calm. 'I have to admit, I'm surprised the SIO isn't here himself.'

'*Herself.* DCI Jordan's SIO on this one, but to be honest

with you we're so stretched at the minute you're lucky you got me.'

Emma raises her eyebrows. *Does everyone know how to do that eyebrow thing?*

'I guess I should be grateful then.'

Mina turns back to the images on the screen. 'So there's nothing else you can tell me?' If she goes back with just this, will it be enough for Jordan? The DCI had made it pretty clear she needed an ID.

'There's the coins,' she says, selecting another photograph.

'Yeah, Dr Elliot said they were Roman?'

'I'm not an archaeologist but I'd say Dr Elliot's supposition's correct. They're definitely old. And that looks like Latin.'

'Oh. Dr Elliot said you were a forensic archaeologist?'

'I'm a forensic *anthropologist*, as Dr Elliot knows full well. But yes, the disciplines are linked. More so in the US than here. But I'm not an expert on ancient objects.' Emma hesitates for a moment. 'I think I know someone who might be able to help though. If you want I could send him the photos?'

'Please. What about the clothes?'

Emma presses a further button on the remote and the images on the screen flicker and change. 'I can get someone in the lab to go over them this afternoon. We may get lucky enough to find an intact label which may tell us something about her general wealth and status but not a lot else.'

'It would be something.' Mina isn't looking forward to heading back with little more than maybes and further tests.

'What's that?' She points to the photo in the bottom right-hand corner.

Emma presses the remote and the picture in question expands to fill the screen. It looks like a withered snake, coiled up in a metal dish. 'Her belt. Dark brown. Leather. The buckle's pretty distinctive though.'

Mina stares at the screen. It *is* distinctive, familiar too. A silver letter H. 'Hermès,' she says.

'I guess I don't really follow fashion.'

'They're expensive,' Mina says. 'Unless it's a knock-off. My cousin got one down the Christmas markets last year for a tenner.'

'I'll get it sent over to you guys and you can check it out but it's in pretty good shape for a fake. A cheap metal would have tarnished by now so most likely it's the real deal. How expensive are we talking?'

'Seven or eight hundred quid,' Mina says.

Emma whistles. 'That's a big price tag for a woman in her early twenties.'

There's something about the belt that rings a bell with Mina but she can't quite place it. Maybe it's just the conversation with Preya last Christmas, but it feels more recent than that. 'Anyway, like I said, cheers, Emma.'

The woman laughs again. Did she say something funny? Mina must frown because Emma rushes to explain herself. 'I'm new here. I guess I haven't gotten used to the way y'all are so familiar. *Cheers.* I love that expression.' She smiles, making it clear she doesn't mean to be taking the piss.

'Anyway, you are more than welcome. I'll let you know when I get back toxicology and DNA, but we should really run those tests I was talking about.'

'I'll speak to DCI Jordan.' *But don't hold your breath*, she adds to herself.

They swap phone numbers and emails and Emma promises to forward the images and the belt to Mina. Then they're shaking hands again and Emma Ridgeway escorts her out of the building.

Outside, Mina breathes deeply. Even with its usual taint of city pollution, the air feels fresh in her lungs, expelling the sickly, clinical smell of the mortuary. There's a dark cloud threatening to move in on them but it's not raining for now. The belt tickles away in the back of her brain. If it's genuine, then how does a woman that young afford something like that? Mina certainly couldn't. But there are any number of ways, of course, and not all of them are dodgy. *Maybe she's just rich.* An East Asian woman from a rich family? That probably means student. The fact she's here is enough to prove she's from a well-off family. Mina has no idea how much the university charges foreign students to study here but she doubts it's cheap. The age was about right for a student as well.

And that Hermès belt. *Why did it look so familiar?*

She hopes what she's got is enough for DCI Jordan.

The woman in the pastry shop smiles widely at Tyler. 'Hi!' she shouts. 'Table for two . . .' Her eyes fall on Callum and all at once the smile vanishes.

'Thank you,' Tyler tells her, returning her former grin as heartily as he can manage. She hesitates for a moment and then leads them to a booth somewhere near the back of the restaurant, a long way from the front window.

Callum's dishevelled appearance stands out among the sea of white-haired, elderly women who frequent the place. Even more so than Tyler's does, and he doesn't exactly fit in. Next to Callum though, in his stained tracksuit and muddy Nikes, Tyler looks positively wholesome. No wonder the two of them are drawing looks.

It isn't a place he would have chosen, but on their way to the hipster coffee shop he had in mind, Callum's eyes had locked on to the elaborate tarts and cakes displayed in the window, with their ludicrously bright colours and tempting glaze. Tyler didn't have the heart to make a plea for the lad's diet but at least most of them are topped with fruit of some kind.

The waitress, unlike the greeter, barely registers Callum's appearance before switching on a professional demeanour that endears her to Tyler greatly. They order a selection of cakes and Tyler overrules Callum's objections and insists on a sandwich as well. To drink, the lad asks for a Coke; Tyler, a black coffee. They sit and wait for their meal in silence while Callum fills the pocket of his tattered jacket with sugar cubes.

The silence begins to thicken until it's unbearable even to Tyler. 'What's your story then, Callum *Morgan*? What are doing on the streets?'

The lad screws up his face in a dismissive way. 'Shit happens . . . you know.'

'And you're what, eighteen? Nineteen?'

'Twenty.'

'No parents?'

'I thought you was a cop, not a social worker.'

Tyler holds up his hands in surrender and falls silent. If the lad wants to talk he will. If not, then at least he'll get some food inside him. He's not a minor. Tyler can't force him to accept help.

'Me mam,' Callum says eventually. He begins tearing a paper napkin into thin strips on the table-top. 'We don't get on so good these days.'

'What's the problem?'

'She has shit taste in blokes.'

Tyler glances again at the black eye. The conversation, if that's what it can be called, is interrupted by the waitress returning with several plates of food. Callum's hands are twitching before she's even set them down.

'Sandwich first,' Tyler says, and the boy stops with a Viennese slice halfway to his mouth. He puts down the cake and switches it for the sandwich.

Tyler watches him eat and wonders how long it's been since he's had a proper meal, something hotter and more nutritious than a McDonald's cheeseburger bought with a discarded bus ticket. He's not entirely sure this meal counts as all that much better, nutritionally speaking, but at least it has a surfeit of calories and the lad's clearly in need of those.

Close up, the yellow-green bruise on his cheek is more obvious. 'So this disagreement you had, any chance it could come back to trouble you?' Tyler asks, more for something to say than anything else.

'Nah,' says Callum through the last crust of sandwich. He immediately stuffs a cake in his mouth. 'Should have stayed out of it.'

The waitress returns with their drinks, which only Tyler seems to think is odd – what sort of place delivers the food first and makes you wait for a drink? He sips at the coffee, which is a bit weaker than he would like, while Callum finishes his ersatz meal. At one point Tyler feels his mobile vibrate in his pocket and ignores it. He doesn't want to end up in some detailed conversation about a case in front of the lad. It'll only remind him he's sitting opposite a police officer. 'Your mum's latest bloke?' he asks.

Callum goes round his plate, mopping up the few crumbs left with a grubby finger. 'Don't like the way he treats her.'

Tyler treads carefully. He has the sense Callum hasn't been on the street all that long – maybe there's time to get him back on track – but he doesn't want to scare the lad off. 'Maybe I can speak to your mum. Let her know you're all right.' He doesn't say, 'and make sure *she's* all right', but he's thinking it.

Callum snorts. 'Nah, mate. I'm better off on me own anyway.'

There's a woman watching them from behind the serving counter but when Tyler notices her, she busies herself and looks away. He considers his next move. He doesn't want to push too hard, but Callum spoke to him first. What was that, if it wasn't a cry for help? He can't ignore that.

'Why don't you let me talk to her? Now tempers are cooler. I'm sure your mum doesn't want you out in the cold for Christmas. Give her a chance, eh?'

Before he's even finished the sentence Callum begins shaking his head violently. 'No! Just *fucking* leave it, all right?' His voice cuts loudly across the tearoom causing a number of disapproving faces to glance in their direction. Tyler raises an eyebrow and Callum goes on, his voice calmer. 'Look, me mam she's . . . well, she's not all bad, but that other bastard . . . I ain't going back there.'

'Fair enough. What about a hostel then? Let's get you a bed for the night.' But even as he says it Tyler wonders if it's the right call. The last thing he wants to do is put the lad in further danger, and shoving him in a place full of older, desperate men, many of them on drugs, might not be the best idea. Assuming he can even find a spare place.

Again Callum shakes his head. Tyler watches him licking his sticky fingers. This lad didn't come from a good stable home like he did. He didn't do well at school. He fits every profile for a gang member. Despite his obvious intelligence, his prospects for the future were bleak to begin with, and are even more so now he's on the street.

'Excuse me.' The woman who was watching from the counter steps up to the table with her arms crossed in front of her. 'I'm sorry, but I'm going to have to ask you to leave.'

Tyler stares at her. 'Why?'

'Well . . .' Her thumbs move nervously over her biceps. '*He's* not allowed in here. It's the other customers, you see.'

Callum starts to get up, used to being moved on, not bothering with even the slightest resistance.

'Hang on,' Tyler tells him, extending his arm. 'I really don't see the problem. I'm paying for this gentleman. He's not causing any trouble. What grounds do you have to ask us to leave?'

The woman looks round at the other staff at the counter. The waitress who served them earlier looks as though she wants the ground to open up and swallow her. The mobile in Tyler's pocket begins to vibrate again.

'It's company policy, I'm afraid. He's a known, er . . . rough sleeper?' She says the words hesitantly, as though unsure whether this is the politically correct term. She turns to Callum because he's clearly the easier target and whatever sympathy Tyler had left for her evaporates. 'We've had to move you on before. You know you can't sit outside our business and beg for money. It's not fair on my customers.'

The customers are pretending not to be interested while simultaneously straining their necks to hear more of the conversation.

'We're closing soon anyway,' she adds somewhat desperately, exposing the weakness of her position.

'Just a minute—' Tyler begins, but Callum interrupts him.

'Don't bother, mate. I'm going anyway.' He stands and heads straight for the door.

Tyler stands up, about to follow him.

'Er,' the woman begins, 'there's still the bill to pay.'

'You *are* joking.'

'If you refuse to pay for your meal I will have to call the police.'

He ignores the woman, walks past her to the serving counter and speaks to the waitress that served them. He pulls out a business card and passes it across to the woman. She reads his name and rank on the card and her eyes widen. He gets out his warrant card and flashes that too, for added effect. 'I'll be back to settle my account in full *after* I speak to whoever's in charge of this place. Can you ask him or her to call me, please?' The eyes of the waitress move to the woman behind him. 'Or her superior,' he adds. He turns to face the first woman, now scarlet in the face. 'Shame on you,' he tells her, and walks out of the restaurant.

When Mina gets back from the autopsy there's still no sign of Tyler. Or Daley either.

She sits down at her desk, drops her bag and takes a moment to think. She lets her chair swing round and looks across the office. There are detectives everywhere, mostly sitting at computer screens as she is. She smiles to herself. This isn't something they tell you when you say you want to be a police officer, that you'll spend your life shut in a room with dozens of other police officers.

She breathes out heavily. She's frustrated because so much of her job is not about what *she* does but also the actions, or inactions of her colleagues. It's all very well for Tyler to give her autonomy and tell her to get on with it, but she could do with the benefit of his expertise now and again. Would he have told Ridgeway to carry out the tests? Probably. But that doesn't make it the right call. She considers ringing him again but what's the use? She's already left him three messages. He'll either get back to her or he won't. He probably won't.

It's not that she needs spoon-feeding but … *God, does everyone feel this out of their depth when they start?* She's been in this job for a year now and she still feels like she doesn't know what she's doing. That can't all be on her though, can it? Surely Adam *bloody* Tyler needs to take some responsibility.

Or maybe it isn't him. Maybe it *is* all her. Maybe she's not cut out for this.

She allows herself a small, pathetic sigh. In truth, she knows what she should do. She should go straight to Jordan with Dr Ridgeway's request. But that would drop Daley, and possibly Tyler too, right in it. She can't bring herself to do it. Not quite yet. And anyway, how much better would it be to go to Jordan with something more solid? Like an ID on the victim. Maybe with the extra information from the autopsy she can narrow her search a bit.

She's turning back to her screen when she sees Daley arrive and head straight towards Carla. No doubt intent on chatting her up in his usual fashion.

Mina shouts across the room, 'Where've you been?' interrupting the heavy flirting before it can begin.

He winks at Carla and heads over. 'All right, Mina, you don't have to have a fucking go!' The tone's more like the old Daley she knows, and only in thinking that does she realise how changed he is since he got back.

'Dr Ridgeway was looking for you, from Watery Street? You were supposed to meet her for the autopsy.'

'Jesus, Rabbani. I got held up. Can you get off my case?'

'Fine. Well, in case you're interested I went in your place. But if Jordan finds out she'll be all over you.'

Daley says nothing but she can see a tick in his cheek, buzzing away under his left eye.

'Guy, what's the matter? What's going on?'

'Nothing.' He swallows and clears his throat. 'I got held up at the Gardens, that's all. Look, sorry. Thanks for covering.'

An apology and a thank you? He really isn't himself.

'She wants to run some more tests but I wasn't sure if I should authorise them. Do you want to talk to Jordan about it or—'

'Yeah, all right, I'll handle it.'

'Fine. I'll forward you the report.'

He actually smiles at her. 'Cheers, Mina. I appreciate it.'

'How did it go at the Gardens?'

He sighs dramatically. 'If I have to talk to one more old dear about her begonias I'm gonna swing for somebody.'

She resists the urge to point out he wasn't supposed to be there in the first place. *What's he been doing all this time?* There were still a few statements to take when they'd left yesterday but Mina could have managed that in a couple of hours, at most. Even when she was still in Uniform. 'She seemed nice anyway, the new pathologist. But I wouldn't piss her off if I were you.'

Daley looks away, distracted for a moment by Carla's legs. 'I heard she was a lezza.' He turns back and winks at her. 'You wanna watch yourself there, Mina.'

She opens her mouth to give him another telling-off but he's already following Carla back to the incident board. It seems that whatever that bump on the head did to him, it hasn't completely rearranged his personality. *Shame.*

Dave stands by the door to the Methodist church smoking a roll-up, his coat collar turned up against the cold. He's earlier than he needs to be for the meeting but it's not as though he has anywhere else to be. There are a dozen or so people inside, rummaging through cartons, and filling their bags with packets of carbohydrate-based foods and tinned goods. A large woman with a kindly face smiles at him as she arrives. He holds the door for her and she thanks him.

He remembers the first time he saw this place. He used to pass it almost every day when he first started seeing Lizzie. He'd grab a video from the Blockbuster over the road – now one of those eco-places without a sign, where people fill empty plastic bottles with shampoos and condiments – and a bottle of wine from the offy, and then stride up the hill to her place where she would be cooking spaghetti bolognese. Badly. He smiles to himself. He usually ended up taking over while she cracked open the wine. He never minded how terrible a cook she was. He never really minded anything about her. She could do no wrong. Maybe that's why it went so horribly wrong in the end. If he's honest with himself though, that's not really true. They argued as much as any couple. He has to remind himself of the bad as well as the good.

They used to laugh at the people who came here. People on the edge, with no comfort but the crutch of religion. Dave's always been suspicious of religion. The way it feeds on insecurity, recruiting you when you're at a low ebb. But now, looking back, he sees he wasn't really laughing at them so much as pitying them. Maybe he knew he'd end up here as one of them. It seems inevitable now.

She was so alive back then, not like the dead-eyed Lizzie he remembers from the hospital near the end, as though she'd had all the life sucked out of her. Was he responsible for that? He can't help thinking he was, although his own memory of that time is pretty broken. He remembers those years as though they were a fairy tale he didn't know he was in at the time but would do anything to get back to now. A perfect era of lazy mornings eating croissants in bed. The smell of freshly roasted coffee. The touch of her soft hair on his bare chest. The way she laughed and showered flaky pastry all over the bedclothes and how she'd tease him when he tried to tell her off for it. If he could have her back now he'd put up with any number of crumbs in the bed. He'd put up with anything.

The cigarette burns down to his fingertips. He presses the fag end against the stone wall of the building and the remnants disintegrate under the pressure, flakes of tobacco drifting away on the wind. The large woman inside is staring at him. He realises she's one of the volunteers. She stops short of beckoning him in but he can see she wants to. Everything about her is hell-bent on getting him through that door. Her eyes are hungry to do good, drag him into the warmth of social comfort. The young fella who is what passes for a vicar in this place calls her away to help with some tables while the gannets paw at the food. What are they looking for exactly? They're supposed to be desperate, aren't they? They should take whatever's on offer.

Dave pushes open the door and steps into the warmth of the church. The fat woman smiles at him but he turns away from her and pretends to search the notice boards along the left-hand wall.

Images of the dead hand keep flickering before his eyes. How could he have been so stupid? Looking back on it now it feels like longer ago than a few months. More like a lifetime. No one was supposed to get hurt and he still doesn't know why she did. He went to meet her in the Gardens, just as they'd planned. It was supposed to be a simple exchange.

When he looks back, he wonders if he knew something was wrong even before he got there. But that's his mind playing tricks on him again. How long did he sit there with her dead body? When did he actually decide on the course of action he took? Did it even occur to him to call the police? He tells himself it was because it all felt like a dream; that there was something unreal about that night in the Gardens that made him act without thinking. But the truth is it *did* occur to him. He'd thought about all the questions they would ask. Why was he there? With her? Where did the coins come from? At the very least he would lose his place as a volunteer, and the Gardens was the one thing he had left.

But it's true also that he wasn't fully in his right mind. The mist had descended, as it had on so many occasions before and since. All he remembers is knowing that he couldn't lose her. He couldn't lose anyone else. It was like he was watching the events unfold on a screen. Fetching the wheelbarrow. Taking her to the Marnock Garden where, that very morning he'd been digging the trench for the rose bushes. Even with half the work already done he must have worked most of the night.

What was he thinking? He wanted to keep her safe, that was all. He placed the two golden aurei on her eyes. It seemed appropriate. Something to pay the ferryman, although that was hardly in keeping with her cultural background. And then he'd covered her up and planted the new roses. He planted her in his garden. Keeping her with him, always. Another one of his Lost Girls.

It was obscene. He knows that. In the months since, he has visited her almost every day. Sat with her. Talked to her. And slowly, across that time, he's come back to his senses. He knows now how selfish he was being. She had a family, and even though they weren't always that close, he knew they'd want to know what had happened to her. What right did he have to keep her from them?

He also began to realise he wasn't going to get away with this forever. The ground had started to sag. He'd had to replace some of the bushes, and constantly tend to the garden to keep on top of the shifting ground. Thankfully, no one had noticed yet, but it was only a matter of time. But what could he do by that point? Even if he stole back into the Gardens one night to move her, where the hell would he put her?

The one thing that never occurred to him in all that time was to wonder how she died. He'd always assumed she must have slipped and fallen into the pit. Banged her head on the statue of the bear. A tragic accident. That's what he told himself. She hadn't had the bag of money with her, and that was odd now he thought about it properly, but maybe she hadn't brought the money with her in the first place. Maybe she was there to tell him she needed more time, or that the deal was off. So why is he not so sure about that now?

Dave's stomach rumbles, dragging him back to the present. He glances across the hall, and notes the fat woman's moved further away and is chatting to some 'folks-in-need'. He steps forward sharply, grabs two packets of pasta and a jar of sauce and shoves them into his jacket pockets. Then he hurries back out of the church, around the corner into the car park, and waits for the others to arrive.

That's it!

On the screen in front of Mina, a missing persons' case from earlier in the year. And in one of the pictures accompanying the file, a pretty young woman, smiling coyly at the camera. At her waist, a thin leather strap with a distinctive silver buckle in the shape of an H. It's one of the cases she'd shortlisted this morning. She must have noticed it without really noticing. Could it really be that easy? But there can't be that many people who could afford a belt like that and this ... Li Qiang was certainly loaded. A Chinese student, as Mina had surmised. *Surely it can't be that easy?*

'You're working late.'

Mina looks up to find DCI Jordan standing over her. She jumps up from her seat. 'Sorry, ma'am, I was looking into something.'

'Mina, you don't need to keep apologising for everything.'

'No, ma'am. Sorry.'

They both laugh, cutting the tension, and Jordan perches on the edge of the desk. She has her jacket on as though she's on her way home.

'Is Guy still at the Gardens? I haven't seen him all day.'

Meaning, Daley hasn't told her about the autopsy and the extra tests.

'I think he's still there,' she says carefully.

'How did he get on at the autopsy? Anything we can use to identify her?'

Mina picks her way through the conversation, trying not to say too much but trying not to lie either. 'Dr Ridgeway couldn't tell us much. It's an East-Asian woman, young, maybe early twenties. She was stabbed and she thinks she fell from a height. She thinks she's been in the ground no

113

longer than six months but she can't tell a lot more without running some more tests.' She wants to say, 'It doesn't matter, I've already found her'. But if she does, she's throwing Guy to the lions. *You don't owe him anything!*

'So? Is she running them? When do we get the results?'

'We weren't sure whether you'd want to authorise them. Apparently, it's going to cost. I think Dr Ridgeway wanted to talk to you about it.'

'What?' She looks tired, Mina thinks. And one wrong step away from issuing someone a serious bollocking. 'So why am I only just hearing about this?'

Mina's run out of things to say.

'DC Rabbani, I asked you a question.'

'Yes, ma'am. Sorry, ma'am. I gave the information to DS Daley and he said he was going to handle it.' *Sorry, Guy.* 'He probably got stuck at the Gardens and—'

'Just a minute,' Jordan stands and holds up her hand. 'What do you mean, you gave Daley the info? You mean, *you* attended the autopsy?'

'Yes, ma'am. I took the call from Dr Ridgeway and—'

'DS Daley didn't go with you?'

She hesitates but there's no way out now. 'No, ma'am.'

'Why not?'

'I don't know, ma'am. I'm sure he had a good reason.'

'All right, Mina, that's enough bullshit.' Jordan pulls up a chair. 'Tell me what Dr Ridgeway said. In full, please.'

They sit together and Mina takes the DCI through Ridgeway's report. She outlines her theory about the victim being a student and shows Jordan the distinctive belt. Then it's confession time, and she knows she's left it too late. What should have been a chance for glory is now sullied by the fact she should have led with this. 'Anyway,' she says slowly, 'I think I might have found her.' Mina pulls up the photograph of the missing student, Li Qiang. 'I know it's nothing conclusive but . . .'

'It's her,' Jordan says, nodding. 'Well done, Mina. I just wish you'd come to me sooner.'

'I've literally just found it,' Mina says, but she knows that's not what the DCI meant. 'I'm sorry, ma'am.'

Jordan's face portrays her disappointment but her voice when she speaks is less harsh than Mina would have expected, than she deserves. 'Don't start apologising all over again. Get this information to Dr Ridgeway, immediately. She can get started on a DNA comparison.' She stands and takes off her jacket. 'It looks like I'm not going home after all. I don't suppose there's any sign of DS Tyler?'

Mina opens her mouth with no clear idea of what she's going to say. Tyler had been in earlier but had brushed off any attempt at conversation and buried himself at his desk. She didn't see what time he'd disappeared. Thankfully, Jordan goes on before she has to say anything.

'Never mind.' She drapes the jacket over her arms. 'This is my fault. I've been spreading myself too thin. I thought I had people I could rely on, but it seems I was wrong.' The rebuke stings, even though she knows Jordan isn't specifically referring to her.

'It's my fault,' Mina tells her. She can feel tears beginning to push at her eyelids. What's wrong with her? *Don't let me cry!* 'It's just ...' She trails off, unsure how to articulate what she means, the injustice of it all, the way she feels so out of her depth.

Jordan must guess some of it though, and when she speaks this time, her voice has hardened. 'Are you telling me you can't do the job?'

'No! No, of course not.'

'Good. Because if you're the sort of woman who's going to spend her career apologising for the mistakes of the men she works with, then I've no time for you. On the other hand, if you're struggling and you need help, then all you have to do is ask.'

'Yes, ma'am.'

'I appreciate it's never fun going over someone's head but sometimes it can't be helped. If you want to get on, you can't let anyone else get in the way. It's time to toughen up, girl, or you're not going to last five minutes in CID.'

Her initial upset has morphed into anger and Mina bites her tongue before she says something she'll regret.

'You also need to learn when to hold your temper,' Jordan tells her, her mouth curving into a small smile. 'But it looks as though you're getting the hang of that bit at least.'

Mina watches the DCI head back to her office. She breathes out a sigh of relief at the bullet she's dodged, and wonders which of her two superiors is about to take it instead.

*

Dave waits until he sees Ronnie arrive before he heads back into the church hall. The only person who gets to the hall earlier than Ronnie is Colin, and Dave really can't stand making small talk with Colin. Not that he has to contribute very much because Colin does more than enough to drive the conversation on, on his own.

He's here now, hovering by the door as usual. A short, portly fellow with a mighty nose. 'Good evening, David. How dost thou fare on this delightful evening?' He's the type of man who thinks talking in partial Shakespearean dialogue makes him seem cultured. In Dave's opinion it makes him sound like a twat. He has a new hand-painted banner attached to the table by the door that says, 'South Yorkshire Metal Detectorists and Treasure Hunters Society', and the table itself is littered with flyers advertising the times of future meetings, printed on varying pastel shades of coloured paper. Each one has a treasure chest image in the top right-hand corner – the group's logo.

Dave smiles by way of response and hurries across to the small ring of chairs set up in the middle of the hall where Ronnie's already shrugging out of her thick winter coat. She's a remarkably buxom woman. In her late fifties, he guesses; he's never been brave enough to ask her actual age. She has what Lizzie used to refer to as a 'resting bitch face', but despite that there's something about her he finds attractive.

'Are you still coming on Friday?' she asks without greeting or preamble.

'What's that?'

She sighs heavily and rolls her eyes. 'The Spoken Word thingy. You said you'd give it a go.'

She'd asked him at the last meeting, a week ago. They'd long since established a mutual love of poetry, but he'd wondered if she might be thinking of it as something more than that, perhaps even a date? But that was last week, and last week seems like a lifetime ago. Before they found the body in the Gardens.

'I don't know. I'm a bit . . .' He's not quite sure how to end that sentence. A bit preoccupied? A bit short of cash? A bit sad? There are plenty of bits that are appropriate.

She doesn't wait for him to finish. 'Oh, well, please yourself. I thought you'd like it.' She smiles at him. 'I was hoping you'd come, that's all.' Then she gets up and heads to the kitchen to make a cup of tea. He's offended her.

Nick arrives, gesturing in that easy, devil-may-care way he has about him. He's not a bad-looking kid, really. Probably popular with the lasses. *He'd* know what to do with the attention of a woman. Although, his hair's too long, and very greasy where he's constantly tucking it away behind his ears. 'All right,' Nick says without really aiming the comment at Dave, and then settles in a chair and taps at his phone.

Ronnie returns with two cups of weak tea in chipped white mugs and shoves one of them at Dave. She sits back down next to him. 'Good evening, Nicholas. How are you this evening?'

Nick grunts an acknowledgement and Ronnie turns back

to Dave and gives her eyes a second trip around her head, as though she's saying, 'Kids, eh?' She's not a particularly pretty woman but she does have the most striking eyes. Brown, or hazel, perhaps, with tiny flecks of orange and red. Chestnut, he thinks. Chestnut eyes. Maybe she isn't as old as he's always assumed.

He glances at Nick. Wondering if he's heard about the body yet. Wondering what he will think. Dave feels the mist beginning to close in on him. He shuts his eyes and breathes deeply. Ronnie asks him if he's written anything lately. He shakes his head, unable to risk expanding on an answer even if that means upsetting her further.

When he told her about his poetry she hadn't laughed. That was the first thing he liked about her. Lizzie used to laugh. But she liked it too. Liked the fact her bit-of-rough ex-steelworker fancied himself a poet. But that was another thing she grew tired of.

He realises Ronnie's waiting for him to go on. 'I ... try to but ... with my work at the Gardens ...' Why has he mentioned that?

'Oh my God!' Ronnie puts a hand on his arm. 'I never even thought. That body they've found! You didn't know her, did you?'

'No,' he says, too sharply. 'That is, I don't think they've identified who it is yet. Not that they've told us, anyway.'

'Oh, it must be awful though!' She carries on, detailing what she's heard on the news. He wants to tell her to shut up but he can't, of course. Nick keeps his eyes firmly fixed on his phone screen but Dave thinks he's paying just a bit more attention than he was before. He tries to keep his answers to Ronnie's questions as curt as he can without looking too guilty. Jesus! If he can't manage to fend off a few questions from this lot, how the hell is he going to manage when the police get to him? And sooner or later, they will.

Mike arrives, still in his university uniform, and greets Dave with a nod. He picks up on the conversation readily enough, but far from joining in on the questioning, he takes the role of ally. 'Leave the man alone, can't you?' he cuts in on Ronnie. Even Nick looks up at this point. 'Can't you see how you're affecting the poor bloke?'

Ronnie blinks and stumbles over an apology. 'I'm . . . I'm *so* sorry, David. Michael, you're entirely correct. I should learn to keep my big gob shut. But,' again the hand lingers on his arm, 'you know I'm here for you, don't you? If you need someone to talk to.'

Colin joins them, a folder of no doubt *essential* information tucked under one arm, in conversation with a new fellow.

'This is Stuart,' he says, introducing the lad. 'I know you'll all make him very welcome.' He heads off to fetch another chair.

'Welcome, Stuart,' says Ronnie, extending her hand.

'Hi,' he says awkwardly. 'Stu's fine.'

'Has Colin given you chapter and verse about the horrors of illegal metal-detecting yet?' Mike asks him.

'I think he said something about it.'

'Don't worry,' Mike says. 'We're not all like him.' He

shares a conspiratorial smile but at the last moment his eyes move to Dave's.

Colin gets back with a chair and there are more cups of tea passed round. The conversation moves on. Finally, Nick puts his phone away, which is the unspoken signal that the group's ready to start, and Colin glances at the clock on the wall of the church hall. 'Well,' he says, 'it looks like Deepak's running a bit late, so I think we'd better make a start. Procrastination doth be the stealer of time!'

'Deepak's always running late,' says Ronnie.

The meeting begins, with Colin extolling on them the virtues of proper record-keeping. 'Now, this is the preferred method of logging any finds. You need the date, the location and then a comprehensive list of *anything* you've managed to unearth. This is very important, even if it seems like something banal. You just never know.' This is all for Stuart's benefit, presumably. They've all heard this talk before. Colin takes it so much more seriously than the rest of them.

After ten or fifteen minutes or so there's a welcome reprieve from Colin's droning voice as Deepak arrives. He mumbles a quiet apology for being late and takes off his jacket. He refuses to make eye contact with anyone but as he sits down in his chair, his eyes meet Dave's and Dave knows that he knows. He's put it all together somehow. Well, you wouldn't have to be a genius to do that.

By the end of the meeting, Dave's ready to bolt. What was he thinking? He shouldn't have come here. He sees Colin chatting with Mike at the tea table and he wonders what they're saying. Mike glances in his direction and then hurriedly looks away again.

Ronnie takes hold of his arm once more. 'Are you coming then?' she asks, shrugging back into her coat. 'To the Spoken Word thing?'

And all of a sudden he wants to, more than anything. She's staring at him with those big chestnut eyes and a look he can only describe as … interested. 'Sure,' he says.

'The things one unearths when one isn't looking,' she says cryptically.

'You what?'

'Never mind. Just a thought I had.' And with that she's walking away from him before he has time to think of a way to respond. 'Cheerio, all. See you next week. Happy hunting!' And she's gone.

Dave takes the opportunity to escape too, before any of them can corner him and ask any more questions. He's out of the hall, along the corridor and has his hand on the church door, ready to step back out into the cold, when another hand closes on his wrist. He turns to find Mike staring at him.

'I think we need to have a chat, don't you?'

Tyler sits outside the house on Shoreham Street and watches. He's been here nearly three hours now and there's still no sign of Jude, or Elly either for that matter. It was a long shot, but he can't stop thinking that his brother might have been standing behind those twitching curtains, watching him. Is he there now, peeking out through that sliver of a gap? Or has he already moved on, taking whatever he knows with him?

He leans back in the driver's seat and stretches his arms. This is ridiculous. He hasn't prepared for an all-nighter. He doesn't even know why he came here in the first place.

After a brief trip to the Gardens this afternoon, he'd spent the rest of the day shuffling paperwork, putting his thoughts down on paper and mentally shifting away from CCRU. The boy on the railway line would have to wait a bit longer. It was all very well for them to tell him to drop everything but when he gets back to it – and he will get back to it – he needs to be able to remember where he got to.

Then he'd left the office early and headed home. His plan, on the surface anyway, had been to call Paul, build some bridges. If he couldn't save his floundering career, he might at least manage to do something about his freefalling personal life.

But when he'd got home, the door to the spare room was open and the makeshift incident room had called to him once again. He'd spent what was left of the afternoon reading information he could probably already recite word for word. By the time he'd looked up it was getting dark and the thought of ringing Paul seemed less appealing somehow. His head was clouded with the past and he knew if Paul came round they would only end up fighting.

On some level, he accepts that Doggett's right. The investigation into Richard's death is stalled. In truth, it's been stalled for months, and if it was any other case he would have put it away long ago.

But it isn't any other case. And now he has one final lead . . .

If lead it is. Tyler checks his watch to find it's gone ten. If Jude *is* staying with Elly, he'd most likely be home by now. He can't sit here all night on the off chance Jude might appear. He starts the engine and pulls away from the kerb.

When he gets back to his apartment, he finds a note on the breakfast bar from Paul. Had they arranged to meet after all? He doesn't remember them making any solid plans but the note implies otherwise. Added to that, Paul isn't the type to turn up uninvited, even though he has his own key. Then again, he isn't the type for passive aggression either, but the message is too utilitarian to be anything other than a rebuke.

Food in the fridge. Call me.

Tyler sits down on a stool. Why does he always do this? Why does he always push them away?

The intercom buzzes, making him jump. It's a bit late for visitors, not that he has all that many. Has Paul changed his mind and come back? It seems unlikely. His pride is wounded and now it will be up to Tyler to make the first move. For a brief moment, he wonders what would happen if he didn't.

The entry phone trills again and Tyler lifts the receiver. The camera has been out of order for months now and all he can see on the small black and white screen is static. 'Yes,' he says.

There's nothing but tinny dead air, perhaps the faint whisper of wind, but Tyler has the feeling there's someone there. Listening. He leaves the phone hanging off the hook and bolts out of the apartment and along the corridor. In the stairwell opposite the lift, there's a window that looks down onto the car park from directly above the front door. He can't see anyone but if they're still standing by the intercom, they wouldn't be visible.

He runs down the stairs, bare feet slapping on the cool rubber runner on the edge of each step. At the bottom there's no sign of anyone at the door, just the floodlit, empty car park beyond the glass. Then he sees the scrap of paper lying on the doormat, as though someone has pushed it under the door.

He walks forward and bends down to pick up the note. It's a single sheet of lined paper, all ragged down one side as though it has been hastily torn from an exercise book. It's folded in half and as Tyler unfurls it, he reads the message written sideways in blue ink across the page:

STAY AWAY FROM THE GIRL
IN THE GARDENS.

three

the third nighthawker

Record of Finds

Date: Mon 10th Jul
Time: 19:30
Location: Farm, Hope Valley
Finds: Quatro can, mid to late 80s; copper jug, modern;
collection of toy soldiers, wrapped in tin foil.

The two of them have driven out to a farm somewhere in the
heart of the Peak District. Dave's driving, in his battered old
estate. How the hell the thing is still running, Mike has no
idea. It certainly isn't roadworthy and spits great clouds of
black smoke out into the countryside behind them.

They arrive and park up on a country road. Mike helps Dave
get the equipment out and the two of them hike in silence
across the field. It's a warm summer's evening, which Mike
is grateful for. They don't tell you how much of this metal
detecting malarkey takes place in foul weather.

Dave's quiet as they go to work but that's not unusual; Dave's not exactly a big talker under any circumstances, and with the headphones on they often fall into companionable silence. They've known each other long enough that neither of them feels the need for awkward small-talk any more. It's one of the things he likes best about Dave.

They'd met in a field not dissimilar to this one, a few years back, and Dave had helped him dig up one of the largest finds he's ever had. It turned out to be an old copper bathtub of all things. They reckoned it must have been used by a farmer at some point to feed or water livestock. Anyway, it had fetched a fair price in scrap value and Mike had offered to take Dave for a few pints to thank him for the help. The following week Mike had introduced him to the club.

He'd liked Dave instantly. There was something calming about the man that he'd taken to straight away. And it isn't just him, he sees it in the others too. When Dave walks into the room everyone relaxes. You don't have to impress him, or talk over him, or in any way worry about him judging you. Often, you're not even sure he's aware of the conversation. He's just there. Peaceful, reliable, comfortable. Like your favourite pair of slippers. Or a faithful dog, maybe. An old dog though, with all of the youthful spirit burned out of him.

Mike supposes that's not surprising, given what the man has been through in the past few years. He can't begin to imagine how hard it must have been. Dave rarely talks about his family and Mike only knows as much as he does because it came up in conversation when they first met. Neither of them have brought it up since then, but it's not as though they talk about anything other than detectoring anyway.

So yes, Dave and quiet are old friends. But there's something different lately, Mike thinks, as he waves his detector a few inches above the dry earth and watches Dave walking ahead of him. He hasn't been himself for a couple of months now. Not since they found the coins. In fact ... no, he was as excited as the rest of them when they found the haul. It's more recent than that. It's since the money exchange went tits up. The night the girl disappeared.

'You all right, mate?' Mike asks, as they draw level with each other.

'Huh?' Dave slips his headphones off one ear.

'You've been a bit quiet lately, that's all. I was thinking ... I know it's been tough for you, losing your job and all that. Not that I'm all that flush myself but, I mean ... if you need help or anything.'

'That's kind of you, but I'm fine.'

Mike searches for another opening as they continue scanning the ground together. 'What about your old business? Those pictures you showed me — those knives you used to make — they were quite something. Surely there's still a market for that stuff?'

'There's a market all right. There's a bloke out in Hope who's making a fortune. But it's all on the internet now and that's not really my thing.'

'But you can get help with that now. Start-up advice.'

'I'd still need capital, materials, a workshop.' Dave

shakes his head. 'Anyway, I tried all that before and it didn't work out.'

'But it's different now, isn't it? You don't have . . .' Mike stops. What had he been about to say — '. . . a family to get in the way'? 'Any other commitments,' he finishes lamely.

Dave smiles a sad smile but doesn't say any more. At least he's talking.

'You could have *had* capital by now,' Mike says, because he can't help himself. 'I mean, if that *bitch* hadn't run off with our money.'

'*Hey!*' It's the closest Mike's ever seen to Dave losing his temper.

'Sorry, I know you were close to the lass but . . . well, she did, at the end of the day. Ran off and left us high and dry.'

But then, it occurs to Mike, not for the first time, that they only have Dave's word for that. The day after the meeting was supposed to take place they'd met up in Norfolk Park at the cholera monument as arranged. It was Nick's idea, always with a flair for the dramatic, but they could hardly make the exchange at the club, or in a pub or café, and not one of them was really comfortable inviting the others back to their house. So Nick had suggested the old monument that towers over the city. It was a public place, but quiet enough they could swap bags without drawing undue attention. There was also no CCTV.

But when they'd got there, there was no cash. Just their coins handed back to them. He'd told them the girl hadn't shown up and that he couldn't get in touch with her. He reckoned that she must have done a runner with the cash, but there was something about him that day at the monument. Something different.

'Anyway, she didn't take *our* money,' Dave says now. 'You've still got your Roman coins.'

'Yeah, but the people whose money she *did* take, they're not an overly forgiving bunch from what I gather.'

'We've been over this,' Dave says with the slightest hint of impatience. 'They don't know who we are. They can't find us.'

'You don't know that. What if she told them about us?'

'If she had, don't you think they would have paid us a visit by now?'

Mike treads carefully. They're getting to the heart of things but this is the most he's managed to get out of Dave for months. He doesn't want to ruin it. 'So what *are* we going to do with them? The coins?'

'I don't know,' Dave says. 'Find a new buyer.'

'Can't we go back to the same one? It's not our fault she took their cash.'

'I'm not sure they'd see it that way. Besides, I don't know who they are.' There's something about Dave's voice that has Mike wondering about that.

'We've got to do something,' Mike says. 'I don't feel safe with all that money lying about. It's not as though we can insure it, is it? What did you do with yours?'

'Buried them,' Dave says. 'Like we agreed.'

'Yeah, but where? I mean, your back garden's a bit . . . public. You wouldn't want your landlady digging them up with her lettuce.'

'They're safe,' says Dave, and looks at Mike directly for the first time.

'Yeah, sure. Mine too. I'm just saying we need to think about how we can get rid of them.'

'We *are* thinking, Mike. All of us. No one's come up with an answer yet.'

And that was true enough. Back in the day, Mike had had contacts. People who you went to when you needed help with something not too kosher. But those days were far behind him. Their best hope was probably the internet and, out of all of them, that was Deepak's area of expertise. Only, Deepak seemed to be having his own issues at the moment.

'We need to sit tight a bit longer,' Dave says. 'Let things calm down. We'll think of something.'

Mike lets it go but he's beginning to wonder about his old friend, calming, peaceful, faithful Dave. He barely recognises the man now and he's not at all sure he can trust him. Well, Mike has his own secrets. He's making a plan that doesn't include the others. His exit strategy, he calls it, for when the shit hits the fan. Because he's sure now, that it's going to.

Sooner or later.

The Murder Room's already crowded with expectant faces when Tyler arrives on Wednesday morning.

Jordan had rung him late last night to give him a bollocking about his treatment of Rabbani. He'd taken it stoically. There was no point arguing with Diane when her back was up and his earlier anger at her had dissipated somewhat. He listened patiently while she spoke of 'duty of care' and 'giving something back', and then he apologised and promised to do better, and he could hear from her tone that she didn't believe a word of it. But he did mean it.

His first stop this morning had been at the concierge's office in his apartment complex. There was some pretty clear CCTV footage of the time in question but nothing that covered his front door and nothing that showed anyone coming or going through the main gates. Whoever delivered the note had done a good job of avoiding the cameras.

He'd considered taking it to the documents examiner; fingerprints were unlikely, but there were all kinds of other things to look for. But he'd decided against making the whole thing official for now. There was no surer way of Jordan bouncing him from the case and, perversely, the arrival of the note had only cemented his interest. Was that the point? Did someone know him well enough to try a double bluff? He decides it doesn't really matter. Whether they want him on the case or not, he wants to know why.

With Jordan's scolding still ringing in his ears, Tyler settles himself on the edge of a desk and waits for the show to begin. He sees Guy Daley scowling to himself by the water cooler. This is some consolation, at least. Apparently, Guy had had his own talking-to this morning.

'Okay,' Jordan announces to the room as she walks through the doorway. 'We have a potential identification on the body found in the Botanical Gardens last week. And we have DC Rabbani to thank for it. Well done, Mina. Excellent work.'

Rabbani beams across the room and Tyler's genuinely pleased for her. She's doing well, thriving, despite his lack of attention.

'We'll need to wait for DNA confirmation but it looks very much like this is our girl.' Jordan points to a picture stuck to the board behind her. 'This is Li Qiang.' She butchers the pronunciation, giving the Q the harder sound of a 'K' rather than the softer 'Ch'. 'A biology student from China who went missing earlier this year. I'll let Mina fill in the details.'

'Li Qiang,' Rabbani says loudly, making a much better job at pronunciation than Jordan. 'Known to her friends as Chi. She disappeared, seemingly without trace, back in April. There were no signs of struggle at her student apartment and CCTV showed her leaving in the middle of the night, apparently alone. Wherever she was going, the trail ends once she leaves the vicinity of the university, so either she was picked up in a car somewhere off camera, or the original investigation missed something.' There's a low murmur around the room that tells Tyler she's dangerously close to treading on toes. Perhaps he's taught her something worthwhile after all. 'We'll need to look at everything again but at least this time we know where she ended up – the Botanical Gardens. So I guess we should start by looking at everything along every route from her apartment here,' she points to the map image on the wall, 'to the Gardens, here.' There's a groan as the junior officers in the room begin to take on board how big a job this is.

Jordan picks up the reins again. 'This might be a big pain-in-the-arse to you, but I'd like to remind you that a young woman has been murdered.'

'Actually, ma'am,' Rabbani interrupts. 'Dr Ridgeway couldn't confirm exactly how Chi died.'

There's a palpable silence in the room.

'Yes, thank you, Mina. Good point. But whatever happened to her, she didn't stick a knife in her own belly and bury herself under the rose bushes, did she? So I think we can assume a certain degree of foul play.'

A couple of people, Daley included, snigger, and Rabbani looks down at the floor.

Tyler decides to rescue her. 'Do we know if she was killed in the Gardens?' he asks, giving her somewhere to go. 'Or only that she was buried there?'

'We're waiting for results on soil sample tests, to see if there's evidence of significant blood loss, but that could take a few days. Even then the results might not be conclusive.'

'We should check her apartment again,' Tyler says. 'Just because we have footage of her leaving, doesn't mean she didn't go back.'

'Right,' says Jordan. 'But let's also stay focused on the Gardens. It doesn't strike me as a likely place to dump a body. It speaks of opportunism to me. What about this business of her falling from a height?'

Rabbani's in full stride now. 'There's a few buildings dotted around, including the glass pavilions. And there's the Bear Pit.'

'Maybe she was mauled to death,' Daley announces, raising a laugh among some of the lads.

Jordan shoots him a look. 'Get the SOCO team on it. It's a bit late for trace evidence but you never know.' She turns back to address the room at large. 'Now we have an ID on the body we have a few more resources to play with.'

'Was her daddy rich?' Daley heckles, to another chorus of chuckles.

'She was a foreign national,' Jordan shouts, cutting across the noise in the room, 'here on a student visa. If we fuck this up we have the potential of an international incident, so keep the "daddy" comments to yourself, Sergeant.'

Daley raises a hand in apology.

'However, you're not wrong. Ms Qi . . . *Chi's* family have a great deal of money and have spent a not insignificant amount of it in Sheffield over the past few years. Her father runs an entire province of southern China and not surprisingly is a fully paid-up member of the Communist Party.

138

The Chief Superintendent and the Crime Commissioner will be paying close attention. You do *not* want them noticing you for the wrong reason. Understood?' She pauses for the inevitable mumbled response. 'DS Tyler's going to go over the original investigation and talk to Chi's family and friends again. There'll be new statements that we'll compare to the old ones. Meanwhile, DS Daley will look into any new evidence, starting with the Gardens, and between us we're going to piece together how she ended up there. This case is going to receive our utmost attention. If you're not working with DI Doggett on the Talbot case I want your input on this. Everything else is on hold for the duration.'

The room murmurs its assent and Tyler meets Jordan's eye as she makes a point of looking at him. That had been the other part of the phone call, a not so gentle reminder that this case was now his sole priority. He wonders again just how much pressure she's getting from above.

Jordan takes one last crack at motivating them. 'You've all seen the bad press we've been getting lately over the Talbot case. We don't need any more fuck-ups. Let's get on this and prove to Superintendent Stevens, and everyone else out there, that *this* team at least knows what it's doing.'

Then she returns to her office and the crowd disperses. Tyler waits for Daley to say something unhelpful but he stands there looking lost for a minute, then grabs his jacket and heads for the door.

Tyler turns to Rabbani. 'What's going on with him?'

'Sir?'

'Don't give me all that "sir" bollocks! What's going on with Daley?'

'No idea, Sarge.'

He doesn't believe her. Rabbani's a terrible liar. But he lets it go. For now.

The wind has picked up again and a threatening grey cloud's hanging above them as they pull up outside the house. Chi's sister lives in a terraced property in Crookes. Tyler wonders at this. It doesn't seem like a house where you'd find the daughter of a provincial leader. Jordan had said the family had money but there's no sign of it here. If anything, the property stands out from its neighbours more for its lack of kerb-appeal than anything else. The window frames are old and beginning to rot, and the privet hedge towering over the low garden wall is in dire need of a haircut. There's a faded, yellowed sign stuck to the window with clear tape. It has been hand-written in marker pen on lined A4 paper and placed in a plastic ring-binder pouch. The sign is wet with condensation but is still just about readable. It directs visitors to use the back door, which is pretty much standard operating procedure for terraced houses in Sheffield.

Tyler follows Rabbani down the path to the back of the house where they turn left and cross another property's garden to reach their destination. Rabbani raps firmly on the back door. They don't have to wait long for a response.

'Li Ju?' Rabbani asks, with her thick Yorkshire twang.

'Yes,' the young woman who answered the door replies hesitatingly.

Rabbani introduces them both and asks if they can come in.

'I'm going out soon,' Li says, as though this is an answer.

Rabbani handles it well, smiling softly at the woman. 'It's about your sister.'

Li hesitates for a moment and then opens the door to allow them into the kitchen.

The house is untidy, piles of washing on the linoleum floor and last night's dinner plates vying for room in the sink with this morning's breakfast pots. She asks them to wait a moment and moves through to the living room. Tyler hears a baby cry and the mother cooing quietly for a minute or two. When she reappears, she pulls the door to behind her and says, 'You've found her.' It isn't a question.

Rabbani takes her through the details very professionally and Tyler's impressed with the way she handles the situation. Breaking news to loved ones is not exactly the easiest part of the job.

Meanwhile, he watches the woman in front of him. She's a plainer, perhaps even dowdier version of her sister. Or at least, of the bright exuberant woman in the picture on the wall back at the station, which is as close as he can get to imagining how Chi might have looked in reality. Li Ju, Juju to her friends, stands before them stoically, her arms crossed in a pale pink cardigan in a manner that might be hostile but might just be efficient. She has dark hollows under her eyes that speak of sleepless nights and early morning wake-ups, the cause of which can still be heard mewling to herself in the next room. Her hair's pulled behind her in a short and functional, if careless, ponytail, but there are loose strands waving wispily about her head and it looks unwashed.

'Do I have to identify her?' Juju asks. It's an odd question to start with, but people sometimes say odd things on these occasions. Her accent's very faint. She's been here for five years now, but it's more than that. There's a slight American twang that speaks of her having learned English from an early age, probably from an American tutor paid for by her father.

Rabbani glances to him, clearly unsure how to phrase the fact there's not a great deal left of Chi to identify.

'That won't be necessary, Ms Li,' he tells her without elaborating any further. Best to say as little as possible in these circumstances.

Juju sits down at the kitchen table and exhales loudly. She seems a bit too composed for someone who has just been told her sister's dead.

'You don't seem all that shocked,' he says bluntly.

She looks up at him. 'I knew she was dead. I know it sounds bad, but it's a relief. It's over. No more wondering.'

'That's normal enough,' he tells her, unsure whether it is or not. Everyone reacts differently. There is no normal. But it's worth noting. As is what she isn't saying. She doesn't ask how her sister died, for example, or where she was found. She doesn't ask *how* she was found. It could be shock, but normally people are falling over themselves with awkward questions he can't answer.

'I need to call my father,' she says, and there's something in her voice that makes it sound as though that telephone conversation will be hard for reasons other than the obvious.

'That's being taken care of,' he tells her. 'Your parents are being informed as we speak.' It was something Jordan insisted on. They would need the cooperation of the parents and it wouldn't help if they didn't feel they were being kept informed. Superintendent Stevens should be contacting the embassy right about now.

'It would help if we could ask you a few questions, Ms Li,' Rabbani tells her.

The woman nods her agreement.

'When was the last time you saw your sister?'

Juju looks up from the table for the first time. 'I . . .' She stops. Then she jumps up out of her seat, runs to the kitchen sink and is violently sick.

Tyler hunts in the nearby cupboards for a glass while Rabbani rubs the young woman's back and holds her collapsed ponytail out of her face.

The back door opens and a tall guy with blond hair walks into the kitchen. 'Babe?' He takes in the scene, his face creased with the effort of trying to work out the situation, and then settles for addressing the problem head-on. 'What's going on? Who are you?'

Tyler hands Rabbani the glass and moves to intercept the man. He introduces himself.

'Oh, God! It's Chi, isn't it?'

'And you are . . . ?'

'Ben. Ben Robbins. I'm her . . . partner.'

Juju manages to straighten up and wipe her mouth. She accepts the glass of water from Rabbani with a small wordless nod.

'Perhaps we could all sit down for a moment,' Tyler says. 'Will the baby be okay?'

Juju looks stricken. The sound of the baby's gurgling reaches them all. 'I'll go get her.'

The three of them take a seat at the kitchen table and Juju joins them, a tiny form wrapped in swaddling in her arms.

'She's beautiful,' Rabbani says. 'How old is she?'

'Five weeks,' she says with a dead voice, taking a seat next to her partner. Tyler thinks about how Robbins had hesitated over choosing that word. Partner.

'How are you doing?' he asks. 'Are you alright to go on?'

She pulls herself upright. 'I'm fine.'

'It's the shock,' he tells her, though in truth he's never seen anyone throw up at bad news before. Collapse, pass out, scream the place down, but never throw up. That's a new one.

'Okay, let me take you through what we know.'

Tyler outlines the circumstances surrounding the finding of Chi's body while Rabbani readies her notebook. He chooses his words carefully, aware there's a child in the room. She's obviously too young to understand, but it seems the right thing to do anyway. At one point Ben says, 'Oh God, that body in the Botanical Gardens! Oh, Jesus! No!' and bursts into tears. Juju takes the news without any visible reaction but he has seen that before. Many times. She's going into shock. He's not even sure she's fully taking in what he's saying. He leaves out certain pertinent details: the Roman coins, the state of Chi's body and the nature of her injuries.

'You're sure it's her?' Ben asks, his face twisted into an expression of desperate hope. 'We thought . . . we *hoped* she'd just run away.'

'We have her DNA on file from when she was recorded as missing. We still need to confirm a match but, I'm sorry, the description matches her pretty thoroughly, down to the clothes she was wearing.'

Ben stands up. 'But you don't know for sure? I mean . . . it could be someone else. If you need an identification . . . I mean, I knew Chi well, there's no need for Juju . . .' He stops, reading something in Tyler's face. 'You can't tell who she is from her face, can you?' He sits down again, quietly.

Juju sits in silence, holding the baby. The baby blinks and stares into space.

'Can you tell us when you last saw your sister?'

'It was a few days before we reported her missing,' Juju says. 'Saturday. She came to see if I wanted some old clothes she was getting rid of.'

'Was that usual? Her giving you clothes.'

Juju shifts the baby, causing her to gurgle again. 'She said she was clearing out.'

'Was she going somewhere?'

'I don't know. She didn't tell us she was but . . . we hoped she went away somewhere.'

'And you reported her missing on the Tuesday?'

'Yes.'

'Why was that? I mean, was there something in particular that made you concerned?'

Juju hesitates and glances at Ben. He wipes a tear from his eye and speaks for her. 'We were supposed to see her for lunch on Monday but she didn't turn up. When we couldn't reach her by phone I spoke to some of her friends in the department and they told me she didn't come in that day. She was supposed to be leading a seminar. She wouldn't have missed that. That's what made us worry.'

Tyler watches the man carefully. He's visibly shaking. 'It sounds like you were all quite close.'

Ben sits up straighter. 'Meaning?'

'We were, Detective,' Juju says. 'We were *all* close. We are family.'

'You told the investigating officer that you argued on the Saturday?'

It was one of the few interesting bits of information Cooper had managed to put down in an otherwise shoddy and half-hearted report.

'It was silly. It was the clothes. I wasn't very . . . gracious is the word, I think? I took her offer the wrong way, accused her of giving me . . . I don't know if there's a word for it in English. Her unwanted goods.'

'Hand-me-downs,' says Rabbani.

'Yes. It was silly,' she says again. 'I wish I'd been kinder.'

'You also said you thought she was seeing someone.'

'Yes, I mean, I don't know. She told me she was but ...
I don't know. And she said things sometimes, they weren't
always true.'

'She didn't tell you who it was?'

'I saw her with a guy one day. He looked ... rough.
Dangerous. But she ... talked to a lot of people. I don't know
if he was the one.'

'Why are you asking these things?' Ben says sharply.

Tyler's been waiting for this. 'It's just routine. We have to
look at everything.'

'But surely you don't think we could have ...' He stops.

'Could have what?'

Ben looks back down at the table and ignores the question.

Tyler pushes down a stab of irritation at the interruption.
'Would Chi have had any interest in Roman antiquities?
Coins, for example?'

'I don't think so.'

'Can you tell us exactly what her degree was?'

'Don't you know?' Ben asks. 'Look, what's going on here?
How come the officer we spoke to when Chi went missing
isn't here? What was her name ... Cooper?'

'DI Cooper is ... unavailable,' Rabbani tells him.

Tyler tries to get back on track. 'I know this is difficult, but
we have to go over everything again, in case there's any ...
discrepancies in the original report. It's just procedure.' But
the truth is they don't know very much at all. DI Cooper
has some questions to answer herself about the handling of
Chi's disappearance.

Juju juggles the baby well enough to reach out a hand and place it on Ben's shaking arm. 'She was a PhD student at the Department of Animal and Plant Sciences. I don't know much about her work.'

Ben jumps in again. 'Why would you ask that, about Romans? Shouldn't you be out there finding out who did this to her?'

'Did what to her?' Tyler asks.

Ben splutters over his words. 'Well ... buried her ... I mean, it wasn't an accident, was it?'

'Neither of you have asked me what happened to her. That tends to be the first thing people ask.'

'Well, I ...' Ben trails off.

Juju stands up, the baby still clasped closely to her breast. 'She was killed, wasn't she?'

'It looks that way, yes.'

She stumbles and puts one hand out to the wall to steady herself. Ben takes the baby, holding her awkwardly, as if he doesn't yet know what he's doing. But it's only been five weeks. It doesn't necessarily make him a bad father. Tyler glances around the untidy kitchen again. The couple are clearly struggling.

'Are you okay to go on?' Rabbani asks Juju.

'I ... I need to lie down.'

'We'll leave you be for now,' Tyler says. 'The Family Liaison Officer will be in touch soon. In the meantime, if there's anything you can think of that might be important you're welcome to call either of us, at any time.'

They leave their cards and let themselves out, renegotiating the back gardens to get back to the road.

'Shit!' says Rabbani as they get back to the car. The first spots of the threatening rain patter down on the windscreen. 'Plant Sciences? Is that the connection to the Gardens?'

'What the hell was Cooper playing at?'

'We need to speak with her.'

'That could be difficult, given the circumstances, but we'll see if Jordan can arrange it.'

Rabbani chews on the edge of a nail. 'I thought you'd push them harder than that? Question them before they get a chance to get all their ducks in a row?'

It's such a Jim Doggett expression he nearly laughs out loud. 'It wasn't the best situation, with the baby there.'

'Yeah,' says Rabbani. 'The five-week old baby.'

'Which means Juju was already a couple of months pregnant when her sister disappeared.'

'Not an easy thing to cope with.'

'No.' Tyler glances back at the house through the rain. 'All right, we'll let them get their ducks in a row, but we won't give them too long. I'd rather question them again before the parents arrive on the scene.'

'Where to next?'

'The university.' Tyler checks his watch. 'Let's grab a quick bite first, though, because afterwards I want to swing by the Gardens.'

Rabbani shoots him a look. 'I thought we were supposed to be leaving Guy to handle that bit?'

'And how do you feel about that? Can you honestly say you have total confidence that Guy Daley isn't going to miss something?'

'Just promise me one thing, Sarge?'

'What's that?'

'Promise me you're not going to end up twatting each other.'

'I'm relying on you to stop that happening, Mina.'

Tyler and Rabbani cross the car park, battling against the driving rain. The wind howls around the base of the University Arts Tower, which looms over them like some 1960s monolith. Tyler's always liked the tower, one of the few high-rise buildings visible from pretty much anywhere in the city. A stable anchor at the heart of a sometimes turbulent cityscape.

As Rabbani arrives, an automatic door slides open allowing her into the Alfred Denny Building, home of the Department of Animal and Plant Sciences. Tyler follows her in, shaking the rain from his jacket and wiping his wet palms down his jeans.

The reception area consists of a half-dozen red tub chairs and a small coffee table. Keeping watch over everything is a stuffed Emperor penguin in a glass display case and, above that, the skull of some improbable-looking creature with enormous tusks.

The security guard at the front desk looks up at them with contempt, but after Tyler shows the man his warrant card, the guard transforms, falling over himself to be helpful.

'Yes, sir. I wasn't expecting you, sir.' He jumps out of his seat and then stands there looking uncomfortable.

'We were hoping to speak to the Head of Department.' Tyler turns to Rabbani who checks the information scribbled in her notebook.

'Professor Calderdale,' she says. He'd let her make the necessary enquiries while he fetched them both sandwiches.

The guard's brow furrows. 'Oh, has a crime been committed? Is this about a student? I can assure you we'll all be happy to help in any way we can. Perhaps, er . . . perhaps you could outline the particulars of the case and I could draw up a list of names you might like to talk to. I'd be happy to liaise with the relevant parties and arrange interviews, et cetera.'

Et cetera? Tyler suppresses a smile. 'That's very kind of you Mr . . .'

'Halbert, sir.'

'Thank you, Mr Halbert, but this is more a fact-finding mission for the moment. We simply need to speak with Professor Calderdale, if you don't mind?'

'Right.' He sits back down at his desk and picks up his phone. Tyler moves round the desk so he can see the front of the monitor, more to discomfort the overly zealous security guard than for anything else, but it never hurts to be nosey either. There's nothing untoward on the screen though, not even a cheeky game of solitaire. Just CCTV images on the screen itself, and a number of different-coloured Post-it notes stuck around the edge of the monitor with messages scribbled in blue and black ink. Some stickers too, with what Tyler imagines are supposed to be witty slogans. 'My sister went to Cleethorpes and all I got was this lousy sticker' and more in a similar vein.

He steps back and shares a smile with Rabbani.

After a few minutes a young postgraduate student turns up and escorts them up in the lift to the second floor and into a room with large glass doors and a sign that declares it 'The Alfred Denny Museum of Zoology'.

It's a small room with a very low ceiling, but every possible space is crammed with wooden-framed cabinets with glass sides. Each is filled with a treasure trove of animal bones and skeletons. Every species of bird, reptile and arthropod. Snakes, lizards, elephant skulls. Gibbons, emus, tapirs. There's a collection of sea creatures with impossible numbers of arms, and one whole case devoted to nothing but nematodes, pickled in a viscous yellow liquid. Tyler's not even sure what a nematode is.

'Sarge,' Rabbani shouts from across the room. 'Look! A dodo!'

Tyler guesses the whole thing's probably Victorian, collected on some grand world voyage and donated to the university. A piece of history, if a touch morbid by today's standards. In the very last case, furthest from the door, are four distinct skeletons representing the evolution of man from monkey to ape to hominid. The final of the four is a human skeleton.

'Impressive, isn't it?'

Tyler turns to find the owner of the voice standing in the

entranceway behind them. Professor Robert Calderdale is a giant of a man, well over six feet tall with a bulky figure to match. It occurs to Tyler that one day his skeleton might join the others in the case, as the *next* step in the evolution of man. He has an impressive mane of bright-red hair pulled into a top knot that's a little incongruous to the image of the classic ageing professor of a university department. He's also far younger than Tyler expected, mid-forties or so, and has an elaborate tattoo of a tree, the trunk of which curves down from his right ear and around his neck. Calderdale introduces himself and this time Tyler notices a very faint Scottish burr; it makes him think of the Highland Games, at which this man would no doubt excel.

'He was a criminal,' Calderdale says, indicating the human skeleton in the case. 'If you look closely you can see the snapped vertebrae from where he was hanged.'

Calderdale escorts them back to his office. 'Sorry about the wait,' he says as he follows them into the room. 'It never stops in this place.' He settles himself in the chair behind his desk, the surface of which is covered in books and papers, and offers them a seat with the palm of his hand. 'Now,' he says. 'What can I do to help South Yorkshire's finest?' There's a hint of mockery in his voice, perhaps, but enough humour to allow the statement not to be taken too seriously.

'Li Qiang,' Tyler says abruptly. He wants to gauge the man's reaction.

Calderdale closes his eyes and exhales deeply. 'Ah, yes.' His knuckles whiten as his fingers dig into the desktop. 'I'm sorry,' he says. 'It's just … I've never lost a student before. I mean, of course I have, but … not like that.'

He doesn't seem in the least surprised by their visit. And just like Chi's sister, he makes no attempt to ask any questions. Rabbani's twitching in her seat, desperate to say something, but Tyler stops her with a look. He wants to give the man space to talk.

The silence grows more and more awkward until finally the giant professor caves. 'Chi had a brilliant mind but, to be brutally honest, she wasn't always that good at applying it. She had a lot of potential but didn't put the effort in. We had to have a number of meetings about her work. She wasn't the worse student I've had but I had to upbraid her a number of times and I've no doubt I would have had to again.'

He pauses for a moment and looks out of the window.

'The problem was, she was pretty much untouchable. Her father, you see? As well as the fees paid by him for both Chi and her sister, he's also donated a great deal of money to the university over the years. My hands were tied and she knew it. Between you, me and the gatepost, she would have scraped through with a pass whatever happened, but she was ne'er going to be the next Darwin.'

Tyler notes that Calderdale is talking about his student in the past tense. It has only been a few months since she disappeared. On the other hand, the man must teach hundreds of students every year. Six months might be a long time in academia.

'The point I'm trying to make is, I'm not sure her heart was ever really in her studies, so when she disappeared I wasn't overly concerned to begin with. I assumed she'd run off on an adventure somewhere.'

'What was the nature of Chi's research?'

'Orchids. It was pretty derivative stuff and wasn't likely to further the field of study in any meaningful way.'

'Forgive me, Professor, you don't seem to rate your students very highly.'

Calderdale smiles, the tree-trunk tattoo rippling beneath his neck muscles. 'On the contrary, Detective. Many of them are quite brilliant and as I said, Chi was no exception. She was fiercely intelligent, quite beautiful, and charming beyond belief. But she was also spoiled and childish. And a bit vulnerable, I think.' He stops smiling. 'I'm afraid I might well have predicted what happened to her. I wish I could have done more.'

Tyler looks at Rabbani. They hadn't mentioned to the security guard what their visit was about.

'Professor, what exactly do you know about what happened to Chi?' he asks.

For the first time Calderdale falters. 'I . . . I assumed that's why you were here. I'm sorry, have I got it wrong? The body in the Botanical Gardens. I saw it on the news and then this morning on my way to work I heard it was an East Asian woman. When I heard *you* were here to see me, CID officers, I . . . well, I assumed—'

'That's a pretty big assumption to make, isn't it?'

Calderdale blinks, once, twice, perhaps counting in his head to prevent himself responding in anger. This isn't a man used to having his authority questioned. 'Missing persons might be standard practice in your world, Detective, but they're not in mine. In the last three years I've had students drop out, disappear on holiday without notice, but I usually make it my business to find out what happened to them. In my entire career I've only had one student disappear entirely without trace and there's barely a week goes by when I don't wonder if she's all right. It was hardly a big leap to conclude it was her when the body of a young Asian woman was found in the Botanical Gardens, of all places! If you hadn't come to see me, I would have called you myself.'

'So Chi's work *was* connected to the Gardens?' Tyler asks.

Calderdale looks nonplussed. 'Of course! The Gardens have hundreds of rare specimens gathered from all over the world. Many of my students volunteer there as part of their studies. She loved that place. She probably spent more time there than she did here.'

'It's about the girl, isn't it?' the security guard, Halbert, asks as they pass back through reception.

'Which girl's that, Mr Halbert?' Tyler asks.

Halbert's eyeing Rabbani warily. Tyler flicks her a nod and Rabbani takes the hint, stepping through the automatic doors, back into the driving rain.

'Chinese girl, what went missing earlier in the year? They just said on the news.' He gestures to a tablet propped up on his desk next to the phone. 'They showed her picture and I recognised it.'

Tyler silently tuts, but he supposes Jordan had no choice. The body in the Gardens is big news – nationally, not just locally, and once the family had been informed . . .

'You remember her?' he asks Halbert in what he hopes is a friendly manner.

'I used to see her coming and going. She were a sweet girl. I mean, I never really spoke to her properly but . . . she always had a smile, you know? Not like some of them, with their heads glued to their smartphones, gabbling away in some unintelligible language.'

It's unclear if Halbert's being casually racist, or is talking about students in general.

'Have you worked here long?'

'Fifteen years. There's been a few changes in that time, I can tell you. The Environment Centre was just a pipedream back then, of course, and the restaurants weren't nearly as—'

'So you were here when Ms Li went missing?' Tyler interrupts, attempting to get the man back on track.

'Indeed, I was. I was the one sorted out a lot of the CCTV stuff for them. DI Cooper, weren't it? Aye, she were a po-faced lass. Oh . . . no offence.'

Tyler smiles. 'I won't tell her.'

'I did my best to try and help, you know, for the poor girl but . . . I'll be honest with you, Detective, I don't think my help was greatly appreciated.'

This time Tyler holds back the smile. He's not surprised,

given what he knows of DI Cooper. She's never seemed the sort to put up with well-meaning busybodies. 'Well, I can assure you, Mr Halbert, any information you have for me will be greatly appreciated. I can see you're a man of principle, and it's clear you have your finger on the pulse of things around here.' He wonders if he's not laying it on a bit thick but Halbert straightens in his chair and positively beams.

'Well,' he says. 'You've lucked out, as it happens. There's not many as know as much about this place as yours truly.' Halbert winks. 'Mind like a steel trap, me. I can pretty much tell you the comings and goings around here. And if the old trap lets me down I've got this to back me up.' He pats a large burgundy book with his right hand, almost stroking it. 'I keep meticulous records. It's one of the reasons what made me apply.'

'Apply? For this job?'

'To join you lot. It was me mam's idea originally. Police Community Support Officer. I didn't get in, though. The financial cuts, I reckon. Bloody hell, what those bastards have done to our country—'

Again Tyler cuts him off; he doesn't have time for a political rant. 'That could be useful then, Mr Halbert. I'm glad we can rely on you to help out.' He's beginning to get a bit tired of this. He glances through the glass door at Rabbani, huddled close to the building in an attempt to keep out of the rain.

'I certainly will, sir. If it's in my power to manage it, I most certainly will.'

Tyler turns back to find Halbert eyeing him in that close way again.

'That poor lass,' he says, his placid face breaking into a sick grin. 'Shocking. We all thought she'd run off somewhere. You know, like they do, Chinese. Up sticks and go home without so much as a by-your-leave. To think she were buried in that park all those months. I've probably walked through there a few times me'sen in the past few month. Don't bear thinking about.' He pauses for a moment and then says, 'So, do you have any theories then? Suspects?'

Tyler meets his eye and remains silent.

'I'm just ... it's just ... the sister. She lives around the corner from me. I see her in the supermarket sometimes. I mean, I would never say anything. Not about this.'

'I'd advise you not to.' Again, Tyler lets the silence stretch out between them but this time Halbert doesn't hurry to break it. He pushes harder. 'That's a big coincidence. The fact that you know the victim –' he uses the word deliberately '– in a work capacity and in your personal life as well.'

Halbert's eyes nearly fly out of his head. 'I didn't *know* her, she just lives nearby. The sister, I mean. I didn't even know that until later when I saw her on the news. I mean, if I'd known I might ... well, I would have said.' He glances left and right before going on. 'This won't affect things, will it? I mean, I thought I might reapply. I wouldn't want it to go on my record or anything.'

'That depends what you've done.'

Halbert begins shaking his head, about to set off on another round of explanations and denials, but Tyler jumps in before he can get started. 'All right, as long as you help in whatever way you can, it won't be an issue. Maybe . . . I take it everyone signs in and out of the building? Do you have records? Details from when Li Qiang attended the university.'

Halbert's back straightens. 'Meticulous records! But the students don't have to sign in and out of the building. I can recheck the CCTV footage for you, though. I believe I made a point of keeping the relevant details.'

Tyler bets he did, and knows exactly where to find them too. He imagines his own visit will be going down in the log book, with copious notes about their entire conversation. Thankfully, the man doesn't ask why they don't already have the information he's asking for.

'And of course, there'll be an electronic record of the last time she was in the Environment Centre. Most of her work was in there, I think, so that might help narrow down the window.'

Tyler gives the man his contact details and the security guard gets up for the first time and escorts him to the glass door.

'Well, thank you, Mr Halbert, you've been very cooperative.'

Halbert smiles. 'Call me Mike, please.'

Tyler joins Rabbani in the rain and they set off back across the car park.

'Anything?' Rabbani asks over the sound of the driving wind.

'Not sure,' he tells her. He's certainly an oddball but he might just be keen. On the other hand, how likely is it the man knew Chi and lived a few doors from her sister? It's possible but . . . Tyler can't help hear Doggett's voice echoing around in his head. *I don't like coincidences.*

He glances back over his shoulder and sees Halbert watching them from behind the glass door. He pities the students who cause trouble on his watch. Mr Halbert is *always* watching.

Tyler pulls his jacket collar up against the wind – at least it's stopped raining – and stares at the shallow hollow in the ground that marks the former grave of Li Qiang. She's no longer here, of course, but he imagines he can still see her curled-up remains in the hole. It seems a ridiculous place to bury a body. How could you ever hope to get away with it?

He thinks of the sister vomiting the contents of a light breakfast into a stainless-steel sink and wonders how he would feel if it was someone arriving to knock on his door and tell him Jude had been found in a hole somewhere. It's always been a possibility, one he's considered before. Yes, Jude's exactly the sort who might end up in a shallow grave.

But was Chi?

It was unusual to hear the professor talk about her in terms that were less than flattering. On hearing of the death of a friend, or close acquaintance, most people rush to assure you how wonderful they were, how unlikely to find themselves a victim of crime. As though crime is really that picky.

You might be more likely to be a victim if you fit a certain demographic but that doesn't make you safe. But Professor Calderdale didn't do that. It was a warts–and–all account of a potentially troubled girl. Tyler wonders how accurate it was. They need to talk to the sister again soon.

'Penny for 'em.' Jordan places a warm hand on his elbow.

'I was thinking about siblings.'

'Yours, or hers?'

'Both.'

Jordan pulls on his arm and Tyler follows her back out of the small walled garden. A uniformed officer lifts the police tape so they can duck back under. There's a small crowd of onlookers gathered in the Gardens. Though the scene of the crime is still cordoned off, the Gardens themselves have reopened to the public and the usual gawkers and rubberneckers are doing their best to appear as though they aren't interested while absorbing every detail they can. A camera flashes a couple of times, but whichever newspaper the photographer represents is a bit late to the party; the rest of the press have been and gone.

They follow the path up to the main office.

'What are you doing here, Adam?'

'We found out Chi worked here, as part of her PhD.'

'Yes,' Jordan tells him, 'Mina filled me in. I thought perhaps you had another motive.'

'Just doing my job.'

'As long as you're not trying to rub anyone's nose in anything. You could have called Guy and passed on the information.'

'Daley's a liability.'

'It's my job to worry about that. All you need to do is go over the witness statements from the missing persons' investigation and take new ones. If you can't manage that you're no good to me. And you're no good to Superintendent Stevens either.'

A squirrel darts across the path in front of them and turns over a pile of golden leaves. It pauses for a moment to stare at them and then scampers up the trunk of a tree and disappears.

'He wants to close us down, doesn't he?'

'He's in a tight spot. You know the cuts we're having to suffer.'

'And cold cases are the first to go? Just because the media have forgotten about them, doesn't mean the families have.'

'You don't have to tell me that, Adam. You have no idea how hard I've fought to stop this but—'

'But it's happening anyway.'

Jordan doesn't answer.

They arrive at the small office they're using as a mini incident room. It's tiny, not much bigger than a broom closet, and hardly suitable for the purpose. Rabbani's sitting at one end of a small desk, searching through a box file, while Guy Daley squints at a laptop as though it might offer up the information he wants without him having to make any effort to find it. Daley scowls at him as they enter and Tyler deliberately shoots him an insincere smile.

Jordan spots it though. She slams her hand down on the table-top. 'Enough. You two, settle this now or, short-staffed or not, I'm taking you both off this case and putting you back in uniform. And don't think for a minute that I can't or won't. I'm done protecting the pair of you. Carry on like this and I'll offer you up to Stevens on a plate. Do I make myself clear, gentlemen?' It's a sign of how serious she is that she's forgotten to use the super's rank.

Rabbani's cheeks are blazing and she's staring at a piece of beige paper as though she wants it to expand and swallow her.

'Don't look at her, look at me!' Jordan shouts.

Tyler meets her eye. She looks so much older than she did a year ago. There are lines on her forehead he hasn't noticed before and heavy bags under her eyes. She's under pressure. And he owes her. He owes her more than he can repay.

'Have I made myself clear?' she asks.

'Yes, ma'am.' They speak almost as one, Daley a fraction faster than Tyler.

Jordan gives them one last stare and turns to Rabbani. 'Mina, what have you found?'

Daley catches Tyler's eye and pulls a face behind Jordan's back. It's childish and pathetic but it's also an olive branch. His instinct is to blank the idiot and turn away, but for a split second he sees Jim Doggett shaking his head in that way he does. He hears the gravelly Yorkshireman's voice saying, 'Choose your battles, son.' So Tyler tries something he's never done before. He plays the game. He grins at Daley. It feels fake, and he suspects it looks more of a rictus than anything, but to Tyler's surprise it works. Daley grins back. Then a nod. And another smile.

Is it really that easy? Jordan once told him he doesn't play nicely with others. He figured that wasn't his fault; that it was something he couldn't control. But maybe it is. Or maybe he's changing.

Tyler's missed most of what Rabbani's saying. But he hears Jordan ask, 'So how long was she coming here?'

'About a year or so,' Rabbani tells her. 'The sign-in sheets for the volunteers aren't exactly exhaustive. The bloke who gave me this lot told me there's a lot of volunteers come and go, and 'cos they're volunteers no one really keeps track. There are days missing or incomplete, and it's not like they clock in electronically or anything. It's just initials squiggled on a bit of paper. The earliest record I can find is about a year before she disappeared though, and the last is two days before.'

'What did she do here?'

Rabbani bites her lip. 'None of that's recorded but we spoke to a few of the longer-term volunteers and they remember her well enough. I don't think they get a lot of BAME volunteers so I'm guessing Chi stood out a bit. We're gonna have to talk to everyone all over again. So far all I've got is that she was here once a week, most weeks, helping out with propagating seeds, planting, weeding, that kind of stuff. There's a period over the summer before last when she wasn't coming but we know she went home to China during the holidays so that makes sense. Guy's looking at who else was here on the days she was here, cross-referencing names. We'll go back and talk to them first.'

'And?' she says, turning to Daley.

He looks at his screen again. 'There's a shit-ton of names.'

'All right,' says Jordan. 'Keep going. Start with anyone who's still here now, draw up a list and we'll interview them one by one. If nothing else it will give us another bunch of statements from people who knew her.' She turns to Tyler. 'Any idea why we didn't find this out during the original investigation?'

Tyler hesitates. He doesn't want to be mudslinging again so soon after his attempt to make peace but, at the end of the day, this is his job. 'Well, as you know, after the Talbot fiasco, Suzanne Cooper's suspended pending an investigation. I suspect they'll want to look into a few other cases when they've finished as well.'

Jordan pushes her hand into her side and stretches her back. 'Not exactly by the book then?'

'It's as though she barely bothered. She interviewed the sister, a couple of uni mates, and they made a token effort to look at CCTV, but that's about it. If she made any further enquiries of any kind, she didn't bother to record it. I've literally got a couple of family photos, a plan of her student bedsit, and three very badly put-together witness statements. This was a young, international university student who went missing overnight. There was a lot more she should have done.'

'I'm surprised I don't remember the case,' Jordan says. 'There was another student went missing a year or so back, turned up in Scotland if I remember rightly. But this one doesn't ring a bell.'

'It was the weekend before Jason Talbot went missing,' Tyler tells her.

'That would explain the lack of media interest.'

'Cooper seems to conclude the most likely scenario is that Chi went off with a boyfriend somewhere.'

'What about the family? I'm surprised they didn't kick up more of a fuss.'

'It's certainly curious.' Tyler judges this is the best chance he's going to get. 'We need to talk to her. Cooper.'

Jordan circles her hips, working the kinks from her back while she thinks. He thought she might blow up again, tell him to wind his neck in but she seems to be giving it due consideration. Surprisingly, Daley's doing his best to convey support, gently nodding his agreement with Tyler's assessment. Surely it can't be that easy? One smile and the man rolls over and shows his belly?

Finally, Jordan shakes her head. 'We can't go there. Not right now. For one thing, the union will be up in arms and, for another, even if she is in the shit, Cooper's still got plenty of influence higher up.'

Tyler bites his tongue. It's only what he expected but it rankles no less for that. Rabbani's looking at him as well, urging him to push the point, but this isn't the time. He's not going to give up though.

Dave pulls up in the pub car park and gets out of the car. The choice of location had been Mike's. It's one of those old cosy country pubs in the Peak District that, at this time of year, is only busy at the weekend when the bikers are out in force. It has nooks and crannies, where people can have conversations in hushed tones without drawing unwanted attention.

Mike had wanted to go straight to the local pub after the club meeting last night but Nick had persuaded him it wouldn't be a good idea. Too much chance of someone they knew seeing them, and although they had a perfectly good reason to be together, they've all grown a touch paranoid over the past few months. That was gold for you, Dave suspected. They might as well be Californian prospectors, or whatever dubious official had hidden the gold originally back in the Roman times.

Added to their paranoia, Deepak had been adamant he needed to get home, it being a school night. So they'd made the arrangement for this evening instead. Somewhere remote with fewer eyes on them.

When Dave walks in, he clocks Mike and Nick already ensconced together in a booth near the fireplace. Deepak isn't here yet, but then Deepak's always late. They watch Dave as he crosses to the table, their eyes full of mistrust. That saddens him. More so than he would have expected. He's lost the trust of these men who have become so much a part of his life. They're the only friends he has and, for that reason more than any other, he determines to tell them the truth. He shouldn't have lied to them in the first place but it seemed necessary at the time. That, of course, is what all liars think.

They wait for Deepak as long as they're able but eventually

the silence grows overwhelming and Mike says, 'Tell us what happened.'

'She was already dead,' Dave says simply.

His two friends look at each other and he can see the suspicion in their eyes. He tells them the whole story: finding Chi, burying her, walking away. He tells them the only reason he lied was to protect them, which is not strictly speaking true, but is something he has managed to partially convince himself of in the intervening months.

'What the fuck did you do that for?' Nick asks.

'I don't know. I wasn't thinking straight. All I could think about were the coins, and you lot, and the fact they would link me to her and everything would come out.'

Mike and Nick look at each other again. Then Mike says, 'You could have just left. Even if they made the connection, even if the coins *had* come to light, the worst the police would have done would have been to take them away from us.'

'That's not strictly speaking true,' Nick says. 'There's an unlimited fine for not reporting treasure. Or up to three months in prison.'

'Yes, thank you for that, Nick. You don't need to start quoting Colin!'

'I would have lost my position at the Gardens,' Dave wails.

'For God's sake, mate, they don't even pay you!'

'I couldn't leave her there, not like that.'

'So you buried her?' Nick asks.

He doesn't know what else he can say. They're right, he knows they are. It was a stupid thing to do.

'Do you believe him?' Mike asks Nick. Nick hesitates but nods, and Dave lets out the breath he didn't know he was holding.

'Okay,' Mike agrees. 'You're no murderer, I know that much. Bloody hell, mate!'

'I know.'

Mike goes on. 'All right, the police don't know anything. I was able to establish that much.'

'You've spoken to them?'

'They came to the university this morning. I managed to offer my services and inveigle my way into the investigation.'

'Class! Well done, mate,' Nick says, and Mike can't keep the satisfaction from showing on his face.

'They're stumbling around in the dark. Lead detective didn't seem all that bright, if you ask me.'

'But won't they link the girl with you both?' Nick asks. 'There must be hundreds of witnesses to the fact Dave knew her and you even worked in the same department as her.'

'By that reckoning, you go to the same uni,' Mike points out. 'So you're hardly in the clear either.'

'Yeah, but I didn't know her or anything. I never met the girl and they can't prove I did because I didn't, did I?'

'And I didn't know her that well. Only to say hello to.'

It hurts Dave to hear them distancing themselves from his problem, but he can hardly blame them.

'The main thing is,' Mike goes on, 'there's no link to us as a group. They don't know about the coins.'

But they do, Dave realises. Because by now they will have

found the coins he left on her eyes. His face must give him away because Mike asks, 'Do they?'

He has to be honest with them. These people are his friends. They deserve to know the truth. 'No,' says Dave, 'I don't see how they could know about that.'

Mike leans back in his chair. 'Okay then, all we need to do is keep schtum. They'll find who killed her, or they won't. Either way, it's got nothing to do with us, right? In the meantime, we keep our heads down like we've already been doing.'

'What about Deepak?' Nick asks. 'You know what he's like. He never wanted to be part of any of this to begin with.'

'Leave Deepak to me,' Mike says. 'I'll deal with him. All he has to do is keep quiet. Out of all of us, he's the last one they should link with the girl.'

'Chi,' Dave says.

'What?'

'Her name was Chi.'

Mike stares at him. 'Fine. One more thing,' he says, leaning forward again. 'Whatever happens, if one of us gets caught, for whatever reason, we keep the others out of it. Agreed?'

By 'one of us', he means Dave.

'Agreed,' says Dave. Nick nods.

While Mike and Nick finish their drinks – Dave hasn't got round to buying one and decides not to bother now – Mike does his best to put their relationship back on an even keel. 'Any plans for the weekend then, boys?' he asks, only a hint of the strain of the previous conversation showing.

'I said I'd take that new bloke out,' Nick says. 'Stuart. Show him the ropes.'

'Don't go mentioning anything you shouldn't,' Mike reminds him.

'I'm not a complete idiot! Anyway, he seems sound enough. He's an art student at Hallam.'

Dave listens to them bicker. It will be good for Nick to have another younger man in the group. He's in danger of becoming old before his time, hanging around with the likes of them.

But Mike's attempt to fan the flames of bonhomie fail, and soon enough he and Nick are draining their drinks. None of them suggests another round.

Outside Dave says his goodbyes and climbs into his battered Volvo. Mike waves to him, standing next to Nick. They obviously arrived together and are leaving together, which makes sense since Nick doesn't drive. But as he pulls out of the car park, Dave glances in the rear-view mirror and sees them share a look.

He thinks about that look all the way back to the city. They don't trust him, he realises. And now he doesn't trust them. For a moment there, he convinced himself he had friends, but he doesn't. All they're interested in is their share of the profits and making sure he doesn't jeopardise that.

He's on his own.

Thursday morning brings another freezing downpour and the temperature drops another couple of degrees. Mina spends the morning taking new statements from the volunteers at the Gardens but none of them have much to add to what they already know about Chi. She leaves Daley at the Gardens and heads back to the office to look over the original missing persons' report again. It's not something she's had much experience of, so far. She'd been involved in a handful of cases back in uniform but only doing the grunt work. She'd been hoping Tyler might take her through it, but after a morning coordinating Uniform in their thankless task of checking CCTV cameras across the city, he seems to have disappeared again.

From what she can see, though, he wasn't wrong. It was a shoddy investigation. Even Mina, with her limited experience, can tell that much.

DI Cooper had been running the missing persons' unit for more than ten years before her recent suspension. She didn't always find the people she was looking for, but no one could have done more to try. Until six weeks ago, it would have been hard to find anyone with a bad word to say about her. It still is, in fact, with talk around the watercooler suggesting Cooper is being hung out to dry as a sacrificial lamb over the Talbot case. The press are demanding someone pays for the death of a 5-year-old boy, and Suzanne Cooper fits the mould. It didn't matter that for most of the time Cooper had been looking for the lad, he was most certainly already dead.

Which makes this case even more bizarre. Mina's been over several of Cooper's other cases, to familiarise herself with the other detective's methodology, and Chi's disappearance stands out a mile by comparison. Why? Why didn't she do the job she'd done a hundred times before? Everyone had bad days, weeks even, and obviously she would have been distracted by the search for a 5 year old. No one could blame her for that. But someone who cared about the job as much as Cooper obviously did would have gone back, surely? Her conscience would have pricked away at her until she was forced to look at the case again. Or at least make sure someone else did. But she hadn't. The last dated record in the file was less than two weeks after Chi vanished. *Two weeks?* Mina had spent longer than that looking for missing dogs.

She can't believe Jordan hadn't agreed to them talking with her. And she *really* can't believe Tyler hadn't tried to argue more.

The more she sits there, thinking it over, the more worked up she gets about the whole thing. She's sure there's something in this. And they need every lead they can get. Everyone keeps telling her to take the initiative, that they can't spoon-feed her all the time, so maybe she should do just that.

Slowly, an idea begins to take form in her head.

Doggett appears in the office mid-morning and heads straight for Tyler.

'I need a favour,' he says. Doggett outlines his problem; Jason Talbot has an aunt in West Bridgford, apparently, who's willing to talk about her brother's temper and his controlling behaviour. She's saying that she saw Talbot the week before

Jason disappeared and was worried that he was even more worked up than usual. Doggett needs someone to go take her statement. 'It might not sound like much but I'm willing to take whatever I can get at this point.'

'Why didn't she come forward earlier?'

'Same reason as the wife. Too scared of him. It looks as though her conscience has got the better of her though.'

'Can't you send Daley? Or someone from Nottingham?'

'Nottingham are being particularly unhelpful but to be honest, I'd rather it was you. I don't want her scared off again.'

'Flattery will get you everywhere. I don't know if Jordan will be all that thrilled though.'

'I've already cleared it with Diane. She said you were next to useless at the moment anyway and it would be good for you to get out of the city.' Doggett grins at him but then the smile fades. 'Please, son. There's no one else.'

Ignoring how this statement contradicts the previous reason given, Tyler reluctantly agrees. He could do without what will be a good three hour round trip but it does at least give him an opportunity to make a house call of his own on the way.

Coincidentally, Shannon-Marie Morgan lives in a street not far from the home of the murdered Talbot boy and Tyler half-expects to see Doggett parked up somewhere, keeping his beady eye on things.

The front of the house is a mess, the garden a small patch of jungle pushing its way slowly but inexorably across the path. The gate's missing, fallen disused among the overgrown foliage. He also spots a rusted motorcycle and what might once have been a microwave oven. The whole place looks like a vision from a post-apocalyptic future. He rings the doorbell but when he hears no noise from inside, he decides to hammer on the door as well.

Eventually, a dark shadow behind the glass staggers towards the front door. For a moment, Tyler remembers another door with frosted glass and a dark shadow behind it. He shivers and the hair stands up on the back of his neck.

The door opens slowly and a sharp-faced woman with her hair tied back in a ponytail opens the door and peers out at him.

'What?'

'Shannon-Marie Morgan?' He raises his warrant card.

'Oh, fuck's sake!' she says, and then turns and wanders away from him, back into the house. Taking this as the only invitation he's likely to get, Tyler follows her in.

The inside of the place lives up to the promise of the front garden. The whitewashed walls are dirty and dull, covered in a decade or more of scuff marks from mishandled furniture and nicotine stains. The whole place reeks of tobacco and marijuana. There are toys and books scattered up the stairs that speak of younger children somewhere. Tyler can hear them, high-pitched squabbles that might be coming from the garden or from upstairs, it's difficult to tell. He follows Morgan into the front room where she collapses back onto the sofa that she's presumably just vacated, finishes the text she's written on her way back from the door and takes up watching the television. She lights a cigarette and curls her legs up on the sofa underneath her.

'I ain't seen him in weeks,' she says, her eyes failing to leave the flickering screen. 'What's he done now?'

'It's nothing like that. Do you mind if I sit?'

In response, Morgan gestures with her cigarette towards an armchair. Tyler lifts an iPad off the chair, slips it onto a table and sits down.

'It's about Callum,' he tells her, and then, when she fails to show the slightest trace of interest in what he's saying, adds, 'Your son.'

She turns and looks directly at him for the first time since she opened the door. 'I know who he is. Whatever it is, he had nowt to do with it. You can't come in here, accusing him of shit. This is 'cos of Brent, i'nt it? You fit up one of m'sons and now you're back to—'

'No one's accusing Callum of anything, I just need to talk to you about him. You know he's living rough at the moment?'

She snorts, apparently satisfied he isn't about to cart away her second eldest child and put him away too. He knows all about her older son, Brent Morgan. Shannon-Marie Morgan wasn't always a Morgan. She was formerly a McKenna and the McKenna family had something of a history with South Yorkshire Police. As soon as he'd dug up Callum's address he'd known what he was getting into. So much so he'd hesitated about coming here on his own. Jordan would certainly have something to say about it. But it's not that far out of his way and he can't help thinking he owes Callum something. A chance, that Diane Jordan once gave to him.

And anyway, Brent was put away two years ago for a five-year stretch, for attempting to steal some farm equipment and half-killing the farmer in the process. And Tyler can handle the likes of Shannon-Marie. Her father, on the other hand, is another matter.

Joey McKenna is the sort of old-school villain who'd give Reggie Kray a run for his money. He was a minor member of the Johnson Gang who pretty much ran the east side of Sheffield throughout the 1980s. Those days are long gone and all the old gang are either dead or serving life sentences. All except Joey. No one ever managed to make anything stick to Joey. On the surface he's a respectable businessman these days, with a portfolio of property and assorted clean-cut enterprises, and if no one can quite piece together where the start-up capital came from, well, it isn't enough to give Joey a headache, even if it is for his accountants.

'That's not my problem,' Shannon-Marie says now. 'He was the one chose to fuck off on his tod. No one forced him.'

Earlier, he'd thought it almost endearing how keen she was to defend her son, indifferent parent that she may be. But whatever inbuilt instinct to protect her child she has hardwired into her seems to have come loose.

'So he's welcome to come back then?' he asks.

Her eyes flick over to him and then back to the TV. 'He comes and goes. He don't get on with Mark.'

'Mark?'

'Boyfriend,' she tells him, and it's a strangely odd word coming from this 44-year-old woman.

'Is Mark home?'

'Work,' she says.

There's a noise from somewhere further back in the house, a door opening and then a voice. 'Shannon, love?'

'In here, Dad!' Marie shouts. She sits up in her seat, stubs out the cigarette and turns and looks at Tyler properly for the first time, the hint of a grin on her face. He can read what she's thinking, it's written all over her face. Now we'll see what's what. And Tyler suddenly understands who she was texting a few minutes ago.

Joey McKenna walks into the room.

Cooper had been a bit frosty on the phone. Distant. But Mina supposes that's understandable; the woman must have a fair bit on her mind at the moment. When Mina asked if she could drop by for a chat about an old case, the DI replied with a curt, 'It's not as though I've got anything else on.'

Suzanne Cooper lives in a run-down block of flats on the Arbourthorne Estate. It isn't the best place in the city for a lone police officer to find herself and Mina's grateful she's not in uniform. The lift's out of order but given the stench of urine in the lobby she's not sorry to have to walk. By the time she reaches the fourteenth floor, however, she's long since changed her mind.

Cooper opens the door to her flat, blank-eyed, as though

she has no idea who Mina is and cares even less. When Mina explains she says, 'You'd better come in then.'

The flat is not much more than a bedsit, although the bedroom is at least separated from the living area by a stud wall. There's no door, though, just a faded, flower-patterned curtain, stained with nicotine. There are a number of cardboard boxes stacked against the wall, and more piled up behind the sofa. It looks as though Cooper has only just moved in and hasn't unpacked properly yet. Where she's going to put the stuff is anyone's guess.

Cooper lights up a cigarette the minute she sits down, as though the two actions are intrinsically linked, and judging by the overflowing ashtray on the coffee table they are. There's a tumbler of whisky on the smeared glass surface as well. Whether it's from the previous night or not, Mina can't tell, but it's a bit early to be today's. There's a laptop as well which, when Cooper sees Mina looking at it, she closes sharply.

There's an awkward silence where Mina struggles to work out where to begin. 'How are you?' she asks.

'Fucking A,' Cooper says, and blows smoke at the ceiling.

'So ... I wanted to talk to you about a missing persons' case you were involved with shortly before ...' She hesitates, unsure exactly how to word it.

'It's fine,' Cooper says, 'you can say it. Before I was hung out to dry by the big boys.'

'Sorry.' Mina feels her face heat.

Cooper holds out a palm in what seems to be a half-apology

of her own. 'Don't be. It was only a matter of time.' She stubs out her cigarette end. 'Anyway, technically they can't do anything at the moment as I'm on the sick. Stress.'

'Oh, right. The union are helping though, right? And if Doggett manages to catch—'

Cooper interrupts. 'No,' she says. 'It's too late for that. He was looking for a reason to get shot of me and now he's found it.' She picks up her cigarette packet and extracts another.

'Who? Doggett?'

'Doesn't matter.' Cooper lights her cig and takes a deep drag. 'So, what's this about? Which case?'

Mina reminds her of the details of Chi's case, few of them as there are in Cooper's report.

'Of course,' Cooper says, burying her head in one hand, her hair falling dangerously close to the tip of her cigarette. She straightens up again. 'Yeah, I remember it. What's your interest, exactly?'

'The body that was found in the Botanical Gardens.'

'It's her?' The first real emotion Mina has seen darts across Cooper's face. 'You're sure?'

Mina nods. 'Can you remember much about the case?'

Cooper leans back in her chair, holding her cigarette up in one hand and propping her elbow on the other as though she's a Hollywood actress from the 1940s, the image somewhat distorted by the stained tracksuit top and cracked nail varnish.

'Of course I can remember it. It was only a few months ago. Li Qiang. Botany student. Had a sister called Juju and a boyfriend or several. It seemed likely she'd run off with one of them. We found two packed cases in her room, full of clothes. It was a bit more than you'd need for a week in the sun.'

The packed cases were labelled on the sketch Cooper had drawn of the room. 'Actually, that's one of the things I wanted to ask you about. Didn't it strike you as suspicious she didn't take the cases with her? If she'd run off.'

Cooper's eyes narrow. 'She was Chinese. They're always leaving stuff behind when they go home.' She finishes the second cigarette and thankfully doesn't start on a third; Mina's not sure she could take any more smoke. She sees Cooper eyeing the whisky glass though, and wonders if it isn't so much a remnant from last night, as an early start this afternoon.

'My brother's a landlord,' Cooper goes on. 'He says they leave a right mess behind, most of them. They're not bothered about the deposit, just count it as part of the rent.'

'But Chi wasn't going home, was she? She hadn't finished her studies.'

Cooper folds her arms across her chest. 'There was no passport, no ID, no credit cards. All the personal stuff was gone. It made sense she'd gone away. Besides, she was deemed low risk so there was no reason to assume she was . . .' Cooper trails off and Mina wonders if she's now thinking about what actually happened to Chi. She hopes she is.

'That's something else I was a bit confused about. Was she low risk? She *was* a foreign student.'

Cooper checks her watch and stands up. *That's all I'm going to get.* Mina prepares to be kicked out. But instead, Cooper picks up the whisky tumbler and crosses to the kitchen counter to pour herself a drink. 'The initial investigating officer flagged the case as high risk because she was a foreign national, that's why it ended up on my desk.' She pours a generous measure of whisky and leaves the top off the bottle, a statement of intent. 'I downgraded it,' she says, returning to the living area.

'Why?'

Cooper sits back down. 'I can't remember. Anything else?'

Mina holds her temper in check. *Why isn't she taking this more seriously?* 'Yes,' she says, looking down at her notes. 'I'm assuming a check was made with the Department for Work and Pensions? Only, there's nothing in the file.'

Cooper stares at her. She takes a sip from her glass.

'There's nothing from the DVLA either, or any request for info from the Chinese embassy. Did you make a check of car-rental companies or—'

'Who sent you?' Cooper interrupts. She goes on, without waiting for Mina to answer, 'You see, I'm trying to work out what this is? I assume you're here to help stitch me up, though? Right?'

The change of attitude from Cooper takes some of the wind from Mina and she finds her anger fading. 'No, it's not like that.'

'If you're from IPCC, I have the right to representation, and to be interviewed by a senior officer.'

183

'Like I said, we're just trying to find out what happened.'

'What department are you?' Cooper asks.

Mina hesitates. 'CCRU.'

'You're Tyler's bloodhound? What's his interest in this? I know he likes to hang people out to dry but he tends to go for the jugular himself, not send some green-arsed constable to do it for him.'

'Look, you've got to admit, you didn't exactly exhaust every angle on this before you decided to shunt it away, did you?' Mina can feel her heart hammering in her chest. She's losing a battle she only now realises she's fighting.

But her own anger seems to calm Cooper somewhat. 'Who knows you're here?' she asks, the hint of a smile on her lips.

Mina's face is on fire again.

'Tyler *didn't* send you, did he? You're here on your own.'

'I'm sorry,' Mina says. 'I didn't mean to cause any offence, I just want to understand why. Why did you give up on her? I know you had all you could handle with the Talbot case but it was less than two weeks! If you had a good reason for shelving the case, just tell me!' By the end she's almost shouting, but it has an effect. Cooper's on the back foot again. She reaches for another cigarette and Mina notices her hand shaking.

She lights it slowly, taking a deep drag on the nicotine. 'I feel sorry for you,' she says, before blowing out the smoke in a thick cloud. 'I used to be like you once. Everything all black and white. Right or wrong. You've got a rude awakening ahead of you.' She downs the last of the whisky and bites her lip. She glances at the door, then the window, almost as though she's checking if there's a chance she'll be overheard. She pauses a moment longer and then says, 'Ah, fuck it! Screw 'em! It doesn't matter much now, anyway.' She stubs out the fag half-finished and leans forward, her elbows on her knees. This time, when she speaks, she sounds more professional, a hint of the woman she used to be. 'It was hard to get them to talk, but Chi's friends agreed on one thing – she was seeing someone. They didn't know who but it was a recent thing and he wasn't too good for her. The sister, Juju, had seen him once and she obviously didn't approve. She didn't say it outright but I got the impression Juju thought Chi was planning on going away as well.'

'Juju told us the cases were hand-me-downs that Chi had offered to her.'

'She was clearing out, that was the point. Given the amount of money she had, it would have been easy enough for her to buy new stuff when she got where she was going. The easy assumption was that she intended to travel light, especially if she was running off with some bloke.'

'Did you look into her financial records? Did she make any large withdrawals before or after she disappeared?' They were still waiting for that information themselves – dealing with a Chinese bank was causing Daley some difficulty, apparently.

'Of course, I did! I'm not an idiot.'

The silence is palpable. Mina can hear the fridge humming from the other side of the room. Cooper gets up and fetches herself another drink. Mina wants to say more but something tells her to stay quiet and give the woman the time she needs to compose herself.

When she returns, she curls up on the chair and holds the whisky glass close to her chest. 'I said it was an *easy* assumption. I didn't say it was mine. There was pressure from above. You may not have figured this out yet but there's always pressure from above. Chi's father was some bigwig in China and he didn't want any scandal, apparently. So he put pressure on someone who put pressure on someone else, and all that pressure filtered down until it landed on the poor sod at the bottom of the heap. That would be me.' The self-pity is back. 'I was *told* to let it go.'

Mina has no idea what to say. It isn't unusual for cases to be shelved, she knows that. If resources are tight and leads are failing. But not that quickly, surely? 'Okay,' she says. 'But you had two weeks, you must have done something more than sketch her flat and interview three people? How come the financial check isn't recorded in the file?'

'What?' Cooper looks genuinely puzzled. 'Of course I did more than . . . oh, that bastard!' She barks out a scathing laugh. 'He really is trying to fit me up, isn't he?'

The laugh turns into a sob and Cooper buries her face in her hands. Then she takes a deep breath, puts down the whisky glass and wipes her face with the sleeves of her track-suit top. She stands up. 'I think you'd better go now.'

Mina gets up and allows herself to be ushered back to the door. Then she turns back. 'Can you at least tell me who gave you the order?'

'It's better you don't know.' Cooper wrenches open the door and half pushes Mina out into the hallway.

Mina manages to turn and get a foot over the threshold. 'Who told you to shut down the case, please? Then I'll go, I swear.'

Cooper slams her hand against the wall in frustration and lets out another sob. She wipes her face again with one hand. Then she stops and Mina knows she's going to tell her.

'Who do you think?' Cooper says, her voice a little slurred but still full of venom. She looks down at her feet. 'The same person who shuts down everything. Including my career.' When Cooper finally looks up, Mina's shocked by the depth of pain in her eyes. 'The Eel,' she says. 'That slippery bastard Stevens.'

Joey McKenna fills the room.

He's a big man, tremendously well-built but not fat. In fact, considering he's in his mid-seventies he's in remarkably good shape. He's handsome, despite his years, but it's more than that. This is a small front room in a rundown part of the city but Tyler suspects he'd feel the same way if they were meeting in the Cutlers' Hall. There's something about this man that radiates authority and command.

Tyler stands up. He has no intention of having any inter-action with the man from a seated position. He's already at a significant height and weight disadvantage and he begins to reassess the wisdom of coming here alone.

'Who do we have here, then?' Joey asks, with his faint

Scottish burr, and never have six words sounded more threatening.

'He's a copper, Dad,' Shannon-Marie says, crossing her arms. The television show she couldn't draw her eyes from earlier has now ceased to exist. There's a new show in town.

Tyler isn't a man who's easily cowed but he knows how to read a situation and is as much a slave to biology as anyone else. He feels the adrenaline surge through his limbs, preparing him for whatever comes next. Fight or flight. He takes a deep breath in order to steady his hands and voice, and then reaches carefully for his warrant card and unfolds it for Joey.

'I'm DS Tyler, Mr McKenna. I'm here about Callum.' He hates how timid that sounds, but he isn't here to ruffle feathers. Not yet anyway.

McKenna takes the warrant card from him and inspects it carefully. He's a man who prides himself on detail. Tyler has no doubt the man has memorised his warrant number and ten minutes after he gets out of here, assuming things go that well, Joey will have found out everything there is to know about DS Adam Tyler.

McKenna flicks the warrant card closed and passes it back to him. Tyler takes it but the man doesn't let go immediately. It's only a split second but it's designed to push home a point. McKenna's the alpha here.

'Well, Detective Sergeant, how about you tell *me* what you want with my grandson, eh?' It's an innocent enough sentence but it comes loaded with meaning. If Tyler says the wrong thing now he's in a world of trouble.

'I've bumped into him a couple of times this week. On the street. It seems he's having a bit of a hard time of it and I was hoping I could straighten things out for him at home. See if we can't manage to get a roof over his head tonight. That's all.'

Joey digests this information, his eyes boring into Tyler's as though they're reading his soul. 'Aye,' he says. 'That's good of you, Detective Sergeant. He has his issues, our Cal, but he's a good lad at heart. I didn't know he was on the street.' He glances at Shannon-Marie, who looks down at the floor.

Tyler considers mentioning the bruises and cuts on Callum's face but decides against it. It might be better for Shannon-Marie, and for Mark, if McKenna doesn't find out the true extent of his grandson's misfortunes. 'I don't want Cal to become another statistic, Mr McKenna. The longer he's on the street, the more chance there is he gets involved in something he can't handle.'

McKenna pushes his tongue round the inside of his top lip. 'Like I said, that's good of you, Detective.' He steps forward suddenly. Tyler's a little over six feet but this man manages to look down on him. 'However,' he goes on. 'It strikes me that doesn't fall within the usual remit of CID now, does it?' His eyes narrow. 'So I'm left wondering what your true motivations are in this.'

'No motivation other than what I said.'

McKenna analyses him closely. 'Aye, well, I'll take you at your word. This time. But you can't just come round here asking questions, matey. That's not how it works. Our

189

Shannon-Marie, here,' he throws a fat palm in his daughter's direction, 'she's a bit highly strung, you know what I mean? I don't like seeing her bothered. So why don't we take this outside and we'll see what we can do about sorting things out, eh?'

Tyler's not stupid enough to ignore this thinly veiled demand but neither is he going to allow McKenna to have things all his own way. He pauses for a moment, making it clear to them both that he's choosing to leave, not being pushed out. At this point it's a minor distinction but a small victory. He turns to Shannon-Marie. 'Thank you for your time, Mrs Morgan. I'd appreciate it if you'd think about what I said. Maybe reach out to Callum. If you can.' A small victory, but a victory nonetheless.

He steps around McKenna and into the hallway. The kids are still playing noisily upstairs somewhere. All the way to the front door he can feel Joey McKenna's hulking presence right behind him. He resists the urge to look back. No reason to let the man know how rattled he is, and if McKenna's still involved in anything shady, he's unlikely to raise his profile by taking a pop at a police officer in his daughter's hallway. Unlikely to. But then again, McKenna's known for having a short fuse. If the red mist descends, all bets are off.

McKenna escorts him to the front gate, a curious smile fixed on his face.

'Tell me, Detective Sergeant Tyler. You wouldn't be related to *Richard* Tyler, by any chance?'

A cold chill moves through Tyler's body causing a wave of nausea to rise up in his stomach. 'My father.'

McKenna frowns, as though digesting the information, but something tells Tyler this isn't news to him. 'Is that right? Yeah, I can see the family resemblance. Small world, eh?'

'You knew him.'

'Mostly by reputation. We were on ... opposing teams, you might say.' He smiles widely and there's a twinkle in his eyes that's as charming as it is chilling. 'We met a couple of times though. He seemed a fair sort.' McKenna nods. 'Aye, awful business, what happened to him. A man taking his life like that. It's hard to fathom.'

Tyler feels his hands shaking again. Keep it professional. 'I want you to know, Joey,' he says, using the man's first name deliberately, 'I'm not trying to stitch anyone up here. I was looking out for your grandson.' He tries to sound as straight-forward as he can, appealing to the man's feelings as a father and a grandfather. He wonders how far those feelings stretch though. Looking at the state of the Morgan family home and knowing the relative size of McKenna's bank balance, it seems they don't stretch all that far. 'But if you want to make this personal, I'm sure I can find a reason to come back here.'

He expects McKenna to start playing the heavy again but the man laughs. He holds up his hands in mock surrender. 'Just an observation, lad.'

Another wave of cold sweeps through Tyler's body.

McKenna glances back at the house, his eyes taking in the squalor just as Tyler's did earlier. 'Shannon-Marie,' he says shaking his head. 'She's not the best housekeeper. I'd buy her somewhere better but she'd only destroy that too. I help out where I can, make sure the kids get all those technological doodads they're so keen on. But the trouble with our Shannon is she's easily led. This new fella she's got . . . well, I think perhaps it's time he moved on.'

'Mr McKenna, I understand you're worried about your family, but I have to caution you against taking the law into your own hands—'

McKenna's laugh is heartfelt. 'DS Tyler, you are a card. You've fair made my day with that one. If I thought he'd laid a finger on Cal, or our Shannon, he'd be six feet under by now. No, it's not like that. Shannon's a bit troubled, that's all. All the smarts skipped a generation there, landed squarely on young Callum's shoulders, thankfully. Her and Cal have never seen eye to eye but this new fella doesnae help any.' He reaches out with his oversized hand and places it squarely on Tyler's shoulder. 'Don't you worry that clever little head of yours, I'm nae gonna kill the twat. I'll have a quiet word and he'll be gone by morning. Then I'll find Cal and make sure he has a roof over his head.' McKenna stares at him thoughtfully. 'Thank you,' he says. 'For the information about Cal. I reckon I owe you something for that. I shall have to have a wee think and see if there's anything I can do to help you in return. I'll be in touch.' McKenna lets go and turns back towards the house.

'If you know something . . .' Tyler can't bring himself to mention Richard but he's sure McKenna knows exactly what he's talking about.

McKenna turns, grinning from ear to ear. 'I know all kinds of things, DS Tyler.'

'You're not above the law, McKenna.'

'You really are a chip off the old block, aren't you?'

And with that, Joey McKenna turns and walks back into his daughter's house, closing the door behind him.

Dave sits in his flat, flicking through old photographs he keeps in a shoebox under the bed. The meeting with Mike and Nick has made him edgy, as though seeing the distrust in their eyes has made everything more real. He isn't going to get away with this. He can stay clear of the Gardens for as long as he wants but sooner or later the police are going to come calling. And if his friends doubt him, the police aren't likely to give him an easier ride.

He finds a picture of Lizzie and him, taken in the hospital near the end. It's probably the last photo he has of the two of them together. He can see the strain in her eyes and remembers the stiff feel of her arm round his waist, as though she couldn't wait to drop the pose.

They'd met in the coffee shop by the hospital. She was late, but he didn't hold that against her. When she arrived, she was wearing the scarf he'd bought her the previous Christmas and for a moment he wondered if it was a sign. An attempt at a rapprochement. A peace offering, at least. But then he saw her face as she glanced across at him before turning to join the queue at the counter, and he knew he was wrong. He wasn't sure exactly what the look represented. Frustration? Despair? Utter contempt? Take your pick. It certainly wasn't the way she used to look at him anyway.

She ordered a soya milk latte and, because she'd rushed straight from work, a granola bar that she ate in tiny broken-off portions, nibbling the nuts and grains like a bird at a feeder. He used to find this endearing about her but that day, he remembers, he wanted her to shovel the food in her mouth as though she couldn't get enough of it. He wanted her to do something with passion again, if only to remind herself she could.

'You okay?' he asked her as she sat down, and immediately regretted it. It was the kind of asinine greeting they used to hate from others. The kind of remark that, if someone had said in the past, would have caused them to raise their eyebrows to each other; and then later, perhaps naked and sweat-soaked, they would lie in bed together, her back curled into the contours of his body, and dissect the personality of the person who made it. Their way of affirming that it was the two of them versus everyone else, always. And forever.

He watched her face for some recognition of this thought process, a smile to convey she felt the same way. But she didn't meet his eyes. 'Fine,' she said.

They sat in silence and he watched her gnaw at the granola, staring out of the window at the rain that had begun to fall.

She said, 'I had a call from your mother last night.'

'Oh?'

'She wanted to know if there'd been any change.'

'And?'

'I told her there hadn't, obviously.'

'Sorry,' he said. 'She worries, and if I'm not available . . .'

He trailed off, hoping she might wonder why he wasn't available. But she didn't ask. 'I got some work at the university,' he went on. 'Just nights. Cleaning. But I can't have my phone on me.'

She didn't respond to this news but said, 'Well, I'd rather she didn't ring, to be honest. I don't know what to say to her.'

'I'll talk to her.'

'Fine.' She was biting the inside of her cheek, the way she always did when she was pained or troubled about something. Then she saw him watching her and stopped. She looked away, out of the window again. 'It's good,' she said. 'About the work.'

'Thanks.'

She dusted the crumbs from her fingers and picked up her coffee. 'We should get going. She'll be waiting.'

He brought his own cup to his lips but the coffee had grown cold. She started to stand up and he couldn't help himself. He reached out and took hold of her wrist.

'Lizzie,' he said, on the verge of saying so much more.

But she pulled her arm away. 'Don't,' she said. 'Not today, please. Nothing's changed. Let's get ...' He knew she was about to say, 'get this over with' but she stopped herself. 'Let's get moving, okay?'

He got up, slipped on his jacket, and followed her out into the rain. It was a heavy downpour but it wasn't as though they had far to go. Ahead of them, outside the emergency admissions entrance, an ambulance stood idly by, its occupants no doubt haring through the corridors of the Children's

Hospital at that very moment, delivering another precious, broken cargo.

She pushed her way ahead of him through the crowd of smokers gathered outside the door. He looked up for a moment, letting the rain batter against his upturned face, washing away any trace of tears.

Later, in her room, Rachel had taken the picture of them together. 'Come on, Mum, Dad. Smile!' she'd told them, and struggled to hold the phone steady as she pressed her finger to the screen.

Mina stands on the platform waiting for the tram to arrive. She's been there fifteen minutes and they're supposed to run at least every ten at this time of the day. Still, the crowd of people on the platform's growing so that's a good sign. There's a young woman with a pushchair, and two kids who keep jumping down on the track and hurling stones at each other. An elderly woman keeps glancing at Mina as though she might attack her, and behind her are a couple of teenaged lads, smoking a cigarette that may or may not be legal.

She thinks about DI Cooper again, and the sad little flat. Is that what lies in store for her? She hears her mother's voice in her head. *You need to start thinking about your future, Amina. You girls today, you think – it's never too late. But soon it is too late.*

Bollocks to that! But it's not so much that her mother is wrong that gets to her. It's the thought she might be right.

Surely, Cooper could afford better than that though? On her salary. If it came to it – and the way things are at home, it just might – Mina reckons she herself could afford a nicer place than that on her own meagre salary. It's not as though anyone got rich being a copper, but Cooper's a DI; she can't imagine Jim Doggett living like that. Well, maybe the booze and general untidiness fit, but that flat was tiny. It looked as though she'd just moved in as well. Why would she choose to live there of all places?

The tram finally arrives and Mina takes a seat right at the back so she can keep her eyes on everyone. Her thoughts stray to her mother. It's not as though she doesn't want to meet someone. But she wants to make a career for herself first. Something unassailable, so that there's no talk of staying home and looking after babies. Does she even want babies? Does she even want a husband? She's not sure she does. Most of the time. But the thought of ending up like Suzanne Cooper, alone, drowning her sorrows . . .

Why the hell would Stevens tell her to shelve the case? Is it just as Cooper said? That there was pressure from the family. That was bad enough but . . . the alternative is unthinkable. Surely, Stevens couldn't have had anything to do with . . . No, that's ridiculous! The father then? Why was he so keen to brush things under the carpet? But he was in China at the time. He couldn't have possibly murdered his own daughter. Not personally, anyway.

Back at the station, her afternoon is taken up with trying to fill in the gaps in the initial investigation. She chases up Daley's request with the Chinese bank and makes enquiries with both the embassy and the passport office. But her thoughts remain scattered and she ends up going back to Cooper's original file. *What else is missing?* Did Stevens really go so far as to remove information from the report? Why? Cooper seemed to imply it was to make her look bad but what if it was more than that? She should have taken the file to Cooper's. Maybe the DI could tell her what was missing. She could go back, but she has a nasty feeling the woman wouldn't want to talk to her again.

It doesn't take much – a brief check on the internet and a call to a couple of estate agents – and she discovers she was right. Suzanne Cooper *has* just moved. A month ago, from a half-decent semi in Loxley that she sold, to her current apartment where she now rents. *Money troubles.*

She loses herself in her own thoughts, doodling idly on a notepad all the while. Cooper didn't strike Mina as the sort who'd take risks on the stock market, and she certainly didn't have an obvious shopping problem – there was nothing of any worth in the flat as far as she could see. There was that laptop though, that Cooper had snapped shut when she saw Mina checking it out. *Porn?* Unlikely. *Gambling.* That makes more sense but the only way to tell for sure would be to delve into Cooper's finances and there's no way Jordan would authorise that. *Does any of this even matter?* No doubt the IPCC will find anything there is to find and she doubts any of this has any bearing on their case. Unless ...

'Working late, Mina?'

Doggett's voice makes her jump and she immediately feels guilty. He has that effect on her.

'Just trying to get my head round something, sir.' She glances down and notices she's written Stevens' name down on the pad and underlined it. Twice. She scratches it out with her pen.

Doggett plops himself into a swivel chair, sitting the wrong way round, and scoots it up to her desk. 'What have you got?' he asks, sticking his large, hairy nose quite literally into her business.

'I'm looking at the original investigation,' she says. No need to tell him about her visit to Cooper's house. She's pretty sure he wouldn't approve.

His leg bounces up and down causing the wheeled chair to squeak alarmingly. 'And?'

'I dunno,' she admits. 'It all seems a bit ... weak.' How much should she say? She's not paranoid enough to think Doggett has any axe to grind with her. Until he spoke to her then, she wasn't even sure he still remembered her name. *Why is he talking to me?* But she does remember how easily he dropped her from CID after her brush with death last year. Tyler told her it was because he felt responsible somehow, but that was just Tyler trying to make her feel better about things. Uncharacteristically. The real reason is that Doggett thought she didn't have the right stuff. He'd made that clear enough. On the other hand, he isn't Stevens' biggest fan either ...

'But?' he prompts.

She decides to trust him. 'Do you know DI Cooper?' she asks.

'She's a good copper,' he says, interpreting her meaning correctly. It's unnerving how good he is at that.

'It's just . . .' She still doesn't want to admit to him that she's spoken to Cooper. 'The case was shelved a bit quickly, for a missing persons' case. You'd think she'd have given it longer than a couple of weeks.'

Doggett shrugs. 'Depends what else she had on. This was back in April, right? When Jason Talbot first went missing? Some cases take priority over others. Especially kids.'

She can't get over how matter-of-fact he is about things sometimes. She wants to tell him what she's found out, about Stevens, and Cooper's potential gambling problem. Her troubled financial situation. But it's all hearsay and speculation. *He paid her! He paid her to drop the case.* It was a ridiculous thought. *Why would he do that?* But now the thought was in her head she couldn't shake it.

Doggett's watching her closely. 'I don't know what lessons DS Tyler's been teaching you, but don't make this a witch-hunt, eh? Going after Suzanne Cooper won't do you any favours. If you want my advice, leave the feather-ruffling to Tyler, he's good at it. You stick to the case.'

Maybe he's right. Maybe she's seeing conspiracies where there aren't any. So Stevens told Cooper to drop the case. It might not be right but it was the way things were sometimes.

'Okay,' she tells Doggett. 'Thanks, boss.'

Doggett grins at her and gets up.

'Sir, while I've got you, I was wondering . . . I mean, I

know you turned down my application to join the Murder Team, but I really think I could be an asset.'

The smile fades from Doggett's face. She's gone too far.

'You've got a job to do, Detective Constable. I suggest you focus on that before you start auditioning for the big leagues.'

She drops her head. 'Yes, sir.'

Doggett looks down at her. 'Look,' he says, 'if in doubt, go back to basics. It's not all running around all over the place interviewing suspects. Sometimes you have to put in the leg-work in a different way. My advice is to stop trying to run before you can walk.'

That's the second piece of advice he's given her without her asking. That's not really fair when she thinks about it; she offers up a reluctant thank-you and he disappears back into the bowels of the Murder Room. Only then does she realise she didn't even ask him about his own case.

She checks her watch. Her shift ended half hour ago. She should head home and listen to whatever new wonderful piece of information her mother has about Ghulam and his bride-to-be. Or she could stay here and work? It's a no-brainer, really.

She picks up her mobile and calls Guy Daley.

'Ay-ay, Miiiiinaaaaa! What's up, love, missing me?'

So it's *that* Daley, this time, is it? She counts to five before she answers. 'Have you finished the statements from the volunteers yet?'

'Mina, don't start!'

'I wasn't having a dig, I was offering to help!'

'Oh.' He tries to sound contrite without losing face. She doubts it's something that comes easily to him. 'Cheers, mate. But I'm just about done.'

'Anything interesting?'

'Not really.'

'Why don't you send them over anyway and I can take a look.' She expects him to argue and she's ready with explanations about being at a loose end and how a new pair of eyes might help, but in the end he simply agrees and hangs up.

What the hell's going on with him? He's so changeable.

While she's waiting for the email to arrive she starts looking over the employment records she requested from the university. An hour later she finds something. And this time she thanks Doggett for his advice for real.

The Nottingham trip is a complete bust. The aunt wasn't home. Either that, or she'd changed her mind again and refused to answer the door to Tyler. He'd made a few enquiries with neighbours and spoken to the local police so that they could follow things up but that was as much as he could do. He'd rung Doggett to give him the bad news.

'Ah, well,' Doggett had said philosophically. 'Maybe she'll have another change of heart.' And with that he'd hung up, without a word of apology or thanks.

On his way home, Tyler answers a call from Rabbani.

'Where the fuck have you been?' she snaps without saying hello.

'Mina. Always a pleasure. I was looking into something.'

'Whatever! Look, I thought you might like to know I spoke to DI Cooper today.'

'You did *what*?' He doesn't mean to shout it.

'Well, you obviously weren't gonna get round to it and we needed to do something.'

Tyler takes a deep breath before he says something he might regret. 'I was going to speak to Jordan about it again tomorrow.'

'Oh,' Rabbani goes quiet for a couple of seconds. 'Well, if you told me this stuff I'd know, wouldn't I?'

Tyler takes another deep breath. 'What's done is done. Let's hope Jordan doesn't find out. So what did you learn?'

'Not a lot, except that she was told to drop the case by Superintendent Stevens. Why would he do that?'

'It's not that unusual in a missing persons' case. If there's no real evidence and the missing person is an adult.' But then something occurs to him. A nasty thought that creeps up from somewhere deep in his mind and demands to be heard. He pushes it away, unwilling to confront it yet.

'Sarge?'

'Sorry, what?'

'I said, there was plenty of stuff they hadn't tried yet. No contact with the embassy, or anything?'

'What was Cooper's take on it?'

'She said the father had piled pressure on from above. Stevens told her Chi had run off with a boyfriend and the parents didn't want any more shame coming down on the family. I don't think she'd have told me that much but she's obviously pissed that Stevens didn't back her over the suspension. She also said that there was information missing. Things she had done, like contact the bank. She implied that Stevens must have removed it from the file.'

Why would he do that? Tyler listens to Rabbani as she outlines her theory about Cooper's gambling problem.

'Sarge? What if he paid her to drop the case?'

'Why on Earth would he do that?'

Rabbani doesn't answer but in the back of Tyler's mind that thought creeps up again. *A conspiracy.*

'There's something else,' Rabbani says. 'I've been going over the statements and looking into the volunteers at the Gardens.'

'I thought Guy was handling that bit.'

'Yeah, but he's not, is he?'

Tyler pulls up at the gates to his apartment and waits for them to open, the nasty thought continuing to pick away at the threads of his consciousness. 'Then what *is* he doing?' He notices a car pull up behind him and follow him into the compound.

Rabbani doesn't answer but goes on with her own discovery. 'I also took a look at the employment records from the university. There's a name that comes up on both lists. A bloke named Dave Carver. He was let go from the university earlier this year but he was there when Chi was there.'

'And he works at the Gardens as well?'

'As a volunteer. But Sarge, get this . . . He's also the one that found the body. *And* he's got a criminal record for assault.'

Tyler gets out of the car and locks the door. 'Okay. That's definitely worth a look.'

'Worth a look? He attacked some bloke in the street and nearly killed him.'

He's vaguely aware of the other car pulling into the empty space next to him. 'Okay, I'll be in first thing, all right? We'll go over everything then and see what we've got.'

He hangs up on her before she can argue.

'DS Tyler?' says a voice behind him.

Tyler turns and something hits him, hard, in the face. The punch is strong enough to send him straight down onto the brick-paved path. He manages to get his hands out to save his head but feels the skin on his palms rip and a sharp judder travel up them and into his body. A boot hits him deep in the stomach, doubling him over, and then a second connects from behind, burying itself into his right kidney.

The air rushes from his lungs even as the pain ripples up and down his spine. He thinks there are two of them. One of them bends over, his mouth so close to Tyler's ear he can feel the shadow on his face and smell the man's cologne. It's sickly sweet – orange blossom, layered over the stench of stale body odour. His head is spinning but he hears the words the man whispers clearly enough.

'You were told to stay away from this. Next time won't be as pleasant.'

Another boot to his stomach, but less forceful this time. Still enough to leave him gasping for air.

He manages to get up on one arm and angle his head far

enough in time to see them get back in their car. Two of them, dressed head to toe in black, including balaclavas. He tries to make out the registration but his vision is blurred. The car speeds back towards the gate.

He tries to get up, to get back down the path but his body won't respond. He collapses again and listens to the gates creaking open and shut and then the sound of the car engine as it rumbles away into the night.

He's lying there, drifting in and out of consciousness, when the nasty thought returns in full and settles in the back of his mind. *Conspiracy.*

four

the fourth nighthawker

Record of Finds

Date: Wed 8th Nov
Time: 00:15
Location: Drakehouse Estate, Bradfield
Finds: small indeterminate piece of metal (tin?), zipper attached to torn Levis, men's size 42 waist (worth washing?), assorted coins (2p — 1994, 5p — 1980, 50p — 1982 — check prices on internet!)

It's not a great night to go out, but at least it's stopped raining. Deepak stays clear of the city, wanting to be as far from the scream of police sirens as he's able to get. His anxiety is bad enough at the moment — at one point he even thinks there's a car following him — and police attention is the last thing he needs. Instead he drives north-west to Bradfield and the reservoirs. He picks a field he hasn't visited before, finds a quiet lane to park up the car and sets out across the wet ground into the night.

It's not as cold tonight either, and the ground squelches beneath his feet. The wetter the ground, the softer it is and the easier it is to dig. Not that he's expecting to find much out here; these places have been dug over so many times you'd probably have to go deep into the bowels of the Earth to find anything even vaguely of worth.

He loses himself in the quiet buzz of his headphones for a couple of hours but his thoughts keep skating right back to the problem. He couldn't wait to get away from the detectorists' meeting tonight. He nearly didn't go at all but then he thought he'd better show his face, if only to prevent one of the others doing or saying something stupid. And now Mike's set up this pub meet for tomorrow. Or today, technically, since it's now past midnight. He doesn't want to be anywhere near Dave Carver, or any of them for that matter. He still can't believe how far he's become involved as it is. What was he thinking?

When Nick came up with the idea of nighthawking the archaeologists' site he hadn't been keen, but he'd let them persuade him it would be a laugh. And then they found the coins and everything changed. He should have tried harder to convince them to declare it to the coroner. Maybe they would still have got some money for finding them, whatever Mike Halbert believes. And even if they didn't, they could have at least enjoyed the notoriety that would have come from unearthing a significant archaeological find. That was no small thing in itself. Who knows what that might have led to?

But instead he'd kept quiet. And the longer things went, the harder it was to row back on the decision. Every time he pulls that shoe box out from under the bed and examines those three perfect golden aurei, he can't help thinking about the money they represent. But doing shady deals under cover of darkness? How had that come about? He never would have thought Dave capable of anything like that. He could see Mike getting involved in it, but Dave?

When you lie down with dogs you get up with fleas, as his old man used to say. He's been following the news reports about the body in the Gardens. It didn't take a genius to figure out who that was. And judging by the faces of some of the others at the meeting last night — Dave's included — he isn't the only one who's worked it out. He didn't stick around to find out though. He can't believe Dave could have killed that woman but . . . when he'd looked in the man's eyes, he wasn't so sure. He'd told them that she never turned up. But that clearly wasn't true, was it?

A dog barks and a security light comes on at a distant cottage. He freezes but the barking dies down and there are no other signs of life. He carries on across the field, the hum of the detector in his ears.

He should go straight to the police, turn Dave in and the rest of them too. Before one of them does the same to him. But he has more to lose than the rest of them. He's a teacher, for heaven's sake! If he ends up inside for failing to declare treasure, he'll never work again. Then again, the penalty for aiding and abetting a murderer is probably a fair bit more than six months. He should never have gone along with any of this.

By the time he makes it to the far side of the field, he's

found precious little and he decides to call it a night rather than head back on another sweep. His nerves are shot and he needs to be somewhere warmer where he can think the whole thing through properly. He follows the road back round to where he parked the car. There's not much in the way of street lighting out here but the light pollution from the city is enough to see, without using his torch. And there's the occasional flash and crack of distant fireworks. Bonfire night seems to go on for weeks these days.

When he gets back to the car, he sits for a few minutes and examines his finds with the courtesy light in the car. Just as he'd thought, crap. He tidies his backpack away and starts the engine. He'll go tomorrow. To the police. He's bound to get off with a suspended sentence if he's the one who turns the others in. All right, it's not exactly cricket, as his father would say, but he really doesn't owe these people anything. He doesn't even have anything in common with them, except a hobby.

But, he thinks as he puts the car in gear, that's not entirely true, is it? When it comes down to it he's just the same as those other sad bastards, grubbing around in the dirt, looking for a better life.

Then something grabs him by the throat and he feels the cold bite of steel on his neck. 'Give me the coins,' says a voice from the back seat.

Deepak screams.

'DS Tyler, DC Rabbani, with me.' Diane Jordan passes them without stopping and disappears around the corner towards her office.

Rabbani glances at him, the worry etched into her brow. How the hell is he supposed to know? Whatever it is, it isn't good.

They hurry after Jordan, Tyler's aching ribs causing him to wince with every step; however bad the news is, it won't get any better if they keep her waiting. Tyler tries to catch Doggett's eye as they pass through the Murder Room but the DI is neck-deep in paperwork and doesn't look up.

In Jordan's office, they stand shoulder to shoulder, like naughty school kids hauled in to see the headmistress. Jordan doesn't leave them hanging for long. She isn't the sort to play psychological games. When there's a problem she comes straight out with it.

'Sit down,' she says, and they each take a seat across the desk from her. 'Why do I have Superintendent Stevens ringing me at eight in the morning to tell me he's received a complaint about one of my officers?'

Rabbani looks at him but before he can speak, Jordan goes on. 'It seems he had a call last night from DI Cooper, who is under the impression we're trying to build a case against her for negligence.'

Rabbani squirms in her seat.

'My fault,' Tyler says, before she can dig herself an even deeper grave. 'I asked Mina to have a gentle chat with her, but it seems they got their wires crossed.' He moves his foot so that his shoe is tight up against Rabbani's own and hopes it's enough that she gets the message.

'I should say they did.' Jordan turns to Rabbani. 'You're in agreement with DS Tyler about this sequence of events, I take it?'

Rabbani squirms a bit more, presumably caught between her desire to be truthful and a desire not to drop him in it any further.

After a few moments Jordan takes pity on her. 'All right, Mina, don't tie yourself up in knots. I'll accept DS Tyler's version of events, unconvincing as it may be.' She looks back at him. 'Not the best idea to send a newly installed detective constable in to talk to someone of Suzanne's experience. Not very politically minded, shall we say?'

'No, ma'am,' he admits. 'I don't know what I was thinking. But then, politics has never been my strong suit.' He risks a glance at Rabbani, who's growing steadily pinker in the cheeks.

Jordan is giving him that look she's so good at. He's surprised he hasn't already heard something about the fat lip he's sporting. Of course, he should have already told her what happened last night, but if he does she'll bounce him off the case. She's obviously curious but has probably decided it's better if she doesn't know.

'Superintendent Stevens isn't the only person who fielded a phone call this morning,' Jordan says. 'Would you like to hazard a guess who I heard from half an hour ago?'

'No, ma'am.'

'Very wise. The manager of a certain restaurant called the central switchboard this morning wanting to make a complaint about one of our officers. There are no prizes for guessing who. Apparently this officer caused something of a scene in her establishment and refused to pay the bill.'

Damn. He'd meant to ring the restaurant yesterday but Doggett's errand had distracted him. He's surprised the manager hasn't rung sooner. Maybe she was plucking up the courage. 'It wasn't like that,' he says.

'I really don't care. Thankfully the switchboard put her through to me and I talked her out of an official complaint on the condition you would apologise and settle your account.'

Tyler looks down at his feet. It usually has the right effect in these circumstances. 'I'll sort it.'

'Yes, you will. Do I need to remind the pair of you how important this case is?'

'No, ma'am.' They speak in unison.

'For God's sake, Chi's parents arrive in the country next week to collect what's left of their dead daughter, do you really want to be the one to tell them we have no idea what happened to her? Because it can be arranged. Superintendent Stevens and I are agreed on that much at least.'

Rabbani snorts. 'If he was that bothered about Chi, he wouldn't have shelved the original investigation.'

Tyler stares at Rabbani, who looks as though she herself can't quite believe she's spoken aloud.

'Mina!' Jordan's voice is strangled. She runs a hand over her face.

'Sorry, ma'am, but it's true! That's the only thing he's bothered about. He knows DI Cooper told me he made her drop the case.'

Jordan glances at Tyler but he says nothing. He doesn't want to sell Rabbani down the river but he's not ready to bring Jordan in on this yet. Not until he's had a chance to work out exactly what it means.

Jordan says, 'Please don't tell me you seriously think Superintendent Stevens is involved in the death of Li Qiang.'

There's a short pause during which time Tyler again presses his foot hard up against Mina's.

'No, ma'am,' she says at last.

'Thank heaven for small mercies!'

'But I do think he cut short DI Cooper's investigation, either for his own benefit or . . . I don't know, political pressure or something.'

Jordan closes her eyes. When she opens them again Tyler can see how hard she's trying to hold her temper. When she speaks her voice is lower. 'Between you, me and these four walls, you might well be right about that. It happens. But, think what you like about whether that's legal, moral or anything else, I'm strongly advising you to keep those thoughts to yourself. Understood?'

Mina bites her lip. 'Yes, ma'am.'

'You're supposed to be finding out what happened to Chi.' Jordan slams her hand down on the desk. 'Both of you!'

Rabbani drops her head and mumbles another affirmation.

Jordan turns back to Tyler. 'Enough of this nonsense. Get back to the case you've been assigned.' As they get up to leave, she adds, 'I can only help you so far. Last chance, the pair of you. Make it count.'

'What do you think?' Mina asks.

She and Tyler have been holed up outside the suspect's house in a CID Vectra for almost three hours. They've already been to the door but there was no response to the intercom. Jordan agreed to work on a warrant but she wasn't too excited about their chances of getting one considering the only thing they have on the suspect is a minor affray for assault. She suggested their best chance was the landlord and Daley was supposed to be handling that for them. The trouble is, Mina's not sure Daley even took in what she was telling him, let alone whether he's acting on it.

'I think it's a bit thin, to be honest,' Tyler says, and the words sting. 'I mean, we all know Stevens is a bit dodgy – they don't call him the Eel for nothing – but it's a long leap from there to a conspiracy to commit murder. What possible reason could he have for murdering Chi? There's no evidence he even knew her.'

He's right, she knows that.

'Anyway, let Jordan handle Stevens. He's a bit above both our pay grades.'

'All right, you don't have to keep on.' It's almost as though he's trying to convince her not to get involved. No, she's the one jumping to conclusions. Maybe she's got it wrong about Carver too. She met the man at the Gardens and it wasn't as though he was giving off an evil vibe or anything. Intuition. That's what you're supposed to have, to make a good copper. Tyler's got it, Doggett's got it. God, even Daley has flashes of inspiration sometimes but, if she's honest with herself, she's just not sure she has got it.

Tyler's looking at her.

'What?' she asks.

'It was good work, Mina. Tracking down Carver. That's how it works; we follow the evidence. We look into everything, no matter how small. Everything's small until it's not.' He smiles and the scar on his face turns it into a much larger gesture than he means it to be. She notices again the fat lip he came in with this morning but decides not to give him the satisfaction of asking. He won't tell her anyway. He winces and reaches a hand round to rub the small of his back.

'Sciatica,' he says, when he sees her watching him.

There's something he's not telling her. And not just about his appearance. First shutting down her theory about Stevens and then trying to distract her with flattery. *How am I supposed to do my job if he won't talk to me?*

'Shit!' she says.

'What?'

'We've been staking out his house because, as far as we know, he hasn't got a job, right? He was fired.'

'Right.'

'But we forgot he *does* work.' She watches his face crumple into confusion and then the grin's back.

'The Gardens!' Tyler says, starting the engine. 'I can be there in five, ten maybe, depending on traffic. Call Daley and tell him to keep his eye out. You'll be all right on your own for a bit, won't you?'

'What? No way! You're not ditching me again.'

'Mina,' he says, turning in his seat to face her. 'We can't let Guy handle things on his own. You've seen what he's like at the minute. But we need someone here too, in case Carver comes back.'

She can't think of an argument against that except . . . 'So why don't *I* go and back up Daley, while *you* wait here?'

Tyler laughs. 'Wait for Carver. If he gets back, ring me, I'm five minutes away.'

'Or ten, depending on traffic.' But there's not much she can do except save herself the ignominy of him ordering her, so she gets out of the car and slams the door. It's the only weapon she has left. Even if she knows how ineffective it will be.

Dave's given up trying to avoid the Gardens. It only makes him look more suspicious and at the end of the day he still has responsibilities. He made a promise to Chi when he laid her to rest, that he'd finish the work she'd started. Silly, really, he thinks, as he sets about tending the delicate stems. It isn't as though he knows all that much about propagating plants, and certainly not orchids, but it still seems important to try. He knows she's not coming back, and that whatever experiment she was attempting will never be completed, but he can't bear to part with the plants that remain. He's surprised the lead volunteer, Chloe, hasn't tried to sell them yet. He suspects she hasn't even noticed them, tucked away in this dusty corner of the glasshouse.

This was the place where they'd first met. He was ferrying bags of compost between here and the Long Border at the time. Sweaty, backbreaking work with the wheelbarrow – he hadn't been cleared to drive the trucks at that point – but he didn't mind. It was good, honest work and kept him in shape. Every time he came in she would look up, smile and then turn away. Such an innocent, childlike gesture, and so familiar to him it was almost unnerving.

On the third trip he plucked up the courage to speak. 'Looks like tricky work,' he said, gesturing to her tiny fingers as they separated seeds.

She grinned. 'Not really,' she said, placing the tips of her fingers across her lips to cover her smile. The gesture made him ache with sadness. 'It's good. I like it. It reminds me of home.'

They chatted for nearly an hour that first day. She told him her name, what it meant, and how to spell it. She told him about life in Kunming and her father's nursery, and how she had grown up around flowers and plants. She told him about her studies and introduced him to the basics of genetics, which he said sounded fascinating even as he struggled to hide how little he understood.

He felt he could listen to her talk all day, every day. She was so young and vibrant and full of energy. Fiercely intelligent too, and charming. At one point she held out her soil-covered fingers and told him to feel the particular ridges on the edge of a leaf. He wondered if she was flirting with him, but discounted the theory almost immediately. There was a vast age gap between them and, although he'd heard some younger women found older men attractive, he wasn't deluded enough to think that he was one of them.

In the end, it was the afternoon sun sweeping round and catching the edge of the Pavilion that made him realise he was in danger of not finishing his own job. He made his excuses and thanked her for taking the time to talk with him. She'd smiled at that. 'It is nice to meet you, Dave,' she said, smiling and once again covering her mouth; once again, for a brief moment she was someone else. 'I'll be here next week. Say hello.'

So he did, although he didn't linger too long, not wanting to give her the wrong impression. This time though, she sought him out afterwards, found him sitting on his favourite bench in the Marnock Garden at the end of his shift.

'I thought I would see what you do,' she said, and laughed like a child. And so he told her.

Over the weeks that followed, they fell into an unspoken arrangement. Sometimes he would visit her, sometimes she would visit him, but not a week went by without them chatting idly and easily for at least half an hour. They told each other their stories and they both listened. He told her things he'd never told Mike, or Deepak, or any of them. He told her things he was never able to tell Lizzie, even before things fell apart.

Equally candidly, she told him about the boys in her life. There were many, although he was never sure quite how serious these flings were. She guessed at how uncomfortable these stories made him so she began glossing over the details, referring to them in her stories as 'that guy I was dating for a bit' or 'a boy who took me on a date once'.

He realised soon enough that what he'd mistaken on that first day as flirtation was as natural to her as breathing. She was like that with everyone, and he was glad she wasn't interested in him romantically because that wasn't what he wanted from her. He suspected she felt the same way. There was no doubt she was beautiful; he saw the way other men looked at her, even older men like him. But she liked the fact he didn't look at her the same way. She almost said as much one day, as they sat on his bench and breathed in the sweet scents of the garden. 'It's so peaceful here,' she said. 'I feel ... at rest.' And there was something in the way she said it, and wrapped her hand around his forearm, that made him think that by *here* she meant *with you*. Every man she'd ever met, from her father onwards, had wanted something from her. Dave was no exception, but his want was basic and easily fulfilled – her company, half an hour or so, once a week. A reminder of the time when he sat in this garden with another young girl, who covered her lips when she giggled.

*

There's no sign of Daley in the little office by the main gate so Tyler wanders through the Gardens. It's turning into a much better day now the rain has stopped and even the sun is managing to burn its way through the cloud cover above. He fields a call from Rabbani who tells him she can't reach Daley. He tells her he's arrived so she can stop trying and sit tight for the time being.

There are quite a few people milling about and he wonders if this is usual for the time of day or whether the Gardens is attracting more attention than normal thanks to recent events.

Finally, after circumnavigating the paths and criss-crossing the lawns he finds Daley sitting on a bench next to a fish pond not far from the main entrance. He's sitting still, staring into the water, but his mind's clearly somewhere else.

'What's going on, Guy?'

Daley looks up, startled. 'Eh? Oh, all right, Tyler.'

'What's going on?' he asks again.

'Just taking a break. That's allowed, isn't it?'

'Where's your phone? We've been trying to reach you.'

Daley pulls out his mobile and checks the missed calls. 'Sorry, mate, I had it on silent.' He presses the screen a few times, presumably altering the settings. Tyler notices his hand shaking.

'Are you okay, mate?' The word feels odd on his lips but if Daley wants to play nice, Tyler isn't going to get in the way. 'You don't seem your normal self?'

'Yeah, 'course, what's the score?' he asks, turning to give Tyler his full attention.

Tyler outlines the situation regarding Dave Carver.

'Right,' says Daley. 'There's a log book where the volunteers sign in and out in one of the greenhouses. Let's check that first.'

They walk down the path in silence, through the trees, disturbing another squirrel who appears to be taking advantage of the break in the cold to gather a bit more food for the winter. The Marnock Garden where the body was found is still cordoned off with tape, although no longer guarded. The forensic team have done all they can but no one's in a rush to open the space up to the public. Tyler supposes the people who run the Gardens may even want to do something different with the area now. Will anyone even want to visit it as it is? To sit on the memorial benches and remember that a young woman's corpse was found buried there.

'That's him!' Daley shouts.

Tyler looks up to see a shabby-looking man sitting on one of the benches.

'Hey!' Daley shouts. 'Police! Stop right there.' And predictably, the man jumps up and runs.

'Dammit, Guy!'

Carver has a good head start, and disappears through the gap in the wall. Tyler follows. He makes it to the path in time to see Carver bolting across the grass towards the far side of the Gardens. Tyler goes after him, his bruised torso and aching kidney screaming at him with every jolt of his shoes on the grass. Before he's even halfway across the lawn, Carver has slipped into the bushes on the far side and is out of sight again. By the time Tyler fights his way through the rhododendrons, the man has disappeared.

Tyler jogs back and forth, following each path while he hugs his groaning ribs. There's no sign of Carver anywhere. It's possible he managed to scale the outer wall but it seems unlikely in the short space of time he had. If he did, there's no way Tyler's following him up there, not in his current condition. He has to choose a direction. He turns right. The path winds up through the trees and leads directly to an entranceway that leads into the stone enclave of the Bear Pit. A man in a white Tyvek protective suit is picking at the statue of the brown bear. The SOCO looks up.

'Did you see a man run this way? Long, shabby coat?'

The SOCO shakes his head and Tyler lets out a sigh of frustration. He turns and looks back down the path he came along. Not a soul in sight.

'DS Tyler?' the SOCO calls. 'You might want to look at this.'

Tyler turns back and steps under the archway into the circular pit, the cold stone walls towering above him. He hasn't been here since he was a child, when Richard would lumber, bear-like, out of the hole in the wall and Tyler and his brother, Jude would go screaming around and around in circles with their father chasing them.

'What is it?' he asks.

'Blood,' says the SOCO. 'Not much. The rain will have washed most of it away but the luminol still picked it out. Enough to indicate someone had a serious injury here at some point. I found a sample here, sheltered by the curve of the bear's leg where it meets the torso. Enough for a DNA test.'

Tyler looks up at the rim of the pit above. If it's Chi's blood, she didn't go over those railings by accident. Knifed first, then thrown into the pit? He moves back through the archway and turns up a narrow path at the side that rises steeply to the top. From above he looks back down at the forensic scientist below. The height is dizzying and he wonders what it would have been like to stand here and watch the bears below. Or to fall, your life's blood spilling from the wound in your stomach.

'You'd better check up here too,' he shouts down to the SOCO. Then he heads back down the path and onto the lawn. There's still no sign of Carver.

'So why did he run?' Rabbani asks.

'Who knows?' Tyler says into his mobile. 'But that's certainly one of the questions I will be asking him. I wanted to let you know, in case he's headed home. I need to have a word with Daley and then I'll re-join you.'

He's about to hang up when Rabbani speaks again. 'Sarge?'

'What?'

'I'm desperate for the loo.'

He suppresses his laughter. 'I won't be long. Promise.'

He picks his way back through the Gardens to the main entrance and finds Daley deep in conversation with the volunteer coordinator. Yes, David – Dave to his friends – is a very good volunteer. No trouble at all. A bit quiet but very reliable. He's been with them for years.

No trouble at all. Tyler can imagine Doggett's response if he'd been involved. *It's always the quiet ones, lad. Watch out for the quiet ones.*

'DS Daley, can I have a word?'

'Yeah, no worries.' He turns back to the coordinator. 'Sorry, love, official police business, you understand? I'll catch up with you in a bit, all right?'

The woman falls over herself to oblige and disappears into another office.

'Guy, what the hell's going on with you?'

'What?'

'You know what. Ah, I haven't got time for this. Have you finished the statements from the volunteers?'

'I might have done, if you hadn't interrupted me.'

'You've had days on this! What have you been doing out here all this time? You're not here for the fresh air!'

'Oh, fuck off, Tyler! What the *fuck* have you been doing that's so *fucking* important?'

It looks as though the truce is over. Tyler does his best to be reasonable. 'I'm just saying, Jordan's already read me and Mina the riot act this morning. If I were you, I'd come up with something useful, or move on. I don't know what's going on with you but you can't hide out in the park forever. *Mate.*'

Daley scowls at him but doesn't answer back.

That worries Tyler even more.

*

Tyler drums his fingers on the dashboard.

The passenger door opens and Rabbani climbs back in.

'Find somewhere?'

'Café on Broomhill High Street. I felt bad about not buying anything so I got you this.' She passes him a paper bag which he opens to find a lemon-curd-covered Cronut.

'Aw, Mina, you shouldn't have.'

'No, probably not.'

He chucks it onto the back seat.

Tyler watches a woman steering a pushchair up the hill ahead of her, while she drags a young kid behind. They watch her all the way to Carver's house, where she stops and begins struggling with the gate at the end of the path. Tyler glances once at Rabbani and then they're moving as one, out of the car, across the road, and up the garden path behind her.

'Excuse me, love.'

He lets Rabbani do the introductions. The woman gives a fairly typical response, frowning at first, then showing her relief that whatever they want has nothing to do with her. Then curiosity, as she hurries to tell them all about the fellow who lives upstairs. Dave, he's called, although she doesn't really know him. Keeps himself to himself for the most part but seems harmless. She stops short of asking what he's done and lets them into the building without any argument.

Rabbani helps her with the pushchair into the ground-floor flat, then asks if they can come back later and ask her a few more questions. She agrees excitedly. Then she stands in the doorway trying to ignore her kid screaming to get out of the pushchair, watching them head up the stairs.

The first floor has two cheap wooden doors with apartment numbers stuck onto them. Neither one is quite straight. Then a further set of stairs heads up to the attic. Tyler knocks loudly on the door numbered '4' but there's no response.

'Have a nosey upstairs, would you?' he asks Rabbani.

As soon as she disappears round the bend, Tyler pulls out his wallet and extracts a supermarket reward card he always forgets to use. He tries the door handle and, although the door's locked, it gives a little. It's an old-fashioned Yale lock. He slips the card into the gap between the door and the jamb and joggles it until he feels the catch give.

Rabbani gets back in time to see the door swing open. 'Sarge . . .'

He wonders how she manages to convey quite so much with just one word.

'Door's open. We should probably make sure everything's all right.' He moves into a short hallway. 'Mr Carver. This is the police. I'm DS Tyler. I'm here with my colleague DC Rabbani. We're coming in. Please make yourself known if you're in here.'

No response. The hallway has two doors leading from it. The first is the bathroom. The door's wedged open and their noses are assaulted by the stench of mildew and damp. It's clean and tidy though, apart from the black mould gathered in the corners of the ceiling. Tyler pushes on the second door at the end of the corridor. It's a very small space considering that it passes for three separate rooms. The kitchen area is essentially a small length of Formica work surface punctuated with a two-ring gas hob and a stainless-steel sink. A microwave takes up most of the rest of the space. He supposes it might be possible to find room enough for a chopping board but certainly nothing else. Underneath there's a single cupboard door and a fridge. There's enough space to open the fridge door without it meeting the bed, but only just.

The sofa-bed takes up most of the rest of the room, and it doesn't look as though it's ever used as a sofa. There's also a tiny fold-down table and a narrow wardrobe but that completes the furniture. Interestingly, there's no television. His own preferences aside, Tyler appreciates this isn't the norm. In fact, he's not sure he's ever met anyone else who didn't have an oversized screen at the centre of their living space.

'Sarge,' says Rabbani again, hovering in the doorway behind him, perhaps worried about committing any further infraction, or possibly unsure if there's enough room for her to get in.

'All right,' he tells her. 'We're just having a quick look.'

The room's so tidy Carver might not be living there at all. But a quick glance into the wardrobe confirms he hasn't done a bunk. Not yet, anyway. Tyler wonders how anyone can make do with so little. He thought his place was minimal but this guy makes him look like a hoarder. In the single kitchen drawer he finds one knife, one fork, one spoon, a couple of cooking utensils, and a passport. At least they know he's not planning to flee the country. But this can't be all Carver has. Can it?

There's a flash from the window and he turns to see Rabbani has her phone out.

'Orchid,' she says, pointing at a plant on the windowsill.

'Interesting.'

Tyler glances again around the room and then drops to his knees, his aching ribs complaining as he folds himself down. Under the bed there are a few clear boxes, filled with carefully folded clothing for the most part. And a shoebox, its lid knocked enticingly off kilter. There's a photograph poking out as though it has been pushed carelessly back into the box. Tyler extracts it.

'We shouldn't be here,' Rabbani says from above him. 'He could be back any minute.'

'Wait outside. I won't be long.'

The picture is of a young girl. Perhaps six or seven? Red-headed, green eyed, smiling at the camera. It looks like a holiday snap, taken in a Mediterranean country of blue skies, strong sun and historic architecture. Tyler doesn't recognise the landmark though. Somewhere in Greece, maybe?

He looks round the empty room once again. 'Where have you gone, Dave Carver?' He gets up, feeling his ribs groan again under the strain, and inches his way round the foot of the bed to the window. It is in fact only half a window; the other half has been cut off by the cheap partition wall that's been added to separate this main living space from the bathroom next door. The smell of mould is stronger here. The window looks down onto a charming and well-maintained garden that speaks volumes for the landlord's skewed priorities.

Tyler glances again at the photograph. Wherever he's gone, Carver didn't mean to go without this. He slips the photo into his pocket and retraces his steps out of the flat.

Mina hangs up the phone as Tyler finishes interviewing the woman next door. Between them they've managed to speak to the other residents in the house and the closest neighbours, those who are at home, anyway. Not one of them knows a single detail more about Dave Carver than the woman with the pushchair. *He keeps himself to himself. He seemed harmless.*

'Daley's turned something up,' she tells Tyler. 'It looks like Chi had a job, working at some bubble-tea place on Division Street. He's headed there now to talk to the owner.'

'How the hell are we only just hearing about this? I can't believe how he's been dragging his feet on this.'

'Maybe your little chat with him helped,' she suggests, failing to mention what Daley had actually said. *Tell the prick I finally came up with something useful.*

'I doubt that,' Tyler says. 'Anyway, I'm not leaving him to cock this up. We'll meet him there.'

'What about this place?' She can't keep a hint of petulance out of her voice and hurries to qualify her meaning. 'I mean, do you want me to stay? It doesn't look like Carver's gonna show but ...'

He thinks about this. 'All right, but just until Uniform get here. I should have grabbed that passport while I was in there. When they arrive, leave them to watch the house but tell them to try and keep a low profile. They're to ring either of us if Carver shows but I don't want them approaching him on their own.'

'You really think he's that dangerous?'

'This is Uniform we're talking about. I don't want them spooking the man and letting him escape. Ah, here they are now. That's lucky.'

Mina tries to hide her disappointment as Tyler goes to give the uniformed officers their instructions. She's had a thought about that orchid. Something she didn't want to get into with Tyler in case she's wrong. She'd been hoping for some time away from him to check it out.

She joins him at the car and says, 'Look, if it's all right with you, can you drop me at the station? There's something I want to look into.'

He studies her across the roof. 'That's cryptic.'

'Yeah,' she says, holding his gaze without blinking. 'It's annoying when people take themselves off without giving you any good reason, isn't it?'

He grins at her. 'Touché, Constable.'

As Tyler turns onto Division Street he sees Daley parking up on a meter.

'Ticket?' Tyler reminds him as they meet at the kerb.

Daley laughs. 'Yeah, good one.' Then he realises Tyler's serious. 'Nah, it's alright. I know this lass, works at the council. If I get a ticket I take her for a drink and she sorts it. Cheaper than the fine, anyway.' He winks at Tyler.

As they walk up the road, Daley fills him in. 'It's one of

these bubble-tea places what are all the rage with the Chinks.'

'Can you turn off the racism for five minutes?'

'What? Nah, it don't count if they're Chinese, does it?' He laughs. 'Only joking,' he adds, holding up his hands in mock surrender.

Tyler should take it further but this new-found camaraderie that seems to have sprung up between them makes life a lot easier and he's already jeopardised it once today. But that's how these things work, isn't it? *I'll let this one go. I don't want to rock the boat.* He's been the butt of the joke too often to not say anything. 'Keep it to yourself. No jokes. I don't want to hear it.'

Daley scowls but it's less aggressive than his usual disparaging look. 'Don't get your knickers in a twist, Duchess.'

Tyler tries to wrestle things back on track. 'I don't remember anything about a bubble-tea place in Cooper's original investigation.'

'That's because she missed it.' Daley tries his best not to look smug and fails miserably. 'I, on the other hand and contrary to popular belief, have been working. I finally got the girl's bank statements.'

'Any sign of any large deposits or withdrawals?'

'Nothing that would support the theory she was about to do a bunk. But I did notice a lot of entries from this tea place, "Cha Cha Cha", would you believe? A lot of payments, but there were a few receipts as well. Spaced a good few months apart. My guess is she mostly got paid cash in hand. Or else she was a regular customer but only worked for them once in a while.'

'That's quite a big thing for Cooper to miss,' Tyler says, half to himself. Unless it was part of the information Stevens removed from the file. Was Rabbani right? Did he have some reason for closing this case down quietly?

After Tyler finally managed to crawl his way back inside last night, he'd gone straight to the trestle table and the piles of paperwork Doggett had given him regarding Richard's death. It hadn't taken him long to confirm the nasty thought that had come to him, lying on the pavement outside his apartment. The unsolved cases Richard was looking into before he died – they *did* all have one other thing in common. They were all cases where Stevens had either been SIO, or the direct line manager of whoever was.

Tyler hadn't really noticed that before because, in and of itself, it didn't mean anything. Stevens must have worked hundreds of cases over the years and now he was pretty much everyone's line manager. So why in the light of what Rabbani said – of what Cooper implied – does Tyler feel differently?

It wasn't news that Stevens had a reputation for impatience when it came to solving cases. The running joke was that the Eel only liked two types of case, ones that he could solve easily or ones that got his name in the papers. Preferably both. Most people thought that was how he'd got to where he was today, by massaging percentages, focusing on cases that had a high probability of conviction, rather than allo- cating resources to something that might take months to get a result. It was something the IPCC might be interested in if someone had evidence but it would be very difficult to prove. This case was a good example. Stevens could justifiably argue that the disappearance of a 5-year-old boy took precedence over a missing Chinese student in her twenties. He was paid to make those decisions. It had to be more complicated than that.

A conspiracy. That was the word Richard had used. A conspiracy implied more than one person. He needed to speak to Cooper himself and see if there was more to this than he was seeing. There had to be. But for now, he figured it was best left alone. And that meant keeping Rabbani off the trail as well.

'Here it is,' says Daley.

Cha Cha Cha has a bright-green neon sign that flickers. The place is heaving with young Asian adults. Students mostly, many of them newly arrived in the country no doubt, given that it's still early in the university year.

Inside, the noise is incredible, the hubbub worthy of a pub near to closing. But none of these people are drinking. Nothing stronger than tea anyway. They head to the serving counter where Daley flashes his warrant card and asks to speak to the manager. There's a noticeable lull in the level of conversation at this point and Tyler's sure the news of their arrival is working its way around the room. If Tyler knew the Mandarin word for police, he's sure he'd be able to pick it out over and over again among the conversations and avoided gazes. He remembers working a case as a young PC, a hit-and-run that involved tracing a particular man through the Chinese community. He'd been given the run-around again and again until finally, by the time he'd identified the driver, he was on his way back to China never to be seen again. So he knows from experience how hard this is going to be. Not necessarily because any of these people have anything to hide, but simply because they're schooled in the art of avoiding authority. He can hardly blame them. Authority means something very different in China. He'd seen that first-hand during his travels. They're going to have to squeeze and squeeze to get the tiniest piece of information and, just like that case all those years ago, he has a feeling the answers might come too late.

A young woman emerges from a back room. 'Mr Daley?' she asks.

'Detective Sergeant,' Daley responds, clearly oblivious to the interest being surreptitiously paid him by the audience.

Tyler sees the woman's expression tighten and hurries to undo any damage. 'I'm DS Tyler. Thank you for seeing us. Perhaps you have a room out the back we could talk in?'

She hurries them through a doorway into the back office and gathers up the paperwork lying on the desk. She does her best to hide it from them, but they aren't here on behalf of the Inland Revenue or Immigration, or whatever department it is that she's scared of. And he doubts there's anything in those papers that will lead them to the murderer of Li Qiang.

'You're the one I spoke to on the phone?' Daley asks, making no attempt to pronounce the woman's name, assuming he even thought to ask for it.

The woman nods. 'Lee So Jung. Manager.'

'Li?' Tyler asks. 'Any relation to Li Qiang?'

'No. Different.' She spells it for him. 'No family.'

It's a common enough name, so it could just be a coincidence. The English spelling of foreign names can be arbitrary. On the other hand, just because they spell their names differently in Pinyin, doesn't mean it isn't the same character in Mandarin. He makes a mental note to get someone to check Lee's background.

'But she did work here?' Daley asks.

Lee starts to nod but then turns into a wobbly gesture that could mean anything. 'On and off,' she says. And then, perhaps realising she's admitting to too much, she giggles.

'All right, love, we're not here to look into your business dealings. We just wanna know about Chi. Who her friends were, who she hung out with. You get me?'

Tyler half-listens as he glances round the office. There's the usual laptop and box files that you might expect. Some spare uniforms, the same white overcoats that the waitress behind the counter was wearing but in varying sizes. His eyes move on, cataloguing the room for information. There's a corkboard on the right-hand wall that's partially covered in photographs, staff and customers, he supposes, the former all wearing the white overalls. There are one or two Caucasian faces but the majority are Asian.

He steps back out into the corridor where there are a couple of other doors. He opens one to find what is essentially a cleaning cupboard lined with shelves of bottled chemicals and cleansers. The door on the opposite wall opens into a unisex toilet that seems to have had limited attention from the bottles in the store cupboard. He returns to the office where Lee's still answering Daley's questions with one-word answers. She looks up at him as he comes in and Tyler wonders what this tiny woman is trying to hide.

Tiny. The word echoes around his head. He glances again at the uniforms hanging from the hooks. Varying sizes. But in fact, all of them bar one are fairly small. One is large, *much* larger than the others.

'Whose uniform is this?' he asks, interrupting Daley in mid-flow.

Both Lee and Daley turn to look at him as though he's lost the plot.

'For everyone,' says Lee, but he can see in her eyes she's avoiding the question.

'This one,' he says, tugging hard on the thick cotton. 'Who wears the big one?'

Lee's gaze flicks between Tyler and Daley. 'Owner,' she says, simply.

'You're not the owner?' Daley asks, his head flipping back round.

'No. I say. Manager.' Her voice has grown curt and her accent has grown conveniently thicker. She's withdrawing.

'We'll need to speak to the owner,' Daley says. 'Is he here?'

Lee says nothing.

Tyler looks back at the photos on the wall. He moves across and scans the faces. One photo is a group shot of

Asian faces in white overalls. But on the right-hand side of the picture stands a tall blond man he recognises. He looks much younger in the photo than he does now, but he didn't have a baby back then. The man's looking to his left, at something – or someone – off the edge of the photograph. There's a hand just visible on his right-hand shoulder, as though someone has their arm draped around him. The photograph has been cropped.

'Is this him?' Tyler asks, pointing to the tall blond man.

Lee flicks her head in a gesture that manages to convey the affirmative but has a healthy dose of the *go-fuck-yourself* about it as well.

'Where is he?'

'Supplier.'

The conversation's degenerating, collapsing in on itself. Lee's growing colder on them as they press the attack.

'What's his name?' Daley demands, not helping matters.

Lee begins muttering to herself and clutching her hands into fists.

'His name is Ben Robbins,' Tyler says. He tries to moderate his tone, loosen the tension in the room. 'Ms Lee, I've already met Mr Robbins and I know where he lives and who he lives with, so there's really no reason to hide the truth from us.' But it's too late. He's seen this before. As stalling tactics go it's a fairly effective weapon. She begins shouting at them in Mandarin and her face contorts in what can only be described as anguish.

The door to the shop opens and a number of people flood

through into the corridor and fill the doorway of the office. Before long everyone is talking at once in a language that effectively excludes them.

Daley looks horrified. He clutches at his belt and Tyler realises he's reaching for his baton. He seems to have forgotten he's not in uniform.

Tyler raises his arms, a universal gesture of surrender. When he speaks, it's loudly but calmly, keeping his voice measured and controlled. 'Okay, we're not here to upset anyone.' The crowd of people, both shop workers and customers as far as Tyler can tell, buzz around them like a swarm of angry hornets. Two of the girls in white uniforms cluster around Lee and placate her, forming a protective cordon worthy of loyal workers round their queen. Tyler suppresses the urge to pull out his warrant card again. 'Detective Sergeant Daley and I are leaving,' he says, emphasising the title, reminding them who they are.

But Daley seems frozen in place. Sweat has broken out on his forehead and his hand is still at his side, as though clutching the phantom baton. Tyler grabs his arm and half-pulls him out into the corridor through the crowd. As they step back into the shop, Tyler sees Rabbani arrive at the front door and silently thanks her for her timing.

'What's going on?' she asks, edging her way past the Formica tables to reach them.

'Get Daley out of here,' he tells her. 'And call for backup. No blues and twos. I just want a few extra bodies.'

Tyler sees them out the door and then turns back to face

the crowd. He's damned if he's going to let them chase him out entirely.

Mina ends the call and slips her mobile back in her pocket.

'What the hell happened in there?'

She can see Tyler through the glass dealing with what's beginning to look increasingly like an angry mob. He's talking calmly and with authority, displaying none of the effects of the adrenaline that must be streaming through his veins. It's certainly streaming through hers. She's not sure whether she should go back in and help or whether that would make the situation worse.

'Guy?' She turns to check on him. He's staring up the road in a world of his own. She reaches out and touches his arm. 'Guy?'

'What?' he says, returning from wherever he was. 'Mina?' He glances around as if getting his bearings.

She glances back inside and is pleased to see the crowd beginning to disperse, the hubbub dying down. 'What happened?' she asks again.

'They just went fucking mad. One minute we were asking questions and the next they're all chattering at us in gobbledygook.'

He's obviously shaken but it would make it so much easier to care if he wasn't such an arsehole. 'Are you okay?'

He scowls at her. 'Yeah, course. It was just a bit hot and . . .' He trails off and she lets it go. For now.

'Do you think we should go back in?' she asks him. 'I don't want to rile anyone up again.'

Tyler's sitting down now, talking to a young woman in a white overall. A larger, older woman who might as well have the word 'boss' tattooed across her forehead is standing over them talking animatedly. Tyler has his notebook out and is jotting things down in it. Both women are talking at once and Mina comes to the realisation the younger woman is translating the older woman's words.

'Looks like he's got it under control.' Daley spits a wad of phlegm onto the pavement and Mina shudders. *Why does he have to be such a dick?*

A car speeds up Division Street and screeches to a halt on the opposite side of the road. Tom and Jess from the Murder Team. A patrol car arrives shortly behind them.

Tyler sees them and gestures to the two women to hold on a moment. He steps out of the shop.

'You all right?' Mina asks.

'Fine.' He speaks to them as a group. 'Right, I want statements from everyone in the building. A couple have probably slipped out the back by now but there's not much we can do about that.'

'What are we asking them?' Tom asks.

'I'm not bothered, to be honest. I just need them to know they can't fuck us about. If we can shake anything loose relevant to the case, all the better. Start with their take on what just happened. Make it seem as though you're on their side. Imagine you're IPCC. Ask them what Daley and I did, how we behaved, all that stuff. Get them onside. Then I want information. Particularly, whether or not they knew

Li Qiang, and anything they can tell you about the owner, one Ben Robbins.'

'Robbins? Bloody hell,' says Mina.

'What do you want me to do?' Daley asks.

Tyler hesitates. It's a fraction of a second but Mina notices it.

'You'd better get back to the station, Guy. See what you can find out about this place. How long it's been open, employment records, all that. You put us on to it, so it makes sense for you to finish what you started.'

'Yeah,' says Daley brightening. 'Yeah, okay. I can do that.'

Daley takes off back to his car and the others file into the tea-shop.

'What happened in there?' she asks.

Tyler watches Daley disappear up the street. 'I'm not sure. Some sort of panic attack, maybe? We're gonna have to say something to Jordan.'

She can't help thinking that what he really means is, *you're* going to have to say something to Jordan.

'Right, come on. Let's get this over with.'

Mina follows him into the shop.

'You don't have any right to come in here and harass my customers.'

Ben Robbins is back from the cash-and-carry, or wherever it is he gets his supplies from.

He hadn't taken too kindly to finding his business disrupted, so in the spirit of fair play Tyler agreed the shop could stay open in exchange for a table at the back where his detectives could interview the staff and customers. Then he'd taken Robbins into the back office and begun his attack.

'Why didn't you tell me Chi worked here?' Tyler asks, turning the blame back on Robbins.

'It didn't come up.'

'You didn't mention it to DI Cooper either.' Of course, he can't be sure about that, given the state of her investigation, but it's a calculated risk. The way Robbins is avoiding his eye tells him the gamble's paid off. 'You had a much longer talk with her.'

'I don't know ... I didn't think it was relevant.'

'Not relevant?' Tyler's pacing back and forth in the tiny office space. He'd offered the chair to Robbins, another gamble; it would put him more at ease, being in the managerial space he was used to, but it also gave Tyler the height advantage. It's hard to maintain authority with someone standing over you. 'What if her disappearance had something to do with someone she met here? A customer, perhaps?'

'She hadn't worked here for a long time before she ... before she disappeared. I honestly didn't think about it.'

Tyler stares at the pictures on the wall and lets Robbins fill in the details.

'She used to help out sometimes, in the early days when I was setting up. I was an undergraduate in Business Studies. I could see there was a big influx of Chinese students coming to the city and I saw a gap in the market. That's how I met Juju in the first place.'

'And Chi? When did you meet her?'

'Chi came to the UK the year after Ju. By the time she arrived we'd been together for a few months.'

'And when did you start seeing Chi?' Tyler asks.

'What? I . . .'

Tyler plucks the photo frame from the wall and prises open the back.

'Hey! What do you think you're—'

Tyler pulls the photo free and drops the frame and its glass onto the desk with a clatter. The photograph has been folded rather than cut, which is what he'd suspected from the look of the edge, and been hoping for. He unfolds the glossy picture and sees the woman who has been exorcised from the picture. Chi. It's her hand on Robbins' shoulder, and the way they are looking into each other's eyes tells Tyler he's right. At the time this picture was taken, they were more than just good friends.

'Why are you hiding her then?'

Robbins' face colours. 'It's not what you think. It's difficult for Juju. When she comes in here, she doesn't want a reminder of . . .'

'Of what? Of her sister? Or the fact you were seeing her?'

Robbins is quiet a moment and then he admits, 'We dated for a while.'

'Talk me through it,' Tyler says, more gently now he's getting what he wants.

'When Chi first arrived, Juju and I were . . . well, it wasn't going great. I was tied up with the business all the time, she had her studies. We broke up. A couple of months after that, Chi and I hooked up. We weren't together very long. It was stupid really. It shouldn't have happened.'

'How long?'

'A few weeks, on and off. I'm pretty sure she was seeing other guys as well.'

'What did Juju think about you getting together with her sister?'

'She didn't mind, honestly. Like I said, she had her studies and was busy.'

'But she knew about the two of you?'

'Yes, of course,' Robbins says. He looks up. 'Hey, wait a minute, you can't think—'

'I think it's an odd situation, that's all. So then, after your not-that-long, on-and-off relationship with Chi, you got back together with Juju?'

'You make it sound sordid. It wasn't like that. Chi was a bit of fun. Juju and I were the ones meant to be together, obviously. We just lost our way for a bit.' He almost sounds as though he's trying to convince himself. 'Chi had tons of boyfriends. All that repression back home made her cut loose when she got here. She went off the rails a bit. Juju and I were worried about her. It's one of the reasons they argued that day.'

'I thought they argued over clothes?'

'Yeah, I mean, it was about clothes but it wasn't, you know? Juju wanted Chi to calm down a bit, get on with her studies. They come from a pretty strict family and if their dad found out what was going on he'd . . .' Robbins trails off.

'He'd what ... kill her?'

'That's not what I meant.' Robbins tries again. 'Look, when she missed uni we panicked, that's why we reported her missing. But then we began to convince ourselves she must have run off with some bloke. DI Cooper said her passport was gone and ... well, we figured this was her way of punishing us, disappearing without a word like that.' He looks down at the desk. 'For the first couple of months anyway. Then time went on and we still didn't hear anything, and then the baby came and ... I guess I'd begun to think the worst. I never said that to Ju, obviously.'

Tyler looks again at the photo, studying the coy smile on Chi's face. So far he's only seen the one photo of Chi when she was alive, and he notices something now that he hasn't seen before. 'They're very alike, aren't they?' he says. 'Juju and Chi.' There's a year between them but they could be twins, apart from the fact Chi looks vibrant and shining, and Juju when they'd met her had seemed tired and dull. Was it just the baby? Or had Juju also convinced herself her sister wasn't coming back?

Robbins looks down at the desk and says nothing.

Tyler asks if he can take the photo and Robbins nods his assent.

'All right, Ben, that'll do for now.' Tyler slips the photo into his pocket, next to the one he recovered from Carver's flat. 'I strongly suggest you have another think about what you might not be telling us, however irrelevant you think it might be.'

Tyler turns and walks out of the office.

*

After the bubble-tea place it's a relief to be back in the Red Deer, an old-fashioned pub serving proper alcohol. Doggett pays for their drinks while Tyler finds a quiet spot by the fireplace. The hearth isn't lit and the damp from outside feels as though it has followed them in and is settling down with them.

Doggett slaps a pint glass down on the table, causing a small tsunami of beer foam to erupt over the side and flood down the glass. 'Cheers,' he says, then takes a hefty swig from his own drink, smacks his lips and sits down on a stool across from Tyler. His leg immediately takes up its default rhythm under the table, jiggling the floorboards and causing more tidal disruption to the surface of their drinks.

Tyler takes a long sip of his pint and when he puts down the glass he's surprised to see a good third of it empty.

Doggett chuckles. 'I heard you had your hands full today.'

Tyler raises his eyes heavenward, and takes another long draught.

'Did you at least get something out of it?'

He's not sure if he has the answer to that yet. Some of the staff admitted to remembering Chi vaguely but none of them could, or would, tell them a thing about her they didn't already know. Of course, any one of them could be downplaying their connection. He'd tasked Daley with the background checks and that at least would eliminate anyone who wasn't in the country at the time. The biggest shock of the day had been the fact that Daley hadn't argued with him but jumped at the chance to do something deskbound.

But they did at least have one solid lead.

'The owner, Ben Robbins. Who also happens to be Chi's ex-lover and father of her sister's baby.'

Doggett whistles loudly and Tyler feels something wet touch his leg. He looks down to see the terrier wag its stubby tail and snuffle around his ankles. He'd forgotten the thing was there. Seeing it brings back uncomfortable memories of the night he rescued the bloody thing from a fire. He reaches up subconsciously and touches the thin scar tissue on the back of his neck. Doggett bends down and tickles the dog behind the ears. 'That's opened things up a bit then. And with your gardener fella on the run, it looks like you're finally making some progress.'

There was still no sign of Dave Carver but at least they'd convinced Jordan of the necessity for a proper warrant. The fact he'd run from Tyler hardly made him look innocent.

'What about you?' Tyler asks. 'Any developments?'

Now it's Doggett's turn to sigh. 'The bastard done it. I know he did. I can smell it on him. I can see it in his squinty eyes and all over his sweaty bald head.'

'But you can't prove it.'

Doggett taps his mobile against the edge of the table. 'Alibi. The wife's sticking to her story and there's sweet FA I can do to budge her. The worst thing is, I think she knows he did it. But somehow he's convinced her it was an accident.'

'It's hard to imagine a mother choosing a husband over her son.' But even as he says it, Tyler thinks of Callum and Shannon-Marie. Maybe it wasn't so unusual. And besides, his own mother had opted for a life without husband or sons when she chose to run away, so what did he know about it?

'She wouldn't be the first,' Doggett says. 'He's all she's got left. She's clinging to him like a flamin' life raft. A rotten, rat-infested life raft, but when you're all at sea . . .' Doggett drains the rest of his pint before going on. 'Meanwhile, the squir-relly bastard is turning it on for the cameras and demanding *we* do something about finding whoever's responsible for the death of his precious boy.'

'And the media put pressure on the Police and Crime Commissioner, and she puts pressure on the Eel and . . .'

'. . . so on, ad infinitum! Still,' says Doggett, visibly perk-ing up, 'I'll find a way to get the creepy fucker.' Doggett winks and checks his watch. 'Another?'

'You supposed to be somewhere?'

'She's taking me out tonight. Bloody poetry night or something.'

'What sort of poetry?'

'I don't bloody know. Poetry's poetry, isn't it? All that staring at clouds and flowers, and contemplating the meaning of your navel. She might as well be taking me to the opera!'

Tyler suppresses his smile. 'Maybe you'll enjoy it.'

'A bunch of hairy lesbians and blokes in turtlenecks sharing their angst? Bollocks to that! Still, I've got a bit of time left yet. Don't want to be too early, eh? One more for the road?'

'I'll get these,' Tyler says, holding up his empty glass. 'For the condemned man.'

'May the Lord ha' mercy on his soul.'

When he gets back from the bar, Doggett points to his lip and says, 'I don't suppose you're going to tell me what happened to your face?'

Tyler runs his tongue over the split. It's closed up a bit but the swelling's still obvious. 'Minor disagreement,' he says, and then, 'How much do you know about Superintendent Stevens?'

'The Eel?' Doggett squints at him over his pint. 'Don't tell me he did that?'

Tyler laughs. 'No. Those cases Richard was looking at, apart from the fact they were unsolved, they did have one thing in common. Stevens was SIO on them, or overseeing them in some way.'

'Along with hundreds of others I've worked on over the past twenty years.'

'Cooper told Rabbani that Stevens put pressure on her to stop investigating Chi's disappearance.'

'So what if he did? It's his job to make sure resources go where they're needed. Jason Talbot was missing at the time, remember?'

'You also told me someone shut *you* down when you tried to investigate Richard's death. Shall I have a guess who?'

Doggett's silence is testament that he's right.

Tyler leans forward and drops his voice. 'You told me Richard was looking into a conspiracy. What if it was a conspiracy on the force? Who's better placed to cover things up than the man at the top?'

Doggett takes a mouthful of ale. 'I'd be lying if I said the thought hadn't crossed my mind over the years. The man's a Grade-A pain in the arse, and he certainly isn't bothered about who he steps on as he climbs his way up the greasy pole. But he's also a rule-follower. The sort of bloke who'd find a penny in the street and hand it in to his local cop-shop.' The dog starts whining under the table and Doggett reaches down and tickles its head. 'But let's say you're right and Stevens deliberately turned away from investigating those cases before he'd exhausted every angle. We'll put a pin in the "why", for the moment – maybe he's focusing on the cases that bring him the most glory? I don't know. But anyway, if that was the case, your dad would have gone straight to the IPCC. They would have investigated and, absolute worst-case scenario, Stevens would have been forced into early retirement on a nice fat pension. That's hardly reason to kill someone.'

'Maybe there's more to it than that. Something we haven't seen yet.'

'But where's your evidence? You can make up daft theories about anyone you like, but we're gonna need more than that.'

Tyler sits back in his chair and folds his arms.

'What about your brother? Any news?'

Tyler admits that there isn't. The dog whines again.

'I'd best take his nibs outside before he piddles all over the carpet.' As he gets up, Doggett places a hand on Tyler's shoulder. 'Let it go, son. I'm sorry I told you any of this. You can't let it ruin your life. Or your career. Just let it go.'

Tyler sups at his pint and lets the noise of the pub wash

over him. The new barman arrives at the table and smiles at him. 'I thought he might want some water,' he says, holding out a round metallic dog bowl. Doggett gets back and the barman fusses with the dog for a minute but his eyes keep returning to Tyler.

When he leaves, Doggett says, 'You know what you need.'

'Don't.'

'A bloody good shag.'

'Thank you for that.'

'A man has needs. If one of the barmaids in here batted her eyelids at me like that I'd be all over her.'

'Haven't you got a poetry reading to get to?'

Doggett grimaces. 'Ah, that's the problem. A man'll put up with most things if he's got a bird giving him what he needs.'

'Please stop, I think my ears are bleeding.'

'And our Ronnie is bloody good at giving me what I need.'

Dave's one of the first to arrive at the Spoken Word night. It's being held in the back room of a run-down pub near the Victoria Quays. He hasn't been in here for years but the old place hasn't changed a great deal. It's comforting to see it still standing, in need of work perhaps, but stubbornly resisting the bulldozers that have taken down everything around it.

He orders a pint and scrapes together enough coins to pay for it. He'll have to nurse it for a good while since he hasn't got enough for another one.

He shouldn't be here really. That was a near miss in the Gardens, but at least now he knows the police are properly on to him. If he'd been any slower that detective would have had him. Thankfully, his knowledge of the Gardens had paid off and he'd managed to shelter behind the big oak until the bloke had passed and then double-back to the Eccy Road entrance. After that, when he realised he couldn't go home, he'd spent a good part of the day just driving around. Then he figured out they were probably looking for his car as well so he'd ditched it and found a place to hole up until he could decide what to do.

No, he shouldn't be here at all. But he wants to know if there's a chance. If Ronnie's really interested in him, maybe he can still put all of this right. He doesn't know how but there must be a way back somehow. What has he done that's really so awful?

He sips at his pint and loiters near the bar. He's never been a big drinker but it occurs to him he fits in here. He's about the same age as the other punters and he reckons he probably has a similar story. These people have been left behind too. In one way or another.

Ronnie arrives in a bubble of noise and light, surrounded by assorted hangers-on. There are a couple of women of a similar age and background to Ronnie herself, who twitter around her like she's the mother hen. And a short, wiry scruffy-looking man, about the same age as Dave. He doesn't seem to be anywhere near as thrilled to be here as the others.

Dave's not sure if Ronnie's the organiser of the event, only that she invited him, but she's the one who approaches the bar and demands to know where they'll be setting up everything, and enquires as to whether or not they have access to a microphone. This last request receives a less than enthusiastic response from the young publican who, Dave imagines, is more concerned as to whether or not any of them are going to order any drinks. His concerns are mollified by the scruffy man, who orders a pint of bitter and a whisky chaser with all the urgency of a man who's had a long day and fully expects the evening to be longer.

When she notices Dave standing unobtrusively at the end of the bar, Ronnie lets out a stifled cry of delight that stirs him in unexpected ways. She seems genuinely pleased to see him.

'David! How lovely! Now the gang's all here.'

His pleasure at being included is tempered when he's forced to shake hands and suffer a number of air kisses brushing his cheek.

'Will you be reading this evening?' Ronnie asks him.

'Er . . . no, not tonight.'

'Oh, and there's Sarah-Jane!' she says, with much the same air of excitement she had when greeting Dave, this time directed at a young woman with green hair and very pale skin. Ronnie launches herself towards her, leaving Dave unsure if he's supposed to follow.

The scruffy fellow orders a Dubonnet and lemonade, and then grunts something at Dave. It takes him a moment to realise the man's providing him with a name. Too embarrassed to admit he's missed it, Dave offers his own in return.

'You a poet as well then?' asks the man.

Dave apologetically admits that he is and gets the sense the man's disappointed. Then Ronnie returns and pushes everyone into a room at the back of the pub where the main event is to take place. As they move down the corridor the scruffy man passes the Dubonnet to Ronnie and she leans in and kisses him on the cheek. It's a far more intimate gesture than the kiss she gave Dave.

The first half passes painlessly enough. Dave manages to sit to the left of Ronnie, with the scruffy man taking the seat to her right. Several people read, including the woman with green hair who mumbles into her laptop incomprehensibly, her voice rising and falling with the rhythm of the sentence yet still somehow managing to sound monotonous. Dave claps along with everyone else.

Then there's an interval and the scruffy man's out the door and headed for the bar like a whippet from a trap, which finally gives Dave the chance he's been waiting for.

'Hi,' he manages.

Ronnie smiles at him and raises her eyebrows. 'Having fun?'

'It's . . . wonderful.' It sounds ridiculously lame to his ears but she doesn't seem to notice.

'I thought Sarah-Jane was rather marvellous, didn't you?'

He can't remember which one Sarah-Jane was but he agrees with her. 'So,' he says, trying hard to think of something – anything – that might get her talking again. 'Are you going to be reading?'

'Oh, Sarah-Jane! You were marvellous, darling!' And his

opportunity's lost as Ronnie's off across the room leaving him sitting alone once again.

'Do I know you?' asks the scruffy man when he gets back. He has a tray this time, with two pints, two whisky chasers and another glass of Dubonnet and lemonade. He rests the tray on the seat and picks up one of the shots of whisky.

'We met earlier,' says Dave.

'No, I mean, before then. You look familiar for some reason.'

Dave smiles weakly.

Ronnie returns to claim her drink and there's something about the way she takes it, without so much as a word of thanks, that makes Dave realise there's more between the two of them than just friendship. And all at once he realises he's been an idiot. She's not interested in him. Not in the way he thought. Mike had it right all along. She's just a gregarious woman who collects people like others collect trinkets.

'I see you two are getting along famously,' she says, contrary to the evidence offered by the stony silence that's fallen between them.

The scruffy man raises his pint. 'I was just telling your man here, I thought I recognised him from somewhere.'

'Crikey,' says Ronnie. 'Not in a work context, one hopes.' She chuckles and, when Dave fails to respond, she adds, 'Jim's a detective, you know? With the police.'

He does his best to take this information casually but Dave feels sure his face must change because scruffy 'Jim' is peering at him curiously from behind his pint, his eyes weighing Dave up as though he's a plump fish he's about to land.

'That must be ... interesting,' he manages.

'You'd be surprised.'

'Oh, Jim has to deal with all manner of gruesome things, I'm sure. Of course, he won't talk about any of it, will you, darling? It makes him quite the most irritating man I've ever met.'

Jim smiles without letting any feeling touch his face. 'At least I'm not a poet.'

Ronnie laughs. 'I've no doubt he's working on that grisly business in the Gardens. Have you heard any more about that, David? So awful. That poor girl. A student, they said.'

Dave can feel the mist descending on him, his face breaking out in a sweat. God, not now! It feels as though he hasn't spoken for hours and the ferrety policeman, Jim, is looking at him steadily from under his bushy eyebrows.

'Still, it's the parents you've got to feel for. I suppose they'll at least know what happened to her now. But my God, murdered? Butchered with a knife. It doesn't bear thinking about.'

'What?' Dave can't help himself. 'What did you say? I thought ...' He thinks back to that night in the Bear Pit. There *was* a lot of blood for just a bump on the head but ... No! He would have noticed a knife wound, wouldn't he? It's all so vague.

'Oh, Lord,' says Ronnie. 'Listen to me prattling on. I'm so sorry, David. I've done it again. Me and my big mouth.'

Dave gets up. 'I ...' He has to get out of here. 'I need some air.'

'Oh, David, don't go. I'm truly sorry. We'll change the subject. Dave works there, you see,' she says, turning to Jim.

'Works where?'

He has to resist the urge to run. He can feel the sweat gathering in the folds of his shirt. But if he bolts he'll only raise the suspicions of the detective even further. The mist moves ever closer and it's all he can do to hold it in check. He makes for the end of the row of chairs, sees the detective getting up as well. Ronnie's trying to explain, 'It's the shock, I shouldn't wonder. Let him get some air and then perhaps ...' The rest fades away as Dave makes it out of the function room, along the corridor, and back into the main lounge of the pub. He staggers through the crowd, feeling the policeman's eyes on him all the way.

Outside, he breathes deeply and hurries around the corner out of sight, just in case the detective should decide to follow. He stumbles past the dog rescue place, upsetting the dogs behind the wall and sending them into a cacophony of ferocious barking. He sees a small figure step from the door of the pub, blowing smoke into the night air. It's him. The ferrety detective. The man glances up and down the road as though looking for something. Or someone.

Dave turns and hurries across the ring-road towards Kelham Island, the sound of the dogs baying at his heels all the way.

*

Tyler lingers in the pub after Doggett's gone. Every now and then the cute barman looks across and smiles. He hates to admit it, but Doggett wasn't so far off the mark. Maybe it would be good to distract himself. For a while, at least. He still hasn't rung Paul, but maybe it's not too late. He chickens out though and texts instead, asking if he wants to come over. He'll stop at the supermarket on the way home, make a nice pasta. As long as he can keep Paul from the 'we-need-to-talk' conversation it might turn into a nice relaxing Friday night – just what he needs.

The text back is curt – *Half an hour. Don't be late* – but offers a small ray of hope in the form of a smiley emoji at the end.

Tyler drains his glass and heads for the door, smiling his thanks to the barman in a manner he hopes isn't too encouraging.

Outside, there's a car parked against the opposite kerb.

'You're a hard man to find,' says Joey McKenna, leaning against the driver-side door. There's another figure inside the car but it takes Tyler a moment or two to realise it's Callum. He makes no attempt to get out of the car. His face is hidden in shadow but there's enough glow from the street lighting to pick out the bruises and cuts that pepper his face.

'What happened?'

McKenna's mouth turns up in a sardonic smile. 'Says he fell over.'

'Right.'

'He knows if he tells me who's responsible I'll break the fella's legs.'

'I've warned you about saying things like that in front of me.'

'Oh, come on, Adam. We're old friends now, eh? No need for all that nonsense. Anyway, he's keeping mum.'

'How *did* you find me exactly?'

McKenna smiles. 'I like to keep my finger on the pulse of the city. When someone comes sniffing around my family asking questions, I take an interest. And it's not too hard to find out the favourite drinking hole of a notorious copper like yourself, DS Tyler.'

As before, McKenna's words somehow manage to hover right on the line between camaraderie and death-threat.

'What do you want from me, Joey?'

McKenna's face changes and he looks properly serious for once. 'The lad told me what you did for him.'

'It was only a couple of cakes. He was hungry.'

'Not that. Although, that alone was a kindness not many would bother with. I meant the phone snatch. You let him off.'

'There was no real harm done. That doesn't mean I'll let it slide again though.'

'Still. It says something about you, son. It caught my attention. And now you've done that, I need a favour.'

Tyler steps back from the car and raises his hands. 'I'm not having this conversation. If you want to talk to me, you can come into the station and see me.'

McKenna laughs, a big bellyful of a laugh that makes the hair stand up on the back of Tyler's neck. 'We both know that's not going to happen. Anyway, this is more a personal favour.'

Tyler turns and starts to walk away.

'Hear me out. *Please!*' McKenna almost shouts the last word and there's a hint of desperation to it. 'My boy, Cal, here. He needs a place to stay. I can't protect him on the streets. Too many people know of his connection to me.' The admission must stick in his throat. 'Nowadays, it's all drugs and Russians and Eastern Europeans, and what some of them do ... well, it doesnae bear thinking about. It's not the game it used to be, I'll tell you and, if I'm honest, my name doesnae carry quite the weight it used to either.' A man like Joey McKenna doesn't admit things like that to anyone, let alone a police officer. He must be desperate.

'You should speak to his mum, then.'

McKenna cocks an eyebrow. 'You've seen that place. I'm ashamed to admit it but it's no place for the lad. I'm working on getting rid of the boyfriend but even if I could get him to go back he wouldn't stop for five minutes.'

'Again, I should warn you about making threats to—'

'Oh, calm down, Adam. I'm nae gonna kill the bastard. I'll pay him some money so he fucks off. Just like the last one. With a wee suggestion that it might not be a good idea if I ever see him again. The old carrot and stick routine. But, that aside, he doesnae want to go back there and to be honest, I can't blame the lad.'

'So *you* take him in. I'm sure you've got room in that mansion of yours.'

McKenna flicks his car keys over his fingers. 'Aye, now that's where it gets a bit awkward. You've not met my Tina, have you? Lovely young girl, she is, but she's not big on family at the end of the day. She'll come round eventually or I'll send her packing too, but it's early days at the moment and I don't need the lad cramping my style.'

So the man's concerned about his grandson but not so concerned he'll disrupt his love-life?

McKenna must pick up the thought in Tyler's eye because he straightens and his voice turns defensive. 'I'm levelling with you here, son, because I think I can trust you — I don't want him there. I don't want him mixed up in ... anything. Do you understand? He idolises his old granddad and that's all well and good and as it should be, but I don't want him trying to impress me by following in the family business.'

It's a stunning admission. McKenna's virtually admitting that not all of his affairs are squeaky clean. There's still some kind of operation being run from Joey McKenna's home.

Again McKenna seems to read his thoughts. 'Don't bother passing this on to anyone. If they raid my old place they won't find anything, you can be sure of that. But it would be a costly mistake. For a start, it'll cost me the substantial fees my lawyers demand. But it will also cost your superiors a whole heap of bad press, and it will cost you my undying ingratitude. That's the highest cost of all.'

'What do you want from me, McKenna? I can put in a word with sheltered housing if you want?'

McKenna laughs again. 'No, lad. That won't do. I want *you* to take the boy in.'

'What?' He laughs, and then realises McKenna's serious. 'You've got to be fucking kidding me!'

McKenna raises the eyebrow again and Tyler wonders how far the man's having to hold his infamous temper in check. It doesn't pay to rile a man like Joey McKenna. He needs to remember that.

'You've got a spare room, haven't you?'

'How do you know that?'

'I know where you live. They're two-beds.'

Tyler laughs again, but it's a cold, mirthless sound that comes out of his mouth this time.

McKenna goes on. 'What better example to set for the boy, eh? A police officer. I can't think of a better role model. He'll be fine on the couch if you've no spare bed.'

'Jesus, is there anything you don't know about me?'

'I know a lot of things about a lot of people,' McKenna says, and then he steps forward faster than Tyler would have expected the man could move and places a large palm on Tyler's shoulder. He leans in close and whispers, 'I could tell you a thing or two about your old man for a start.'

'What?' Tyler pushes him away.

'You heard me. You scratch my back and I'll scratch yours. You want to know what your father was up to before he – what are we calling it? – died? I can get you that information. All I'm asking for is a goodwill gesture that might encourage me to ask questions in the right places.'

Tyler feels the burns on the back of his neck crackle in the cold air. There's a ringing in his ears that's making it hard to concentrate on anything McKenna's saying. His hands are shaking and he has to clench his fists several times to get the feeling back into them. Callum gets out of the passenger side of the car. In the stark streetlight, the bruises on his face look even worse. McKenna's saying something, explaining to Callum what's going to happen.

'I haven't agreed to anything!' Tyler's voice sounds petulant to his own ears.

'You're going to though, DS Tyler.'

'What's to stop me taking you in? If you've got information pertinent to the investigation of a crime you're obligated to reveal it.'

'Come on, Adam, old son. This isnae my first rodeo, nor is it yours. You know where that takes us – all the way back to lawyers and superior officers and difficult conversations, and then no one gets what they want, least of all our Cal, here.'

Tyler looks at Callum Morgan. He has his eyes fixed on the ground and his hands pushed deep into the pockets of his tattered hoody.

'Don't blame the son for the sins of the father,' McKenna tells him. 'Or the grandson, in this case.'

The sins of the father. He remembers Gary Bridger's words that day in the canteen, the day he'd earned this scar on his cheek. 'They say it runs in the family,' Bridger said. 'Like father, like son.' They'd told him his father was a bent copper, that he'd been on the take and couldn't live with himself. Tyler had never believed that. Was McKenna now saying it was true?

'Come on, Adam,' McKenna says. 'Cal will stay out of your way and not cramp your style too much. And obviously, I expect you to keep your hands—'

Tyler raises his hand. He's damned if he's going to take that from the man after everything else. 'As far as I'm concerned, your grandson's a kid. At best, a vulnerable adult. I ask you to do me the courtesy of not finishing that sentence.'

McKenna holds up his own hands. 'I apologise. I can see you're a man of honour and I appreciate that. It's something sadly lacking in today's world.'

A man of honour. He's not so sure of that. Not that he has any interest in Callum other than to help the lad out, obviously, but there are different forms of honour. He can't believe he's considering this. If Jordan finds out she'll crucify him. Taking in the grandson of a known gangster. Bloody hell, she won't need to. If this gets out, every officer on the force will be queueing up for a turn.

'This information you have about my father. Tell me what you know and I'll think about your request.'

McKenna tuts. 'It doesnae work like that, pal. Besides, like I said, I need to make a few enquiries first. But trust me, this is worth your while.'

Trust him.

They stand in silence for a few moments before McKenna continues. 'I'll tell you what, you agree to put a roof over

Cal's head for a short spell and I'll give you something else, as a bonus, right now.'

'What?'

'Your pal Jim Doggett's been fishing around our neck of the woods lately looking for that lad's murderer. Word on the street is, the father's in the frame. You should tell him there's a houseboat down on the canal. *Shy Meadows*, it's called. He'll no doubt find what he wants there.'

'How do you know about that? If you had something to do with that—'

This time it's McKenna's turn to raise his hand. 'I would ask *you* the courtesy of not finishing *that* sentence, boy. I've done a fair few shady things in my past but no one, *no one* gets away with calling me a kiddie-killer.'

Tyler inclines his head in acknowledgement. 'How do you know about this boat?'

'Talbot's father did some work for me back in the day. I remember them spending a lot of time down there. I'd say if the man had something to hide somewhere, that's probably where you'd be likely to find it.'

Tyler exhales a long breath. He can feel the adrenaline pulsing round his body. 'A roof,' he says. 'Just until he can find a more permanent solution. But that's a few days at most. The fewer the better as far as I'm concerned, and I'd appreciate it if we could keep this arrangement between the three of us.'

'Deal,' says McKenna.

'I also expect to hear whatever you know about my father

by the time he's gone. If not, maybe we'll start paying a bit more interest in who's coming and going from your place.'

McKenna smiles widely. 'Of course, Detective Sergeant. And there's no need for threats. You can trust me.'

five

the fifth nighthawker

Record of Finds

Date: Fri 10th Nov
Time: 14:30
Location: Beach, Cleethorpes
Finds: lump of old iron, indeterminate — possibly from a ship; large bronze nail, industrial; thrupenny bit, 1954!

Ronnie's in a foul mood as she steps off the tram at the University stop and begins the final slog up the hill to home. She's still fuming about the poetry evening. She's not sure she's ever had two men run out on her before, not in the same night anyway. First Dave disappears for no apparent reason — well, maybe that *was* her fault — and then Jim goes as well, without so much as a goodbye. The bloody cheek! Added to that, her feet are killing her. She regrets deciding to walk the last section, but there's something too decadent about travelling by taxi.

At least she's done her ten thousand steps for today, though. Cleethorpes had been nice but she isn't sure she'll be rushing back. She found virtually nothing of interest on the beach. She should have listened to Colin when he told her beachcombing was a waste of time. But then it hadn't been entirely wasted, had it? She'd enjoyed her day. She'd found the thrupenny bit — that had been exciting! When she looked it up on eBay on the train home, she found one that had sold for £9.20! That's by far the most valuable item she's ever found, although she's not quite that desperate for an extra tenner. It will make a nice memento anyway.

And at least the beach was better than sludging around in some grubby field like the rest of them. The Nighthawkers they call themselves. She laughs. Bunch of bloody kids playing secret societies. She's heard them whispering to each other at the meetings, arranging clandestine operations. It's all a bit daft but that's men for you. Not that she hasn't had a go herself, mind, just for the thrill of it. But she's getting on a bit for night-time shenanigans, especially illegal ones. No, she'll stick to the beach. At least you can finish the day with fish and chips.

She looks up at the windows of the Children's Hospital. She can never pass this place without thinking about the poor mites inside. At least that's something she was spared by not having kids.

She thinks she might be going off the whole metal-detecting thing anyway. She only really joined the group in the first place because she figured it might be a good place to meet men. She'd taken to Dave straight away, with that damaged-bird vibe he gives off that she finds so irresistible in men. But it had been so hard to get his attention.

And then Jim Doggett had come along. Not at all her usual type but, she had to admit, the sex was incredible. She'd thought those days were behind her but he'd awakened something in her that she didn't realise was slumbering. Such a shame that she has to end things but . . . well, you can't base a future on one thing alone, least of all that. And it's all getting a bit too much really, he has such an insatiable appetite. The next one — as well as having a lot to measure up to in the bedroom department — will be the kind of man who sees a lady home at the end of an evening.

As she turns up Northumberland Road, she becomes aware of someone behind her. It's not that unusual; lots of people use this as a cut-through to Crookes but she likes to stay aware of her surroundings. It's dark on this street and the trees crowding in from either side add to the oppressive feel. She hears him getting closer, at least, she assumes it's a 'him'? But she refuses to turn around. She's not some flighty young thing in danger, and she won't let that rubbish the media pour in your ear about how the country's going to rack and ruin affect her. She won't live her life in fear of getting old like some of her friends do. She won't be that person.

But she can't help quickening her pace. Still, he draws closer. She speeds up a bit more but the hill's taking its toll now and she's not leaving him behind. She glances back without meaning to, sees him just a few paces behind, face covered by a hoody and the shadow of the trees. Even as she's turning again she realises there's no one else around. She's on her own with him. She's speed-walking now — heel, toe, heel, toe — her breath catching in her throat and her chest heaving.

And then she hears him start to run.

No!

She runs too, adrenaline shooting through her body and washing away the fatigue. She can't outdistance him, though, and all at once he's on top of her. She cries out but his left hand closes round her throat, cutting off her air. He says something about coins but, with the terror, and the blood pumping in her ears, she can't really make it out.

She just has time to curse Jim Doggett for abandoning her before she sees the glint of the knife.

For someone with as few belongings as Callum, he manages to make an inordinate amount of mess. There are two hoodies, a jacket and a spare pair of jeans lying chucked across the back of the sofa; two empty pizza boxes piled on the kitchen counter; and half a dozen beer cans dotted across the floor.

He lies snoring on the sofa, one leg angled awkwardly over the arm and pointing skyward, like a severed limb Tyler once saw poking up out of a recycling container.

He does his best to tidy without waking the lad, although the crunch of a couple of tin cans could never compete with the guttural, animal snoring that permeates the room. If he can sleep through that he can sleep through anything. After a few minutes of tiptoeing around his own kitchen and wondering if he should leave Callum some money for food, Tyler catches a glimpse of himself in the oven door. What the hell is he doing? There's another grating crescendo of grunts that reverberates up his spine and Tyler snaps, slamming the cutlery door closed. Twice.

The snoring stops but Callum takes another ten minutes or so to surface properly. He sits up, stretches and yawns expansively. 'All right, mate?' he says. 'What time is it?'

'Time you got out there and started looking for a place to live.'

'I'll have a coffee if you're making one, cheers. Hey, I was thinking, I can get you a cheap telly if you want one? There's this bloke I know . . .'

Tyler ignores him. He makes coffee and toast while Callum heads into the bathroom to begin the day with five minutes of hacking up phlegm.

'What did you get up to over the weekend?' Tyler asks. He hasn't seen much of the lad since he moved in.

Callum drops back onto the sofa, shovelling toast into his mouth as though it might be the last meal he has for a while. 'I had to get the rest of me stuff, didn't I? Mate of mine was looking after it for us.' The *rest* of his stuff equates to a large rucksack, of the type serious campers might take with them, or a gap-yearer on a round-the-world-trip, and a smaller holdall bag more suited for the gym.

'You came in pretty late last night.'

He has to remind himself he isn't the lad's surrogate father. On the other hand, he can't *afford* to have anything happen to him.

Now it's Callum's turn to do the ignoring. Tyler lets it go. It might be better if he doesn't know too much about what Callum gets up to.

'Sorry about your bloke,' Callum says.

'Don't worry about it.'

He'd rung Paul on Friday night to cancel their date; McKenna hadn't left him much choice but he had a feeling Paul wouldn't see it that way, so he explained nothing, just told him something had come up. It hadn't helped that at that exact moment Callum had chosen to shout, 'Fucking hell, mate, you don't even have a telly!'

On Saturday morning Paul arrived with the few belongings Tyler had left at his place – a toothbrush, a paperback book, a pair of jersey shorts – in a Sainsbury's carrier bag, just as Callum stepped out of the bathroom with a towel wrapped round his middle. Never had the end of a relationship looked so bleak.

Tyler tried to explain, the two of them huddled in the bedroom while Callum had the run of the apartment. It wasn't enough.

'You don't get it, do you?' Paul asked.

Tyler thought he got it full well and tried to explain again that Callum was the grandson of a friend who needed a place to stay.

While Paul gathered together his own stuff – *four* carrier bags – he finally spoke the words that, Tyler suspected, had been playing on his mind for some time.

'It isn't the kid,' Paul said. 'Jesus, Tyler, if it was as easy as that, I'd let you *have* your fun. But the trouble isn't that you want to see other people, it's that you don't want to see me.' He stopped, his shoulders falling as though he'd been defeated in an argument Tyler hadn't taken part in. Paul reached across and put his hand on the back of Tyler's head. 'There isn't room for me here,' he said. Tyler didn't think he meant the apartment. Then they kissed. It was brief, passionate and final. There was no way back from a kiss like that.

Paul was on his way out the door when he turned and said, 'Because I still care about you, you need to know something. It isn't normal to have a detailed copy of your father's autopsy report stuck to the wall. Whatever's going on with you, Tyler, get some help.' And then he'd left.

Tyler looks across at Callum now, curled up again under a blanket, his breath rumbling and sonorous, on his way back to the land of dreams. He clears his throat loudly. 'I'm heading to work,' he says. He gives Callum fifty quid in cash. 'Get yourself a clean shirt. For interviews. I've made you an appointment at the job centre, eleven o'clock.'

'You're not me dad, you know.'

Tyler opens his mouth and then closes it again. He'd been about to say, 'As long as you're living under this roof ...' but the words took him back to another time, Richard and Jude shouting at each other while he listened from the top of the stairs.

Callum pushes his tongue into the side of his mouth and picks up the money. 'Look,' he says, 'I know you didn't want me here and ... well, I wanted to say thanks, yeah?'

Tyler inclines his head in acknowledgement. 'Let's have a chat tonight. I'll bring back some beers and help you put together a creative CV.' He points to his laptop, and in doing so realises it isn't facing the same way it was when he left it. He'd been doing some research last night, sitting at the breakfast bar in the kitchen. Now it's facing into the living room. Callum has wandered away and is looking out of the window. Tyler flips open the screen and sees the

Windows password screen. Did he close it down properly? He doesn't always. Maybe Callum wanted to look something up. It's password-protected anyway, so it doesn't necessarily mean anything.

But as he returns the laptop to its case, he wonders what else the lad might get up to while he's got the flat to himself. After Paul's final stinging rebuke, Tyler had spent most of Sunday packing up the research in the spare room into boxes and pushing them under the trestle table. It was all still there though, for curious eyes. Confidential information about police cases, about his own father's death.

Before he leaves the apartment, Tyler digs out the keys he never uses from a drawer in the kitchen, and locks both bedroom doors.

Tyler's on his way in when he gets the radio call directing him to a property in Pitsmoor. It's a two-bedroom flat above a beauty salon. When he arrives, there's a uniformed officer standing at the bottom of a flight of fire-escape stairs. He looks queasy.

'PC Khatri?' he asks, pulling on a pair of disposable gloves.

'Arjun, sir.'

'Arjun. I'm Tyler. You okay?'

'Yes, sir. It were a bit of a shock, to be honest.'

Tyler pulls on some disposable shoes and chucks another pair to Arjun. While he waits for the guy to get dressed he has a quick look around the general area and notes the CCTV camera above the beauty salon window. It's pointing the wrong way but, if they're lucky, it might have caught something.

'No joy, sir,' Arjun informs him, following his gaze. 'I stuck my head in the shop just now. They reckon it hasn't worked for years.'

'Right,' says Tyler. 'We're never that lucky, are we? Up here?'

'Yes, sir.'

He starts up the stairs with Arjun in tow. 'Take me through it.'

'Call came in from the school where he works. He didn't come in to work on Thursday last week. That's pretty unusual apparently. The Head came out to visit on Friday but no joy. They thought he might be sick but when he didn't show up again this morning they rang it in. I came up to check and broke in.'

At the top of the stairs the front door to the flat has been pulled closed but left ajar. Tyler pushes it open with the tips of his gloved fingers and sees the splintered wood where the door's been forced. He steps into the kitchen and the first thing he sees is the metal detector lying on the wooden kitchen table. There's mud encrusted around the rim of the sensor at the bottom end. Dried mud. Other than that, the rest of the room's clean and tidy. No dirty pots in the sink, no food on the stove. The room's cold, and a brief touch of the radiator confirms there's no heating on. It's a cold enough day to warrant heating, especially if you're off work because you're sick.

'Through there, sir.'

Tyler moves past the table towards a corridor at the far end of the room. As soon as he steps through the doorway the smell reaches him.

'Door at the end.'

He moves slowly, glancing through the open doorway on his left. The living room's tidy, with a large flat-screen TV and a laptop and tablet lying out in full view on the coffee table. Not a robbery then.

The doorway diagonally opposite opens into the bathroom and then they reach the last door. The bedroom presumably. Tyler reaches for the handle.

'I should probably warn you. The window was open. There's a fair number of flies.'

Tyler hesitates. 'Cheers.' He puts his free arm up to cover his nose and mouth and pushes down on the bedroom door handle.

The stench hits him first. It's something you never get used to. At least, he hopes you never do. Then he hears the loud buzz of the insects. The body's lying on the bed, not end to end like someone sleeping, but crossways, as though the man fell as he died, leaving his feet trailing on the floor to the right-hand side. The face is turned away from them, towards the headboard and the far wall. It's not immediately obvious what killed the man but there's enough blood pooled on the floor to make it clear it's too late for the paramedics. Even with his limited knowledge of forensics, Tyler can tell the man's been lying here for days. The blood pool on the floor has already dried and darkened.

Tyler inches his way carefully round the bed to the left, making sure not to touch anything. The eyes of the corpse are wide open and glassy. His mouth's open in a small o, as though he's surprised to find himself in this state. Tyler supposes he would be. As he's watching, a fly emerges from the mouth, crosses the man's face and starts licking at his pupil.

'Are we sure it's him? What was the name again?'

'Jayashankar. Deepak Jayashankar. I asked the school to text me the photo they've got on file. It's definitely him.'

But Tyler doesn't recognise him as anyone involved in the case. 'Control said you specifically asked them to send someone from the Botanical Gardens case? Why?'

Arjun grimaces. 'I had my phone out, checking the ID, and then a fly landed on my hand and I freaked. I'm sorry, sir. I'll tell the SOCOs where it fell and all. Only, when I bent down to pick it up I saw it. Under the bed.' He points with his head, encouraging Tyler to look for himself.

Tyler squats, his ribs still grumbling from the pummelling they took on Thursday. Under the bed, lying just out of sight from a standing position, is a small gold coin stamped with the head of a Roman Emperor.

'Right,' says Tyler. 'I see.' But he doesn't. Who the hell is this Jayashankar? And what has he got to do with the death of Li Qiang?

Mina stares down at the empty slab and blinks. 'Do we know how he got in?' she asks, making an effort to keep her voice level.

Emma Ridgeway hesitates. 'We got it all on camera. He came straight in through the back.'

'Show me.'

Emma pushes the empty gurney back into the wall and closes the freezer door. Mina follows her back into the office and waits while she pulls up the relevant footage on the CCTV monitor. It doesn't take long; she's obviously watched it several times already this morning.

They watch the grainy black and white images on the screen. It's clearly him, Dave Carver, the man they've been looking for. He pulls open the back door and walks right into the building. They see him hesitate for a second, then pull a discarded overall from a hook and slip his arms into the sleeves. They follow his progress on camera as he moves through the building. He passes any number of people but none of them give him a second look. Yes, Mina thinks, it's easy for a man like Carver to be anonymous if he wants to be. There's nothing furtive in the way he moves. He makes no attempt to hide his face from the cameras, wears no mask. He doesn't need to. He's an anonymous man. A cleaner, a technician, a background person with a walk-on part. He moves through the corridors like a stagehand dressed in black walking on to change the furniture in between scenes. You know they're there but you choose to ignore them.

They're both silent as Emma cues each camera and presses play and Carver moves from one field of vision to another. For moments he's out of view and then there he is again, passing the end of another corridor, collecting an empty trolley from one room, moving it into the next. At one point, one of the doctors or technicians holds a door for him and Mina sees him nod his head in acknowledgement to her.

In the privacy of the morgue he doesn't hesitate, but neither does he hurry, opening one freezer door after another, unzipping each body bag until he finds what he's looking for. Who he's looking for. Then, and for the first time, he falters. But there are no witnesses here other than the camera. He lifts Chi's remains . . . gently, yes, Mina would use that word. There's a reverence to it that makes the hair stand up on her arms. He scoops up the misshapen body bag and transfers it to the empty trolley he's brought in with him. It doesn't seem to cause him any effort. Carver's not a particularly big man but Chi was no heavyweight when she was alive either, and now the remains probably weigh less than an average-sized pet dog. She certainly struggles less.

He closes the freezer door behind him and then he's leaving the same way he came in, although he opens the loading bay this time, rather than manhandle the trolley through the doorway. The final piece of footage sees him loading the body bag into the back of an unidentifiable estate car. At least this image is in colour so Mina can see that it's blue. Presumably the Volvo they've had an alert out for.

It's that easy.

'Shit,' she says.

'It's been nice working with you.' Emma smiles weakly.

'They can't hold you responsible for this, surely?'

'You don't think Elliot's gonna take the heat for this? He's been on my back since I got here. My transfer here wasn't exactly his idea and since I was the duty supervisor this weekend, I'm pretty damn sure he'll try and make me the scapegoat.' She makes a bleating noise.

Mina smiles at the weak joke. 'We'll get her back.'

Emma claps a hand across her mouth. 'Oh, God!'

'What?' Mina can't see how this gets worse.

'Her parents. They're due to arrive in the UK this afternoon. They're supposed to be picking up her body tomorrow.'

Mina reaches out and puts a hand on her arm. 'You're not responsible for this.' She turns back to the frozen image of Dave Carver carrying the feather-light body of Li Qiang. For all its creepiness, she can't shake the feeling there's a tenderness about the image.

'Okay, look,' she says. 'We've already got an all-ports warning out for him. He won't get far. We'll find her. Maybe even by the end of the day.'

Emma looks at her and nods.

'Can you burn me a copy of the footage?'

'No problem.'

Mina looks back at Dave Carver's face on the screen. With the level of detail visible it's hard to tell for sure, but it looks very much as though he's crying.

Dave's breath billows out in a cloud and catches on the jagged glass of a broken window. He's five storeys up but he can still make out the young professionals setting off for work far below. Stepping from their chrome-fixtured inner-city apartments, dressed in tight clothing, they begin their short commute through Kelham and into the city centre. Some may be travelling further, he supposes. Turning right at the corner for the tram stop at Shalesmoor that will take them on to the railway station, and then on to Manchester or Leeds. They'll spend the day in their air-conditioned offices making money for people they never meet, before trudging home again. Maybe they'll stop at a champagne bar after work to meet friends, or head to the gym. He does not envy them. That was never the life he wanted. He once had a taste of it though, when he was with Lizzie. She lifted him up, made him stretch for things he didn't know he wanted. But it isn't the champagne and expensive restaurants he misses. It's the sense of belonging that she gave him, the sense that someone else needed something from him. He'd never felt that before. He'd give anything to get it back. He doubts he will ever feel it again.

His eyes stray to the bench on the far side of the workshop but then he pulls them away again; he can't go there yet. He shivers as a drop of rainwater falls from a sodden ceiling tile and slithers down his neck. He pulls his jacket tighter around him and tucks his legs up on the windowsill.

Chi had needed him. It was a small thing he gave her, he knows that, and it wouldn't have lasted forever, but their weekly chats on the bench helped her. She was such a lost soul and he felt he owed it to her to help in the small way that he could. He listened. She told him about her life growing up, wanting for nothing but a father who loved her and didn't take every opportunity to point out she was a disappointment to him. A second disappointment.

Now what use is he to her, or anyone for that matter? Homeless. Jobless. On the run from the police. He tries to find the point at which he could have done things differently. It's not like that though, really, is it? It's never one flick of the dice, but rather a series of seemingly inevitable events.

Again his eyes are drawn to the large bag lying in shadow on the work bench. No! He can't think about that. About what he did.

The rest of the building's empty apart from a couple of busted-up stools and the mould-coated walls. He figures he's safe enough here for now, but it's not somewhere he can live forever. He can't go home, obviously, but if he could find a way to get in somehow, just to grab a few items – a sleeping bag, a blanket – it might make life here tolerable for a few days at least. He assumes hotels and B&Bs are out of the question, even if he could afford them. They'll have put a stop on his bank cards by now, or be watching the activity on them at least, but since there's no money in his account that's hardly an issue.

He can't drive anywhere; they're bound to have the make and reg of his car by now. He stashed the Volvo at the back of the building. The only people who go round there are smack-heads and he doubts any of them will report it. He probably should have ditched it somewhere else but there's a chance he might need it again.

What is he going to do?

The bag on the workbench creeps back into his vision. No matter how hard he wishes it, it isn't going to go away.

What had he been thinking?

After the Spoken Word night and the close call with the copper he'd spent most of the weekend holed up here. He'd found some fragments of metal and a few old work tools scattered around. It was quite therapeutic really. It had been years since he'd lost himself to his knife-work and the hours slipped by without him having to think about anything too deeply. By Sunday evening he had fashioned a half-decent blade, or as best as he could manage under the circumstances. But then, once again, the cold and damp crept back into his bones. If he spent another night on the floor he wondered if he would wake up. He was almost tempted to find out but as he huddled under the bench, shivering, the temptation to find warmth and shelter overrode his self-pity.

So he'd found a quiet pub nearby, and spent the last of his cash on a pie-and-pea supper and a lime and soda. The news was on in the background, muted, but with those tickertape subtitles staggering across the bottom of the screen, and then the local bulletin came on and *she* was the lead story. Li Qiang. The missing Chinese student who had been found abandoned in a shallow grave in the Botanical Gardens.

That was the word they used, abandoned! It made his blood boil. Nothing could have been further from the truth. He hadn't abandoned her. He'd tended to her all these months, sitting on the memorial bench. Talked to her, laughed with her, just as he always had done when she was a little girl and ... No, that wasn't her but ... the point was, he would never abandon her. Never!

Dave breathes deeply, watching the cloud of water vapour emerge and dissipate in front of him. Stay calm. He can't afford to lose his mind. It's the only thing he has left. It was just that damned news report. Those subtitles sliding along the bottom of the screen, putting down half-truths and outright lies in black and white, as though they were facts.

He doesn't remember making a conscious plan but he must have worked it out on some level. Afterwards he realised he knew where she was only because the reporter had been standing in front of the morgue, telling the viewers how he had *abandoned* her, gesturing at the red bricks behind her as though that soulless, clinical place was better than the garden she had always loved. Talking about Rachel ... about Chi, and how devastated her parents must be, when, if anyone was responsible for abandoning her it was them! And then, that last piece of information. The fact they were on their way to the UK to repatriate her remains. He couldn't let that happen. Her father never wanted her when she was alive, why should he get her now? Is that what she would have wanted?

That's what had spurred him into action, made him stand up and walk out of the pub. He'd driven to the mortuary on autopilot. He'd had a job there once, a couple of years back, a temporary security guard position, so he knew the security was pretty lax. He knew the back door was usually unlocked.

He knew where the spare uniforms and passes were kept and how few people were around at that time of the day. He knew all of this even though none of it had consciously crossed his mind. If he'd been caught, he's not even sure he would have run. But he hadn't been caught. He had got her out and he'd brought her here.

He looks again at the sad bag of bones on the work bench. What had he been thinking? What the hell should he do with her now? Dave buries his head in his hands. All he knows is that he can't lose her. Not again. Why do all the things he loves get taken away from him?

Dave looks up.

That's the point. He didn't lose her. She was *taken* from him. Ronnie had said as much the other night and her words had been etched into truth by the ticker tape subtitles. *Stabbed to death and buried in the Botanical Gardens.* He might have been the one to bury her, but there was a question that remained unanswered.

He brought her here to keep her safe. To do that, he needs to find out who killed her and make them pay. Only then will she be at peace.

Maybe they both will.

Tyler's sitting halfway along one side of the conference table with Rabbani next to him. He wants to tell her to stay calm and follow his lead but it's a bit late for warnings. Diane Jordan is seated at the end of the table to their left. Dr Elliot and his new American colleague, Dr Emma Ridgeway, are seated at the other end of the table, one looking as though he's ready to explode and the other as though the bomb's already gone off.

Superintendent Stevens enters the room and Tyler, Rabbani and Jordan stand up. He's wearing his best dress uniform, the buttons all shiny and polished, the creases in his trousers so sharp they could cut you if you walked too close. He waves them back to their seats and takes the chair opposite Tyler, removing his cap and placing it carefully on the table. He turns it minutely to the right so that it's straight, and the badge catches the light from the window and shines directly in Tyler's left eye. It's doubtful he's done it on purpose but, then again, you didn't make it to superintendent without knowing the odd trick or two.

Through the glass wall of the room, Tyler can see Doggett trying to catch his eye. The man raises his eyebrows in support and Jordan gets up and closes the blinds. When she sits back down Tyler notices the Eel staring at him intently, his expression unreadable.

'Right,' Stevens says. 'What do I need to know? Diane?'

Jordan looks relatively tidy this morning although Tyler can see the now familiar bags have been hidden beneath a touch more make-up than is usual. 'It's likely Chi was killed on the day she went missing.'

Stevens raises a hand and cuts her off. His head whips the opposite way along the table to Elliot. 'Cause of death?'

Elliot, well used to dealing with jumped-up officers with delusions of grandeur, asserts his own authority by turning on the woman next to him. He leans back in his chair, swivels it to face her, and raises a thick, greying eyebrow.

Ridgeway shifts in her own chair and pushes a stray lock of hair behind her ear. 'Blood loss is most likely, given the blunt trauma to the head and the knife wound. We're still waiting on toxicology reports.'

Tyler feels a bit sorry for the woman. No doubt Elliot will make sure none of this shit lands on his doorstep.

'Go on,' Stevens says. His hand, which has been stretched out to Jordan all this time, now drops back to the table. But again his eyes rest on Tyler.

Jordan picks up where she left off. 'Our main suspect is this man Carver. He volunteers at the Botanical Gardens where Chi's body was found, he used to work at the university as a cleaner in the department she was studying in, and . . .' she pauses for a moment, '. . . he absconded from DS Tyler to avoid questioning.'

Stevens picks up her unfinished list. 'And then he walked into the morgue and stole the girl's body out from under our noses.'

Nobody speaks. The silence draws out before them and Tyler can feel Rabbani beginning to shuffle in her seat. He stills her by pressing his leg against hers again.

'And now we have another body,' Stevens goes on. 'A physics teacher. Anyone want to fill me in on that?'

It's Tyler's turn. 'We believe his death's related but we're not sure how. A coin was found at the scene matching the ones found in the Gardens. A gold Roman aureus. We've spoken to an antiquities expert who's identified them as aurei. They're rare, extremely rare. Potentially worth as much as half a million apiece. The one found at Jayashankar's place was under the bed rather than placed on the body so it doesn't look as ritualistic as the two we found on Chi's eyes. Our theory is the killer dropped it by mistake.'

'How's this man connected to the girl?'

'We're looking into that. Obviously, we might know more when we get the postmortem results.'

Elliot clears his throat and shoots Tyler a glance. 'The SOCOs are still on scene,' he says. 'But it looks pretty cut and dried. Knife wound to the stomach. Been there for a few days, at least.'

'The same as the girl,' says Stevens. 'So are we looking at the same killer?'

Tyler inclines his head. 'It seems likely, but at this point we can't say for sure.'

'I can look again at the knife wound,' Ridgeway says, 'maybe establish if it's the same weapon.'

'And how are you going to manage that without a body?' Stevens asks.

Ridgeway manages to remain professional. 'We do take photographs, Superintendent.' She leaves it there.

After another long silence, Stevens says, 'Mr and Mrs Li arrive from Shanghai this afternoon. I will be travelling to Manchester with the Police and Crime Commissioner and Councillor Matthews to meet them. Does anyone have any suggestions about what I should tell them? That we found their daughter, who has been buried in a park for the past seven months, but then we lost her again?' His eyes dart from one side of the table to the other but ultimately rest once again on Tyler. 'Any suggestions? DS Tyler?'

Tyler knows why he's getting the brunt of this. As always, the Eel's looking for a way to pin this on someone else. A troublesome, failing department perhaps. He's hoping Tyler will provide his own rope. But at least that means he hasn't found a way to do it yet. If Tyler mentions his cosy chat with Joey McKenna on Friday night, or the fact McKenna's grandson's currently dozing on his couch, it would be more than enough. 'No, sir,' he says.

Stevens turns back to Jordan. 'Where are we with finding Carver?'

'We've issued an all-ports warning and everyone's aware this is their highest priority. Unfortunately, we've still got a lot of resources tied up with the Talbot case.'

'And where are we with that? It's dragging on a bit, isn't it?'

'Jim's convinced the father's responsible. I have to agree, he seems the most likely suspect, but we don't have enough to arrest him.'

'We can't waste time on lost causes. If Doggett can't find something new we need to move on.'

'As you'll be aware though, sir, the first seventy-two hours of an investigation are key and—'

'DI Doggett has already had that and more. He's managed to achieve very little as far as I can see. Time to scale it back.'

Is this how it works, Tyler wonders. Maybe the man's just

impatient, so focused on getting results that any case with no obvious lead gets wrapped up and filed away somewhere. Or is there more to it?

'What about the press?' Tyler asks.

Stevens turns his head very slowly back in Tyler's direction. 'Leave me to worry about the press, Detective. With a body-snatcher on the loose I'm fairly certain they'll lose interest in what is, at the end of the day, just another domestic killing.'

Tyler wonders what Doggett would have to say if he could hear this conversation. Assuming he's not outside listening right now.

'Our main priority – the only priority anyone in this department has – is to find that body. Preferably before I get to the airport, but I'll settle for the end of the day. Is that understood?'

'It's a shame we didn't put that much effort in when Chi went missing in the first place, isn't it, sir?' says Rabbani.

Tyler tries the leg trick again but this time she bats it away with a swipe of her own knee.

'Detective Constable Rabbani,' Jordan snaps.

But Stevens raises his hand at her again. 'It's all right, Diane. If the young lady has something to say . . .'

'The young lady,' Rabbani says, smiling sweetly, 'is wondering why the original investigation into Chi's disappearance was shelved in just two weeks. Maybe you could ask her father why he didn't care if she were found. Or maybe you already know the reason. *Sir.*'

'Mina!' Jordan's voice is strangled.

Stevens smiles. Or at least, does his best impersonation of what he thinks a smile's supposed to look like. 'I suggest, Detective Constable ... Rabbani, was it? I suggest you concentrate on finding this man you and your mentor here have let slip through your fingers on three occasions now, and you can leave the questioning of high-level diplomats to me.' He stands up.

Jordan leaps to her feet and Tyler stands too. Rabbani's a bit slower but manages to get up eventually. Stevens takes pains to fix his hat back on his head, all the while his eyes focused on Tyler, before he leaves with a curt, 'Dismissed.'

Jordan collapses back into her chair and lets out a deep breath. 'Find that bloody body. I don't care what it takes.'

Elliot and Ridgeway file out of the room and Tyler and Rabbani start after them.

'DC Rabbani,' Jordan says behind them. 'A word.'

Rabbani looks at Tyler in supplication but there's nothing he can do for her. She'll have to learn to take her medicine, the same way they all do. He mouths the words 'good luck' to her and leaves the room, closing the door behind him. But when he hears Jordan start shouting it actually puts a smile on his face. Well done, Rabbani! He's never felt more proud.

Doggett looks at him with a wry grin on his face. 'How far have you cocked things up this time?'

'Not as badly as Rabbani.' The whole office stops for a moment as Jordan's voice erupts from the meeting room.

Doggett chuckles. 'Good lass. Listen, I need to talk to you about something. The other night at this poetry thing . . .'

'How did it go?'

'About as well as you'd expect. Thing is . . . He was there, your man Carver.'

'What?'

'I wasn't sure at first but I checked the photos this morning and it was definitely him. He's a friend of Ronnie's. I'm sorry, lad, if I hadn't been so preoccupied with Talbot, I might have recognised him sooner.'

Tyler can't believe it. Who is this man, Harry Houdini? 'How does Ronnie know him? Can we use her to get to him?' He sees Doggett scowl and corrects himself. 'I mean, can she tell us anything about him?'

'That's going to be a problem. She isn't talking to me. I left early that night. I rang her this morning once I realised who Carver was but she was a bit pissed off with me. Can't blame her, really. She walked home alone and to make things worse some bloke tried to mug her.'

'Is she all right?'

'Says she is. Reckons this bloke wanted money off her, so she kicked him in the knackers and ran.'

'Still, that's pretty rough.'

'Yeah, I'm gonna pop round in a bit and make sure she's all right. If she'll let me. I'll try and convince her to make it official but knowing Ronnie she'll just brush it off. I'll have a word with her though, see if she can tell me anything about Carver.'

'Fine, but can you make it sooner rather than later? Rabbani and I are hanging on a thread here.'

'The Eel?'

Tyler nods. 'You should know, he's after closing your case down now as well.'

'He can certainly try.'

'There's something else too.'

'Oh, Christ! Here it comes.'

'Not here.'

'Christ with a cherry on top! All right, give me ten minutes and I'll meet you outside by the lunch van; it's near enough breadcake time, I reckon.'

It's nearer fifteen minutes by the time Doggett shuffles out of the building and joins him in the queue with a dozen other hungry mouths. Most of them are office workers but there are some who could easily be civilians from the station, so Tyler keeps his voice low.

'I need you to know something. I don't want you to do anything about it, or even say anything, I just need someone to know what's going on in case . . .'

'In case it comes back to bite you in the arse. I get it. Go on then.'

Tyler takes a deep breath and then outlines the situation with McKenna and Callum.

Doggett's eyes grow wider and wider through the telling

but somehow he manages to hold his tongue until Tyler's finished. Then he says, 'My God, lad, you don't half know how to fuck up, don't you?'

'I think Diane mentioned something about that in my last appraisal.'

They shuffle forward in the queue and Doggett says, 'I don't suppose there's any point telling you not to do this but I will tell you one thing. You won't listen but at least it'll clear my conscience. Joey McKenna's an evil bastard. Rotten to the core and out the other side. Oh, he thinks himself an honourable sort, last of the old-school crims, but in truth he'd stab his own grandmother in the back if there were money in it for him. He'll certainly try to use whatever hooks he's got into you for his own agenda.' Doggett stops and rubs his chin with his hand. 'On the other hand, there's a small chance he might know something about your dad. They ran across each other a number of times. There's also a chance he's making the whole bloody thing up mind, you realise that?'

Tyler doesn't answer.

'Christ,' Doggett goes on, 'how do you manage it?' He's looking at the ground now, as though he's debating with himself more than Tyler. 'Bloody hell, but this is a ball-ache I don't need.'

'There's something else,' Tyler says.

'Go on then, might as well be hanged for a sheep as a lamb.'

'He offered me ... a bonus, he called it.' Tyler tells him about the houseboat on the canal but Doggett is surprisingly reticent.

'It wouldn't hold up in court. I can't magically find evidence on a formerly unknown-of boat in the middle of bloody nowhere! How would I explain what made me look there?'

They step forward again, the smell of cooked meat and frying onions wafting to them from the hatch in the van.

'Look into the boat first, see if you can find a connection with Talbot, then massage the evidence trail a bit.'

'Have you heard yourself?' Doggett asks him.

'You've done worse in the past.'

Doggett looks at him closely. 'But you haven't. What's going on with you?'

'Fine. Don't use it. I just thought you'd want to know, that's all.'

Doggett clicks his tongue in the back of his throat. 'I suppose, worst case scenario we could say it was an anonymous tip. Alright, I'll look into the boat. As for McKenna, thanks for telling me and dropping me right in it and all. Christ, who am I kidding? I was the one sent you on this bloody fool's errand in the first place.'

'If he knows something about Richard . . .' Tyler leaves it there. He can see the cogs whirring in Doggett's brain.

After a moment or two Doggett asks, 'What's this young grandson of his like then?'

'Cal? He's a bit lost but I think he just needs a leg-up, that's all.'

'Drugs?'

'Not that I can see.'

'That's something. I guess you're committed now anyway. You don't want to make an enemy of Joey McKenna. But get him out of your place as soon as you can. And watch yourself, you don't want the boy crying foul or saying you touched him or something.'

'Why is that always the first thing anyone thinks of?'

'All right, all right. Don't get your knickers in a twist. But don't be so bloody naive either. If I've thought it, there'll be others think the same. One word from the lad or Joey or both and your career's up shit creek. And that's not a euphemism. You can do without any more scandal, given your history.' They both step forward again. 'Find him a place and get him out. ASAP! Then we'll talk to Joey McKenna together.'

'I don't need you to—'

'Maybe not, but you've got me anyway.' Doggett finally reaches the window in the side of the van. 'Roast pork and all the trimmings, please, love. Not too stingy on the apple sauce, eh?'

And with that the conversation's over.

Mina goes out of the office for lunch.

She thinks it's probably best given the circumstances. If one more person grins at her and asks her what Jordan said, she's going to put her fist through the nearest wall, whether the nosey bastard's face is in the way or not.

She walks down the towpath along the river. It looks as though it's about to rain again at any moment. So she'll get wet. That'll set off her mood nicely.

Fuck the lot of them! *Fuck* Jordan and her insistence on toeing the line when it comes to senior officers who clearly know less about doing their job than she does! *Fuck* Adam Tyler and wherever the hell he's gone now! *Fuck* Guy Daley and his unwanted advances and crazy-headed psychodramas!

First Jordan tells her if she wants to get on she needs to not let anyone get in the way, and then she tells her to keep her head down and do her job without rocking the boat. *Which is it?* Stevens is up to something, she *knows* it. Why aren't they taking this more seriously?

She kicks a stone off the path and listens to it plop into the river, sending ripples out across the water. Maybe she *should* just keep her head down and get on with it. She's supposed to be running a background check on Ben Robbins so that's what she'll do. That's *all* she'll do, and not a damn thing more until one of them instructs her to. They want her to work to rule, fine. She'll do just that.

It doesn't rain, but by the time she gets back to the station, her mood's darker than ever.

'There you are!'

The voice takes her by surprise, coming from under the walkway where the office workers go for a smoke. It's Jim Doggett.

'Yeah, I'm here. Why? What have I done now?'

He makes no comment about her tone but his face makes the point for him. 'With me, *DC* Rabbani.' And with that he walks away from her and round towards the car park.

She follows him and he stops by a battered old Saab she recognises as his preferred ride.

'Right,' he says. 'Have a guess where I'm off to this afternoon?'

Mina knows she's not supposed to have an answer so she settles for, 'Sir?'

'I have to go and see a young woman, not much older than you are, whose 5-year-old boy was kidnapped, beaten, and then strangled to death. She's going through pretty much the worse thing any human being can go through. And guess what I have to do?'

Rabbani stays silent.

'I have to break her. I'm going to have to look that woman in the eye and somehow force her to accept that the man who did this to her beautiful boy is also the man she shares a bed with every night. I have to convince her she's to blame so that she crumbles, and the person who's really to blame doesn't get away with it. Or, for that matter, do it to someone else's poor little boy.'

'I'm not sure why you're telling me this.'

'I'm telling you because you've just had a roasting from the DCI. We've all been there and more than likely each of us'll be there again at some point. I wanted to make sure you remember why we do this. I want you to think about what made you want this job because if you give up and bury your head in the sand now, at the first setback, then you're not suited for it. That's not a problem. You can get yourself transferred and move on. No harm done. But I don't think you're going to do that, Mina. I think, if you were that sort of person you wouldn't have made it this far. The question is, am I right, *Detective* Constable Rabbani?'

He doesn't wait for a response, just throws his cigarette end on the ground and walks away.

Tyler slams the door of his car and clicks the lock button on his key fob. As he crosses the car park he sees the security guard, Halbert, getting up from behind his desk.

The man meets him at the door, his face animated but a bit strung out, as though he's coming up on a drug high. 'Hello again, Detective, what can we do for you today? Professor Calderdale isn't here at the moment.'

Tyler follows him into the reception area and the man resumes his position behind the desk. 'Actually, Mike, it's you I've come to see.'

'Oh?' Halbert swallows and tries to smile.

'Any chance you know a man named Deepak Jayashankar?'

Halbert thinks about this. 'I don't think so. The name doesn't ring a bell.'

'Really? Are you sure about that?'

Halbert makes another show of thinking about it. 'No, no I don't think so.'

'No, you don't know him? Or no, you're not sure?'

'What's this about?'

Tyler moves round the desk. The Post-its are still there, or new ones at least, with different messages scrawled across them. The stickers are the same though. There's one with a picture of a metal detector and the slogan, 'Detectorists do it holding their shafts!'

'Mr Jayashankar has been murdered.'

'What?' The shock on Halbert's face seems genuine.

'Are you all right, Mike? You seem a bit upset for someone who didn't know the man.' Tyler taps the sticker with his left forefinger. 'You see, we found a metal detector in his house and that got me thinking about where I'd seen one recently.'

'I . . .'

'How about David Carver?' Tyler asks, moving back round to the front of the desk. 'Does that name ring a bell?

Halbert hesitates.

'Careful, Mike. You don't want me thinking you've got something to hide, do you?'

'Dave? Yeah, he used to work here? He was one of the cleaners. Nice bloke.'

'That's right. He also volunteers at the Botanical Gardens where we found Chi. The student whose sister you live along the road from.'

'I told you the truth before,' Halbert says, beginning to break. 'I barely knew her, I swear.'

'But you do know Dave?'

'A bit.'

Tyler brings his hand down on the reception desk. 'Don't lie to me, Halbert!'

'I'm not! Honestly, I'm not!'

Tyler changes tack, softening his tone. 'I've been doing a bit of digging, Mike. Your application to join the PCSOs.

You told me you got rejected because of budget cuts, but that's not true, is it?'

Halbert's face collapses, the smile disappearing completely.

'You were rejected because you were once a member of the British National Party.'

'That were a long time ago. I were just a kid. I didn't know anything back then.'

'Maybe. Or maybe you still have prejudices. Maybe you took a knife to Mr Jayashankar because you didn't like the colour of his skin.'

'God, no! I wouldn't!'

He's guilty, Tyler thinks. But not of murder. He looks ashamed of his past, but do people really change that much?

'Please, you have to believe me. I'd never . . .' There are tears in his eyes.

'So you do know him?'

'Yes, but . . . I only know him as Deepak. I . . . I got confused about the surname. I didn't know what it was.'

'But now it's coming back to you?'

'We're both part of the same club.'

'The metal detectorists' club?'

'You know about that?'

'We've spoken to Ronnie,' Tyler says. 'She told us all about you, Mike. And your friends Deepak and Dave.'

Halbert's eyes stay firmly fixed to the floor. It seems genuine, not just an act.

'Now. How about you stop lying to me, and tell me what you know about this.' Tyler already has the picture ready on his mobile. When he shows Halbert the coin from the murder scene, the man's eyes widen.

'I . . . I don't know anything.'

Tyler's had enough. 'Fine. Have it your way. How about we continue this conversation down at the station?'

The house Lizzie Gordon lives in is a beautiful Victorian semi on a tree-lined street in Nether Edge. It's perhaps no more than ten minutes' walk from Mina's house yet it could not be more different.

On the way there, Mina keeps reliving the conversation with Doggett. She feels her face burn every time she thinks of it. Well, there's nothing she can do about it but move on. She's sure Doggett's forgotten it already. And he was right. This is the job – the career – she's always wanted. She *can* make a difference. She can make a difference to Chi's parents. If she can find her body, and ultimately her killer.

She climbs a small flight of stone steps to the front door and presses the doorbell. There's a long wait and she's about to press again when she sees a figure through the glass.

Gordon's a pretty, middle-aged woman with immaculate dress sense. She answers the door with a wide smile and only a touch of the anxiety most people have plastered across their face at a visit from the police.

'Lizzie? I'm DC Rabbani. We spoke on the phone.'

'Yes, of course. Please come in.'

Mina's escorted into a spotlessly clean and well-decorated front room. No children, then. She *is* wearing a wedding ring however. The room's huge, big enough for two sofas, and they end up with one each. Gordon offers her no tea or refreshment, which is a bit weird. It's normally the first thing people ask.

Mina comes straight to the point. 'It's about your ex-husband, David Carver?'

'Yes. You said as much on the phone. What's he done?' She doesn't seem overly shocked or worried.

Mina hesitates while she decides how much to say. 'We're interested in talking to him about a case we're investigating and unfortunately he appears to be missing.' She winces at her choice of words. She doesn't really want to imply he's in danger, but on the other hand, that might not be a bad thing if it gets the right response. 'Can I ask, have you seen him lately?'

'No. I can give you the last address I have for him but I honestly don't know if he's still living there. It was a flat in Broomhill.'

'Yes, we have that, but he hasn't been home for a few days now.'

Gordon looks at her closely. 'I suppose you're not telling me everything, but that's fine.' She carries on before Mina can jump in. 'No, really, I don't think I want to know.' She wipes a hand across her forehead, pushing back her fringe. 'How much do you know about Dave?'

'Not a great deal, to be honest. We know he works at the Botanical Gardens and that he was let go from his post at the university a few months back. We know you were married for nine years and divorced five years ago.'

Mina can hear Tyler's voice in her head. *Shut up! Let the woman talk.*

'I didn't know about him losing his job at the university. But he always loved the Gardens. He—' Abruptly her face drains of colour and her hand reaches up to cover her mouth. 'Oh God! The Gardens. I saw it on the news! You can't think ...?' But it's clear from her demeanour that's exactly what *she's* thinking.

'We don't know what to think, that's why I'm here.'

'Oh God, I feel sick.'

Mina waits for her to recover. 'Can I get you a glass of water?'

'What? No, I'm fine. Sorry.'

This is getting her nowhere. 'Mrs Gordon? Lizzie. Can you tell me what sort of man Dave is? Does he have a temper? I'm sorry to ask this but, why did you break up exactly?'

Gordon sits up straighter. 'It wasn't like that. Dave ... Dave's the gentlest man I've ever met in my life. What sort of man is he?' She thinks for a moment. 'He's kind. That's the word I would use. More than anything else. We met when I was a postgrad and Dave was teaching evening classes in metalwork. A friend of mine was really into jewellery-making at the time. We laughed about how quietly spoken he was. Good-looking, too. We both flirted mercilessly with him and gave him a pretty hard time. But what I remember most is how gentle he was with his hands. You don't expect that from someone who works with metal, do you?'

311

Gentle. It's the same word Mina had thought of when she'd seen the CCTV footage of him handling Chi's body.

'I asked him for his number as we were leaving, it was a joke more than anything, but he gave it to me. And then, a few days later, I found myself ringing it. I couldn't get him out of my head. We were married just over a year later but it took us a while to get pregnant, nearly two years. I've thought about this a lot over the years and to be honest, I'm not sure I really loved him. Not at that point. But when we finally had Rachel and I saw him holding her, something changed. I knew I'd made the right decision. This was a man who would never hurt me, or our child. He was everything you could ever hope for in a husband.'

Mina reassesses the room. She would never have dreamed a child lived in this stark place. Where were the toys?

'Something went wrong.'

Gordon smiles, but it's a sad kind of smile. 'Dave was always a bit ... damaged is probably the word. He'd gone into the steel industry just at the point everyone else was leaving. He was struggling to hold on to a way of life that's passed. He's very old-fashioned in lots of ways. He lost his job and things got hard for us. I probably wasn't all that good a wife, to be honest. I didn't really help him as much as I should have and, looking back on it now, it's obvious he was depressed, struggling to cope, but all I cared about was how we'd pay the bills and put food on the table. It put an enormous strain on our relationship but honestly, the harsh words and the temper tantrums ... all of that came from me.

It used to drive me crazy he wasn't *more* concerned about stuff. But that's Dave. He's a bit of a closed book. He doesn't share easily.'

This all makes a certain kind of sense. Did it all boil over one day? Was that it? Chi got in the way on the day the man finally snapped.

'Then Rachel got sick,' Gordon says. 'Leukaemia. It took three years. We watched her ...' Gordon's voice breaks but she swallows and carries on. 'We watched her just fade away. She was seven.'

'I'm so sorry.'

'It broke us, I suppose. Or maybe Rachel was all we had by that point. Maybe without her there was no *us*. By the time she died I'd already moved out and I was staying with a friend. The last time we even spoke, other than practical things like the divorce and the sale of the house and everything, was the day before Rachel's funeral. On the day itself we didn't say a word to each other. I couldn't even look at him. I know that sounds ...'

'It sounds like you both went through a terrible ordeal.'

Gordon wipes her eyes with her fingers. 'I'm sorry. I'm not sure this is what you wanted.'

'No, it helps.'

'You think he killed that girl? The body they found?'

Again Mina hesitates. 'Do *you* think he could have?'

Gordon doesn't hesitate. 'No,' she says without even considering it, but then her eyes betray her. She's considering it now. 'At least ... The Dave I knew could never ... I mean, I never even heard him raise his voice to someone. But I guess you hear stuff like that all the time, don't you? "I can't believe it." "He seemed so ordinary."'

'Can you think of anywhere he might have gone? Anywhere at all.'

Gordon considers it for a while but comes up with nothing. 'He doesn't really have anyone, not that I know of. His family are all gone. Other than his precious garden I can't think of anywhere.'

Mina thanks her and leaves her card, just in case.

When she gets outside she has to stop for a moment and breathe in the fresh autumnal air. Gordon had seemed so certain to begin with. 'No.' But then she let herself think about it for a moment and realised Carver *was* capable of killing. Who wasn't, given the right circumstances? We might not want to believe it but it was true.

But Mina thinks again of the image from that camera, Dave carrying Chi's body out of the morgue. So gently. Then again, people are capable of being more than one thing.

six

the sixth nighthawker

<u>**Record of Finds**</u>

Date: Mon 13th Nov
Time: 14.25
Location: River Sheaf
Finds: Hubcap, BMW (3 series?); shopping trolley, ASDA;
baked bean tin, Heinz; iPhone 5, screen cracked

When Nick gets back to halls he passes a group of girls in
the foyer.

'Ladies,' he says, winking at them and pushing his long hair
back. He reckons it's probably his best feature, his hair. Makes
him look a bit like Thor.

They giggle and he can't help but straighten as he walks
past them to the lift, wondering if maybe he has a chance with
one of them. But as the lift arrives and he gets in he hears
one of them whisper, just loudly enough to be heard, 'Oh, my
God, did you see the state of him.'

The doors close and the smile on his face evaporates. Well, who gives a shit what they think? He can get laid any time he wants on Tinder, so fuck 'em!

He looks down at his muddy Converse. There are grass stains and mud splatters all up his ripped jeans. He supposes he probably is a bit of a mess. He sniffs at an armpit. But if that stuck-up bitch had spent the last four hours walking along the riverbank digging through brambles she might look a state as well. It had been worth it, though. The iPhone was no doubt locked but he should be able to get a decent price for it. And even the hubcap might go on eBay.

He usually comes back with something worthwhile when he hits the Sheaf. It's his own secret dig site, he's never told the others about it. He was planning to take that new bloke, Stuart, down there at the weekend, figured it would be a good place to start his training. But when they'd met up, the guy made some excuse about his detector not working and suggested they hit the pub instead. They'd ended up chatting for a bit over a couple of pints in the student union and then calling it a day.

The beauty of the Sheaf site is, he doesn't have to do much digging. The Sheaf runs right through the city, underground for the most part, but here and there along its length are sections where the river cuts up and out into the open. Over the years these places have become lost wildernesses, sandwiched between apartment buildings and businesses. Finding a way down to them can be tricky, which is probably why most people who drop things there tend to abandon them.

The lift doors open, he steps into the hallway, and immediately notices his door's open. He's sure he locked it but . . . He steps up to the door and pushes. The lock's all bust-up. Shit!

He hurries into his apartment. The place is a mess but that's nothing unusual so it's hard to know if anything's missing. No, his laptop's still there. And there's only one other thing of value anyway. He rushes over to the bookcase and reaches behind the textbooks on the bottom shelf. He can't find it.

He pulls the books off the shelf. Then pulls everything off the other shelves too. He knows where he left it but . . . what if he forgot he'd moved it? Maybe it's a mistake. He pauses, looking around the room. He gets them out sometimes, to have a look at them. Maybe last time he put them back somewhere else. They have to be here. Somewhere!

He searches for forty-five minutes, turning the room upside down. There really aren't that many places to search, just the main room that functions as bedroom, living room and kitchen all in one, and the bathroom. He searches them both again. In the end, though, he has to accept it. The empty cigarette packet is gone, and so are the three coins that he'd hidden inside it.

It's only then, as he sits down on the floor and buries his head in his hands, that the thought comes to him. Whoever took them, knew exactly what they were looking for . . .

Mina presses cancel on her mobile as Tyler gets back from the interview room. 'How did it go with Halbert?' she asks him.

'He's clammed up. He's admitted to being part of this detectorists' club, and that he knows both Carver and Jayashankar. There are numerous calls to both of them logged on his mobile, but nothing in the past couple of days.'

'That makes sense,' Mina says. 'We know Carver's ditched his mobile or we'd have him by now.'

'He's not admitting to anything about the coins either. He's clearly lying but we don't have enough to arrest him. He's started making noises about the fact we can't keep questioning him so I'm letting him have a breather and then Daley's going to have another crack at him before we let him go.'

'Are you sure he can handle it?'

'Who knows? But I'm not getting anywhere so it's worth a try. What's going on with him anyway?'

'I'm not sure. I asked Emma about it and . . .' She sees him frowning. 'Dr Ridgeway? I managed to catch her before the meeting this morning. I didn't mention Daley by name but I described what he's like. Changeable, moody, irritable. The way he fades in and out like that? She did that doctor thing, hedged her bets, wouldn't diagnose on the basis of a description et cetera, et cetera, but one of the things she mentioned was post-traumatic stress disorder. Do you think this is about what happened last year? His injury?'

Tyler reaches up and touches the burned skin on the back of his neck. She's not even sure he's aware of it. 'We should tell Jordan,' he says.

'Let me talk to him first, Sarge. Maybe I can convince him to speak to someone.'

He seems to consider it but doesn't give her a firm answer before changing the subject. 'Any sign of Chi's body?'

'The last footage we have of the Volvo is on the Parkway yesterday evening. After that, no sign. Uniform are looking at more road traffic cameras but nothing so far.'

'He might still be in the area then?'

Mina nods. 'The ex-wife couldn't think of anywhere.'

Tyler taps the photo he took from Carver's house, now pinned up on the incident board. 'At least we have a good idea who this is.'

'Yeah, Lizzie Gordon's story checked out. Rachel Carver. Only child. She died in the Children's Hospital six years ago after a long battle with leukaemia.'

'A hard thing to go through. The final straw, maybe. He'll go back for this eventually. We need to keep eyes on his flat.'

The two of them stand staring at the board for a few moments.

'Stevens is going to crucify us over this, isn't he?' Mina asks.

'Not until tomorrow, at least.' Tyler smiles. 'I just heard

from Diane, the plane's been delayed. A woman took ill on the flight so they had to divert.'

'Well that's one piece of good news.'

'Not for the woman on the plane, she died. But it means they're being held in Dubai for a few hours. Stevens and his entourage are staying in Manchester tonight so they can meet the plane first thing in the morning. We've got a short reprieve.'

'I might be able to add to that,' Mina says. 'I'm not sure it helps us find Carver but it might be significant.'

'Go on.'

'The orchid we found in Carver's place. It's very rare, apparently. One of the volunteers at the Gardens identified it and the DCI put me on to a contact she has in Defra – the Department for Environment, Food and Rural Aff—'

'Yes, thank you, I know what it is.'

'Anyway, that was him on the phone just then. I think we need to speak to Calderdale again. I think Chi's PhD might have been a cover for something.'

Tyler scuffs at the concrete floor with his shoe, breaking down the clump of soil at his feet and grinding it into smaller and smaller pieces.

Rabbani looks equally irritated, not least because she's taking the brunt of the lead volunteer's discomfort. She's a nervous, twittering woman Rabbani introduced as Chloe, who has picked up on their frustrations and is somehow managing to magnify them and reflect them back.

The greenhouse is busy with volunteers, though the volunteers themselves do not appear all that busy. They gather in small groups and discuss the Gardens in hushed whispers – who's planting the Mediterranean Garden without permission, why Gareth can't be trusted with the alyssums, whether or not the funding will come through for the pond. The one thing they do not discuss is the presence of the police. He and Rabbani are the elephant in the room. Or the body in the flowerbed.

Tyler interrupts Chloe as she launches into a new monologue extolling the virtues of the man they're waiting for, and suggests to her that they relocate somewhere quieter. But rather than offer an alternate location she begins harrying the volunteers out of the glasshouse and on with their jobs. They go reluctantly and slowly but they do at least go.

There are four long tables running the length of the greenhouse. Tyler knows, thanks to Chloe, that, although they are currently bare, come Saturday they'll be covered in a cornucopia of bedding plants and cuttings for sale to the public. When they first arrived, she'd told them she had high hopes for this month's sale, given the interest being paid to the Gardens since the grim discovery last week.

He sits down at the end of the second table and Rabbani joins him. As Chloe sees out the last of the gardeners, a quiet descends on them, enough to make out the birdsong that is the constant backdrop to the Gardens.

'Perhaps we should make a start?' he suggests.

Chloe takes the seat next to Rabbani, and Tyler begins.

'Mina tells me that you don't think the orchid we found comes from the Gardens.'

'It's not our sort of thing, at all. We've never really done all that well with them given the climate, and we only have limited greenhouse space. It's so incredibly rare, as well. If what Detective Rabbani says is true. No, we've never had anything along those lines.'

'Could Chi have found it somewhere though?' Rabbani asks. 'You told me yourself that some of the seeds you get are mixed up, or get misidentified. Mislabelled.'

Chloe thinks about this. 'I suppose it's possible. But we've never had anything like that. It's such a rarity . . .' And she's off again, falling over herself to apologise for not being more help.

Tyler sighs and notices Rabbani's face twitching with equal irritation. It makes him smile and lightens his own mood considerably.

Chloe breaks off in mid-ramble and declares, 'Oh, here he is!' She jumps out of her seat and rushes to meet the latecomer.

Professor Calderdale arrives unhurriedly and makes no attempt to apologise for being half an hour late. 'You've started without me,' he says with a hint of passive-aggressiveness that sends Chloe into another round of apology and explanation.

'Please sit down, Professor,' Tyler tells the man, and the red-headed giant pulls out the chair opposite Chloe's, spins it 180 degrees and sits with his arms along the backrest.

'What's this all about then? You made it sound urgent. I've had to find cover for my afternoon lectures.'

'It's about your ex-student,' Tyler counters. 'The dead one we found in the flowerbed over there.'

Chloe gasps but Tyler's not interested in her reaction; he keeps his eyes fixed on Calderdale.

'Poor Chi. I still can't believe it.'

Chloe begins another volley of apologies and 'how-awful-for-you's', but rather than wait for her to die down Tyler speaks right over her. 'We've come into possession of a rare orchid that we have reason to believe may have been stolen from the Gardens. We were wondering if you knew anything about it.'

Rabbani shows him the picture of the plant on her phone.

Calderdale feigns some surprise but isn't very convincing. 'Goodness. That's . . . some orchid.'

'You know of it then?'

'I *am* a professor of Botany, Detective Sergeant.' He makes a show of looking at the photo again. '*Phragmipedium kovachii*? Native to the Andean cloud forests of northern Peru. I'd need to examine the stem to be certain but it certainly looks the part. It was only identified for the first time about fifteen years ago. Very rare, critically endangered. Wherever did you find it?'

'In the possession of a suspect who seems to have had a close connection with Chi. A man named Dave Carver.'

'I can't say I recognise the name.'

'Carver worked as a cleaner at the university until a few

months ago. In your department, in fact. He was fired, or let go, not long before Chi went missing.'

'The university has a lot of cleaners. I have to confess I can't say I know very many of them.'

'You told us Chi's work involved orchids,' Tyler continues. 'Perhaps you could tell us about her thesis and why she was working here, specifically. I understand you got her the job?'

'I was telling them, Robert, how we have a lot of your students helping out—'

'I'd appreciate it, Chloe, if you could allow Professor Calderdale to answer please?'

Chloe falls silent and looks down at the table top.

Calderdale crosses his arms. 'Chi's thesis concerned morphology. She was revisiting certain taxonomic groups from a molecular genetics angle. After your last visit I dug out the relevant file. I can send it to you, if you wish? I'm not sure how much sense it will make to the layman. But orchids were only a part of her research. Her wider thesis—'

'Her father sells orchids though,' Rabbani interrupts. 'In his nursery in China.'

'You'd need to ask him about that.'

'But you do know him, don't you, Professor?' Rabbani looks down at her notes. 'In his capacity as the Head of the Chinese Academy of Science Institute in Kunming? You were at the same conference together in 2010. And again in 2014. I reckon you must have had a number of dealings with the man, on a professional level, over the years?'

Calderdale remains impassive. 'I have, Detective. I'm not sure what you're trying to imply by that.'

'We're not trying to *imply* anything, sir,' Rabbani says. 'But we're imagining a few things. For example, we *imagined* that while she was working here in the Gardens, Chi discovered a rare plant no one knew about. Maybe she thought it would make a nice present for her dad and decided to snatch it and pop it in the post to him. From what I know about these plants – and I have to confess here, I'm only speaking as a layman – I've heard these orchids are pretty hardy things. So maybe she could have wrapped it up and popped it in the post. Risky, maybe, but not every package gets scanned by Customs. On the other hand, this is a very, *very* rare plant, isn't it? Maybe the only one of its kind. To someone who has the necessary expertise to propagate it – I believe that's the term – it could be worth a lot of money. Even the smallest chance of it being lost or intercepted by Customs and Excise might put her off that idea. So we're *imagining* she might have got some help. From a trusted mentor and friend, perhaps. Someone who knew her father. Someone who could have arranged for the plant to be sent overseas through more official channels, with the necessary clearance to sign the relevant documentation. I believe it's called a CITES permit, is that right? You have that clearance, don't you, Professor?'

'I do.'

'So that got us imagining some other things. Maybe this wasn't the first time she'd done this. Maybe it wasn't a coincidence she got the job here in the first place. *Maybe* it's not even a coincidence that Chi ended up studying at a university under a professor who has a long-standing acquaintance with her father.'

'They do say it's good to have an active imagination.' Calderdale stands up. 'But since, by your own admission, you can't even link this mysterious orchid with Chi, let alone me, I would suggest you keep your imaginative hypotheses to yourselves. Now, I need to be getting back to my lectures.' He turns to Chloe. 'I'm sorry you've been dragged into this, Chloe. I'm appalled the police are allowed to operate in this manner and I'm certain the university lawyers will be interested in making something of this. I'm sorry if this has caused you any embarrassment.'

Chloe begins apologising all over again but this time there's something less heartfelt about it. They've given her food for thought, if nothing else. Calderdale storms out and Chloe chases after him.

'He's right,' Tyler tells Rabbani. 'We don't have anything except conjecture. I was hoping we might rattle him a bit and he'd let something slip, but he's too good for that. Too well protected, I imagine. He doesn't seem in the least bit worried about us finding out the truth.'

'Do you think he was involved?'

'With plant smuggling? Your friend in Defra seems to think so and that's good enough for me. You'd better let him know what happened here, by the way. If Calderdale begins covering his tracks, it might give them something they can use.'

'What about Chi?'

'That's another matter, isn't it? Let's assume she was smuggling plants out of the country. What reason would Calderdale have to kill her?'

'Maybe they fell out? She decided she didn't want to be involved anymore, was going to tell someone.'

'How did Carver end up with the orchid then? And where do the Roman coins fit in?'

'I don't know,' says Rabbani.

'I'm not saying you're wrong but I can't see how it all connects up. Too many maybes. I'll take a closer look at Calderdale. See what else I can find out. In the meantime, you need to track down Carver and find that body. Maybe he can tell us what Calderdale's involvement is.'

'What if we can't find her?' Rabbani asks.

Tyler looks at his watch. 'We still have a few hours. It's going to be a long night though. You'd better wear something warm.'

'Carver's flat?'

'You and Daley, I'm afraid; I've got something else on. You'll want to pick up that orchid too. It's material evidence now and if it's worth as much as you say it is, we'd best not leave it lying around.' He stands up. 'At least the parents' arrival tomorrow gives us one opportunity.'

'Sarge?'

'What better way to find out if Chi was smuggling plants to her father than to ask him.'

Rabbani closes her eyes. 'Stevens'll shit bricks.'

'As someone recently said to me, might as well be hanged for a sheep as a lamb.'

'Eh?'

'Never mind.'

Now the clocks have gone back and the nights are drawing in, it's nicely dark by five, but it's still a bit early for what Dave has planned; there are too many students still milling around. It's a risk. But a calculated one this time, and no more of one than he's already taken. There's a small chance Calderdale might have knocked off early but, whatever else might be said about the man, he was always a hard worker, staying in the office until nine, ten o'clock some nights. Doubtful he's changed his habits in the past few months, but in the worst-case scenario, at least Dave will have a roof over his head until morning, somewhere the police are unlikely to look. Dave can wait. He's good at waiting.

He crosses the car park at the base of the Arts Tower, the wind battering at his overcoat and swirling eddies of litter and leaves around his feet. It's now that he's most vulnerable. People here might recognise him, there are security cameras, but again he's not enormously worried. He doesn't seem to worry much about anything anymore. When the worst thing that can happen to you has already happened, what is there left to be afraid of?

Dave holds his old pass against the pad on the door to the Controlled Environment Facility and is only mildly surprised when the light turns green and the door buzzes giving him permission to enter. Security's always lax in big organisations. Databases take time to update, people forget things. Case in point, *he'd* forgotten he still had this pass tucked away in his wallet. But if it hadn't worked he could have broken through the fire exit at the back. It would have been noisier and riskier though. He presses the button that calls the lift and waits.

He never liked Calderdale. He's one of those men who don't even see the menial staff. The cleaners and night watchmen, the cooks and secretaries and drivers who actually enable the university to function. A surprising number of the professors weren't like that, taking the effort to greet you when you walked by. But not Calderdale, always nose-deep in his work.

The lift arrives and Dave gets in. There are Tensa-tapes that can be pulled across the entrance, to be employed when the lifts are used to transport hazardous substances. There are a lot of hazardous materials in this building. Dry ice, for example, which were it to be exposed in the confined space of the elevator would instantly suck the oxygen out of the air, killing the passengers. The lift descends two storeys and opens onto a long featureless corridor that always reminds Dave of those *Doctor Who* episodes of his childhood. A Dalek might come careening around the corner to exterminate him at any moment. But tonight, the only danger here is Dave. *He* is the hazardous substance.

When he arrives at the appropriate lab his feet stick to the tacky white paper laid into the floor in the doorway. It's there to keep things in and to keep things out. There are pathogens kept in this lab. Genetically modified seeds, vulnerable plants and organisms. But it's not enough to keep him out.

Dave knew who she was before he saw her. He always did. It was that infectious laugh that so often preceded her. He looked up from the rubbish bin he was emptying to see Chi bounce into the laboratory with that embarrassed smile on her lips, those childlike dimples in her cheeks.

Calderdale looked up from the bench where he was working. 'There you are. I thought I was going to have to send out a search party.'

She saw Dave in the corner of the room, smiled coyly, and sent him a small, shy wave. He found himself beaming across at her. Whenever they bumped into each other like this, in the environs of the university, they didn't acknowledge their friendship openly. For his part he didn't want to embarrass her. He felt that her colleagues and fellow students might consider the age gap between them untoward in some way, even though their relationship was platonic. It was strange that when they were in the more romantic, public environment of the Botanical Gardens, he didn't feel the same way.

Calderdale told Chi to sit, rather sharply, Dave thought, and they began to discuss her dissertation. Dave went back to work.

It was only gradually he became aware of the atmosphere in the room. He looked up and began to focus on their conversation. *Failing. Unlikely to pass unless you begin to put a lot more work in. I don't care who your father is.* Chi was crying, drops of salty water, too big for her diminutive face, sliding down her cheeks to hang from her jaw. If anything, this seemed to infuriate Calderdale further.

'Turning on the waterworks isn't going to help. I suggest you think again about what you do and don't want to be involved in. Do you think your father's going to be impressed you've changed your mind? Eh?'

Chi shook her head.

'There's no need to talk to her like that.' Dave couldn't help himself. The words were out of his mouth before he even thought about the ramifications.

Calderdale blinked at him, as though registering his presence for the first time. 'This has nothing to do with you. Get the fuck out of my lab, man, before I fire you!'

He couldn't afford to lose another job. But still, it wasn't right. 'It doesn't matter who you are, you don't have a right to talk to people like that.'

'Please,' Chi said, her cheeks glistening with tears. 'It's okay.' *Just go,* she mouthed to him.

So Dave packed up his trolley and wheeled it out of the lab. He glanced back once to see Chi with her head down, nodding demurely. Agreeing to whatever it was Calderdale was asking her to do.

The following week, back in the Gardens, he could see she was still upset. He tried to make her talk about it but she wouldn't. What was Calderdale making her do?

To change the subject he told her about the coins. It was stupid really, and it broke his promise to the others, but he wanted to cheer her up. He'd taken to carrying one of them round with him and he slipped it out of his wallet now and showed it to her. Her eyes grew wider as he told her the story of the Roman find, even admitting to her the dubious legality of their treasure trove, and their dilemma as to what to do with it.

'I might be able to help,' she said. She knew someone who might want to buy them, quietly, without any attention. She could speak to the man in question for him, if he wanted? She wouldn't tell him the man's name but that should assure him that she wouldn't divulge his name to the man in question either.

He felt a bit guilty that he hadn't run it past the others first but when he told them later they agreed readily enough. Over the next couple of weeks, as they met to solidify the details of the deal, he felt the bond between the two of them strengthening in conspiracy. And it obviously wasn't just on his part because the last time he met her there, a few days before the date they'd agreed for the exchange, she seemed closer to him than ever.

She clutched his arm at one point and laid her head on his shoulder. Dave's face grew heated and it was the first time he was conscious that someone else might see them. Might think their relationship was ... something sordid.

'What's wrong?' he asked, noticing her eyes were wet and glistening.

'Nothing,' she said, pulling away from him and wiping her face. 'I . . . I'll miss this.'

'Are you going somewhere?'

He saw her pull herself back together. She laughed. 'No, I mean . . . when I graduate.' She smiled at him and then he saw an idea come to her. 'Wait here,' she said, and hopped up from the bench.

And as he waited there, the spring sun shining down on him, the birds singing, he felt somehow that all their problems were about to be solved. He hadn't mentioned to her that he'd lost his job. It seemed Calderdale paid more attention to the little people than Dave gave him credit for. They'd let him go the very next day. Resource allocation, they said, but he knew the real reason. Calderdale had spoken to someone.

Then she was back, a plastic bag clutched in her hand. 'For you,' she said.

'No, I can't take—'

'Please. I want you to have it!' She seemed almost desperate. 'It was to be a gift for my father but . . . I want you to have it. To remember me.'

'I'm hardly likely to forget you.' He took the bag from her and opened it to find a plant cutting of some kind. He was about to pull out the cutting – an orchid, was it? – when she closed her hand on his.

'No,' she said. 'Don't show anyone. Our secret.' She put her delicate finger to her lips and shushed him. Then she giggled.

'Thank you,' he said. 'I'll treasure it.'

He reached into his inside jacket pocket and pulled out his knife. It was the last one he had left, but he didn't hesitate; a gift received meant a gift given in return. 'Here,' he said.

She took it cautiously, her fingers caressing the intricately carved handle.

'I made it,' he told her, and felt guilty for being boastful.

She flicked open the blade and ran a finger along the polished silver steel.

'Careful,' he said, closing it into her hand. 'And maybe don't flash it around in public too much. Keep it at home, yes?'

'It's beautiful,' she said. And then, all at once, she was crying and running away from him.

'Chi? Chi!' He tried to go after her but she was much too fast for him.

He didn't know then, but it would be the last time he saw her alive. He thought, just as she pulled away from him, he might have heard her say she was sorry. But he couldn't be sure, and he decided he must have misheard her. After all, what could she possibly have had to be sorry about?

He's been thinking about that last meeting a lot recently. He should have known something was wrong. Was Chi scared that day? Did she know something was going to happen to her? If so, Dave can only think of one man who might be responsible. And as though the thought has summoned him, Calderdale appears around a corner, his white lab coat flapping open round his legs.

He's a big man but Dave doesn't consider this. He lashes out with a tight fist that catches Calderdale right on the nose. The professor spins away with a sharp cry, and Dave uses the momentum to push the man forward, through the open door of one of the controlled environment capsules, his fists raining blows on him the whole time. Calderdale loses his footing and goes face down into a tray of green stems. Above them, the heat of an African sun burns down from a hundred tiny lights set into the ceiling. A fan intermittently pumps moisture into the atmosphere in short bursts.

Calderdale lies prone on the ground, groaning and holding his nose. There are traces of blood visible between his fingers. 'Wha . . . what do you . . . ?' he stammers, the words distorted by what may well be a broken nose.

'I want you to tell me what you did to her. To Chi.'

'What?' Calderdale focuses on Dave's face. 'You! But I . . . You don't work here anymore.' His voice is confused, desperate. 'I'll . . . I'll have you arrested.' Calderdale tries to get back on his feet but Dave pushes him back down.

He picks up a discarded trowel. 'No,' he says. 'You're going to tell me what happened to her. What you did to her.'

He turns and pulls the door of the capsule closed, in case there's anyone else working nearby. Someone who might hear the screams.

Tyler knows something's wrong as soon as he gets back to the apartment but he can't quite put his finger on it.

'Callum?'

He moves into the kitchen and puts the six-pack of lager down on the breakfast bar. There's no sign of him. No, that's not precisely true. The blanket's tossed on the floor next to the sofa, the plate of crumbs from this morning's breakfast is still on the coffee table. But Callum himself is gone, and so is his stuff. The spare key is on the windowsill with a message scribbled on the back of a supermarket receipt:

thanks mate this not good thogh
see you out their

Tyler wonders if this is what he noticed when he first walked into the apartment. This absence of human habitation. He's never been the type to get lonely but he has to admit this feels ... odd. Different. Maybe it's the finality of the end of his relationship with Paul, not having someone to ring and talk to about things. Although, now he thinks about it, that wasn't something he did very often. But maybe he'd got more used to having someone there than he realised.

He runs a finger over the cardboard container of the six-pack. He has to admit he was actually looking forward to talking to someone, even if that someone was only Callum, and the talk would have consisted of several rounds of badgering the lad into looking for work – he'd rung the job centre earlier, to check if Callum had made it to his appointment; he hadn't.

But now Callum's gone. And Paul's gone, and it's back to business as usual.

He cooks himself some pasta and settles down to his other task for the evening – researching Calderdale.

The professor's a busy man. Aside from his various academic achievements, a brief internet search brings up photos of Calderdale at various civic events, pressing the flesh with the movers and shakers of Sheffield commerce and industry. There's even one photo of him standing a few feet away from Superintendent Stevens, but that's probably not all that surprising. The Eel would turn up to the opening of an envelope if there was a free meal in the offing.

He finds the same connections Rabbani mentioned in the interview, the conferences in Sweden and Luxembourg attended by Chi's father, but it's easy enough to link him to any number of people, all around the globe; there are pictures in Texas, Oman, Vietnam ... and that's just on his Facebook page. If he's up to something, he certainly isn't trying to hide it.

And then he sees a picture that changes everything. A series of pictures, taken at an event held at the Cutlers' Hall. The room's crowded with guests but in the foreground of the picture Calderdale's smiling his lazy smile, his expansive arm wrapped around the shoulders of the mayor. But it isn't the subjects of the photo that interest Tyler so much as the figures in the background. He isn't sure at first, but he searches for more pictures and eventually finds one that shows the man's face in its entirety. Joey McKenna, large as life and equally as smug, hobnobbing with the great and the good.

What is it about seeing McKenna and Calderdale in the

photo that bothers him? McKenna's legit now, at least as far as his public image is concerned, and he probably has connections with any number of prominent local dignitaries. The two of them aren't even talking to each other in the photo and, though he looks on for another half-hour, Tyler can't find another image that puts them closer than a couple of metres apart. But it bothers him, nevertheless.

Calderdale was connected to Chi and now, based on these photographs, McKenna has at least some tacit connection with Calderdale. Could that imply a connection between Joey McKenna and Chi as well? Tyler begins to think about timing, and the nature of coincidence. He hears Callum Morgan saying, 'You stalkin' me or summat?' and reflects on the fact that could be applied the other way around. Didn't McKenna turn up a little too quickly when his daughter texted him? Almost as though he was waiting for that text. If McKenna was involved in Chi's death somehow, then his remarkably timely appearance and his promise to deliver Tyler the answers he's been looking for take on a new light.

His first encounter with Callum, outside the restaurant, could only have been chance, couldn't it? But what about after that? What if Callum isn't as destitute – or as removed from the family business – as McKenna made out? Callum goes to his granddad and tells him about his close encounter with a nosey detective. Tyler had even given the lad his card. It wouldn't have been hard for McKenna to research him. Then Callum turns up again outside the station, with a sob story about his troubled home-life, and Tyler rushes off on his white steed. Is he that predictable? Or maybe that just made it easier for McKenna. If he hadn't taken the bait, they'd have engineered a meeting some other way.

And then they both approach him at the Deer, Callum all bloody and beaten – that was a dark thought – McKenna asking a small favour, and promising the moon on a stick in return, the one thing Tyler wants more than anything: the truth about his father's death. McKenna could have made up all that stuff about Richard.

All for what? To get Callum inside the investigation and see what Tyler knew, how close he was getting. But surely they didn't think Tyler would keep sensitive information about the case at home?

Tyler shivers, his skin prickling with goose bumps. That's exactly what he's been doing. Not anything relevant to Chi's case, but maybe *this* case isn't the one they're interested in. Or not the only one anyway.

He grabs the key to the spare room from his laptop bag and heads out into the hallway.

As soon as he opens the door to the spare room he knows he's right. The box files are still stacked under the trestle table where he left them but they could easily have been searched and put back. They've had all day, after all. The door was locked but he doubts that would cause any real trouble to someone in McKenna's employ. Assuming Callum didn't have the skills, he would have just got someone else in to help.

And he knows now that that's what happened. Because

there's one distinctive difference to the room. The same thing he noticed when he first walked into the apartment but was unable to put his finger on. It's stronger in here, in this air-locked, preserved environment.

The entire room hangs heavy with the sickly sweet scent of orange-blossom cologne.

On Tuesday morning Mina and Tyler sit side by side at the conference table. Mina can feel Tyler's foot going up and down under the table and she's glad he's as nervous as she is, even if he's hiding it better.

After Uniform took over at Carver's place this morning, she'd just about had time to rush home and shower before racing back for this meeting. She'd kill for even half an hour of proper sleep. Spending the night in a car with Daley had been everything she'd thought it would be. When he wasn't ladding it up or making suggestive comments, he was playing games with irritating noises on his mobile. At one point she'd tried to talk to him about what happened at the bubble-tea place but he wasn't having any of it. He was the cocky, self-assured dickhead he always used to be and, although on the one hand that was somewhat reassuring, on the other, that was the very last version of Daley she wanted to be trapped in a car with.

Through the glass partition they see Stevens arriving with Mr and Mrs Li. They appear younger than Mina imagined, even through their grief. Stevens introduces them to the DCI and Jordan shakes each of their hands; Mina can almost read the sorry-for-your-loss speech on her lips. Then she's gesturing to the boardroom and is presumably outlining Tyler's request to speak to them. Contrary to what they'd expected, Stevens' eyes light up at this. He seems pretty happy about the whole idea. That can't be good.

The Lis have to walk through the Murder Room to reach the conference suite, and Mina and Guy have spent the last half-hour taking down pictures of the couple's dead daughter. She hopes they didn't miss anything. There's not a single sound coming from the office now, a stark contrast to the normal frenzy of the place.

Jordan introduces them. Stevens closes the door and the blinds as well. They all take seats round the conference table and, just as he did before, Stevens places his hat on the table and adjusts it until he's sure it's straight.

'These are the lead detectives working your daughter's case,' he tells the Lis, his eyes fixed on Tyler.

Jordan jumps in at that. 'I'm the Senior Investigating Officer,' she says, as though she isn't correcting her superior. 'Detectives Tyler and Rabbani work under my supervision.'

Stevens smiles without humour.

'Please,' Mr Li says in a quiet, gentle voice. 'We do not understand. You say she is missing, Qiang? But, we thought you had found her?'

'It's complicated,' Jordan says.

'Perhaps DS Tyler might explain?' Stevens suggests.

'Yes,' says Tyler. 'Mr and Mrs Li.' He turns to face them directly and they both look at him, ready for answers he doesn't have. It's the first time Mrs Li has looked at anything other than the floor or the table. 'Your daughter's body was found buried in the Botanical Gardens just over a week ago. An autopsy was carried out. She had been stabbed and fell from a significant height but we don't believe she suffered.'

Mina doesn't remember Emma saying any such thing but she's not about to contradict him.

'She was buried in a shallow grave. It's our belief that this all happened on the day she disappeared.'

He's trying to minimise their suffering, Mina realises. If Chi died the day she disappeared, there's nothing her parents could have done differently. Of course, that lets them off the hook too. They can't be held responsible for not finding her. The Lis don't seem to care either way, they just want answers.

'Two nights ago,' Tyler says, 'Qiang's body was stolen from our morgue.'

Mrs Li gasps and places her hands over her mouth.

'We believe the man who took her body is the same man who buried her.'

Surprisingly, Mrs Li recovers first. 'This man . . . he is the one who killed our daughter?'

Tyler glances at Jordan before he goes on. 'We believe that's the most likely scenario, although, as I said, we don't know for sure what happened.'

Mr Li is shaking his head. 'But how do you know this? How do you know this is our Qiang? This could be any girl, you find!'

'I'm afraid there's no doubt,' Jordan says. 'We have DNA on file from Chi . . . from Qiang's belongings.'

'This could be mistake!'

'There's no mistake, Mr Li. I'm sorry.'

The man continues to shake his head but says nothing more.

Tyler clears his throat and Mina knows what he's about to say. *Here we go!*

'Mr Li, it would be helpful if we could ask you a few questions about your daughter. We understand Chi's PhD thesis involved plants. You work with plants too, is that right?'

'Tyler,' Stevens says, his voice dripping with warning.

Jordan adds, 'Adam, this isn't the time.'

But Mrs Li raises a thin, crooked hand. 'We will answer your questions, if it will help.'

'It will help,' Tyler tells her. 'We need to find out as much as possible about Chi and her life here.'

Mrs Li smiles for the first time. 'You all call her Chi? Her friends call her this too. She has many friends.'

Tyler smiles back and turns to Mr Li. 'Chi worked in the Botanical Gardens where her body was found, and we have reason to believe that before her death she was in possession of a very rare orchid. It's possible she intended to send it to you. You run a nursery in Kunming, is that right?'

For Tyler, it's a very rare attempt at diplomacy – 'in possession of', rather than 'stole'. But the inference is there.

Stevens interrupts. 'What is all this, Tyler?'

Tyler pushes on. 'Mr Li, is this something your daughter

might have been involved in? Might she have taken this plant for you?'

Li begins talking in Mandarin. Mrs Li snaps back. The sentiment behind the words is clear. She's telling him off, sharply.

'We're looking into the possibility that the theft of this plant may have had something to do with Chi's death. If you know something, now's the time to tell us.'

Again Mrs Li begins talking, but this time Mr Li holds up a hand and she stops.

'My daughter,' he says, 'she was good girl. Not thief.'

'No one's suggesting—' Stevens begins, but Tyler interrupts him.

'We believe Chi was taking plants from the Gardens, rare specimens that she was sending home to you with the help of Robert Calderdale.'

Stevens stands up. 'DS Tyler, that is enough! I apologise, sir.'

But Li's looking at Tyler. 'You say this has something to do with him? Calderdale. He did this to my daughter?'

Tyler hesitates. 'It's possible he was involved.' He's pushing it now.

Li looks properly shaken for the first time. 'I do not think . . . I . . . No. This cannot be.' He gets up.

Stevens escorts him from the room, ushering further apologies and explanations all the way.

Mrs Li starts after them but stops and turns back to face Tyler. 'Please,' she says, her eyes flicking to Mina. 'Please find her.'

Mina can't speak but Tyler says, 'We will.'

Jordan escorts her out and they watch from the boardroom as Stevens begins one final angry exchange with Jordan before they leave.

'Uh-oh,' says Mina.

'Yes,' Tyler says. 'I think that covers it. Come on, there's somewhere we need to be.'

Juju looks even more tired than the last time Tyler saw her. She has hooded eyes and a small lick of hair standing out at right-angles from her head. Her clothes are rumpled and thrown on, a grey sweatshirt with wet patches on her left shoulder where the baby's been sick. She opens the door and then simply turns and walks back into the kitchen.

They follow her in. The kitchen's a mess of baby toys, leftover food and unwashed dishes, but someone's obviously in the process of trying to do something about it. There are bottles of antibacterial spray and oven cleaner on the dining table, and two cupboard doors stand open displaying the disorganised chaos inside. Juju goes back to the sink and begins to scrub the remnants of crusted food from a plate.

'I'm sorry if this is a bad time,' Tyler tells her, failing to hide his own tiredness and irritability.

'When *is* a good time?' Still she carries on cleaning.

'Could you just stop that for a moment?' He doesn't mean to snap but she does at least stop, although she fails to turn round.

Rabbani touches her on the arm. 'Why don't you come

and sit down, eh? I'll put the kettle on.' She ushers the woman across to the dining table and Tyler passes her a tea-towel he finds draped over the back of a wooden chair. Juju wipes her hands and sits down with the linen cloth still clutched between her fists. Tyler takes the seat opposite and Rabbani fills the kettle.

'I'm sorry,' Juju says. 'It's just . . . my parents are coming.'

'You haven't seen them for a while?'

'Not since . . .' She doesn't need to finish. Not since her sister went missing.

'Is your little girl all right?' Rabbani asks.

'Sleeping. For once.' And Juju manages a short smile that dissipates as soon as it forms.

'And Ben?' he asks.

She flinches. 'At work, I think.'

Tyler exchanges a look with Rabbani. It was Ben they'd been hoping to speak to.

Juju picks up on it. 'Whatever it is you need, I can help you.'

Rabbani looks to him for permission and Tyler nods.

'We think Chi was involved in something,' she says. 'We think she may have been stealing plants from the Gardens and selling them using her contacts at the university.'

Juju says nothing but it's clear this isn't new information.

'We also believe your father was involved,' Tyler adds.

Juju clutches at the tea towel. 'I don't know the details, but she wasn't doing it for the money. Our father paid for everything.'

Tyler notices her use of the past tense. *Paid* for everything. Meaning, he no longer does? 'I guess that makes him a hard man to say no to.'

'If he asked her to do this, she would do it. Out of duty.'

'We thought Ben might know something,' Rabbani prompts. 'They were pretty close at one point, weren't they?'

Juju flinches again at the mention of her boyfriend. She's clearly on edge about something.

'Where is Ben?' he asks.

'I don't know.' She starts to add something, stops herself, and then, as though utterly defeated, goes on. 'He didn't come home last night.'

'Is he seeing someone else?' Rabbani asks. Tyler hadn't thought of that.

Juju fails to take umbrage at the question. 'Maybe. I don't know. He isn't around much but I don't know if there's anyone else. Maybe he just doesn't want to be here. He says he feels trapped. By the baby. This isn't what he wanted. It isn't what I wanted either. He forgets that bit.'

'The day Chi went missing,' Rabbani goes on. 'You said you argued. Was it because of Ben?'

Two tears roll down Juju's cheeks in perfect symmetry.

'Was she still sleeping with him?'

She wipes her face with her sleeve. 'No, it wasn't like that. She didn't want him.'

'But he still wanted her?'

She doesn't answer, which is answer enough.

'After she left that day,' Tyler asks, 'did Ben go after Chi?'

'I don't . . . No, of course not.' She glances up at the ceiling, presumably to where the baby's sleeping.

There's a noise in the yard and then the back door opens and Ben Robbins walks in. 'Oh,' he says, stopping in the doorway. 'What's going on?'

Juju bursts into tears, scrapes back her chair and runs into his arms.

'Hey, hey, what's happened?' He wraps his arms round her and she cries on his shoulder, while he rubs her back. 'What the hell have you been saying?' he asks over her shoulder.

Tyler doesn't want to give them a chance to talk to each other. 'Mina, why don't you take Juju upstairs while I have a word with Ben?'

Robbins tries to object but Rabbani's already taken her cue and is prising the small woman from his arms.

'I just need a few words, Ben. You don't mind, do you?'

Robbins reluctantly lets go and the two women disappear up the stairs.

'Take a seat, Ben.' Tyler gestures to the dining chair recently vacated by Juju, as though this is an interview room at the station rather than their own kitchen. Robbins sits down.

'Juju said you didn't come home last night.'

'Oh, I had a lot of paperwork to catch up on. I ended up falling asleep at the shop.'

'At Cha Cha Cha? That can't have been comfortable.'

'Yeah, I have got a bit of a crick in my neck.' He adds

credence to this by working the left side of his neck with his hand.

Tyler changes the subject. 'When was it you broke up with Chi? Exactly.'

'We just sort of grew apart. We were never exclusive or anything.'

'Did you know she was stealing from the Gardens?'

Robbins' eyes flick up to the ceiling. 'Did Juju tell you that? Yeah, we knew what she was up to. We tried to stop her but she wouldn't listen. She never listened to anyone, about anything.' He laughs. 'It's one of the things . . .' He stops but the words hang in the air. *One of the things I loved about her.*

'So it was never that serious between you, right?'

'Yeah. No. It wasn't.' His eyes go back to the ceiling and this time when he speaks, his voice is lower. 'I wanted it to be though. It was Chi who wanted to keep things casual. I know that makes me look bad. You're going to say I killed her because I was jealous or something, because I couldn't have her, right? But that's not what happens in real life, is it? People don't do shit like that. I just decided to keep my distance from her, that's all. I moped around for a bit and then I got on with my life.'

With her sister. Tyler says nothing.

'You don't believe me.'

'I think it would be easier to believe if you'd told this story to DI Cooper seven months ago. Or to us, the other day. What about the plant smuggling? You could have told us about that. Did you not think it might be relevant?'

'I dunno. We didn't know much about it but . . .' Robbins looks back at the doorway and his voice drops even lower. 'Ju doesn't have the best relationship with her family. They weren't exactly pleased when she told them she was pregnant, and us not being married or anything. They've stopped sending her an allowance and . . . well, it's not about the money but . . . that's why I came home, now. Today will be the first time I've even met them.'

'You knew her father was involved and you didn't want to make things worse between them.'

'Honestly, I didn't want anything to do with it. I told her to stop but, like I said, Chi never listened to anyone.'

Rabbani comes back into the room.

'What about the coins?' he asks.

'What coins?' Ben looks up. 'Wait, you mentioned that before, didn't you? Roman coins?'

It's a detail they've managed to keep away from the media up until now, thankfully. Robbins' confusion looks genuine enough.

'All right, Ben, we'll leave it there for now.' Tyler pushes his chair back and stands up.

Robbins stands too and glances at Rabbani.

'She's having a lie-down,' she tells him. 'She'll be all right.'

Robbins shows them out but before he can close the door, Tyler stops him with a hand on the glass panel. 'Do you know a man named Dave Carver?' he asks.

'What? No, I don't think so.' The answer comes too quickly.

Tyler lets go of the door. It closes in his face.

'I asked her about the guy Chi was seeing,' Rabbani says as they walk back down the ginnel. 'Cooper told me Juju said she'd seen him once.'

'And?'

'She couldn't remember much about him. But he was short, skinny. Darkish hair.'

'Not Ben, then. Unless she's deliberately trying to throw us off.'

'She could have been seeing both of them?'

They reach the end of the path. 'What now?' Rabbani asks.

'We're not finished here yet. But let's wait in the car for the moment.'

'Eh?'

'I thought we'd have another crack at Chi's parents, without the Eel breathing down our necks this time. And now we know where they're going to be today.'

Rabbani grins at him. 'You sure? The super won't be none too pleased if we upset them again.'

'Mina, when you're this far in the shit, there's really nothing to be gained by stopping digging.'

'You know what, Sarge?' Mina says with a smile. 'I think you've been hanging out with DI Doggett too much lately.'

'God help us all.'

They sit in the car and watch the house for a good couple of hours.

Mina struggles to keep her eyes open, and Tyler clicking

his fingernail against the window is having a strangely soporific effect on her. She knows he's frustrated. They still have so little to go on and he's taking it personally. He's taking risks, with both their careers. She's surprised they haven't already had another call from Jordan. Chuffin' hell, did the man know how to piss people off! They're one complaint away from the Eel pulling the plug on CCRU for good. He might have done it already and they just hadn't found out yet.

What then? Bounced back to Uniform? Or would Doggett take her on? She doubts it. But what other options were there? The old-boy network wasn't going to work for her.

'Here we go!' says Tyler.

A long dark car with diplomatic plates pulls up, and the driver hops out to hold the door for the Lis. Mr Li gets out first and looks up at the house in front of him as though this grubby terraced property represents all that's wrong with the decadent capitalist West. Mrs Li joins him and touches him lightly on the arm, breaking his reverie. The two of them walk towards the front door and then Juju appears at the end of the ginnel and beckons them round the back. They move reluctantly, as though this short tunnel between the houses might swallow them up for ever. The driver gets back into the car and pulls away.

'Are we going then?' she asks.

'Let's give them a few minutes to get settled. I'm guessing they've got a fair bit to talk about.'

They sit in silence for a few more minutes and then,

because she can't bear it any more, Mina asks, 'What do you think the coins are about?'

Tyler says nothing for a few moments but the tapping starts up again, so she knows he's thinking. Finally, he says, 'The metal detectorists. I think they found them somewhere.'

'But how does that involve Chi? You're not telling me she was into metal detecting?'

'What would you do if you found some Roman coins from antiquity? Assuming you knew they were worth a lot of money.'

'I'd hand them in to the authorities.'

Tyler huffs out a laugh. 'Let's assume you're less civic-minded than that.'

Mina thinks about it. 'I suppose I'd try and sell them.'

'Would you? How? You can't just take them down Cash Converters, or stick them on eBay.'

'Point taken. But I wouldn't take them to a Chinese Botany student.'

'Unless you already knew she was involved in something less than legitimate.' Tyler abruptly stops tapping. 'All right, let's go talk to the Lis again.'

They get out of the car and cross the road, retracing their steps of a couple of hours ago. When they get there, Tyler raps smartly on the back door and Robbins opens it.

'Just a couple more questions,' Tyler says, pushing his way back into the house without waiting for an invitation. Everyone's gathered there in the kitchen. No one's speaking though. They've clearly interrupted a tense moment.

'Mr Li,' Tyler says. 'Our conversation was interrupted earlier. I hoped you might have had time to think about what I asked you.'

'Have you found my daughter?'

Juju gasps and buries her face in her hands.

'I need to know what your daughter was doing. Was she stealing for you? Is that why she was here? I need to know who else was involved.'

'This is ridiculous. I don't have to answer these questions. I am a diplomat representing the People's Republic of China—'

'I thought you were a father, who wanted to find out what happened to his daughter.'

'How dare you? Do you have any idea what it is like to lose someone like this ... to not know what really happened to them?'

Tyler hesitates for a moment at that, but rallies soon enough. 'I don't want to have to arrest you, sir.'

'Please, stop,' Juju cries out and covers her ears.

'You cannot arrest me!'

'I can if I think you're obstructing my investigation.'

Mrs Li grabs her husband's arm and begins shouting at him in Mandarin. Li pulls his arm away and gets out his mobile. He makes a call, shouting at his wife the whole time. She gives as good as she gets. Li retreats into the living room and his wife follows. Juju runs after them both. Tyler tries to follow but Ben, who's been standing quietly by the door throughout the whole confrontation, steps in front of him. 'No,' he says.

Tyler stops.

'You're done. This is still my house, so unless you have a warrant or you really intend to arrest someone, I want you out. Now.'

Tyler holds the man's eye.

'Sarge,' Mina warns. Still he doesn't move. 'Sarge!'

'All right, Ben. We'll see ourselves out.'

They step back into the garden and Mina pulls the door closed behind them. 'That went well.'

Tyler kicks the garden wall and a loose brick tumbles out onto the path.

'Feel better?'

The door behind them opens again and Mrs Li steps out, pulling the door closed behind her.

'Please,' she says. 'One minute.' She holds her cardigan close around her. They wait for her to go on.

'He will not tell you but much of what you say is true. Qiang was always close to her father. Juju, she is more like her mother, yes? But all this business – the plants – it is not linked to Qiang ... to her death. You ask your questions like you think he is involved. He is not. He was in China with me.'

'We can't ignore the possibility the plant smuggling was a factor, Mrs Li. Chi was found in the Botanical Gardens, the place she was stealing from. We need to know who else was involved.'

Mrs Li hesitates, then says, 'Professor.'

'Professor Calderdale?'

'He organised transport. Papers.'

'What about a man named Dave Carver? Have you heard that name before?'

Mrs Li thinks for a moment. 'I do not know this man but there was someone else.'

Mina glances through the window to where Ben's hovering inside by the hall doorway and Mrs Li correctly guesses her thought.

'Not this boy,' she says, flicking her head back over her shoulder at her prospective son-in-law. 'Qiang told me about him too. How he liked both of them. This is why we do not approve. Juju only ever cared about her studies and now . . . *a baby!* All wasted on this *bèn dàn!*'

'Someone else then?' Mina asks, trying to get her back on track.

Mrs Li nods. 'She told me she loved him.'

'When was this?' Tyler asks softly.

'One week, maybe two before. We argued. She told me he had money. A big family. This would make her independent . . .' she trails off. 'We thought she had run off with him. That is why we asked for no fuss. My husband . . . he did not want your newspapers causing trouble. It is his position, you see?'

Could it have been Dave Carver? Nothing about that description fits what they know of him. 'Do you know his name?' Mina asks.

Mrs Li shakes her head. 'She knew him through the Professor.' She glances back at the door. 'Calderdale. He is

359

just one of them. They all work together. My husband gives them money for their city, they give him ... opportunities.'

'What sort of opportunities?'

There's a loud shout from inside and Mr Li comes racing towards the door.

Mrs Li reaches for the handle. 'Please,' she says as she opens the door, and her voice is almost drowned out by the shouting of her husband from within. 'Find her. Find my daughter.' It isn't a request. Then the door slams shut in their faces. Inside, Mr Li is shouting and his daughter's screaming back at him, tears streaming down her face. Mrs Li joins in and upstairs the baby starts to cry, her tiny voice cutting right across all the other noise, a third generation joining the family conversation. Mina catches a glimpse of Ben standing in the corner of the kitchen looking like a lost child himself. He clearly has no idea what's being said but he can guess as well as she can.

The noise of the argument follows them up the path and out to the front of the house.

'Should we do something, Sarge?'

'I think we've probably done enough.'

As they get into the car, Mina asks, 'What do you think she meant? All that about a group working together?'

'No idea,' he says. 'But I think we need to talk to Calderdale again.'

The black limo pulls up at the kerb, followed by a second car, a four-wheel-drive BMW. Half a dozen Chinese nationals in black suits spill out from the cars and rush towards the house.

A woman in a tight-fitting white blouse and pencil skirt steps out of the limo and heads straight for them. But Tyler's clearly in no mood for a diplomatic telling-off. He starts the engine and pulls away, leaving her standing in the road behind them talking into her mobile. Mina can guess who she's calling though, and she doubts it's the last they'll hear on the matter.

There's a different security guard on duty at the university, no sign of Mike Halbert. Rabbani manages to contact a secretary who tells them Calderdale hasn't been seen all morning but that he might have gone straight over to the Controlled Environment Facility. They wait in reception for someone to be found who can escort them to the relevant building. Tyler finds the delay unbearable. He keeps expecting his mobile to ring and for Jordan to tell him they're off the case.

Finally, a PhD student arrives and asks them to follow her. The building she leads them to is on the opposite side of the Arts Tower. It looks no bigger than a large shed, but once they're inside they enter a lift and descend into an underground laboratory stretching all the way back under the car park. It's a network of stark white corridors and air-locked doors designed to keep something in, or out, Tyler's not sure which.

The PhD student escorts them round the lab but there's no sign of Calderdale anywhere. 'Hang on a minute,' she says, and sits down at a desk to access a computer. After a few minutes of scrolling and clicking she says, 'That's weird.'

'What?'

'According to the log, Rob used his card to access the lab last night but he never left.'

'Is that unusual? Could someone else have opened the door for him?'

She concentrates on the screen. 'There wasn't anyone else here last night . . . no, wait! There was another entry at 17:05. It's a general access card. The cleaners use them. They left again at 18:22. Then nothing until this morning.'

'Could he have left with the cleaner?' Tyler asks.

'It's possible . . .' she says, trailing off.

'But not likely?'

The student looks up at Tyler and bites her lip. 'Rob's a bit of a stickler for the rules. This whole system was put in so he could keep an eye on who was coming and going. He likes to lead by example.'

'So he's not likely to break his own rule and forget to sign out.'

The student cocks her head to one side, allowing that this was the case.

Rabbani inches round the desk and whispers, 'Dave Carver worked as a cleaner at the university.'

Tyler looks round the room. 'What's in all these cabinets?'

'They're controlled environment rooms where we conduct experiments on plants. We can replicate any environment we want, from anywhere in the world. It's the biggest facility of its type in Europe.'

'Can we see inside them?'

She moves to the nearest door and opens it. The inside's dark and misty, the air thick with moisture. There are trays of green shoots lined up against one wall.

'We need to check them all,' he tells her.

They move along the row, one by one, and all of a sudden there's a sense of urgency to their movements. With each empty unit they speed up. When they get to the end of the first row they turn the corner to find more units running down both sides of the corridor. 'Mina, you take the right-hand side.'

'Some of the rooms may be locked,' the student says, moving ahead of Tyler and leaving him to check the first door while she goes to the next. 'They'll need a code to override them.'

'Let's focus on the open ones first.'

There's a clunk behind Tyler, and Rabbani shouts, 'Here!'

The lights inside are bright and hot as the sun. Tyler supposes that's the point. Calderdale's tucked under a workbench in a foetal position. His eyes are closed but he stirs at the noise.

The student cries out when she joins them at the door. Tyler turns to her. 'Can we turn these off?'

'It's a pre-set programme. It can be deactivated but I don't know—'

'Okay, go get a glass of water. Now! And phone for an ambulance,' he shouts after her as she races back down the corridor.

'We have to get him out of here,' Rabbani says.

It's not an easy manoeuvre, extracting Calderdale from under the bench. The man's big and bulky and Tyler wonders for a moment at the ferocity behind Carver's attack, to have been able to overpower someone of Calderdale's size and build. But then, Calderdale's used to fighting with words. Assuming this even was Carver. They don't know for certain.

Someone has been at the man though. There are cuts and abrasions all over his face. Both his eyes are beginning to blacken and he has a deep gash on his temple that's dried in the heat.

Together they manage to drag him into the air-conditioned corridor and Rabbani slams the door shut behind them. Calderdale stirs and opens his eyes.

He tries to croak something but it turns into a cough. The student gets back with the glass of water and gives it to Tyler. 'Ambulance is on its way.'

'Go upstairs and wait for it,' he tells her, and presses the edge of the glass to Calderdale's ragged lips.

The woman disappears and Tyler pulls the glass away as Calderdale starts to cough again. He has reddened blisters forming along his hairline. 'Slowly,' Tyler says. 'Who did this?'

Calderdale stares at him but doesn't answer.

'Who?' Tyler snaps.

'Cleaner,' Calderdale croaks.

'Dave Carver?'

The professor nods.

'Why would he attack you?'

Calderdale reaches out for the glass of water but Tyler moves it out of his reach.

'Sarge?'

'Quiet. Tell us, Robert.'

'Sacked him.'

'This seems a bit of an extreme reaction to losing your job. That was months ago.'

'DS Tyler!' Rabbani says sternly.

'. . . thought I killed her . . .'

'Chi?'

Calderdale nods again.

'We know Chi was seeing a boy,' Tyler says. 'We know she somehow met him through you. Who was it, Robert?'

'Can't,' he says. 'Please! He'll kill me . . .'

'Sarge, you can't do this!'

'Just give us a name.'

Calderdale eyes the glass. 'Stu . . . Stuart,' he says.

Rabbani snatches the glass from his hand. 'For fuck's sake!' She holds the water to Calderdale's cracked lips.

'Thank you for seeing me,' Emma Ridgeway says.

'Of course, no problem.' They shake hands and Mina fetches a second chair across from an empty desk.

'Where is everyone?' Emma asks, looking around the unusually quiet room.

'Big case,' Mina says.

After they'd seen Calderdale off in the ambulance, Tyler's phone had rung and Mina had waited to hear the bad news.

But it wasn't quite the bad news she'd been expecting. Doggett had finally had a breakthrough in his case after an anonymous tip. But when he'd gone to make his arrest, the father of the murdered boy, Talbot, had compounded his sins by taking his wife hostage. Tyler had raced off to help Doggett and Jordan at the scene. Mina had offered to go too but predictably Tyler wouldn't hear of it. Her sole priority was to find Chi's missing corpse.

'So,' Emma's saying, 'I wanted to bring this to you in person because ... well, I don't know how much longer I'm gonna be around.'

'Elliot still throwing his weight about?' Mina asks.

'I can handle Elliot. I've handled far worse. But it's his show, and if he wants me gone there's not much I can do about it.'

'I'm sorry,' Mina says. 'What will you do?'

'Hey, I'm not done yet. I still got a few cards to play. Besides, there's plenty of jobs out there. It's just a shame, that's all. I was kinda hoping to stay here for a while, put down some roots. Especially as I just started making new friends.' She smiles.

Mina hears Daley's voice in her head, *I heard she was a lezza!* She feels the blood rushing to her face. 'Oh,' she says. 'I ... I'm not ... I mean, I appreciate the compliment but ...'

Emma looks confused and then gets it. 'Wow, I guess news really does travel fast in this place. Yeah, that's not what I meant. Like I said before, I just don't have many friends here.'

Mina's face is on fire. 'I'm sorry. I didn't ...' She closes her eyes. 'Oh God, I really need the ground to open up and swallow me right now.'

'Don't worry about it,' Emma says, but she sounds disappointed. Not in being rejected, presumably, but in Mina's assumption.

'Look,' Mina says, biting the bullet, 'I'm really sorry, Emma. I'm an idiot.' She wants to blame Guy Daley for putting stupid thoughts in her head. But in truth this is her fault. Her prejudice, pure and simple.

Emma says, 'I'm used to it.' She lets Mina off the hook more easily than she deserves with a forced smile. 'If it's any consolation, you're not even my type.'

'Oh.' For some reason, that stings a bit, even if she isn't interested. But she doesn't have the right to play the injured party in this. 'So what *is* your type?' she asks, and then regrets it. *Stop trying to virtue-signal!*

'When you meet my wife, you can ask her.'

'Oh.' Mina feels another wave of shame. How has she managed to get this so wrong?

'Really, don't worry about it,' Emma says, and sounds more genuine this time. 'Do you wanna hear what I got or not?'

Emma takes her through the lab results, most of which are negative. Things get a bit easier as they get back on to work topics and before long the two of them are tossing ideas back and forth like well-established work colleagues. Mina has a minor revelation. *This is friendship.* Has it really been so long since she made a new friend that she mistook it for something else? She's never been all that good at female friendships.

She has her family, of course, dozens of cousins her own age, but she's never really thought of them as mates. They're just ... there. It's not as though she can talk to them about dead bodies or anything. If it isn't boys, family problems, or the Kardashians, they're not interested. Same applies to her friends from school. She's always been the outsider.

'You are a coconut!' her mother once told her. 'Brown on outside, white in middle.'

'Mama, where do you get this stuff from?' she asked.

'Podcast,' her mother announced with all the technical authority of a woman whose doctor-son had bought her an iPhone for Christmas.

The trouble is, Mina thinks, to some extent her mother's right. And the fact she grew up the product of two differing cultures is only part of the problem. She's a police officer, too. And no matter what culture you're from, that's a whole different club. Outsider doesn't even begin to cover it.

For all the information Emma's extra tests have produced, none of it really tells them anything they didn't already know. It makes Mina think again about Stevens and his constant cost-cutting. She appreciates for the first time how hard it must be to decide how far to allocate resources to any given case. How can you know what you're doing is worthwhile before you get the results? Stevens didn't know Chi was buried in the Gardens waiting to be found when he made his decision to scale-back the case. And he based that decision on the evidence amassed at the time, evidence that pointed to the fact Chi had probably run off with a boyfriend. Should he have ignored that evidence? Gone with Cooper's gut? In Chi's case it turned out Cooper was right, but she didn't get it right in the Talbot case and now a child was dead. They had to make key decisions all the time, all of them, including Stevens. They wouldn't always get it right. The only thing that counted was the price paid when they didn't. *What will be the cost when you get it wrong?*

'Now,' Emma says, drawing Mina out of her thoughts. 'Deepak Jayashankar.' She opens another file. 'He died of a single knife wound to the thorax. He was really unlucky. The blade didn't even penetrate that deep but somehow it managed to slide right between the ribs and severed his thoracic aorta. He would have been dead in minutes. For that reason, Dr Elliot believes this was a professional hit.'

Mina picks up on something in her tone. 'You disagree?'

Emma hesitates. 'There are easier ways to kill someone and be sure of it. Gunshot to the head would be cleaner and more conclusive. I know you guys don't have the same firearms culture here but even with a knife, I can think of a dozen ways of assuring a more effective killing stroke. Kidneys, throat. If you were aiming for the heart you'd go up and under the ribcage. You just wouldn't go for the most heavily armoured part of the body.'

'So . . . ?'

'So I think it was an accident. There were signs of a struggle in the room. If the knife was between them, and the assailant was taller than Jayashankar, maybe the knife just slipped into him. In any case, there would have been a fair bit of blood splatter. If you can find the knife in question there's bound to be trace evidence on it. Oh, and one more thing – it's a different knife to the one that killed Chi.'

'You're sure?'

'The knife went in deep enough for the hilt to cause a slight bruising around the wound, so I can tell you you're looking for a blade about seven inches in length.'

'Doesn't that contradict your theory of an accident?'

'Not necessarily. The bruising was very slight and if the victim was moving forward at the time . . .' She demonstrates by stepping towards Mina and thrusting an imaginary blade between them. 'It could have been pressure enough. In Chi's case, her body was in a much more advanced state of decomposition so it's hard to say for sure, but my guess is the blade would have to have been no more than four or five inches to inflict the wound it did. I've included some photographs of the sort of thing you might be looking for.'

Mina's mobile vibrates and she apologises before taking the call.

'Detective Rabbani? It's Lizzie. Lizzie Gordon.' Dave Carver's ex-wife.

'Hi, Lizzie. Everything okay?'

'Yeah, I was . . . I wasn't sure if I should call but—'

'It's okay, Lizzie. What is it?'

There's a pause and Mina's beginning to wonder if the woman has hung up before she speaks again. 'I thought of another place. That he might have gone. I mean, I can't be sure or anything, but I was talking to my husband and he said I should ring and—'

'You did the right thing. What have you thought of?'

'When Dave was first made redundant from the steelworks, he tried his hand at his own thing. I think I told you that we met when he was teaching metalwork? Anyway, he had his own business. He made artisanal knives that he sold on the internet. There's a big market for it, especially in America. Then Rachel got sick and he – well, with less time to devote to the business it folded. But he loved that old workshop. When things got really bad, with Rachel I mean, he used to go there sometimes. Just to get away from me, I think. I'm not sure he even knew I knew about it.'

'Just a minute.' Mina fumbles with her notebook. 'Okay, do you have the address?'

Mina takes down the relevant details. 'One more thing,' she asks. 'Dave's business. Do you remember what it was called?'

When she ends the call, Emma's looking at her expectantly.

'Carver's ex-wife. He used to sell bespoke knives on the internet.'

It takes them no more than a few minutes to find historical information about the company on the web. As they flick through the images of the products on offer, they find at least three that Emma thinks could have killed Chi but nothing that matches the type of blade that killed Jayashankar.

'You're looking at something more like a chef's knife,' Emma says. 'A Sabatier maybe?'

Mina thinks for a moment. 'We're looking for two killers then?'

'Or someone who likes to kill with different knives? Carver could have gotten rid of the knife that killed Chi. It was seven months ago.'

Mina thinks fast. They need to check out that address. If she managed to get Chi's corpse back before Jordan and the others returned, well, it certainly wouldn't hurt their chances with Stevens. But then she thinks about the last time she went off on her own, and what that nearly cost her. She shudders at the memory of the smoke filling her lungs. Even now, when she gets a cold, the infection goes straight to her chest. And every single time, her mother reminds her how foolish she was, how lucky to be alive.

She leaves a message for Tyler and then tries ringing Daley but there's no answer. She supposes she could grab someone from Uniform but if she's wrong, and Chi's body isn't there, that will just add fuel to Stevens' fire. 'We need to get that body back.'

'Fine,' Emma says. 'So what are we waiting for?'

'I can't let you come.'

'Why not? You just need backup, right? In case something happens.'

'But you're not police.'

'Missy, I can handle myself, don't you worry.'

'It's not that, it's just ...' Mina can imagine what Jordan will say when she finds out.

'I already have the address. I'm going, whether you like it

or not.' Emma smiles. 'Look, Chi was *my* responsibility. All we have to do is check the place out, right? If we think we're on to something, you call it in?'

'I guess.'

'Come on then!' Emma jumps out of her chair, leaving Mina no choice but to follow.

But as they leave the building and head for the car, that question keeps buzzing around in her head. *What will be the cost when you get it wrong?*

The address from Lizzie Gordon takes them to an empty office block on the outskirts of Kelham Island.

It takes a while in the rush-hour traffic but eventually they manage to get clear of the ring road and here the streets are quieter. This is the heart of the old industrial Sheffield, now a patchwork of new-build apartment buildings and run-down old factories, with a hipster pub or barber shop dotted in between. It's the up-and-coming part of town that's been up-and-coming for the past twenty years or more.

'I hear there's some good bars around here,' Emma says. 'Nice place for a first date, huh?'

Mina feels her face flush again. 'You're not going to let this go, are you?'

'Not for a good while.'

The building in question's enormous, an eight-storey monolith without a single glass window intact. A lot of the old industrial property around here has been demolished now but there are still odd buildings like this one that everyone seems to have forgotten about, painted with thick coloured lines of graffiti and strangled by vines. The remains of dead Buddleia sprouts out of every orifice in the building's face, like hair sticking out of an old man's nose.

It's starting to get dark and it's beginning to spit with rain as they step over a rusted chain across the entrance with a sign hanging from it by one corner that reads: 'No Parking. Access needed at all hours.' It doesn't look as though access has been needed here for years. They cross a weed-pitted car park that looks like a location from a zombie film.

The entrance to the building's boarded up, as are the windows on the ground floor. There's a fat waste-pipe running the length of the front of the building with some kind of orange effluent pouring from every joint along its length. To the left of the main entrance, a faded sign mounted on the wall still lists the ill-fated businesses that used to trade here. Mina traces her finger up the plaque until she reaches the fifth floor. 'Sheffield Steel Knives', Carver's old business, is on the fifth floor.

'It wasn't the most original name, was it?' Mina asks quietly.

'No wonder the company folded. Why are we whispering?'

There's a padlock on the door, securely fastened.

'We could try round the back?' Emma suggests.

Mina hesitates. This is how it starts. You wander into an empty building and all at once you're trapped and fighting for your life. It's like every one of those stupid horror films Ghulam used to make her watch. She should just call it in.

But she doesn't. She heads round the corner of the building with Emma.

The side of the office block's hidden from the road by the blank façade of the building next door. Some kids have taken advantage of this fact and have decorated the entire wall with a black and white tag that's clearly meant to be a word, but neither of them can work out what it says.

'It's kinda beautiful in a way,' Emma says. 'I mean, they've got talent.'

'Yeah, but is it art?'

At the back of the building things are even more overgrown and they have to fight their way past more of the Buddleia, its dead brown buds scratching Mina's face.

The back door's padlocked too, but the lock's attached to a length of chain that extends far enough that they might be able to slip inside.

'What are we waiting for?' Emma asks.

'Someone's been here,' says Mina. The grass leading up to the door is flattened.

'There's no one here now. Unless they're sitting in the dark.'

That's not the most comforting thought. Given what she's learned about Dave Carver, it strikes Mina he might be exactly the kind of guy who would sit in the dark. None of this is exactly by the book. Jordan will go spare. But since she's barely clinging to a job as it is, what difference does it make? What was that expression Tyler had used about shit and digging?

'There's no car out front,' Emma says, reinforcing her

argument. 'We'll hear if anyone arrives. Or we'll see the headlamps through the window.'

'Maybe, but—'

'Come on, Mina! Where's your sense of adventure.' And with that Emma pushes on the damp wooden door and wriggles her way under the chain.

'Wait . . .'

But she's already inside. Mina glances once back the way they came and then follows Emma into the building.

Inside, it takes a while for her eyes to adjust to the dark.

Emma's somewhere across the room, her voice echoing back through the darkness. 'There's nothing here. The whole place is empty.'

'He could be upstairs,' Mina whispers. 'Fifth floor, remember?'

'I guess the elevator's out? Hey, there's some kind of work-bench over here.'

Mina catches up to Emma and together they move through the open-plan space towards the door on the far wall. They find nothing but dust and dirt and, finally, a wooden-handled chisel of some kind. Emma picks it up and tests the weight in her hand before gripping it like a knife.

She sees Mina's questioning look. 'I grew up in Little Rock.'

'Yeah, well, you're not in Kansas anymore.'

'Arkansas, actually.'

'My point is, there's no right to bear arms in Sheffield.' But Mina doesn't insist she put it down.

At the far end of the building they find a small partitioned office, empty, and another door that leads into a stairwell.

'Fifth floor, huh?'

'Shit.' But Mina has to admit, she doesn't want to go back now. 'I'll go first,' she says, pushing ahead.

'How gallant!'

'Fuck off!'

Emma laughs, the sound echoing and dying away in the damp hallway. They climb the stairs slowly, Mina testing each with her weight before moving on. But they're concrete and feel solid enough. She wishes she had her baton with her. On each floor they do a quick recce through the doorway, both of them holding their mobiles up to cast light around the rooms. Every floor's as empty as the first.

When they reach the fifth floor, Mina stops dead.

'What?' Emma says behind her.

'I thought I heard . . .'

What exactly? She's not sure but it was definitely something. She listens, hard, but she can't hear it now. Probably just a rat. She wishes she hadn't thought that.

She reaches out slowly for the door handle in front of her. One deep breath and then she pushes the door open wide. 'Police!' she shouts, stepping into the room and preparing to duck.

But the office is as empty as all the others. There's enough light filtering in from the city outside to see there's no one here. Mina moves fully into the room and Emma steps up to join her, brandishing her chisel.

'What's that?' she asks, squinting into the darkness. 'On the far side.'

They cross together, keeping so close to each other Mina can feel the doctor's arm brushing against her own. And then they can see what it is. Lying in full sight on top of the work bench furthest from them is the familiar form of a black body bag.

'She's here!' Emma says. 'It's gotta be her.' She starts towards the body.

'Shh!' Mina whispers, and this time she's sure she heard something. The sound of footsteps, echoing up the stairwell behind them.

They both drop into a crouch behind the bench. Emma reaches out and grabs Mina's arm.

'Shit!' Mina says. 'Shit! Stay quiet.' She can feel her heart hammering in her chest and the hair standing up on the back of her neck. She can't decide what to do. Should they backtrack as far as possible and risk meeting him on the enclosed stairwell? Or are they better waiting here and confronting him in the relative open of the office? Every decision has a consequence. *What will be the cost when you get it wrong?*

But before she can do anything, she hears him enter the room.

Mina and Emma stare at each other as they listen to the footsteps coming closer. Emma nods as if to say, *we got this.* Mina nods back. She uses her finger to indicate Emma should go right while she goes left. Emma makes an *okay* symbol with her fingers. The footsteps grow louder until they're almost on top of them.

Mina counts them down with her fingers, three, two, one . . .

They move in unison, jumping up. Mina shouts, 'Police!' while Emma just screams, a blood-curdling, primal scream, the chisel thrust forward in front of her like a spear.

Tyler stumbles backwards and falls on his arse. 'Jesus Christ!' he shouts.

seven

the first nighthawker

Record of Finds

Date: Tue 14th Nov
Time: 19:06
Location: Botanical Gardens, Sheffield
Finds: None

They must be here, he knows that much now. The last of the coins.

His heart's hammering in his chest as he sweeps the ground with the detector. Is it the thrill of being back here in the Gardens? The fact that the last time he was here he uncovered a corpse? Or is it simply that he's so close to realising his plan. He's nearly won. He's nearly managed to take everything from them, and prove he was right into the bargain.

He feels a stab of guilt about Deepak. But not as much as he might have expected. Did that make him a monster? He hadn't meant to kill him. He'd followed Deepak on that trip out to Bradfield and taken the opportunity to search his car. But then Deepak came back and he'd panicked, and acted too soon. The balaclava wasn't enough. Deepak had studied him in the rear-view mirror all the way back to the city, had time to get his nerve up and think about a plan of action. In the bedroom, as he handed over the shoebox with its golden treasure inside, something must have finally clicked. Deepak called him by name, questioningly at first, as though testing out his theory aloud. But once he knew who his attacker was, he lost the last of his fear. They struggled, the shoebox clattering to the floor and spilling its contents across the bedroom carpet. He only raised the knife by instinct. It was self-defence, really. And Deepak had virtually thrown himself onto it. He couldn't be held responsible for that, could he? He watched the life drain out of the man faster than he ever could have imagined possible. There was no chance of his being saved by an ambulance so there was no point in calling one. Why should he let this man ruin his plans? So he collected up the coins — just two of them, to hear them talk you'd think there were more — and left. He did his best to wash the blood from his hands in the canal, and then, he'd been so paranoid about leaving a trail, he'd spent half the night roaming the streets. To think, they didn't even find the poor fellow for days. He needn't have worried.

The detector moves on across the uneven ground. They have to be here somewhere; it's the only thing that makes sense!

Ronnie was a mistake as well, although a less costly one. He'd never been 100 per cent sure she was involved but the way she was always fawning over Carver made him suspect her more. It was pretty obvious she didn't have a clue what he was talking about though, when he'd held the knife to her throat and demanded she hand over her portion of the Roman coins. He really should have guessed that out of all of them, she would be the one to fight back. He'd paid for that mistake all right, the memory of it still burned deep in his crotch.

The kid, Nick, was easy. It's not hard to get into those student places and the lad had hidden his portion of the treasure, three coins this time, so poorly — behind a book on a shelf? Why not put them in a freezer bag behind the peas? What a cliché! — the whole thing hadn't taken him more than twenty minutes.

And then there was Halbert. The easiest of all. He'd slipped into his place earlier today using the spare key the man kept hidden under a pot by the back door. The coins were mixed in with a handful of loose change he found in a ceramic dish by the back door. Another three. He could imagine Halbert congratulating himself on how clever he was being, hiding the treasure in plain sight.

Which left Dave Carver and brought him back here. He's long had his suspicions about the Gardens, especially after a search of Carver's flat came up empty, but it's just such a huge area to search and he knows he hasn't got time to keep coming back. Maybe he should cut his losses, make do with the eight coins he already has. But that would mean leaving a portion for Carver, not to mention the fact that Carver's coins, if sold, might lower the value of his own. So here he is, back where he started. It was the obvious place, given how much Carver worships the place. He's been following them all for weeks now, recording their movements, working out their routines and likely hiding places. And Carver spends more time here than anywhere else. He visits every day and sits on that damned memorial bench to . . .

He stops, the metal coil of the detector humming faintly over a bare patch of earth. He turns to look at the bench. Of course! He checks his watch. He doesn't have enough time and anyway, he'll need something to get those paving stones up. He can't believe he didn't think of this before.

Yes, he's made some big mistakes over the past few weeks, but hopefully that was the last of them. Maybe, he can still get away with this . . .

There's a party atmosphere in the Murder Room that belies the grisly nature of the day's events. The truth is, it's good to have something to celebrate, even if it is a bit macabre.

Doggett's triumph is the main topic of conversation. The houseboat turned out to belong to Talbot although it was still registered in the name of his maternal grandfather which is why they hadn't found it sooner. A forensic search uncovered the bench seat where Jason's body had lain for almost six months while presumably Talbot panicked about what to do with it. He'd made a good job of the clean-up but not good enough. It was enough for an arrest warrant and Talbot had finally cracked, taking his wife hostage.

Tyler had seen some of what happened with his own eyes and he's heard variations on the story from a dozen different sources now. Jim had gone in alone, at the behest of the kidnapper. He had managed to keep Talbot talking as he held an antique pistol to his wife's head. Talbot told his story in quiet, precise sentences, explaining why he killed his 5-year-old son. The boy had back-chatted him once too often, and anyway, Talbot wasn't even sure the boy was his. All this to the backdrop of the wife's teary testimony to the contrary. He'd seen red when the boy got scared and voided his bladder. He'd been so sickened by his so-called son's cowardice, he'd shaken him, hard. Until he'd stopped breathing. Doggett didn't point out how far this account differed from the forensic evidence of strangulation. He just stood patiently and listened to the confession. Then Talbot tried to justify the elaborate steps he went to, in order to fake the boy's kidnapping and murder. The DNA they'd taken from the parents to eliminate them from their enquiries had proven one thing, the boy *was* the legitimate son of his father. It was this information Doggett chose to impart while Talbot pressed the cold barrel of his gun against his weeping wife's temple. And then Doggett had talked the man into giving himself up.

It didn't really matter that they later found out there was no ammo in the gun, nor that Doggett swore blind he could tell as much from the empty chamber he'd seen as he'd stared down the barrel. DI Jim Doggett was still a hero by anyone's standards and there was talk of long-overdue promotion rattling around the office, as though anyone who spoke of such things actually had a hand in them. Tyler supposed it was possible. Sometimes it was less a case of what you'd actually done and more a case of what you were perceived to have done. Doggett wouldn't be the first promoted for reasons politic, any more than he was the first whose career had stagnated for the same reason. Anyway, as far as Tyler was concerned, he deserved it.

'Congratulations,' he tells Doggett when he manages to get a moment alone with him.

'Lot of bloody nonsense,' Doggett says, but Tyler can see a

glint of what might be pride in the man's eye. 'I hear you've been ruffling feathers yourself. Stevens is out for your blood.'

'Isn't he always?'

'What about the info from Ronnie? Any good?'

'It was. Thank you. How's she doing?'

Tyler sees Doggett's brow crease. 'Fine. But if you need anything else from her, you'll need to speak to her directly.'

He knows Doggett won't appreciate any sentimentality. 'I'd say it was her loss but I'd be lying.'

'They come and go, eh? C'est la vie.' Doggett lets out a long breath. 'I need a drink. How about it?'

'Not off the clock yet. Just waiting for Mina to get back from the morgue.'

Doggett grunts out a laugh. 'I wish I could have seen your face when they went for you.'

Tyler grins. 'I honestly don't know who was more terrified.'

'The new doc, eh? Who'd've thought she had it in her? Still no sign of Carver then?'

'He's gone to ground again. Uniform are staking out the building but with all the fuss the SOCOs made recovering the body, he could have seen the lay of the land and been away before anyone noticed.'

'At least you've got the body back.'

'A stay of execution at best.'

'And what about your house guest?' Doggett asks cautiously. 'How's that going?'

It was a good question. Had Callum found what he was

looking for, whatever McKenna had sent him for? There was no way to know, short of asking him.

'He's cleared off.'

'Well, that's something worth drinking to.' Doggett pats him on the shoulder. 'You sure you don't want one?'

Tyler's tempted but he shakes his head. 'Mina and I have one last appointment tonight.'

Dave gets to the meeting early again so he can watch them all go in, standing hidden in the bushes at the side of the building. Colin's first, as always, lugging his great shopping bag of useless leaflets into the hall where he will fan them all out into neat piles that no one will touch. Then Ronnie turns up, looking troubled for once – he hopes *he* isn't the cause of that – and Nick right behind her. Before Nick manages to get through the door, Mike arrives and they chat for a moment. Dave's too far away to make out what they're saying but he has no doubt they're talking about him. He briefly considers announcing himself to them. Would they help? No, it's too late for that. And given the course of action he's focused on, there's a fair chance they might try to stop him, or even turn him in. Besides, they're only interested in the money, not about what happened to Chi.

Nick seems upset, angry even. He accuses Mike of something but Mike shakes his head vehemently and touches him on the shoulder. Whatever he says must convince the lad because things seem to calm down and they walk into the church together.

Dave lets them go. They're not the reason he's here.

It had taken a long time to get anything out of Calderdale but the man had broken eventually. Dave looks down at his bloodied and bruised knuckles, just visible in the moonlight. It doesn't matter. Only one thing matters now. Finding the man who hurt her.

He assumed that was Calderdale, to begin with. Even back then, at the point Chi arranged the deal, he'd considered the idea Calderdale might be the buyer. He'd had trouble with that idea, at first, but after a while he convinced himself there was a certain satisfaction in taking the money of the man who had caused him to lose his job.

But as he'd stood there, towering over the professor's broken form, Dave realised his mistake. Calderdale was only an intermediary himself. He protested his innocence with every punch and kick Dave laid on him and Dave was beginning to believe him. Calderdale might be a big man, but he wasn't a fighter. And he doubted he was a killer either.

So the questions changed. *Who do you work for? Where did the money come from? Who was Chi's contact?* At first Calderdale thought he was talking about the plants, but Dave assured him he didn't give a shit about any of that.

'The coins,' Dave told him. 'Who put up the money for the coins?'

Calderdale pretended not to know anything but Dave could see the man was lying. After a few more hits, the man caved. 'All right,' he said, 'all right! Please, just stop.'

Dave let him catch his breath.

'I heard about the coins later, I had nothing to do with it. But you don't want to mess with these people, honestly.'

'Name,' Dave said, stepping forward.

'Stuart! Everything went through Stuart. That's all I know.'

The name meant nothing to Dave at first, but with a bit more encouragement Calderdale described him. 'Young, skinny lad, dark hair. Another one of the girl's lovers.'

Dave gave him another kick for that.

And then it came to him. Stuart. A student, like Chi. The newest member of the detectorists' club. The people who put up the money for the coins must have found them, and presumably they wanted their money back, or the coins. Or both. And that meant the others were in danger. If these people, this Stuart, had killed Chi, they wouldn't balk against killing him either, or Mike, or Nick. Or even Ronnie! They might not know she had nothing to do with it. But that didn't make sense. Why would this Stuart kill Chi before he got his hands on the coins? Unless it was an accident? Or maybe Chi changed her mind and tried to back out of the agreement? It doesn't matter, the point is, this Stuart has the answers he needs.

At least he knows the others are all safely inside – except Deepak, but Deepak's always late, it didn't mean anything. Now he'd deal with this Stuart.

He doesn't have to wait long. He feels the mist closing in on him as soon as he sees the lad, but this time he lets it. He steps out from the bushes and hurries across the car park, intercepting Stuart before he can reach the safety of the lit church hall.

'Hello, Stuart. How are you?'

The lad frowns at him. 'Dave, right? Yeah, good, mate. How's you?'

'Good,' Dave says. 'Very well, thank you.' His voice sounds like it's coming from a long way away. He knows he isn't behaving quite right but a part of him's still in control enough to know that it doesn't matter. Let him be suspicious, the man's greed will lead him where Dave wants him to go.

'I know who you are.'

'Yeah?' Stuart says, his eyes flicking back and forth, checking to see who else is around. 'Is that right?'

'You were friends with Chi,' Dave says. 'You were going to buy the coins from us.'

Stuart says nothing.

Dave goes on. 'What happened to Chi that night?'

'How should I know, mate? I wasn't even there.' He crosses his arms. 'I heard you were, though. Maybe you can tell me what happened.'

It wasn't as though Dave expected him to admit it. Not that easily. 'What if I show you instead?'

'Show me what?'

'The coins. I still have them. We can still do a deal.'

Stuart's eyes look past Dave towards the safety of the church hall.

'We can go now. I'll show you where they are.'

'I don't have that sort of money on me.'

'That's okay. I trust you. We're all in the same club now.'

'Sure. Okay, mate.' He's looking at Dave strangely, as though he knows he has something planned. 'I haven't got a car though, so you'll have to drive.'

'We can walk. It's not far.'

Stuart eyes him, cautiously. 'After you then, mate.'

They leave the church hall and head down the hill, keeping a wary distance from each other. He knows Stuart doesn't believe him. But the lad's curious. His greed palpable. He thinks he can handle Dave. And maybe he's right. He might even be armed, with the same knife he used to kill Chi. It doesn't matter. Dave's the dangerous one, and Stuart's the one who's going to pay. For Chi.

On their way, Rabbani fills him in on the situation at the morgue. 'It was all a bit tense, to be honest, Sarge. Some bigwigs were there to do an audit or something. One bloke looked like he'd give the Eel a run for his money.'

'Your new friend in trouble, is she?'

Rabbani smiles. 'That's just it. Turns out she was the one that called them in the first place. Apparently she was worried about the way the place was being run when she first started. She sent them an email weeks ago. Chi's body going missing made them pull their fingers out and now they're going over the place with a fine-tooth comb. Emma's not the one needs to worry, if you ask me. You should have seen Elliot's face when they turned on him.'

'Pretty, was it?'

'As a picture.'

By the time they pull up outside the church hall though, all the merriment has left them both. Rabbani hesitates with her hand on the door.

'What is it?' he asks, as she stares up at the cross on the side wall. And then he remembers the last time she visited a church.

'Nothing,' she says. 'I'm fine. Come on.'

He follows her into the church. There are only four of them and they all look up as Tyler pushes open the door to the hall. He recognises Mike Halbert, and by process of elimination the only woman present must be the eminently shaggable Ronnie. The other two, an older, fussy-looking man and a young, long-haired student type, he doesn't recognise, but neither of them are Dave Carver. He feels a wave of disappointment, even though the chances of them stumbling across him here were always going to be slight.

'Hello, Mike, good to see you again,' Tyler says, before turning to the others and introducing himself and Rabbani.

They interview them separately, well, three of them, at least. Halbert refuses to say anything more without a solicitor present and encourages the others to do the same.

Thankfully, it's Doggett's former squeeze, Ronnie, who leaps to their defence. 'Don't be ridiculous, Michael. We don't have anything to hide. Where do you want me?'

He interviews her first while Rabbani talks to the young student, Nick, in the opposite corner of the hall. Ronnie's helpful but doesn't tell him a great deal more than he already got via Doggett, except for her repeated attempts to convince him Dave Carver's the gentlest of men and that she could believe Mahatma Gandhi more capable of murder than him. When they get to Deepak, her eyes fill instantly with tears. 'Oh, it's just so awful,' she says. 'So, so awful. I can't believe he's gone.'

On the subject of the Roman coins she denies all knowledge, and he has no reason to disbelieve her. He asks if any of the others could have found something like that, to which she laughs. 'This lot,' she whispers, 'could not find their own arse with both hands.' But then she thinks about it. 'It's possible though. I've heard them talk about going out on night digs. It's illegal, obviously, searching on private land, but it does happen.'

He thanks her for her time and decides to swap notes with Rabbani before tackling the final member of the group. Nick was about as useful a witness as any student, according to Rabbani. Although she had a feeling he might be trying to hide something from her. 'I think he probably knows something about the coins.'

'What makes you say that?'

'Because when I asked him if he knew anything about them he said that he didn't.'

'So?'

'So the rest of the time, whenever I asked him anything, he either nodded or shrugged. That was the first and only time I got words out of him.'

'All right, go and keep an eye on them and see if you can learn anything else while I talk to the last one.'

Tyler calls the man over. 'Colin Tavistock,' he says, introducing himself and taking a seat. 'This is my group, actually. I set it all up myself.'

'Impressive.'

'One doth tryeth one's best.'

'What?'

'Er ... nothing. I take it from what Mike's just told me this is about Dave? David Carver? I'm shocked to hear you're looking for him. He was here just last week and none of us can believe he could have had anything to do with ...'

Some witnesses you have to question, others are happy to talk. Colin Tavistock's one of the latter. Tyler listens as patiently as he can while Tavistock takes him through the history of the club, the finer points of metal-detecting, his opinions of his fellow detectorists – *Detectorists! Not detectors, which are the tools of the detectorist, a mistake that many people make* – and any number of other things besides.

When he gets the opportunity to speak, Tyler asks him about Roman coins and shows him the photograph of the coin found under Jayashankar's bed.

'Oh, you should have come to me straight away! I have quite an interest in Roman antiquities. Do you know the rarest of the imperial Roman coins is probably the aureo medallion of Massenzio?' He does his best to impersonate an Italian accent. He's wildly off the mark. 'This one though ...' he inspects the photograph closely. 'Goodness, is it Allectus? My word, this would be worth a fair amount. He was a usurper-emperor, killed his predecessor and was in turn killed himself by his supporters. He planned to take Britain out of the Empire, you know, so some wags call him the original Brexiteer.' Tavistock laughs.

'Have you seen anything like it before?'

'Well, I've seen pictures, of course … but no, I've never *found* anything like this.'

'Are you sure about that, Mr Tavistock? You see, we have reason to believe that Dave and Deepak found a number of these coins. They might even have been trying to sell them, or working with someone else in your club.'

Tavistock puffs himself up in indignation. 'I can assure you, Detective, I would *not* have allowed something like that to happen on my watch. No, it's entirely out of the question. If it were just the one coin perhaps, but any more than two gold coins *must* be declared. That's according to the Treasure Act, 1996. A valuation is made and then the finder might be entitled to a proportion of the value of the—'

'Yes, thank you. I see.'

Tavistock dries up and Tyler takes advantage of the brief silence to gather his thoughts. He glances across to the others. Rabbani's deep in conversation with Ronnie while, opposite them, Mike Halbert sits and sulks and Nick the student plays on his phone. He has his feet up on one of the unused chairs. For some reason Tyler counts the empty chairs. There are three of them. Assuming Rabbani has Colin's place that means two of the empty chairs would be for Carver and Jayashankar, but who's the other one for?

'Mr Tavistock, why do you have seven chairs laid out?'

'Hm? Oh, well, I'd heard about Deepak on the news, obviously, but I couldn't bring myself to put out just the six. It would have felt wrong, you see?'

'But who's the seventh chair for? The four of you here, Deepak and Dave. That makes six. Who's the seventh member?'

'Oh! Stuart, you mean?'

Stuart. Bingo!

'He only joined last week. I don't charge for the first week. Not that I make any money from this, but it covers the room hire and photocopying, and the tea and biscuits, of course. I don't think three quid's a great deal of money but a lot of people do tend to drop out before—'

'Do you have his details? We'll need to talk to him too.'

'Really? He can't have anything to do with any of this, surely? I wouldn't want to put him off coming back if he's—'

'Mr Tavistock. His full name, please, if you have it?'

Tavistock blinks at being cut off yet again but soon recovers. 'I can do you one better than that. If you'll accompany me unto my filing cabinet ...' He laughs and escorts Tyler over to a table by the door that's covered in pamphlets extolling the virtues of various pieces of metal-detecting equipment. He pulls out a box from under the table, lifts from it a pristine black ring-binder, and flicks through the laminated pages.

'Here we are,' he says. 'I always insist on a photograph, you see? I like to make up a name badge for the new starters, with the group's logo on. Then members have something official they can show to people when they are going about their work. I don't insist they wear them in the group, of course, although I sometimes think it would be nice if the others—'

'May I?' Tyler asks, one arm outstretched.

'Oh, of course.'

Tavistock spins the folder round and Tyler examines the photograph of a young man sporting a black eye and a cut on his cheek. The name filled out on the form identifies him as Stuart Smith.

But Tyler knows him as Callum Morgan.

'This way,' Dave says, stepping through into the Marnock Garden, the spade balanced loosely on his shoulder. Stuart walks behind. Dave's not comfortable with the lad behind him but he doubts he'll do anything until he has his hands on the coins.

Stuart looks round the enclosed space. 'Where exactly? This is a big area to search.'

'Over here.' Dave leads him to the memorial bench. 'Underneath,' he says.

He watches Stuart read the inscription on the small bronze plaque:

IN LOVING MEMORY OF
RACHEL CARVER
HER SMILE BRIGHTENED THE DARKEST DAY
HER LAUGHTER WAS A JOY
SHE LOVED THIS PLACE

Then he bends down and slots the edge of his spade between the paving slabs, just as he did seven months ago. He lifts the slab high enough to get his fingers under and then uses his own strength to flip it up and over. Then he goes to work while Stuart holds a torch. It isn't easy to get the right angle with the bench positioned above the hole, but he manages to get a couple of spadesful of earth out before switching to a trowel.

Stuart watches him. 'Was she your wife, mate?' he asks.

Dave stops digging and looks up. Stuart has let the torch dip and is staring at the bench.

'My daughter,' Dave says, and feels the mist closing in at the edges of his mind.

'Sorry, mate. That's tough.'

After a few more minutes' digging, Dave feels the satisfying crunch of the trowel as it hits the leather pouch he fashioned for the coins. He digs the last of the earth out with his hands, pulls the sack clear of the ground and tosses it straight at Stuart. The boy catches it with a jolt and looks at Dave, warily.

'Is that it?'

'Open it.' Dave watches him do just that, juggling the torch in two fingers as he spills out the two golden aurei into his hand.

'Fuck me! Is this what all the fuss is about?' Stuart says, and Dave's hand closes on the shaft of the spade.

'This isn't all of them, though? She told me thirteen. And where's the money—'

The spade hits him hard on the side of the head and Stuart goes down on the path. The coins drop to the path and roll in opposite directions. The torch bounces end over end, flashing a laser show of white light until it hits a rock and goes out.

Dave stands over the prone figure of Stuart, the spade held tight in both hands.

Stuart clutches his head. 'What the fuck?'

'Why did you kill her?' Dave shouts.

'Shut the fuck up, you *fucking* lunatic! Before someone calls the cops.'

'*Why?*' Dave steps forward, raising the spade high above his head.

Stuart puts up a hand, part surrender, part defence. 'Wait! There's no need for this. I thought we had a deal.'

'I want to know what happened to her,' Dave says, lowering the spade. 'Why did you kill her? She wasn't any threat to you.'

'I didn't, man, I swear. I fucking loved that girl. Well, loved fucking her, anyway.'

The spade goes up again.

'Look, you've got this wrong. Me and Chi, we were mates, yeah? I met her when I used to visit the university for me gran . . . my boss. He had some . . . merchandise he wanted me to sell, and one of his business partners who works at the uni made sure I didn't get any trouble from campus security.'

Merchandise? He means drugs, Dave supposes. 'Calderdale.'

Stuart puts his hand to his head again. 'Yeah, Calderdale. Bloody hell, I'm bleeding here!'

'Go on.'

'That was it, that's how I met Chi. One thing led to another and then ...' He must see something in Dave's expression because again he changes what he was about to say. 'I guess you don't need the gruesome details. Anyway, she told me about your lot and your little coin problem. Asked me if I had any contacts who might want to buy them off you. I spoke to the boss, he liked the idea, and came up with the cash.'

'Why did you kill her?'

'I keep telling you, man, I didn't! I was supposed to come with her that night, to meet you. She came over to mine and we ... well, you know. Then afterwards I must have fell asleep 'cos when I woke up she was gone, her and the money too. She never told me where you were meeting so it wasn't like I could even follow her. I was never here, mate, I swear to you. It wasn't me.'

Dave considers this. It sounds like the truth, and he was never blind to Chi's flirting. He knows she had several boys on the go.

'My ... boss went fucking bat-shit crazy when he found out I'd lost eight hundred grand. I thought he'd kill me. That's why I followed you the next day. Ah, don't look like that, she never gave you up. But my boss isn't the sort of bloke to part with that kinda money without checking who he's dealing with, so I followed her a few times. We knew all about you and your treasure hunters lot, and by then I knew where you lived. I watched you at the cholera monument giving them their coins back and I worked out the deal never got done. When Chi was declared missing, we figured she must have scarpered with the cash. My boss has been looking for her for months now.'

'Why did you join the metal-detecting club?'

'Because they found her body, didn't they? That changed everything. She didn't bloody run off with the money if she was buried here in the Gardens, did she? We thought maybe you killed her and kept the money, so I went into the club under-cover. Only you went on the run then. I went back to the club tonight to see if I could get anything out of the others. I never thought you'd be there, couldn't believe my luck.' Stuart winces at his choice of words and touches his head again. 'But we got it wrong, somehow, didn't we? You didn't kill her either.'

'You weren't the one who dug her up?'

'No, of course not! I didn't know where she was, did I?'

Dave drops the spade. 'You can go.'

Stuart gets up on his knees and begins gathering up the coins.

'Leave them,' Dave says, picking up the leather pouch.

'Listen, mate, you don't want to mess with the people I work for, trust me on this.'

'We had a deal. It's not my fault your boss lost his money.' Dave picks up the spade again to underline his position.

Stuart raises a hand to fend him off. 'He'll come after you. You're best off giving them to me now.'

'Go!'

'Fine. It's your funeral.' Stuart limps away into the darkness, clutching his head.

Tyler's sitting at his desk when his mobile rings.

'Mina?'

'Sarge!' There's an urgency to her voice that makes him sit up straighter and come instantly awake. 'Where are you?'

'In the Murder Room. I thought I told you to get some rest.'

Rabbani had been nodding off by the time they left the detectorists' meeting, her night in the car with Daley catching up on her. It had given him an excuse to send her home while he worked out what the hell he was going to do about 'Stuart Smith'. Rabbani had offered to check him out but Tyler told her it was probably an alias and that he'd look into it himself.

'Still no sign of Carver?' she asks, ignoring his comment.

'Nothing. I was just wondering about the ex-wife.'

'I don't think he'd go there,' she says.

'I meant, is it worth asking her if she can think of anywhere else?'

'That's why I'm ringing,' Rabbani says. 'I was just nodding off and my mind was going over the conversation I had with Lizzie.'

'Go on.'

'She told me that, other than the workshop where we found the body she couldn't think of anywhere else he'd go except "his precious garden". But she didn't mean his garden at home, did she? She meant—'

'The Botanical Gardens.' Tyler considers it. 'He's not likely to go back there.'

'Nothing Carver's done is "likely". Stealing a corpse from the morgue? Evading us all this time? I'd say he's managed to pull off a whole host of unlikely achievements.'

'I don't know.'

'It's worth a look, isn't it? What if he's been there the whole time?'

'We searched the Gardens.'

'Once. Right at the beginning, before we even knew about Dave Carver. What if he went back after that?'

'You think he's sleeping rough?'

'He has to sleep somewhere, and the temperature hasn't fallen that far yet. There's the greenhouses too.'

Tyler nods to himself. 'All he'd have to do would be to make sure he was gone by morning.' It made a certain kind of sense, if you were crazy enough.

'Sarge?' Carla shouts across the room.

'Hang on,' he tells Rabbani. 'What is it?'

'We just got a call from a concerned neighbour. Reckons she heard some shouting and saw a light flashing in the Botanical Gardens. Control thought we might want to look into it rather than Uniform.'

'I'll meet you there,' Rabbani shouts down the phone.

'Mina, wait . . .' But she's already hung up.

*

Daley's quiet all the way to the Gardens. He hadn't wanted to come at all, grumbling that he too had spent a night holed up in a car. Tyler convinced him, using the fact Rabbani was already on her way to shame him into action. 'Come on, Guy. Rabbani's capable enough but we have no idea how dangerous Carver is. I need you on this.'

Daley had reluctantly agreed.

But when they arrive at the south entrance and Tyler gets out, Daley stays sitting where he is.

Tyler bends down and opens the door again. 'Guy?'

He's staring through the windscreen, focused on nothing in particular. Nothing Tyler can see anyway.

'Guy . . . *mate.*' It's worth a try. 'We need to move. Rabbani could be here already.' Given the fact she's coming from Sharrow, and presumably needed to get dressed first, she's more likely to be behind them. But on the off-chance she's gone straight in, she could end up facing Carver alone.

'I can't,' Daley says. His forehead glistens under the interior car light, his knuckles are clenched in his lap.

Tyler doesn't have time for this. 'Fine,' he says. 'You look after yourself for a change.' He slams the car door.

He tries Rabbani's mobile but it goes straight to the answering service. He leaves a message telling her not to follow him in without backup. Uniform should be on their way. But he can't afford to wait. He's not going to let Carver get away again.

The iron gates are locked and it would take far too long to get someone out here with the authorisation to open them.

He takes hold of the railings and hauls himself up. It's not a difficult climb but the spikes at the top cause him a couple of awkward moments. Then he's scaling down the other side and finally drops the last couple of feet onto the gravel drive. He crunches his way up the road to the admin building and the greenhouse where he and Rabbani met with Calderdale. He checks the area but there's no one around. He sticks to the paths but explores every hidden area he can. He listens for something, anything. He can hear traffic passing beyond the park walls, and the occasional rustle in the bushes from a rat or badger or something, but apart from that, nothing.

The Marnock Garden's empty but then something catches his eye. A spade, lying abandoned next to a bench by the back wall. He walks towards it, spots the small hole that has been dug out beneath. He reads the plaque on the bench and knows he's in the right place.

He moves on, exploring the park in the dark. The north entrance is locked for the night. Still no sign of Rabbani or Uniform. He moves on, skirting the Gardens, arriving at the Bear Pit from above. He hears them talking before he sees them. Tyler edges forward and peers over the railings to look down into the pit.

Dave stands in the Bear Pit, the leather pouch clutched in his left hand. He isn't even sure he wants the coins any more – it's not as though they're going to do him any good – but he was damned if he was going to just hand them over to that drug-pushing boy. He reaches out and touches the statue of the brown bear. He hates this place. He hasn't set foot here since that night seven months ago.

Was she really going to run away with the money? He doesn't want to believe it, but that last time he saw her ... hadn't it seemed to him she'd been trying to say goodbye? He knows all at once that it's true. She was here in the park that night, which meant she intended to collect the coins from him. No doubt she would have hidden the money somewhere, and made up some excuse about why she needed to take the coins from him first. He would have believed her too, and let her walk away with the money and coins both.

But what could he have done differently? That's what he wants to know. How could he have stopped all of this from happening? He could have not involved her in the first place but would that have saved her? She was still friends with that boy, involved in things he had no idea about. He's been a fool.

Dave hears something and turns just as the figure tackles him from behind. He jerks to the right, stumbles, and falls backwards onto the loose bark chippings.

'Give me the coins,' says the black-clad figure standing over him. The man's short, a little portly, and he's wearing a black balaclava over his face, but he's recognisable enough even in the darkness.

'Colin?'

'Shit!' says Colin Tavistock. He holds up a large, silver knife. 'Just give them to me!'

'What's going on? What are you doing here?' None of this makes sense.

Colin shakes the knife in his hand. It's a Sabatier, a kitchen knife, the sort everyone has somewhere at home. Simple but very, very effective. Dave finds himself appreciating the craftsmanship even as he struggles to piece together what's happening.

'Just give me the coins,' Colin demands. 'Now. Throw them over to me.'

'No.'

Colin pulls the balaclava off his face and leaves it rumpled on the top of his head. 'I'm not kidding, Carver. I'll kill you!'

Dave laughs. 'Don't be daft, Colin.' He starts to get up but Colin lashes out with his foot and catches him a glancing blow on the right temple. He goes down again, his head spinning and pounding.

'Stay down, Carver!'

Dave looks up and begins to take the man seriously. 'What's this about?'

'Oh, you want to listen to me now, do you?'

'I'm listening.'

'None of you took me seriously, did you? Not really. Didn't want to include boring old Colin in your secret dig. But I found out about it. You're not as clever as you think you are, scurrying around, whispering in corners. I heard you talking one night, from the kitchen. Voices carry in those old church halls, you know. I heard enough to make me curious so I followed you to the pub afterwards. Sat behind you and heard all about your precious Roman find. You didn't even know I was there. I was bloody furious with the lot of you.

I set that club up. I funded it! I gave all of you a reason to get out of bloody bed in the morning and that's the thanks I get? The first time you have a bit of luck you leave me out!'

'It wasn't like that, we just ... we didn't think you'd approve.'

'Approve? Damn right I didn't approve! You were going to sell them for eight hundred thousand! To the right collectors they could be worth ten times that.'

'But you're always quoting the rules to us.'

'*Fuck* the rules! That's just for the benefit of the members. You don't think I'm going to tell them it's okay to break the law, do you? I've been nighthawking since I was a teenager and have I ever bloody found anything worth more than a few quid? Have I *fuck*! And then you lot come along, a bunch of bloody amateurs and bam! The mother lode. Well, I'm not having it. If anyone deserves those coins, it's yours truly. Now, throw them to me.'

Dave hesitates but Colin grips the knife and steps forward.

'You're not going to kill me, Colin.'

'Yeah? That's what Deepak thought.'

'What?'

The knife trembles in Colin's hand. 'I didn't mean for it to happen but ... well, he shouldn't have tried to stop me. *You* shouldn't try to stop me. Come on, here.' He beckons with the knife.

Dave tosses the bag and, as he does, another piece of the puzzle slots into place. The knife. The mist starts to form at the corners of Dave's mind.

The leather pouch lands in front of Colin. Dave watches him slip his rucksack off and lower it to the floor, gently, so the metal detector strapped to it won't get scuffed. He cares more about that damned machine than he does human life. Deepak? He can't believe it. Even if it was an accident, he could have rung for help. And if he could do that to a friend . . .

Colin crouches down and opens the zip with one hand, while the other still waves the knife vaguely in Dave's direction. He drops the pouch into the rucksack and shrugs it back onto his shoulder without closing the zip.

A shape emerges from the darkness behind Colin, but Dave's too lost in his thoughts to take it in properly. He can feel the mist sweeping in across his peripheral vision.

'Chi,' he whispers. The dark shape closes in behind Colin but Dave's only vaguely aware of it.

'What?'

'*You* killed her.'

'What are you on about now?'

The dark shape grabs Colin from behind, one hand going straight to his knife arm. 'Police! Drop it!'

But Colin doesn't drop it, and the backpack with the bulky detector makes it difficult for his assailant to maintain a grip. The two of them are struggling with each other as Dave gets to his feet. Then the shape is flying backwards and Dave is on Colin. They go down in a tangle of limbs, rolling over and over. Dave's screaming, he can hear himself but it's as though his voice is coming from a long way away. 'You killed her,' he shouts. 'You killed her!' He can't stop himself. His fists pummel Colin's face over and over again but now they're barely connecting, as though he has no strength left in his limbs. Dave pulls away from him, staggers back to his feet and only now sees the blood. He looks down and sees a bloodstain expanding across his own belly. There's a rip in his shirt where the knife must have gone in. He falls onto his knees, tired all of a sudden. He can feel something warm running down his leg.

'Oh,' he says, clutching the wound with his hand, the blood bubbling and tumbling out over his knuckles. Then he falls backward and comes to rest against the statue of the brown bear. He looks up through the mist clouding his eyes and sees Rachel smiling down at him.

Tyler listens to the conversation between the men. Dave Carver, not at all what he expected him to be, and Colin Tavistock. He'd written the man off as a joke. So had everyone else, it seems. He sees Tavistock pull out the knife and he knows he has to stop this before anyone else gets hurt.

If he calls it in though, Tavistock will hear him. He texts Rabbani instead, instructing her to call for armed response. She must be nearly here by now. He's picking his way down the overgrown path when he hears the shout. 'Police! Drop it!'

'Shit!' Tyler races down the path, his progress hampered by the bushes and the dark. Branches smack him in the face and then he slips in the mud, falls backwards. He goes down hard, feeling a jolt in his coccyx. He staggers back to his feet and half-jogs, half-slides the rest of the way down the slope. He reaches the entrance to the pit just as Tavistock emerges, darting right, away from Tyler and back up the opposite path towards the top.

Tyler goes after him. The mud pulls at his feet but it slows the other man down too and by the time they reach the top Tavistock's just a couple of feet ahead. There's a chance he still has the knife, that he could whirl at any moment and plunge it forward leaving Tyler's own momentum to do the job for him. Tyler takes the risk. He launches himself at the man in a rugby tackle. They both hit the ground and the air's pushed clear out of Tyler's lungs. He feels a boot kick him in his side but he holds on to the man's legs even as Tavistock twists in his grasp, trying to turn himself right way up.

Just in time, Tyler pulls back, letting go of the legs, feeling the swish of the blade, millimetres from his face. He struggles back to his feet but Tavistock's on him before he can find his balance. He gets his hands out in time to stop the knife. He feels the blade slice across his palm but he manages to get both hands onto Tavistock's wrist. The blood makes it slippery but he holds on even as Tavistock drives him back towards the pit.

The railing hits Tyler in the back, winding him and sending his hands sliding further up Tavistock's arm. The steel blade inches closer. Tavistock uses his left hand to grab hold of Tyler's jeans and lift. He feels his feet come up off the ground and all of a sudden he's arched backwards, trying to stay clear of the knife but dangerously close to going over the edge. He can't let go of Tavistock's arm but neither can his feet get purchase on the railings. Tavistock's pushing him up ... Up and back.

'You don't want to do this!' Tyler shouts, and some part of him's surprised to hear the panic in his own voice. He's reaching the tipping point, can feel the balance of his weight shifting to the other side of the railing. And then all at once the pressure's gone. Tavistock is yanked backwards by something and Tyler's hands are suddenly free to grab the railings. He arches his back and wills himself to fall the right way. Slowly, he pivots back the way he came and slides to the ground on the safe side.

A few feet away Carver's struggling with Tavistock, the two of them locked in an unlikely embrace. Tavistock's knife hand comes free and then plunges back into Carver's side, again and again, but Carver doesn't let go. He holds on with both hands, screams and lifts the man off his feet. And then they're stumbling back the way they came, towards Tyler.

Tavistock's body hits the railing in mid-air and keeps going, the weight of his backpack tipping him up and over, just as Tyler had been a few moments ago. Dave has collapsed to the ground again, his hands clutching his bloody stomach.

Tavistock scrambles for purchase, the weight of the backpack dragging him backwards like a turtle, flipped on end. Tyler reaches out but he's too far away. A shower of golden coins begins to rain out of the opening in the backpack and then Tavistock's screaming and falling. The scream cuts off with a dull thud.

Rabbani emerges from the treeline. 'Shit,' she says, running forward to check on Carver.

But Tyler's eyes are fixed on something else. Guy Daley is lying curled at the base of the Bear Pit wall, his face grey. Around him, a dark pool of blood soaks into the woodchips.

When Ben Robbins opens the door to them, Tyler can see the hope in his eyes. But then he takes in Tyler's bandaged hand and Rabbani's red-rimmed eyes and he's clearly not sure what to think.

'You got him?' he asks.

'Can we come in, please?'

Robbins lets them in and Juju emerges from the living room. Tyler can see by her face that she's ready to talk.

'We've arrested the man who buried Chi in the Gardens,' he tells them.

'That's good,' Ben says, and then, as though he's picking up on some unspoken current in the room, adds, 'Isn't it?'

'He was badly injured but we managed to talk to him in the hospital and he told us what happened that night. He says that Chi was already dead when he found her.'

'Well, he would say that, wouldn't he? Why would he bury her if he didn't kill her?'

'He's in shock,' Rabbani chips in, 'but he's not hiding anything now. He told us how he found the Roman coins and how Chi offered to act as an intermediary so that he could sell them on to a criminal organisation.'

Tyler turns to look at Robbins. 'But you already know that, don't you, Ben?'

'What? No . . .'

'You knew because Chi told you. She was packed and ready to leave, just as DI Cooper theorised. She really was planning to run off with someone. But she was going to take eight hundred grand in cash, and thirteen collectable antiquities with her. The week before she died, she even rang her mother and told her she was in love with someone. It was you, Ben, wasn't it?'

Robbins turns to his girlfriend to begin his denials but he dries up under her stare.

'I know,' Juju whispers. 'I always knew.'

'She told you,' Tyler says. 'That's what you argued about.'

Juju collapses onto a kitchen chair. 'Do you know what it's like to live in someone else's shadow your whole life? Our father named us after flowers. Qiang means rose. It represents strength, power, energy. Ju means chrysanthemum. A very common flower, a symbol of autumn, and of longevity. Traditionally, they're worn at funerals.

'Chi always thought our father was doubly disappointed in her, because she was the second daughter. His second failure. It had cost him a lot, politically but literally as well. There was no way he could risk a third child. But the truth is he made his peace with that. Chi was the one who he treated as the son he always wanted and I was the pale imitation of her.'

'Where's the money, Juju?'

'Upstairs.'

She leads them up with Robbins trailing behind, demanding to know what they're talking about.

On the first-floor landing they follow her into a small box-room. The baby's room. 'I knew no one would look in here,' she says, looking at Ben for the first time. 'No one comes in here. Except me.'

She pulls out a box from under the crib and opens it. Inside there's a large holdall and on top of that, a flick knife. Tyler takes hold of her arms before she can make a grab for it but she doesn't resist; whatever fight she had has long been burned out of her.

'Mina,' he prompts.

Rabbani pulls a pair of disposable gloves from her pocket, snaps them on and picks up the knife. She zips it into an evidence bag. Then she opens the holdall and they see bundles of notes inside. She does a quick search of the bag, mostly bundles of fifties but some twenties as well. She also finds a small travel wallet with Chi's passport and a few other personal documents.

'I didn't know what to do with it,' Juju says. 'The money. I didn't really want it.'

'But you took it.' He lets her go. 'Tell us what happened.'

'I followed her that night. I don't know why. I think I was hoping to find something I could use against her ... and she gave it to me. She spent the night with some boy.' She turns to Robbins. 'You see how much she loved you? Even on the night you were running away together she was sleeping with someone else.'

Robbins' face is pale and clammy.

'I waited for her, hoping I could get a photo of them ... doing it. Something I could show him.' She gestures to Ben. 'But I couldn't get into the apartment building. Then I saw her leave, sneaking out in the night with that bag. I followed her to the Gardens.'

'Dave Carver, the man who buried her – he saw you, just before he found Chi's body. He told us he thought he'd seen a ghost, or imagined it. That's what made me realise. The two of you look so alike. In the state he was in, it would be easy for him to mistake you for her.'

'I followed her into the Gardens to that place ...'

'The Bear Pit?'

'She heard me and told me to come out. She laughed when she saw me. I asked her what she was doing and she told me to go away. We argued again. I begged her not to take him but she wouldn't listen, just wanted me to go before I ruined whatever deal she had going on. I realised how desperate she was to get rid of me so I refused to leave. That's when she pulled the knife on me.'

Juju's shoulders are slumped forward. She has nothing left.

'There was a struggle and I took the knife from her. I—'

'No!' Ben shouts. 'Be quiet, Ju. Don't say any more until we get a solicitor.'

They stand in silence for a moment and the baby begins to cry downstairs. No one makes any effort to go to her.

'Mina,' Tyler says.

Rabbani steps forward. 'Li Ju, I am arresting you for the murder of Li Qiang . . .'

Back downstairs, as they escort her from the house, Ben begins to follow but Juju shouts at him, 'No! You have to take care of her now!'

He turns back, stricken, listening to the baby cry. 'But . . .'

Juju closes her eyes. 'You're just going to have to learn.'

As they march her from the house, kicking their way through the dead autumn leaves, Tyler wants to feel sorry for her. But he can't. He knows Chi didn't go over those railings by accident. She was too small, too slight for that. If it was that easy, he'd be dead too. Her murder might not have been premeditated but he has no doubt it was deliberate.

Still, that was for the courts to decide.

earthly remains

They meet on the hill behind the station, on a bench beneath the cholera monument. It's McKenna's choice but Tyler's thankful for the lack of CCTV in the park, and for the curtain of drizzle that covers the city below them and hides their meeting from curious eyes.

McKenna has brought a thick-set heavy with him who Tyler doesn't recognise. McKenna sends him off to stand under a tree. As he passes, Tyler catches a sickly whiff of orange-scented cologne.

'Detective Tyler.'

'McKenna.'

'I was sorry to hear about your colleague—'

'I'm not here to talk about that.' Tyler can't let himself think about it or he'll start going over all the questions again. He'll start wondering how Dave Carver could take seven separate stab wounds to his torso and yet somehow survive. He'll start asking why Colin Tavistock could fall from the same height as Li Qiang but walk away with nothing worse than a broken arm. And he'll begin picking over what he could have done or said differently, to stop Guy Daley giving his life to prove something.

But the questions will come later. As will the blame, and no doubt Stevens will make sure Tyler's the one who pays the price. Maybe he deserves to. But for now, there's business to finish.

'You let me down, son,' says McKenna. 'Didn't uphold your end of our bargain.'

'I did what you asked. I put a roof over the head of your grandson. It isn't my fault he decided to leave.'

'Aye, I suppose that's true enough.' McKenna pulls out a lighter and puffs his cigar back into life. A cloud of sweet smoke engulfs Tyler's head and floats away on the breeze. 'I'll be needing one more thing from you though, before I impart the information I promised.' He pats his hand on the plastic document case on his lap.

'You've had enough from me.'

McKenna turns in mock astonishment. 'Now, now, Detective, there's no need to be churlish.'

'I tend to get that way when people have me beaten up outside my home. The attack and the note were to pique my interest, and then you sent Callum in, not just to track down your stolen cash, but because you wanted to know what I'd discovered so far about my father's death. You wanted to know if I had anything that might implicate you.'

'You really are a great deal like your father, you know. Full of self-righteous indignation but often wide of the mark. I can assure you, once again, I had nothing to do with the death of your father.' He takes another deep draw on his cigar. 'Now,' he says, exhaling the smoke and once again tapping the folder by his side, 'if you want the full story, there's the small matter of my missing cash. A down payment

I made in good faith for some rather valuable antiquities I was promised.'

'The money's evidence and has been seized by the Crown. If you want to make a claim for it, you could hand yourself in and explain your part in all this.'

'I had another thought in mind. Evidence goes missing sometimes, does it not?'

Tyler laughs. 'You're lucky I'm not arresting you for perverting the course of justice. *And* your grandson.'

'Aye, but you havenae any evidence, have you? Or is it more that you're worried your role in this might get called into question? A wee bit of both, I suspect.'

Tyler gets up. 'We're done here.'

'Don't you want to know the truth?' He waves the documents case in Tyler's face. 'There's enough in here to get you on the right track. You're not gonna walk away from that, are you, Adam?'

McKenna *wants* him to have it. That makes his decision easier. 'I'll find out,' Tyler says. 'Sooner or later.'

He leaves the man sitting in the rain and heads home.

He sees the figure sitting huddled by the front door of his apartment building before he's fully out of the car. The man gets to his feet as Tyler approaches. He hasn't changed all that much over the years, just a few extra creases around the eyes, a few extra pounds around the middle. They stand in the rain, appraising each other.

'All right, bro',' Jude says. 'I heard you were looking for me.'

Three months later . . .

DCI Diane Jordan pulls up, engages the handbrake and switches off the engine. The house is one of a row of Victorian townhouses that tower over Ecclesall Road South. It sits on the side of the hill, raised up from the road, with a flight of stairs leading up to the front door. She's been here a few times over the years but never ceases to be impressed. She hates herself a bit for that. What she wouldn't do to be able to afford a place like this. But that's the problem, there's plenty she wouldn't do. Unlike the man who lives here.

She reaches for the hip flask in her jacket pocket, takes a long swig of whisky and feels the familiar warmth slide down her throat and settle in her stomach. She knows she has a problem, and she'll deal with it. Not AA, or any of that happy-clappy nonsense, though. She'll do it her own way. When she's ready. Just not yet. She puts the hip flask back in her pocket and glances at the plastic folder lying on the passenger seat. She slips it into the glove compartment and gets out of the car.

The doorbell plays a tinkling rendition of the 'William Tell Overture'. Money doesn't necessarily equal taste. When he opens the door, he blinks at her through the darkness. 'Diane, thank you for coming.'

'Roger.'

Stevens steps back and ushers her inside. The house is sweltering. He takes her thick winter jacket and drapes it over a plastic rain mac on the bannister. Despite the heat, there's something cold and uninviting about the place. It's too neat and clean. Even the family portraits on the wall are so perfect they might have come with the frames.

He escorts her into the living room and offers her a tea or coffee. When she hesitates, he adds, 'Something stronger, perhaps?'

'Whisky?'

'One moment.' He leaves the room.

Once again she's struck by how ordered everything is. She's met Jackie Stevens many times, and the kids, but it's as though none of them live here. Where are the toys and gadgets of a normal family? Where's the empty mug from this morning's coffee; the red-wine stains on the carpet; the wax crayon marks on the wall? Nothing. Perhaps this room is Stevens' own, the children banned except on rare occasions. Yes, he's definitely the type to have a room like that.

On the mantelpiece over the empty fireplace there are a number of framed photographs but none of these are family. They're all of Stevens. A group photo of him at the College of Policing. Another on a team-building day at one of those treetop adventure places. One of him shaking hands with the Prime Minister. She recognises a number of the faces in the photos and knows none of them are friends. Far from it, a good number of them actually hate him, though she can't speak for the Prime Minister.

'So!' He speaks from almost directly behind her, making her jump. 'What shall we drink to?' He's holding two tumblers of whisky over ice and passes one to her. She takes it and has to resist the urge to put the glass to her lips and down the lot.

'A quiet life?' she suggests.

He smiles. 'We should all be so lucky.' They clink their glasses together and drink. 'So . . .' he says again.

Here it comes.

'I've decided to disband CCRU. There's nothing they can accomplish that we can't manage with . . .'

As she listens to him outline his reasoning she feels herself grow numb. She's been expecting this, or something like it, for months – years, for that matter! – but it's still a shock. Especially today, of all days, when she finally has the information she needs to force his hand.

She's thinking about the plastic folder in the car when she interrupts him. 'I'm not going to let you do that, Roger.'

It's his turn to be shocked, hearing her speak this way to him after all the years of toeing the line. 'Diane, we've been over this a hundred times. My personal feelings about DS Tyler aside, we cannot afford a department that solely looks into cold cases.'

'Someone left a folder on my desk this morning.'

Stevens stops. He sits and gestures for her to do the same, but she remains standing. The headlights of cars flash through the bay window as they speed past, the noise of their engines deadened by the triple-glazing.

'It was delivered anonymously to the main desk, marked for my attention. CCTV shows what appears to be a young homeless man bring it in, but he does a good job of hiding his face from the cameras.'

'Someone's idea of a practical joke?'

'It doesn't look like a joke. It looks quite serious. It calls into question a number of key decisions you've made recently, and suggests there may have been a financial incentive for you to take them.'

'Please sit down, Diane.' He gestures to the chair behind her and, used to taking his commands, she sits. She takes the first sip of the whisky and feels that exquisite burn in the back of her throat.

He leans forward. 'So what is this? Extortion, Diane?'

'Nothing so sordid. The information will have to go to the IOPC, obviously.' She just hoped the newly formed Independent Office for Police Conduct really did want to make a difference. 'Granted, its provenance is somewhat questionable, but I have enough information of my own amassed to throw behind it. I'm sure they'll let you retire on a decent salary. I regret this, but I won't allow you to damage any more careers.'

'I see.' Stevens nods, slowly. 'So you're finally making your move. This must be some dossier you've received if you think you have enough to take me down. Oh, let's not play games with each other, I know you've been after me for some time. I'm surprised it's taken you this long, to be honest. Very well, I don't have anything to hide, so I'll look forward to meeting you on the battlefield. You should know though, Diane, this will certainly end in resignation for one of us.'

She shivers. There's something threatening in his eyes. *Please, God, let it be enough to be rid of him!*

'Still ...' He stands up and lifts his empty glass. 'Let's at least be civil. Another?'

She hesitates. It's damn fine whisky but ... She stands and sets the glass on the coffee table. 'I should get back.'

'Let me fetch your coat.'

As he leaves the room, Diane's eyes stray back to the mantelpiece. One photo in particular catches her eye. The team-building exercise. Stevens has his arm around Gary Bridger. She'd forgotten they were thick as thieves back in the day. It goes some way to explaining Stevens' antipathy towards Adam. He must hold him responsible for the fact Bridger lost his job after their altercation. Never mind the fact it left Adam scarred for life.

She picks up the photo. She remembers that day. When this was being taken she was still working her way down from the treetops. Richard had offered to wait for her but she'd sent him ahead. No reason for both of them to look bad just because she had a problem with heights. It must have been no more than a week or so before he died. He was so distracted that day. She wishes she could have said something to have helped him.

And then, maybe because she's thinking of him, she sees him in the photo. Standing way off to the right, almost hidden by that daft bandanna Carmichael was wearing. He's staring straight at Stevens, or at least, that's how it looks, his forehead creased as though he has the weight of the world on his shoulders. And suddenly the information in the folder takes on new meaning.

The plastic covers her face before she has a chance to take a breath. His hands close on her throat. Jordan lets go of the photograph and hears the glass shatter against the stone fireplace even as she gasps for air and tears at his fingers. She tries to rip the bag open but the plastic's too thick and her fingers slip off the material. He's so strong. She has time to wonder how he's doing this – don't modern plastic bags have holes in them precisely to prevent this happening? And then her mind flashes to the rain mac on the bannister and she knows her mistake ... *the information will have to go to the IOPC* ... She should have told him she'd sent it already. She shouldn't have told him anything at all. But she couldn't have known he was willing to go this far. *I should have known exactly how far he would go ... Richard ... I'm so sorry ...*

All this goes through her mind in those last few seconds. How could she have been so stupid? It all makes sense now. But it's too late. Too late to tell Adam. Too late to warn him ...

The last thing Diane Jordan sees as the world goes dark is the photograph of Richard Tyler's worried face.

Acknowledgements

No visit to Sheffield would be complete without a half hour strolling the grounds of its Botanical Gardens. Please be assured, you are most unlikely to be murdered. I'm extremely grateful to Jill Sinclair and the staff and volunteers at the Gardens who generously gave up their time to help me. I'd like to make it clear that the characters and events in this book in no way reflect their real-life counterparts. For the sake of the story, I have taken some liberties with the layout of the Gardens so any perceived mistakes are (probably) poetic licence.

I am indebted to Dr David L. Roberts at the Durrell Institute of Conservation and Ecology at the University of Kent, who helped me find the right orchid, and knows enough about wildlife crime to fill a thousand books. Also, my utmost thanks to my good friend Duncan Cameron, Professor of Plant and Soil Biology at the Department of

Animal and Plant Sciences at the University of Sheffield. He was kind enough to introduce me to the Sir David Read Controlled Environment Facility, as well as the Alfred Denny Museum of Zoology, both of which appear in this novel. Dunc himself does not appear, although I may have borrowed his Scottish heritage and one or two of his tattoos. He is a far, far nicer man than Calderdale.

Once again I have found myself turning to Kevin Robinson and his indispensable books on police procedure. Crime writers or, in fact, anyone with a morbid curiosity of these things would do well to take a look at his website: www.crimewritingsolutions.wordpress.com. Any mistakes are mine alone.

This novel would be much the poorer were it not for the critical eyes of both Susan Elliot Wright and Marion Dillon. I wish I could list all the friends and family who have leant me their support through the writing of this book but I'm afraid there isn't enough space. Thank you anyway. Without your belief in me, I definitely couldn't do this.

I have had no fewer than four brilliant editors over the past couple of years. They are: Jo Dickinson, Bethan Jones, Sara Minnich and Anne Perry. Each of them has had a hand in shaping my half-formed ideas into the beautiful book in your hands. But there are, in fact, hundreds of people involved in getting this book into your hands. There are too many to mention, even if I knew all of their names, but a big thank you to the teams at Simon & Schuster in the UK, and G.P. Putnam's Sons in the US. And special thanks to the huge number of booksellers and book bloggers who picked up *Firewatching*, understood what I was trying to do, and shouted about it to anyone who would listen. I'm enormously grateful to you for your support.

As before, the biggest thanks must go to my agent, the always amazing Sarah Hornsley. Without her steadfast belief, this book simply wouldn't exist.

Finally, thank you to the people of Sheffield who took me in some twenty-five years ago with great warmth and affection. Their generosity towards newcomers, be they students, immigrants or asylum seekers, remains inexhaustible. Long may that continue.

DS Adam Tyler will return in

COLD RECKONING

RUSS THOMAS

Soon after the events of *Nighthawking*, a body is discovered
in a frozen lake, its wrists bound. When the body is linked
to a case from 2002, Tyler, DC Rabbani and the CCRU
team are called in. But fresh blood is soon discovered at the
scene and the disturbing events from all those years
ago are dragged sharply into the present . . .

Coming 2022